ONE SHADOW ON THE WALL

LEAH HENDERSON

atheneum

ATHENEUM BOOKS FOR YOUNG READERS
New York London Toronto Sydney New Delhi

atheneum

ATHENEUM BOOKS FOR YOUNG READERS
An imprint of Simon & Schuster Children's Publishing Division
1230 Avenue of the Americas, New York, New York 10020

Text copyright © 2017 by Leah Henderson

$17.99

Jacket illustration copyright © 2017 by John Jay Cabuay

NOV   '17

ATHENEUM BOOKS FOR YOUNG READERS is a registered trademark of Simon & Schuster, Inc. Atheneum logo is a trademark of Simon & Schuster, Inc.
For information about special discounts for bulk purchases, please contact Simon & Schuster Special Sales at 1-866-506-1949 or business@simonandschuster.com.
The Simon & Schuster Speakers Bureau can bring authors to your live event. For more information or to book an event, contact the Simon & Schuster Speakers Bureau at 1-866-248-3049 or visit our website at www.simonspeakers.com.
Book design by Debra Sfetsios-Conover and Irene Metaxatos
The text for this book was set in Stempel Garamond LT Std.
Manufactured in the United States of America
0517 FFG
First Edition
10 9 8 7 6 5 4 3 2 1
CIP data for this book is available from the Library of Congress.
ISBN 978-1-4814-6295-2
ISBN 978-1-4814-6297-6 (eBook)

To my parents,
who continue to dream for me during times
when I have forgotten how

PROLOGUE

YAAY, is that you?" Mor whispered, unsure. He rubbed his eyes, then shielded them from the rays of a screaming West African sun.

His younger sister Amina looked up from mashing yams. "What is it?"

Mor stared past her. "Do you not see her right beside you?"

"See who?" Amina glanced over her shoulder. She searched the dirt path in front of their village home. "No one is here."

"Yaay is."

"Shh . . ." Amina's head swiveled in the direction of their

little sister, Fatima, playing with rocks an arm's length away. "Don't tease about such things."

As clearly as Mor saw Amina hammering a giant wooden pestle into a hollowed-out stump crammed with yam, he saw their mother. "I'm not—"

"Stop it," she rushed to say. Her face was pinched. "She is gone. You know her heart grew too weak to continue its beat."

"Yes, but she's here," Mor continued. "I don't know how, but she's watching you." A calm wrapped around him like the warmth of the sun after being in shadows as he stared at his mother's spirit. He saw her form exactly as he remembered her, with a multicolored head wrap and her sky-blue *meulfeu* dress sweeping the ground. Though something was different. She glimmered and sparkled and glowed. He could see through her as if the wind could tickle her insides before it journeyed on. Still, he knew with certainty it was her.

The family goat bleated, then wandered to the very spot Mor focused on and craned her head up.

"Look—even Jeeg sees her."

"Enough!" Amina swept her hand toward the other ramshackle homes resting in the dirt around them. "Jeeg sniffs the wind. Someone's cooking cassava and she is teased by the smell. Hush your words, especially with Baay now lying in the clinic. Others will think it has been too much for you." Amina leaned the pestle against the crook of her arm and almost whispered, "Is that what you want? To be thought crazy with all this talk?"

"But I'm not crazy. And this has nothing to do with Baay or his accident. It's Yaay I see." And no matter what Amina said, he knew it to be true.

MOR bounced pebble after pebble off a crumbling packed-mud wall behind his family's *barak*. Clouds of powdery dirt exploded with each strike.

"You want to play?" his friend Oumar asked, juggling a makeshift ball made of plastic bags and twine against his knee and foot. "It always makes me forget when I'm sad." Oumar hopped on one foot while balancing the soccer ball on his other.

"I do not want to forget." Mor stared at Oumar over his shoulder. The ball flopped to the ground. "My *baay* is gone. I always want to remember him."

"I didn't mean it that way. I just thought . . ." Oumar picked up his ball, not finishing his sentence.

Mor could tell Oumar wanted to scamper off like his other friends had after the burial. Mor had seen their discomfort and felt their pity pouring off them like sweat. Oumar was no different. Even though he had stayed, he wore his uneasiness. It draped over his shoulders and pressed down on his head.

"Go if you want," Mor said, freeing him. He scooped up a handful of dirt. "We don't all have to feel as if the air is gone."

Oumar's feet moved before the last words had left Mor's lips. "Maybe you'll come down to the field tomorrow," he called back, dropping the ball to dribble.

Although Mor loved the feel of the soccer ball against his foot, he knew he wouldn't go.

Dust and tears stung his eyes as he watched Oumar run away.

His *baay* was gone. And now so were all his friends. Only Jeeg, the family goat, stayed by his side. She was tied to a post, watching a few mourners as they turned for their homes. It had been only six hours since his father's death, and as was tradition, many of the mourners still prayed and played religious songs on the path outside his family's door, remembering his father's life. But Mor couldn't. It already felt like he had lived a lifetime without him. The sting was as great as, if not greater than, when his *yaay* had died. Then he'd had his *baay* and his best friend, Cheikh, to lean on. Cheikh had been more like an older brother, but he'd long since been sent to a religious school in the city, and now Mor's father had left him too.

6

With the exception of a distant aunt, he and his sisters were now alone.

He studied the ground and caught sight of an enormous beetle scampering past his foot. Lost in its movements, he opened his fingers, letting the dirt he clutched rain down on the bustling bug. The shimmering black beetle stopped and started in a manic crawl. Mor took up a flimsy stick and poked the ground, changing the beetle's direction, causing the bug to leave behind zigzags in the sand.

Does this settle the storm within you?

Mor's head flung up. He strained to hear beyond the caws of crows, through the evening prayer call, and over the murmur of mourners. He was certain he had heard someone, but other than Jeeg curled near him, Mor was by himself. Although Jeeg flicked her ears and lifted her head, he knew she couldn't have spoken.

What has this beetle done to garner such attention?

Mor stood straight. He recognized that voice. "Baay?"

You are not a python slithering in the dirt, hampering any life that falls across your path. Do not let your hurt turn you sour. For in an instant that beetle could have scudded into your spear.

"Father, is that you?" Mor spun around wildly, knowing his *baay* could not be there. Could he? Like his *yaay* had been a week before? Mor was sure he had heard his father's unmistakable voice, which held the feathery lightness of a locust's wings, braided with the strength of a plowing ox. It was deep and quiet all at once and always spilled out as an overflowing stream of riddles.

I know you hear me, my son, but are you listening? the voice asked in the growing darkness.

Mor crumbled to the ground and swatted his tears, raking his palms across his cheeks. Dirt ground into his skin when he wiped his face. "I'm going mad," he sniffled. "Maybe Amina was right."

I assure you, you have not conjured a dream or lost your sense. We are here with you.

"'We'?" Mor stopped. He had seen his mother—could it be that they were together? "Is it really you, Baay?"

Yes, my son.

Mor's heart warmed and his tears stopped flowing. "Will you come to Tima and Mina, too?" he asked the purpling sky, hoping his sisters would experience the same. "They will not believe me if you don't. Especially Mina. She trusts little I say."

It is not her role to trust with abandon. She is our questioning child, who takes the cautious road. Her love often prickles only because she does not want either you or the open heart of Tima to be led astray. You are the anchor of this house now. We come to you.

"Will you stay?" he asked, hope rising with his words.

Not always. Now your need is great.

"What about Yaay?" Mor leaned forward. "Why can't I see her?"

You will see her in comfort, and hear me in storms.

Mor searched the space around him. He wanted her now.

"How can I hear you?" He was relentless with his questions, but he didn't care. He wanted to know. To understand. To keep his father close. "And how can you hear me?"

How can anyone hear? his father asked him. *They listen. Are you listening now?*

"Yes, Baay," Mor said, going still.

That beetle was not the cause of your heartache. Do not let it be a victim of it.

A heat spread over Mor's chest. "I know."

You are a shepherd, not a venomous serpent, and have been entrusted with our beautiful flock of two.

Mor lowered his head. Jeeg stared up at him. "I promise to do all you ask of me if you return."

"Promise," you say? His father's voice held a slight coarseness. *You have already made a promise to me, yet here you are sulking in the dirt.*

The image of his father's hand covering his own filled his head.

It was the day after a careless *moto* and a roaring truck had hit his father. His *baay* had awoken in the Balla Clinic, with its tan tile walls, whizzing fans, and rows of occupied beds laden with sugar-white sheets and black, sick bodies. Recognition had brightened his *baay*'s eyes when he opened them to find Mor and his sisters huddled around him.

Mor and Amina had tried to quiet Fatima as she clung to

9

their father's chest, sobbing, trying to climb into the bed. Amina pulled at her legs until their *baay* told her to let Fatima be. A tear escaped Amina's face then. The only one Mor had seen since their *yaay*'s death.

Instead of asking where he was or how he'd gotten there from the roadway he'd been walking along, their *baay* said, "The wind has blown all that I love back around me." He wheezed then. Small tubes extended from his nose and bandaged arms. When he turned his stubbled chin, it sounded like sandpaper scratching wood, not a cheek grazing a pillow. "As one, all things are strong," he continued. "Divided, they are weak and scatter." Their *baay*'s eyes were glassy when they turned toward Mor. In a breathy whisper Mor felt his *baay* speak as if he and Mor were the only people in the room. No coughing strangers, no beeping machines, no crying sisters. "Do not let our house divide. Your sisters need you. And you need your sisters. Do not let yourselves scatter on a gust of wind. Hold tight to one another."

And with a shaky voice Mor heard himself reply, "I promise."

Do you recall your words to me, my son? His father's voice now shook Mor from his memory.

"Yes." Mor had trouble finding his own voice.

Honor your promise. Keep our flock as one.

When the sun had slipped from the sky, and most grasshoppers rested on leafy stems, long after all the well-wishers had gone and his sisters were stretched on their parents' pallet, eyes closed, Mor hunched on a crate outside his family's one-room home. The moon was the village streetlight, shining down on a mix of rippling tin and thatched wood roofs. Black tarps hung under them against mud-brick walls. The footpaths in front of Mor led in every direction: to a neighbor's *barak*, the village well, the beach, or the village center. Staring ahead, Mor wished he would see his parents strolling along the one to his door, like he had so many times before.

He wiped at his eye while Jeeg lay over his feet, as she often did in the breezeless quiet. His eyes, already accustomed to the moonlit darkness, saw Coumba Gueye, their neighbor and his *yaay*'s closest friend, before he heard her approaching on the path. Even though she was not related by blood, she was an auntie to him, a tanta who had always been there. The moon guided her way toward him.

"What's this?" she asked when she was a few steps closer. "Why are you out in the dark with only Jeeg as your blanket?" She reached down and stroked the goat. As she bent, she revealed the melon-size head of her son, baby Zal, with tight black curls budding on his scalp. His chubby cheek was pressed against her back.

"I do not need a candle to see that my *baay* is gone, or a flame to show that my *yaay* no longer sleeps on her pallet. So what do I need to see?" Mor said bitingly. As Tanta Coumba straightened, one side of her mouth curved into a slight smile. She rocked her head from side to side, her head scarf and

11

baby Zal bobbled with her movement. "You are definitely your father's son." She dragged out another small crate, which had been leaning against his home. "The light is not to show you what you do not have, but what you do." Gathering the ample fabric of her *teybass* so it wouldn't dust the dirt, she sat, tucking the dress's excess cloth in her lap. "For you, that flame shines on two precious girls who need their big brother." She motioned toward the doorway.

Mor shifted, recalling his father's words, "our beautiful flock of two."

Tanta Coumba lifted his head with her hand, and she wiped away tears from his cheeks. Tears he had hoped were invisible in the night. But as he looked down, the glow of the half-moon illuminated the smeared, wet streaks on the backs of his hands. He brushed them across Jeeg's fur, pretending to pet her.

"It is okay to cry." Tanta Coumba leaned closer, pulling his hands from Jeeg. "It is a sign you will be a worthy man because you feel. It is a danger to cinch everything inside, becoming rigid like a stick." She stared at him. "Do not become a cold, unfeeling boy, worse than a flea, springing up only to make others itch, leaving behind scabs and unsettled skin. Let your heart and feelings guide you." She smiled. "I know this is what your *baay* and your dear, sweet *yaay* would want of you."

He blinked rapidly, still embarrassed.

At the mention of his parents, though, he wanted to tell her all about the visions of his *yaay* and hearing his father's voice, but he hesitated. Jeeg had been the only one to understand. Amina had sat disbelieving when he told her of their father's riddles. Suddenly he wished Cheikh, Tanta Coumba's other son, were with him. Cheikh would not have needed more proof. Mor's words and his belief would have been enough. His old friend would have known exactly what to say to ease Mor's worry.

When Mor looked at Tanta Coumba, he thought instantly of his friend. Cheikh resembled his mother in so many ways, from their penetrating stares to their oval faces. It made Mor miss him even more. "What is it?" Tanta Coumba asked, distracting him from his thoughts.

"Nothing." He focused on the dirt. "I was just thinking of Cheikh. I wish he was here so I wouldn't be alone."

Tanta Coumba sighed. "I wish my boy was here with us as well. But his father believes the *daara* in the city is better for him." Then her eyes swept over the other *baraks* huddled in the dirt like a pride of slumbering lions. "But remember, you are not alone. You have all of us, and we have you. A child of my friend is my child. I would bring you into my home tomorrow if I had enough to spare, but dear Dieynaba is coming, *Incha'Allah*. Your aunt will look after you as she looked after your *baay* when they were growing up here in this village." She spun her fingertip into the tight-coiled hairs at Mor's temple. They loosened under her touch, then sprang back tight when she released them. "You are strong enough for this." The balls of her cheeks pushed against her eyes.

"Even if my mind has left me?" Mor whispered. Not wanting to think of his *bàjjan* right then and all the changes she would bring.

"What do you mean?" Tanta Coumba asked. Baby Zal shifted but stayed asleep.

"I see and hear what is not there." His eyes and nose tingled as he forced back more tears.

Tanta Coumba watched him for a long while, not saying a word.

"Things I know cannot be," he continued.

"Things like what?" she prodded softly.

Mor picked at a small hole in his shirt, making it wide enough for his pinky to pass through. Realizing he'd created something else for Amina to mend, he withdrew his finger and let the shirttail fall.

"Go on," she assured him. "I'm certain it is nothing I've not heard or thought myself."

Mor wished more than anything that were true, but he knew what he was about to say made it certain his sense was running from him. He blurted it out anyway. "I see my *yaay* and hear my *baay*."

Tanta Coumba looked him squarely in the eyes. "And that worries you?"

Mor's neck and cheeks bristled with heat. He moved to stand.

"Be still." She pressed her warm palm into his shoulder. "I do not doubt your words. Many of us see the dead in our dreams."

14

"But I am not always dreaming. I see and hear them when the sun is bright and when the moon is shining."

She sat for a long while, scanning his eyes. "I often talk to your *yaay* throughout my day. I have since she left us three years ago. Does that make me mad as well?"

Mor glanced her way. Hope flooded his chest. "Does she answer?"

The light dimmed a little in Tanta Coumba's eyes. "Not as you and I are talking now, but in her way, I would like to think she is answering."

Hope crashed against a dam within him. That was not what he meant. She couldn't understand.

"Where does she visit you?" asked Tanta Coumba.

At first he was reluctant. Tanta Coumba waited, swaying back and forth like a blade of grass in the breeze.

"She came the day after Baay's accident," Mor uttered finally, ready to confess. "And a couple days after that."

Tanta Coumba nodded as if she understood. Then she shifted and stared back at Mor. "So she looked in on you when your *baay*'s voice was first absent, when you needed comfort? When he could not speak?"

Mor thought hard. He had not seen it that way, but he realized she was right. His *yaay* had appeared the second day his *baay* lay in Balla Clinic, the day he'd slipped into sleep.

"But only I can see her." Mor pulled on his finger. "I feel a fool."

"Hush now. It is your blessing."

"But why can't I hear her like I hear my *baay*? And why can I not see him as I see her?" Mor's shyness had vanished. He no longer cared if he sounded strange. He wanted to understand.

"We can never fully know why certain things come to be, just that they have." She cradled his hands, stilling his fingers. "Treasure the comfort and guidance they bring. Though, we can seek out a *serigne* if you are so troubled? I am sure he could bring more understanding."

Mor shrank against his seat. He did not want to tell anyone else what he'd seen or heard, even a religious leader, because he knew of people who had been taken away from their families and their homes for thinking peculiar things. Others were laughed at and thought crazy. And he didn't want that. The idea of being confronted by someone else who might question him made his stomach twist. Despite himself, he asked Tanta Coumba another question.

"Will I ever see my *baay* and hear the voice of my *yaay* again?" he whispered.

"I'm sorry, but I cannot say. I can only assure you that you have not gone mad. You will not be locked away for your thoughts. Instead of worrying, be grateful for what you do see and hear. Many would give anything for a word or glimpse of lost loved ones. These are gifts. Welcome them," she encouraged. "And your aunt Dieynaba's arrival will be another blessing. She is saddened not to have made the burial, but she has called your father's old shop and told Mamadou she would arrive in four days' time on the early *ndiaga ndiaya*. So prepare for her arrival, and thanks be to Allah that she provided for your father's stay at the clinic and that she is coming to provide for you and your sisters."

"Yes, ma'am," Mor said, his head full of thoughts. He wished Cheikh would be on that bus from Dakar too. Not just an aunt he hardly remembered. He couldn't imagine what it would soon be like to share his home, and his family's space, with her. After all, it was her home too. And now there was room again in it for her.

Tanta Coumba spread her fingers across her knees, ready to lift herself up. She placed a light kiss on Mor's forehead. He inhaled the fragrant scents of incense and ginger mixed with light sweat as she rose.

"All will be well. Your *bàjjan* is a wonderful soul who has always aided her brother in times of trouble. And now she will lovingly do it again. You will see." Tanta Coumba pinched Mor's cheek when he did not look up. "She will bring sunshine again, *Incha'Allah*."

Then Tanta Coumba stood and turned for home, leaving Mor with his wishes and the night. Without his permission, more tears blurred his eyes as she got smaller and smaller on the path.

When he blinked, his mother's *djiné*, gleaming like stars, leaned against the doorframe of their home. Her spirit smiled down on him. He jumped to his feet and raced to her as Jeeg's *m-a-a* rolled across the air. His heart danced against his chest. The happiness that ribboned through him was strange after so much sadness. He welcomed it and wanted to be locked in his mother's arms, but he almost stumbled through her. He stared up at her as she stared down, so many silent words being spoken between them. He wished he could hear her voice, but somehow it didn't really matter; like Tanta Coumba had said, the sight of her was a relief. A gift. The love in her eyes, the heat of her presence, and the comfort in her smile were all he needed in that moment.

They stayed staring at each other until Tima squirmed inside on the pallet next to Amina. When Mor looked back from the open doorway, his *yaay*'s lips swept across his cheek like a sunbeam peeking through a cloud.

Then she was gone. But Mor's eyes were dry. He reached up to his cheek and smiled, yawning. He thought he was finally ready to close his eyes and dream.

OPEN *your eyes.*

The words sailed through Mor as if his father had leaned close to him, with lips only inches from his ear, like his mother's had been two nights before. The call to prayer hummed in the distance.

Sleep weighed heavy on Mor's lids, and his mind was a web of dreams. It had been a little over two days since his father's voice had first joined him, and he no longer found it strange that his *baay*'s words reached him at any time of day. And in that moment he even stopped questioning why his *baay* and *yaay* did not come together. He was just grateful that they came at all.

Wake, my son, his father's voice echoed. *Sleep when your heart no longer beats like the sabar drum. Do not lie still, expecting to be handed what you need. You are not a fish flapping in the sun, sucking air, hoping to be thrown back to sea.*

Mor twisted on his mat and his eyes slowly opened. He rolled to his side. He had remained there for almost two days, crying and missing his *baay*, and he wanted to stay there undisturbed at least twenty days more. No one had been able to move him so far, not even Amina. She had nudged him in the back with the broom, saying, "Lying like this is not good for you. It is not good for Tima to see. Get up," but her words fell on Mor's closed ears.

But his *baay* was different. He demanded that Mor listen.

Your tears are understood, but your wallowing is not. Rise, his *baay* urged. *Rise.*

Pulling himself to his knees, he obeyed, then dragged the water bucket and bowl from beneath the raised platform that used to be his parents' bed, which his sisters now slept on. He splashed well water Amina had carried in the night before across his face and behind his ears, then over his hands and feet. He took out his prayer mat and knelt, bending and rising as he spoke in hushed tones.

Once he'd finished, he returned his mat to the corner and retied the square-shaped *téere* amulet he wore high on his arm. The tiny leather envelope contained hand-scribbled Koranic verses written by the village *serigne* that were believed to protect the wearer. Years before, his mother had gotten one made for each of her children. She and Baay had worn their protection rings.

He unfolded a clean but faded polo shirt his *yaay* had bought from a pile of previously loved clothing at the village market. Mor yanked it over his head and stepped into a pair of men's khaki pants cut at the knees, cinching a black cord tight at his waist to hold them. After sliding into his sandals, he poured more water into the jars around the room, in case his parents' spirits wanted to take a drink, something many families did for their dead relatives.

Across the cramped room, the only photograph he and his sisters had of their parents, taken with a borrowed camera, rested on a shelf next to a picture of a fellowship leader cut out from a calendar. Mor took the photograph off the shelf and traced his finger over his father's tall, lean body and his mother's swelling belly as his parents embraced under an imposing baobab tree, excited to be starting their family—to be welcoming him.

His parents seemed so happy staring into the camera's lens with slight smiles, as if unsure of what the camera might actually capture. Mor made himself pull his gaze away from their vibrant black faces. As he went to replace the photograph, another of the shelf's occupants demanded his attention. A rusting tomato can perched on the splintered wood.

He glanced at his sleeping sisters, then reached inside the can and withdrew a miniature fabric sack. It protected a pearl button, a tiny seashell, a curl of hair, and a baby's tooth, along with the money he and his sisters had left after their *baay* had used almost all of it to pay for some of Amina's schooling. Mor felt a bit better holding his mother's keepsakes and the money. Just having them near him settled the sadness brewing in his belly.

Let it rest where it is safe, his father warned. *Where it is protected.*

As much as Mor knew he ought to listen to his *baay*, he slipped the francs and keepsakes back into the pouch and slid it all into his pocket. He wanted his mother's treasures close.

As Fatima twisted in sleep, an image of his parents lying there instead came across his eyes. When he blinked, the memory vanished, much like his father's voice had.

Everywhere he looked in the tight, dark room reminded him of his parents. At first his father's work shirt hanging on a nail, his mother's sarongs, now Amina's, neatly folded with a small stack of his father's pants, and their prayer mats joined with Mor's in the corner had been a comforting sight, snapshots that showed they were once there. Now they began to weigh him down, these symbols of loss. The walls of the *barak* felt as if they pressed against him. And the morning air, stale with sweat and slumber, made it hard for him to breathe. He had to get out.

The path between his home and the other *baraks* was deserted except for a swarm of flies buzzing over a garbage heap at the end of the row. He glanced up and down the path, needing to leave the familiar behind, but uncertain what to do or where to go. He knew his father never tolerated idleness, not even in sadness. After his mother died, his *baay* had gone right back to work, tinkering with engines, believing that idleness would have shackled sadness around his ankles like a chain. "Get up, do something that makes your pulse dance and brings sunshine," he had told Mor then. Lost to his memories, Mor let his legs lead him on one of the paths out of the village, sure he would return before his sisters worried about his absence.

With each step, you must grow in wisdom and in strength, his *baay* instructed, accompanying Mor along the roadway. *But remember you are not a lion until challenges do not have you running the other way.*

Mor grew upset. Ignoring what he'd felt earlier, he didn't want to hear his *baay* if he could not have him there with him. He cupped his hands over his ears. "Go away, if you won't stay and show yourself to me." The words tasted bitter as he spoke them, and he instantly wished he could swallow them back. He definitely sounded like a cub.

His father went quiet again, like he had when Mor first ignored his words.

"I didn't mean it." Mor panicked in the silence. "I don't want you to go. Stay with me."

After a few solitary steps his father whispered, *Even when the breeze is silent, I am always with you. But you must find strength, my son. Not bitterness.*

"But I do not know how to be strong."

23

You must find a way.

As his father's voice grew stronger, Mor hoped he might glimpse his *baay*'s spirit, as he had his *yaay*'s. Yet all he saw in front of him was the shadow of the neighboring villages, Jamma and Mahktar, in the distance, set off by the sea. Beside him were the sunken tracks of those who had recently traveled along the roadside, their footprints oval saucers in the copperish dirt. Trees and sparse patches of weed and grass dotted the landscape.

Do you remember how your little fingers could not hold a wrench? Its weight your enemy? But as you grew—

"I was able to hold it, turn it, and use it to help you," Mor finished for him, bouncing on his toes.

Yes, my son. You became strong.

As Mor meandered down the path with his *baay*, his sadness started to slink off of him, curling in the dirt. Soon he was well away from Lat Mata. Stretches of flat land lay ahead and behind him. The salted sea air was cool and sticky against his skin, and all was clear around him. He heard the squeak and yawn and trill of a bell, before he saw the man with thick reddish-brown dreadlocks pedal up beside him on a rickety bicycle. He was muttering to himself as he passed Mor. A squawking bird sat on an open box attached to the back of his bike.

Mor watched as the man grew smaller, pedaling away. Mor's feet were not tired, and his spirits lifted with each word Baay spoke. The day had just begun, so he kept walking. He followed the line of the bike's tire in the dirt until he came to a deep bend in the road caused by a stubborn tree, splitting the path in two. Instead of going left like the man on the bike, he stepped to the right. Then everything inside Mor went still. Without realizing it, he had taken the same path his *baay* had the day of the accident. It was the exact bend in the road that had halted his father's life.

"Baay, are you there?" Mor stopped in the hot bed of sand. He strained to hear. He feared the sight of the accident had silenced his father. "Baay, have you left me?"

3

EVEN under the waking sun an icy frost bit at Mor. A charred, twisted bumper, a sprinkling of shattered glass, and a jagged piece from the truck that had kissed away his *baay*'s breaths hunkered before him. Straggly chicken feathers fluttered, trapped by the sand.

Lift your gaze and walk, my son. Settle your sights on the horizon, not this.

Mor's body shook. Frantic, he took off in a sprint, though his legs and feet could not move fast enough for him. He pumped his arms and mashed his sandals against the dirt, running until pain pierced his sides, knocking out his breath. He nearly toppled over when he stopped.

Except for his ragged breaths, all was silent. Why had he

gone that way? There were so many other roads he could have taken.

It is not important the reason why, only that you had the strength to get through.

Mor continued walking, not convinced it had been any great strength that had helped him. It had been fear. After a few more bends in the road, and many deep, calming breaths, he realized which path he was on. It led toward Mahktar—a village on the ocean, close to his own but not nearly as big. He had sometimes accompanied his father there when the men of Mahktar became too frustrated with a truck's pesky engine. They had often called the yard where Mor's *baay* had worked, asking him to lend a hand. His *baay* could fix anything.

Heading for the beach in Mahktar, Mor pulled out his mother's turquoise-and-ruby-colored pouch, with its painted twirling line of gold, hoping to settle himself, hoping to hear even his father's disapproval at bringing it. Anything would be better than his heartbeat thudding in his ears. But his father said nothing as he stared down at the pouch. Each day of her life, his *yaay* had poured the contents of it into her hand and remembered, thanking Allah for the treasure of her family. When she was unsettled, she had pressed it close to her heart. And at that moment it brought Mor comfort. His *yaay* had always said the *nafa* held her heart because it contained a curl of Amina's baby hair, his chipped baby tooth, the button Fatima had always tried to swallow, and a tiny seashell that had rested between his parents' feet on their wedding day. Mor had thought there was no better place to secure his family's only francs. The money clinked inside the shifting cloth, and he found it strangely reassuring in his hand.

Glancing around, he shoved the pouch deep inside his pocket. When it fell, he hardly felt it against his leg. The money inside wasn't much, but six-year-olds, like his sister Fatima, might think they were rich, while older kids would consider it a lucky find. But a man would know how quickly it could come and go. And at eleven Mor could no longer be a boy, as his father's voice had reminded him; he needed to become a man.

If I tell myself I am a man, am I? He knew he appeared no different from the boy he had been days before. No taller, stronger, or wiser. But within two days everything had changed. Mor kept walking, concentrating on his next steps. The road curved at a short, crumbling mud wall that spread in front of him, the beach beyond it. Weatherworn boats with flaking bright yellow and orange paint hunkered down in the sand or sat tall on hefty logs. Some of the *gaals* were taller than most men.

Over a bridge at the far end of the beach, a higher pink wall wrapped around an outdoor market, dividing it from the road and water. A woman sold the sweetest *bissap* juice there. He thought about getting one to share with his sisters, like he often had with his *baay* when they'd come to Mahktar. Mor threw his leg up and lifted himself over the stunted wall in front of him, dropping into the sand, when someone let out an earth-rattling scream. He spun in the direction of the commotion.

Two boys chased a smaller boy who looked gobbled up by his oversize T-shirt. The bigger of the two wore a stained basketball jersey and fraying shorts, and tripped him in the sand. The other boy, who was rail thin, shouted, "Be still!" while his friend pressed his knee into the little boy's back and slapped his head.

"You know what you're in for," the boy with the jersey warned.

The trapped boy coughed up dirt. Mor could hardly make out his face. It was a sheet of speckled sand.

"Hold him down," demanded another boy, striding up the beach. His skin shone like a crow's wing against the tangerine baseball cap he wore, turned backward on his head. A *sothiou* dangled in the corner of his mouth. The chew stick bobbed up and down between his lips as he spoke. "I'm going to teach you," he said.

He pushed at his shirtsleeves, already above his elbows, yanked up the crotch of his baggy pants, and squatted over the helpless boy while his friends continued to hold him down.

"Who told you to go spying through our doorway and touching our wall?"

"I . . . I didn't—"

"You saying I'm lying?" The boy's face scrunched into a

scowl. "You hear that? He's calling me a *fene kat*."

"No . . ." The little boy gasped for air. When he parted his lips, he took in a mouthful of sand. "I didn't say that. . . ."

"Then what did you say?"

Head in the sand, the little boy couldn't answer. Instead he wiggled and kicked. Sand flew everywhere. One of the boys pinned down his legs.

The boy with the orange cap sprang up and dusted off his jeans. His eyes darted around, at first paying no attention to Mor frozen at the beach wall. Then they traveled the length of Mor's body, and he snarled, baring teeth.

"Do you want some of this too?" He spit, and nawed off flecks of chew stick bark flew.

Mor backed away, meeting the crumbling wall again.

"Then let your eyes find somewhere else to be." He reached down into the sand and pulled up a plum-size rock. Turning back to the struggling boy, he said, "This will teach you to never let your eyes or hands fall on the Danka Boys' door."

Mor closed his own eyes, but the sound of the rock hitting its target made him leap back, almost tripping out of his sandals. The young child's screams stabbed the air. Afraid to look, Mor squeezed his eyelids together tighter, so the light coiled when he opened them again. The trapped boy's hand lay limp in the sand. The oldest boy raised the rock again. Mor's jaw moved. He yelled for them to stop. Or did he? No sound left his lips. His words were as trapped as the trembling boy. Mor watched in disbelief as the oldest boy let the rock fall again, catching it inches away from the boy's injured hand. His chilling laugh hacked at the air.

"You will not go breathing near our door again, will you? Or even sneeze on our path." He swung the rock back and forth in front of the little boy's eyes.

Sand clung to the little boy's face. Tears cleared lines down his cheeks, exposing his dark-brown skin, like streaks of war paint. When he glanced up, his eyes found Mor. It startled Mor, and Mor dropped his head. A part of him wanted to help the boy, but everything else in his mind was telling him to run. Yet his feet would not budge.

Have your legs been hobbled like a mule's? And your mind as well? his father's voice rattled. Mor's head shot up. *You are not an ostrich that can camouflage its head by lying on the sand. You are its white tail feathers. You have been seen and you must act.*

His father's words sparked something inside him. Blood rushed through his toes and fingertips. His eyes took in the beach around him, but unlike the boy with the rock, Mor could find nothing to throw.

Then he saw it. On the other side of the crumbling wall a massive baobab tree stood with a trunk as thick as a rhinoceros's hide and bark as tough as crocodile skin. Pods dangled down from its branches. On the ground under the tree a few rotting pods lay on the path. Even as they decayed, their outer shells were hard as stone. Mor's eyes swung between the tree, the ground, and the boy.

"Ahh-eck," screeched one of the older boys. He vaulted off the squirming boy's legs.

"What's the matter with you?" The boy with the orange cap knocked the rock into his friend's shoulder. "Who told you to get up?"

"Come on, Papis. This little *badola* peed on my—"

"So?" Papis, the boy with the rock, took a half step away from the frightened child. The corner of his mouth turned up in a smile.

"Man, I'm not holding him anymore. He stinks."

"You let go when I say let go, Diallo," Papis warned. "Now hold his legs."

While they argued, Mor scrambled over the wall and headed to the foot of the tree. He knew he didn't have much time. The first pod he grabbed was broken in half. His hand shook as he reached for another discarded pod, then another. They were all smashed. He clawed the ground for a rock, but it was littered only with the flaky white monkey-bread seeds from the pods. Then his hand landed on a sturdy vine, and when he yanked it, a pod the shape of an oversize caterpillar cocoon slid across the dirt. It was as hard as a coconut shell. Perfect.

"Hold him still," Papis demanded again. The rock was high over his head as his words rambled over the beach.

The captured boy bucked and twisted. His eyes locked on to the rock aimed at his head.

"Make him stop." Papis cut his friend with his eyes. "Or the next blow will be for you."

Mor raced back toward the wall and threw himself over it. He ran as close to them as he dared, probably appearing like another nosy child excited to witness something gruesome. He held the baobab fruit by its vine and swung it over his head. When Papis was about to let the rock strike the young boy's head, Mor let the pod sail.

But instead of slicing through the air, knocking Papis over, it whipped across the open space and crashed inches away from Papis's feet. It landed like a glop of millet porridge. Only a tiny shower of sand flung up when it hit the beach.

It might not have struck where Mor wanted, but it had an effect. Everyone stopped. And Mor was immediately aware that he had gained all the attention. Unfortunately, he hadn't thought past making them stop.

The young boy quit writhing as well. His mouth formed a perfect circle.

But he was also the first to react. In that split second of disbelief he shoved against the other boys' loosened grips. He shot up faster than a bamboo firecracker, knocking the boys off balance. He hurtled toward Mor, cradling his limp hand. For a second, time slowed. They stared at each other. Mor saw panic on the boy's face as he passed. In a flash the boy was over the wall and gone. Mor's stomach plummeted to his knees. He knew the boy's panic was for him.

He was a tree standing alone in the plains. He was exposed. And he was now the target.

4

HAVE *you so soon forgotten that beetle? You are it, and it is now you. Get off this python's path.*

Despite his father's advice, Mor still could not move.

Papis stared at the pod lying undamaged near the tip of his sandal. His eyes traveled between it and Mor. His eyelids twitched, but he did not blink.

Mor turned to follow the boy just as Papis and the others lunged.

A high-pitched scream that sounded identical to the voice of his sister echoed around him, coming from his own throat. Mor was too scared to be embarrassed, and his feet were frightened into moving. Papis clawed for Mor, but Mor took off across the beach, parallel to the wall, toward the bridge and hopefully more people. His legs sank in the deep sand under his crashing weight, making it difficult to gain distance. His feet slid against the thongs of his sandals, and with every step he lifted a kilo of sand up with them.

He nearly collided with a woman drying laundry on the beach. She sucked her teeth and yelled after him. He couldn't stop to apologize. But when he turned his head back to shout "Sorry," he saw her sprawled on top of her dried clothes. Papis and his friends had charged past her.

Mor ducked under taut boat strings and hopped over iron stakes, rocks, and broken paddles. When he swerved to avoid a plastic gasoline container, one of his feet caught in a broken wicker basket and ripped away from his sandal. He kept running.

A group of boys sitting on the back of a floating *gaal*, eating fried fish, stared. His eyes darted their way, but he kept going, not sure they would help him. Then Papis shouted down the beach.

"Dankas!"

The sounds of splashing water and the trampling of sand met Mor's ears. Dread propelled him on as he looked over his shoulder and saw the boys from the resting *gaal* taking up the chase.

Mor's heart slammed against his breastbone. Breathing stung. But his soccer legs refused to let him fall. He was smaller but also faster. By the time he made it under the one-lane bridge, he had widened his distance. Tiny waves lapped against the shore, pushing garbage farther up in the sand. On the other side of the bridge seven or eight old boats towered before Mor, with fishermen hanging about. With all the commotion and bodies, he was able to slip behind the end of a boat and squeeze between the tips of two others. He got down on his hands and knees and crawled. He did not make a sound as sharp shards of cut cans and glass hidden in the shifting sand dug into his skin. He kept moving. Then panic rose inside him, slamming at his temples.

The beach lay open before him.

There was no place left to hide. Only foaming surf and sand.

Then, as if the fish had asked the sea to spit the *gaals* from the water to aid him, the sand began to fill. Boats and men came from the ocean, while women with huge, empty tubs came from every direction. The sun scorched Senegal, calling all the fishermen in with midmorning market catches. Sensing his chance, Mor hopped to his feet and weaved through the crowding beach. When his toes dug into the fiery sand, he realized he had lost his other sandal. He turned, frightened by what he might find. He saw nothing but footprints, fishermen, women with multicolored tubs brimming with fish, and the boats that hid his escape. He welcomed the commotion.

The crumbling beach wall and the curving roadway were

almost upon him. A few old *gaals* with dry, cracking paint that hadn't touched the water lay around him. He pressed close to the side of the nearest one. Splintered wood poked his cheeks, palms, and knees. He waited, trying to listen beyond his own heartbeat. Once his breathing slowed, he heard men talking in the distance. But then he heard Papis's gravelly voice.

"Did you see a runt-size *saccee*?"

Mor leaned forward, straining to hear. He must have heard wrong. The clobbering of his heart erupted in his throat.

"A thief, you say?" one fisherman asked. "We've seen many boys. But who has time to tell an aimless child from a *saccee*? We are working men, not children playing at it."

"What did he steal?" came a voice closer to Mor's hiding place.

He could not hear Papis's response, but he knew whatever it was, it was a lie.

Scared, Mor hoisted himself into the *gaal*. It was almost double his height. Sweat dripped off his forehead, and ant-size shards of wood burrowed into his skin. He buried himself under the pile of netting that sat jumbled in the boat's hull. He was completely still. Not even flinching when a tiny fish trapped in the net gave a final flap against his bare leg. The netting smelled of sea salt, fish, and heat.

Mor closed his eyes and tried to be anywhere but where he was.

Then he heard a thump and a sharp bang. Someone was throwing rocks at the boat he was in.

"Come out of there," Papis shouted.

Mor tried to swallow, but there was no saliva in his throat.

"Did you hear me? Come out now!"

Mor sucked in his breath. His body went rigid. Even if he had wanted to move, his arms and legs were anchored where he lay. But his heartbeat was so loud he was sure Papis could hear it. What now? There was nowhere to go. He was caught.

Without warning, someone yanked at the fishing net. He threaded his fingers in the netting and pulled it close. As the person tugged, Mor clenched as much of it as he could in his fists. The netting spread open, but not all the way. Half of it still hid him. The silhouette of the person heaving the net became visible through the plastic strings. But the sun shining from behind the person's head left his features in shadow. Mor thrust his back hard against the hull of the boat. He felt the boy's eyes ferreting him out. And for a second Mor thought he knew him. Then, when he was sure the boy would give another tug, certain to reveal all of him, the weight of the netting fell back on Mor.

"He's not here, man," a voice Mor couldn't place called out. "He must've found another way."

"There is no other way," grunted Papis, out of breath.

"I don't know, man. But he isn't here. If you doubt me,

check yourself." The shadow stayed in front of Mor's hiding place.

"Let's look this way. That runt can't be far."

The shadow left and so did Mor's breath.

They did not know where he was. *But how could that be?* Mor wondered. *If I could see that boy's outline, shouldn't he have been able to see me?* Mor could not shake the idea that he knew the boy. He lay like a mummy for what felt like his full eleven years. When the backs of his legs started to tingle, he ignored them. When his neck locked up and he thought it would snap, he endured it. And when a piece of wood that had been pinching him in his side cracked, wedging a sliver against his hip bone, he did not turn. But when he pressed his hands hard against his sides, his body almost rocketed up.

The little pouch wasn't in his pocket.

The only possession of value he and his sisters had, besides the family goat, was gone. The week his father lay in the clinic, Mor had studied his *yaay*'s treasures inside that rusted Dieg Bou Diar tomato can so long and so often, they had clouded his vision, becoming a muddle of shapes. Though each time he'd taken the can down from the shelf, he'd always felt better seeing them. He wanted to leap up and tear every piece of trash from the beach to find them. He squeezed his eyes shut and tried to remember everything that had happened, but it was useless. He did not know when he had lost the pouch. Or his family's money.

He pushed back a corner of the netting and listened. The distant shouts of the fishermen, the rumbling of churning motors switching off, and the squawks of seagulls rang out around him. Lifting his head slightly, he peeked over the lip of the *gaal*. A small bug marched across the wood and then took flight. Mor watched it fly, wishing he could sprout wings of his own.

There was no sign of Papis or the other boys. But even though he thought he had heard them go, he worried they could be hiding as he was. The afternoon sky filled with the chants for the call of the midday prayer, and the faint voice of a woman singing came to him from a static-filled radio. The water's constant tap against the shore was the nearest noise. Although he heard nothing else, he was still nervous when he poked his head up. He pushed the rest of the netting off anyway and sat up, ready to crawl down from the *gaal*.

"*Jërëjëf*," came a quiet voice, thanking him.

Mor fell back, almost tumbling over the boat's edge. Behind him, a few feet from where he'd hidden, the injured boy from earlier perched on an old *gaal* at the edge of the beach. Shaken, Mor darted his eyes around, worried someone might see or hear. The beach was nearly deserted, except for people sitting in the shade near the bridge. Having carted the fish away, most people had turned their focus to the market. The boy's hand was wrapped in a dirty red T-shirt with a big knot in the space between his thumb and finger.

"Does it hurt?" Mor asked. He double- and triple-checked that no one was approaching and then hopped out of the boat, squinting toward the ground, searching for his mother's old cloth pouch.

"Not much." The little boy looked down at his hand. "They've done worse." He pointed to a healed gash that started at the top of his knee and wrapped around to the back, like a sucking slug.

"What have you done to anger them that much?" Mor nudged a plastic bag aside with his toes, hoping the pouch was underneath it.

The boy looked at him, confused. "You don't have to do anything. . . . They're the Danka Boys. They wake ready to harm, whether you get in their way or not. They enjoy it."

"Enjoy it?" Mor asked, disbelieving. "To be so cruel when you've done nothing? That isn't fair. But my friend Oumar has whispered stories like this."

The boy shrugged. "I'd believe him, and I wouldn't wander over there right now if I were you." He tilted his chin across the bridge. "They took over an abandoned *barak* there. Papis, the one who did this"—he lifted his wrapped arm—"and two others came back here from Dakar a couple months ago. I think one might be from Lat Mata, and another from Jamma. A few others have joined them here, and now you can go nowhere without seeing them, or hearing their name if you're young. They race around like rats turning everything upside down. Not to mention their name is painted on walls all over."

"Lat Mata? That's where I'm from. But there are no boys there like that."

"Then you are lucky," the boy replied. "My *yaay* says groups like that are all over the cities, and that now some of the evil is coming back home. So I should stay away. But as you can see, it does not always work." He glanced at his hand.

Mor found it hard to concentrate on what the boy said. Now that the Danka Boys, as he called them, were gone, Mor was more concerned with finding his mother's pouch and his family's remaining *khaliss*. Even though his aunt was coming to help them, he still did not want to go back home and confess that he'd lost all the money they had. And he'd never be able to meet Amina's eyes when he admitted he'd lost their mother's treasures, too.

"I should have listened," Mor grumbled. "I should have left it in the can."

"What?"

Mor lifted his head but not his eyes. His feet scrunched up, pawing the sand. "Nothing . . . I better go, though."

"Thanks again." The boy pushed his elbow forward, then swung his legs over the back of the boat, jumping down. "Remember, if you see them, go the other way." The boy ran up to the crumbling wall and was gone.

Mor did not waste a second thinking about the boy's warning. Instead he got back on his knees and turned over each piece of trash he saw. Rotting watermelon rinds, shredded plastic bags, and squished bottles flew through the air. The sand was littered, and Mor tossed it all. The thongs of ripped sandals, the fabric of a worn-out school sack, and the limb of a long-forgotten doll were all noticed by Mor. He saw and touched everything, except what he truly hoped to find.

5

FOUR days after the burial, the *ndiaga ndiaye* bringing their aunt to them slowed to a rattling crawl in a cloud of gray-brown smoke. One of the men bracing himself on the ladder at the back of the bus threw a large orange fabric bag down to Mor. It smashed against Mor's face as he caught it, the weight of it almost toppling him forward. Mor was about to place it on the ground and greet his aunt, when she snapped at him.

"Hold it up!" Her flowing *boubou* spilled out of the back door, a sea of blue trimmed with emerald green. It sailed around her like a wave as she hopped down from the still-rolling bus, which immediately picked up speed once her feet had left its back-end platform. "It is too dusty out here.

Don't put it in the dirt." As soon as her sandaled feet, with polished red toes poking from the front, touched the ground, she was off in the direction of their home.

"Yes, Auntie. Welcome," Mor rushed to say as she passed by him. Amina curtsied, shuffling alongside her, as Fatima just stood and watched.

"She is nothing like she is supposed to be," Fatima said, hanging on Mor, causing him to shift before the bag slipped.

"And how would you know?" Mor looped the bag's shoulder straps over his arm. "You were three the last time she was here."

"So?" replied Fatima. "She does not even say hello, and Baay said only selfish people do that."

"She is just tired after her daylong journey from one bus to another. And Baay also said it could mean someone was busy with thoughts in their head." Mor took a step forward, nearly tripping over his own feet in his father's sandals. They were much too big for him but the only choice he had since losing his own. "She could be thinking the same about you. Maybe she is waiting for you to greet her first."

Fatima gave him a look that said she didn't believe him.

"Come now," their aunt shouted over her shoulder, her hand raised high. Gold bracelets clanked around her wrist. "No messing about. The night will be here before the day has truly begun."

"See?" Fatima whispered as Mor stopped to wiggle his toes back into his father's sandal, which had shot off his foot. "How come you have Baay's shoes?"

"Tima, I told you. I lost mine."

"I know." Fatima leaned on him, holding his wrist. "But they look funny," she giggled. "You should just go barefoot. Your feet are getting all dusty and covered with sand anyway."

"Like yours often are." Mor clinched his toes around the leather that divided his big toe from the others. He could never have met his *bàjjan* with no shoes. "Now go and greet Auntie. Do not bring more distance between us."

Fatima dragged her feet.

"Hurry up now," their aunt demanded again. "We have much to do before the *ndiaga ndiaye* returns."

Something about those words didn't settle right with Mor as he picked up his pace, pulling Fatima along. He had hoped that when Tanta Coumba said their aunt would come to care for them, as she had when their *baay* was young, she'd meant in Lat Mata. Mor had forgotten why she never came anymore. As his aunt charged down the road in front of him, sucking her teeth and batting at flies, he remembered how she'd only sent presents and money from time to time since their *yaay*'s death three years before, but she never came home. Worry started to tumble inside him as he thought about her complaints about flies, the absence of a cool breeze, the long, hot day of travel, and no running water. She acted as if her childhood village had a stink she wanted to wash off forever. And that the village well was too far away to do so. Her life was in the city, with running water and, he guessed, no flies, while theirs was in Lat Mata. "Why should we be concerned with the bus's return already, Bàjjan? That is just two days from now," he asked cautiously. Even though she had been brisk since she stepped off the bus, Mor did not want to ruffle her head-dress any more. Besides, their father had left the *barak* to Mor, as the only son. It was his responsibility to see to its care.

Although their *baay* did not have much, everything he loved was from Lat Mata. Mor hadn't had much time to think with the burial, his days of grief, and what had happened in Mahktar, but he definitely hadn't believed she would take them from their home. But now he realized that was exactly what she planned to do.

"We will all be on it," she said matter-of-factly, cutting into his thoughts as if everything had long been decided. "I'm sure you don't have much to collect before we go."

"All" and "go" rung in Mor's ears, slowing him. "I don't want to leave. When would we come back?"

"Never." She halted in the dirt and turned to stare at Mor, who fended off troubled stares from both Fatima and Amina. Fatima's little hand tugged on him, squeezing the life out of his fingers. "There is nothing for you here, and I have made arrangements."

"But the *barak* has been left in my care. I am supposed to take care of it."

"Nonsense. You are not grown. He never thought it was

Allah's will for him to leave us so soon. Besides, you will be starting at a *daara*, and Amina will tend the house of my late husband's sister. You will both be well taken care of."

"And Fatima? What will happen to her?" Mor asked, even though he knew it was better not to press her.

"She will have to remain with me, I suppose. There is no getting around that right now. You can hold a rag and carry a bucket, can't you, child?" Fatima shrank behind her brother, biting her bottom lip—a warning sign that she was about to cry.

"I promised Baay we would stay together. We don't want to be separated. That is not what Baay wanted. We belong here."

"You belong where I say. There is no one here to care for you." Their *bàjjan* continued down the road. "Now do not question me further. Such an insolent tongue."

"I can care for us," Mor said, challenging her.

Dust kicked up as their aunt stopped and spun, her *boubou* coiling around her. Through gritted teeth she said, "With what? You are hardly old enough to wipe your own backside. How can you take care of yourself and two young sisters? No, you will be coming with me in two days and I want no more words about it!"

Right there in the street, around the sights and smells of his home, Mor realized it would take more than just him to convince her that they didn't need to leave Lat Mata. And he needed to do so fast.

As they neared their home, even the light of the day appeared dimmer than usual.

Fatima yanked on Mor, stopping abruptly on the path outside their family's door. "Why did you lie to me?"

"What do you mean?" He turned to her, raising the bag so it did not drag along the ground.

She shook her head back and forth. Her eyelids were rows of wrinkles because she closed them so tight. "Auntie is not nice at all."

"*Nopil*," Mor shushed her. He tilted his head in their aunt's direction, hoping she had not heard Fatima's poor attempt at a whisper. But he had no cause to worry because she had already stepped inside their *barak*.

Then she was back outside in an instant.

"This *bëy* has nibbled at my dress." Their aunt scowled, shooing Jeeg out of the cramped interior of their home. Jeeg bleated and snorted as she was shoved with a square of cardboard. "Goats are for the yard, not where I lay my head to sleep! And this one needs to be brought to the *reykat*."

"No!" Fatima raced to Jeeg. "She hates the butcher."

"My, do all of Fallou's children have loose tongues?" She eyed Amina, who stayed quiet. Shaking her head, their aunt ducked back inside. "I must pray."

Amina and Mor shared another look while Fatima whispered close to Jeeg's ear.

"Don't worry, you are not going to the butcher's. I promise Mor won't let her take you."

Mor stood, uneasy as Fatima made a promise for him. More promises.

"You only nibbled the bottom of her *boubou* because it is green like sweet grass, right?"

Jeeg bleated.

"Shh, Fatima stop," Mor snipped.

"But she doesn't even like Jeeg, and everyone loves Jeeg." Fatima hugged the goat's neck. "I don't want to live with her, and neither does Jeeg."

"What is this?" their aunt shouted, ducking her head back out the doorway. "No water for prayer?" Their aunt let out a tsk. "What if the spirits were thirsty, what would they have to drink?" Mor didn't say it, but he knew Jeeg had probably sipped out of the jars as she always did.

Mor did not meet their aunt's accusing stare, even though he was not in charge of getting the water.

Because of their *bàjjan*'s arrival, Amina had not had an extra moment that morning to take her third trip down to the well to get fresh water after cooking. And since Mor was not expected to mingle with the women busy with their daily chores, he had not even thought to help.

"I am sorry, Bàjjan," Amina said. "I will fetch it now." She bowed slightly, grabbed a cloth and a bucket, and hurried away.

Mor watched her go and then mumbled, "I need to go down there for a moment." He nodded toward a side path parallel to the one Amina had taken.

"I hope it is in the direction of the mosque for prayer. Your sisters are still young, but you are growing. There is no excuse."

Mor knew he should not lie, but he did anyway. "Yes, Bàjjan." He gave a shallow nod.

"Well, give me my *saag*." She snapped her fingers at him as if she were the one in a hurry. "There is no point in you taking it along."

Mor handed it to her and was off, hopping as his foot slipped out of one of the sandals.

"Wait. Where are you going?" their aunt questioned as Fatima dashed after her brother, pulling Jeeg by the neck to follow.

"I'm not staying with you!" Fatima said. "And Jeeg doesn't want to either." She wrapped the cord at Jeeg's neck around her little fingers.

"You insolent children," their *bàjjan* grumbled. "I will cure you of that spiteful tongue."

Mor waited for Fatima to catch up. "Why would you say that?" he asked when she reached him. He kicked off the sandals, picked them up, and ran. "Come on."

"She is mean, mean, mean," Fatima whined, yanking Jeeg along. "Nothing like the stories Baay used to tell of her. And now I know why she always used to send those pretty things. It was so she would not have to come. Wasn't it?" Fatima asked her brother, who also realized his aunt was worse than he remembered.

She had said and done all the right things when Mor's *yaay* died, making sure his *baay* had all he needed. She had even hugged Mor, and Amina, and cradled a crying Fatima in her arms, but now Mor wondered if it was just because back then she wouldn't have to take them home with her. That their *baay* was still there.

The loss stung anew.

At the end of the path Mor saw Amina with some of her friends, pulling long strings from the well. Two girls helped Amina settle her bucket on her head before she turned to hurry back to their aunt.

"Why have you three come to fetch me?" she asked, standing tall, balancing the water bucket on her head without using her hands. "Is there something else Bàjjan needs?"

"We have no other time. We need to talk without her ears gobbling up our words," Mor said, breathing heavy.

"There is nothing to talk about. We must leave with her."

"But we can't."

"What other choice do we have? Do you think I want to cook and clean for others always? Don't you think I know she has made no room for me to continue school? Don't you think I want to stay?"

"Then let's stay. You want to go to that fancy school. Baay said you could. He even put down a deposit. It was supposed to be a surprise."

Amina halted. Staring. It was one of the only times Mor had seen her speechless.

"What? How do you know that?"

"I was with him. He had been saving for months. Next he wanted to buy you a uniform and save more to finish paying for the start of the year. But he . . ." Mor was speechless himself. Then he looked at her. "Don't you see? We have to stay. We can try to make the money on our own."

"It won't be that simple. I'm sorry, but just because you wear Baay's sandals, it does not make you grown like Baay."

"I know that." Hurt pinched Mor.

Amina stared at him. Then bit at her lip. "You were as surprised as I to hear Bàjjan's plan for us, but we have to obey. She is making room for us and no one else will. Iéna Academy was a dream even when Baay said I could go. Even with his deposit. But as you said, he hadn't paid all the fees yet. If he could not get all the money, there is no way we can. And I do not think Auntie would help. Maybe you will be happy at the *daara* and I will be able to go back to school one day in the city. There are schools there, too."

"Amina, you know that is not true! Cheikh has gone to the *daara* and we have not seen him since. When would I ever see you? Besides, she wants to split us up. Is that what you want too? To leave Tima? To get rid of me?" Mor actually sounded unsure, as if she might say that was exactly what she wanted.

"Of course not. Part of me is in you and Tima. I would not be complete without you."

He exhaled.

"But how can we change any of it?" Amina said. She took the bucket from her head. "She will not listen to us."

"I will find a way."

"Brother, you do not even have one hair on your chin. What can you do?"

"He can do anything," Fatima spoke up, pushing between them. "Stop being mean, Mina. Mor can stop her."

"How, Tima?" Amina said. "I am not trying to be mean, I am only telling the truth I see and that each of you needs to see." She looked back at her brother. "What will it help to pretend anything will be different? It is not our path to stay here. We have no *yaay* or *baay* anymore. The money we did have you've taken."

Mor stared at her. She knew the pouch was gone?

"Don't think I did not notice that the Dieg Bou Diar can is empty. I peer inside it each day as Yaay did, as you did, to be closer to the things she loved, and it is gone. Why do you only think of yourself when you make decisions?"

Her words were a slap.

"I don't," Mor whispered. "I am thinking of all of us right now. I know how much you want to go to that school, Mina. I see you looking at that shiny paper with the girls in those clean, new uniforms when you think I am not looking." Amina stared past him. "And Tima does not want to be separated from us. And I want to stay here with all the things Yaay and Baay loved. I can do this. I know I can. I will go to Baay's old shop. They have always told me I am handy with a wrench. I will find work there. I will fix engines like Baay. I was already learning."

Amina's eyes narrowed, but she did not cut in. Encouraged, he continued.

"How much more would you need to start school? Baay has already paid almost fifteen thousand francs. Maybe Auntie can help us get started for the rest if she knows Baay has already given what he had and I will work to find more. I will make sure we do not go hungry each night too. I can. I just need your help."

"How?" Amina asked. "What can I do?" She stared down at the water bucket. "I have nowhere to get money. And even if you take Baay's old job, they will not pay you enough to save for school and feed us. Even Baay did not bring home lots of coins. You will not be able to collect over nine thousand francs in three months' time."

Even with their *baay*'s deposit, that was still a lot of money. More than Mor had ever seen. However, he refused to give up before he had even tried. He watched her for a long time. "If you say you believe I can do it, that's all I need right now. I need to know you want to stay together."

Amina swatted at the corner of her eye so quick that Mor would have missed it if he'd blinked.

"I don't want us to be scattered, but I don't know how we won't be split apart."

If you tug a length of stubborn rope together, as my flock of three, and pull again and again together, you will gain what you seek. Their father's voice swept in.

"If we do it together," Mor said. The image of him yanking a rope with the help of his sisters was clear in his mind. "We can do this, Mina. Baay wants us to try. And we want to be here."

"Yes." Fatima jumped up and down. "I want to try."

Amina exhaled and even gave a slight nod.

"Okay, now go back to Bàjjan. I will be there before the steam over our food is gone." Mor took off down another path before Amina had a chance to protest, or Fatima could follow.

6

WHEN Mor rounded the corner to Tanta Coumba's *barak*, he nearly collided with her.

"Ah, slow yourself, unless you are chased by a lion or something much worse." She smiled.

Even within that instant he felt better than he had all morning. He was hopeful that she might be able to help convince the stubborn ox that was his aunt that he and his sisters should stay. He dropped his father's sandals into the dirt and slipped back into them, smoothing down the front of his shirt.

"I am sorry to bother you when you are about to tend your garden," Mor said, looking down and seeing her hands filled with seeds and a small bowl.

"You are never a bother to me. But why are you not with your *bàjjan*, has she not arrived? I was going to come later and give my greetings after you had time to visit."

"Can't you come now?" Mor asked. "She is taking us away."

"But that is to be expected. You knew that was to happen, right?"

Mor's gaze dropped to his feet. "I thought she might stay here. In her old house."

"This is no longer her home. Her heart lies with the city now." Tanta Coumba's brows came together in concern.

"Then maybe she will give us a little money and check on us sometimes," Mor said, hopeful.

"Come now, she won't leave you children alone."

"She has till now. Baay was in the clinic a week before the burial and she did not come."

"She was away and could not get back for over a week. It was not enough time. I am sure she is very sad about that."

"Well, we took care of ourselves while she was too busy to do so."

"Ease your venom. She came when she could," Tanta Coumba said. "And you were not alone. You had a village of help."

Mor thought about the countless times over the last week Tanta Coumba, her daughters, or someone else was at their door bringing food or checking to make sure they were okay. "Exactly, so we will not be alone now."

"I know you want this badly, but it does not always work that way. Being alone for one week with eyes constantly watching and helping is far different from raising yourself and two young sisters. That would not be easy." Tanta Coumba knocked his nose with her knuckle. "Your *baay* always said your *bàjjan* has a big house in the city where she can care for you all."

"But she won't care for us. She is sending Mina and me away. And she doesn't even want Tima, but she says she will keep her because there is nowhere else for her to go. I'm sure she will leave her with someone else as soon as she can, though. She doesn't want her or us."

"Hush now. That is not true." Tanta Coumba stared down at Mor. "She loves and cares about each of you."

"But Mina won't get to go to that fancy school, and you know how much she wants to." Mor's voice rose in pitch.

Tanta Coumba looked troubled.

Baby Zal giggled and gurgled on a blanket near Tanta Coumba's garden. In Mor's rush to speak with her he had not noticed the naked little boy playing with a carved wooden boat. Tanta Coumba glanced at her son, then back at Mor.

"If she has already decided, I cannot interrupt that."

"But I can take care of us."

Creases appeared at the corner of her eyes. "And how will you do that? You are still a boy that should be in school yourself, learning his numbers and letters, not finding work to care for a family."

"But she wants to send me to a Koranic school like Cheikh, to memorize verses, not learn my math or writing. I won't get to see my sisters, like you haven't seen Cheikh. I know you miss him. I see it."

Tanta Coumba's mouth lay slightly open, as if she was going to speak.

Mor watched her, ready to say more.

"Why are you so sure the city will be bad? You might like it there."

"I won't. My family won't be with me."

"We can't always be with the ones we love, sometimes we have to carry them here and here." She pressed her hand to her heart and then to her temple.

Mor went still. "I have to keep my promise to Baay. He is depending on me to keep us together. I can't lose what I have left of my family. Please help us."

A restless quiet stretched between them.

"I don't know what I could do."

"You could tell her you'll come see us, like you have. You won't need to bring us food, I'll find a way to get us that."

"I don't know. . . ."

Mor was desperate. "I will run if you don't. As soon as she leaves me at that *daara*, I will run back here."

"It is too far for all that," Tanta Coumba said. Her eyes clouded over. "You cannot do such a drastic thing. The big city can be a maze for a boy that has only known fields and open spaces. It will swallow you and spit you out as a different child. You must promise me you will not do this."

Another promise.

"I promise I will if you do not come to change her mind." Mor's boldness was unfair, and his threat turned the air between them sour.

Tanta Coumba's smile had faded.

"I will come," she agreed. "But do not think it will be as easy as stirring sugar in tea."

Shame snaked through him for turning on her as he had, but he couldn't think of that now. Until she came, he had to get back to his sisters and begin to convince his *bàjjan* they were meant to stay.

7

"KAI *legui*. How you have made us wait," snapped Mor's aunt when he reached the doorway of his home out of breath. "Come, come. Our bellies have been rumbling over this good-smelling groundnut sauce and rice Amina has made. You are letting it grow cold."

Stepping in the doorway, he stumbled on a pebble and almost skidded into the pot of food. He knew it was the last of their rice in the dish and there wouldn't have been more if he'd ruined it. Embarrassment crawled around his collar.

"Why are you wearing those ridiculous shoes?" His aunt stared at his feet, swimming in the well-worn leather sandals. "You've been stepping on your own toes since I got off the bus. You may as well go barefoot for all the good they are doing you."

"That's what I said," Fatima giggled, forgetting herself for a moment. Then she clapped her lips shut under their *bàjjan*'s glare.

Mor mashed his toes against the leather.

"Who are you to think you can settle into a man's shoes? Now take those ridiculous things off and come sit down," their *bàjjan* barked. "It won't do to have you falling all over our skirts because you want to play at being a man." She nodded toward Fatima and Amina, who sat on the earth floor while she sat up on the pallet.

Her words stung like a thousand beestings, but Mor clinched his teeth together, holding his jaw closed. He wanted to shout that the sandals weren't ridiculous, that they were his *baay*'s, but he said nothing. He simply turned and slid his feet out of them, and placed them with their shoes by the doorway. When he went to sit down, Fatima wedged herself close, as far away from their aunt as she could be.

Oblivious to Fatima's dislike, their aunt hitched up the enormous sleeves of her *boubou*, creating her own breeze as she sat up. "Now that we are all finally settled, how are you children? You look spindly and thin. I could mistake you for the branches of the baobab." She looked between them, poking her lips out as if making a decision. "How old are you now?" She focused on Amina. "Nine?"

"And a half," Amina said, low.

"Don't you know you should be thick and sturdy like a baobab tree trunk by now?" Their aunt's eyes slid up the length of Amina's body; however, Amina did not seem uneasy.

She probably did not shrink under their aunt's gaze because she knew she resembled their mother in every way. A day did not go by that Mor did not hear someone tell her so. It was obvious to any who knew their parents that Amina would have their height, surpassing Mor's. She was already growing like a reed, with long, thin arms, slender legs, and knobby elbows. Their mother had always said those were the true signs of a beauty to come. Just as a baby giraffe, awkward on its limbs at birth, grows to be elegant and majestic, their *yaay* knew, Amina would do the same.

As their aunt continued to stare, Amina crouched in the dirt, scooping groundnut sauce onto the smoothed-out bed of rice in the gigantic aluminum bowl. "In the city you will become solid and stout. Each of you will." Their *bàjjan* shifted her attention to Fatima, who shrank beneath it.

"And what will we do with you?" their aunt asked, not expecting an answer. "All I've seen is you fluffing about, when you need to be put to work. Many would think you too young, but I do not. Although I cannot trust you will behave living under someone else's roof, cleaning their floors and helping to prepare their meals. I must knock out your idleness first and that poisoned tongue. My brother, rest his soul, was like a cuddly bear with you. A stricter hand is needed to ensure you will be right."

"Yes, Bàjjan," Amina said, nodding for Fatima.

For a moment Mor was only half listening. He stared at Amina, but unlike Fatima, who squeezed Mor's fingers to almost breaking, Amina kept her face expressionless as she placed the bowl in the middle of the four of them. A chunky orangey-brown sauce sat on the pile of white rice, steaming.

While Mor had lost his appetite, Fatima had not. After a few more seconds of pouting, she released Mor's hand and shimmied closer to the bowl. As their aunt scooped her fingers in her section of the dish, Fatima followed behind in her own. She mashed a steaming handful of rice and sauce into her palm until it was a tight-packed ball, and then she dropped it into her mouth. Soon she was asking to dig into Mor's section, after he had gone minutes without taking a second or third bite.

When the last grain of rice had been mopped up by Fatima's little hand, Amina removed the bowl, chewing and swallowing her final mouthful.

"My sister-in-law's family will get good and fat off your cooking." Their *bàjjan* scooted back, giving Amina room to pick up the dropped rice kernels one by one. "There are points you still must learn, but you are showing yourself well." She jimmied a toothpick she'd pulled from her bag between two of her back teeth and wiggled it, making a sucking noise. Continuing to riffle through her *saag*, she said, "Now where is that gunpowder tea of mine?"

As if knowing what their aunt was already about to say,

Amina brought out a miniature red teapot from under the pallet. Flowers once painted on its belly had long since been devoured by black singe from constant contact with the fire. Amina placed the *barada,* with its warming coals, in front of her legs and waited.

"Ah, here it is," their *bàjjan* said, pulling out a bright-green tin. "This is my favorite brand. You can find nothing like it in your village market."

When she opened the tin, Amina reached for the loose green tea leaves, but their aunt pulled the box away.

"Why are you, not your brother, preparing our tea?" their aunt asked. "That duty falls to the son." She held tight to the traditions of *attaaya.* The teapot hovered in Amina's hands.

Amina looked from her *bàjjan* to her brother. "I prepare it sometimes. Baay did not mind."

Their aunt sucked at her teeth again and held the box of special gunpowder tea out to Mor. He took the teapot from Amina and squatted before the *barada.* He crammed a bunch of the loose green tea leaves into the child-size pot. His aunt's full concentration was on his hand, like she was counting every leaf removed from her precious tin. Mor poured in hot water and rotated the teapot, swirling the liquid around the tea leaves. Everyone was silent as he began the ritual of tea service.

Out of the corner of his eye Mor noticed Fatima twisting toward the doorway as her friends skipped by, giggling and screaming in the midafternoon light. Knowing her next move, he pressed his heel into her knee so she would not jump up. She looked down at his foot, then up at him. He said nothing, only shook his head, as unnoticeable as the curve of a moth's antenna—but he knew Fatima had seen it by the slouch of her shoulders. Never stopping his tea preparation, he poured a stream of sugar from a small plastic bag into the teapot. Fatima's body slumped further, and she shot her aunt a cold look, shoving at Mor's heel.

"Do you have a *gunóor* in your dress?" Their aunt pointed her toothpick at Fatima. A small piece of cassava leaf from their dinner dangled at the end. "Even a beetle shouldn't make you squirm so much."

Fatima stared blankly at their aunt. Then her eyes darted to the dirt floor, most likely in search of the bug.

"Why must you move about so?" their aunt continued.

It was evident by her change in tone that she did not favor Fatima as much as Amina.

"So . . ." She switched her attention back to Mor while he poured the honey-yellow sugared tea into a petite glass. It frothed when he emptied it from one glass into another, the liquid tumbling over itself. The loose leaves mixed with each pouring, becoming stronger and darker. However, it still wasn't strong enough for a first serving. When he had emptied the frothed liquid back into the pot to steep some more, their aunt continued. "When I last spoke on the phone with your *baay*, he told me you've already memorized a few passages of the Koran."

Mor tensed. He knew his father had called her once every few months from the phone at the mechanic shop where he worked, but for some reason he did not like being at the heart of any discussions between them.

"You should have been in a *daara* long ago. Your parents never wanted to send you away, but I think it is what you need. Some of our country's greatest leaders have gone to these schools. They will teach you piety. Soon you will learn all six thousand two hundred thirty-six verses."

She said the exact number as if knowing it was a badge of pride.

Mor tried to calculate in his head how long that could possibly take. He knew of boys who had left their families when they were five or six years old and had not returned from Koranic school until they were thirteen or even sixteen. A part of him was curious about the schools, especially since Cheikh had left, but another part of him was glad that, like some of his other friends' parents, his had decided to send him to the village school and have him learn his verses at the mosque. His friend Oumar had heard from his cousin who had lived in Dakar that not all *daaras* were the same. Where some *serignes* were kind, others were not. "You never know what you'll get until you get there," he'd said. Mor worried about what that meant for him if his aunt got her way.

She slid the toothpick between her thumb and finger, wiping it clean, as she looked around their sparse room. "It will not take long to pack your things, I should think. You can leave the few dishes and bowls. You will not need them. I know of someone who may want to move his family in here."

"But Baay told the elders he was leaving it to me." Mor hated the catch in his throat.

"We have already discussed this. That will not happen. There is nothing much here of value anyway." She scanned the room as if it held no history, or memories, or laughter.

Mor couldn't imagine anyone else living here except for his family. His father had built their *barak* with his *own baay* when he was around Mor's age. He had taken pride in every second of their work. Mor's *bàjjan* should have remembered that, like he remembered making shadow puppets on the far wall with his *baay* where the boy chased the lion and won. He could still hear his mother's and sisters' laughter in his ears as they'd watched from the pallet, holding up the *lampe tempête* with cardboard blocking out all but a small circle of light. All their good memories had taken place in that one-room home. Mor looked at the flap swinging over the doorway, wondering what was keeping Tanta Coumba.

"We will need to be ready for the morning bus in two days' time," their aunt continued. "Otherwise we will have to wait days for another, and I need to get back to the city."

"Couldn't we stay behind?" Mor began.

"Your *baay* was in a coma for a week. It has already been too long for you children to be on your own. What kind of *bàjjan* would I be if I let it continue?"

Mor watched her. He wondered where her worry was

69

coming from. She had shown her lack of concern by not taking the first *ndiaga ndiaye* to Lat Mata when someone from the clinic called about her brother's accident. There had been three buses since then, and she had missed two of them. What had she refused to miss instead of seeing her brother? But that was not the question he asked. He knew he could not wait for Tanta Coumba any longer. He would have to convince his *bàjjan* himself.

"We would be fine . . . I mean, we have been fine," Mor rattled, not taking a breath. He knew it was disrespectful to press, but he had to. With all her plans, this was his only chance. "We've had enough food, coal, and butane for cooking and the *lampe tempête*. We've needed nothing more. A-a-a-nd . . . ," he stuttered, thinking fast, "I'm sure I can get a job down at Baay's old mechanic shop. Mamadou said I am always welcome." Before she could cut him off, he continued. "They used to tell me they would always have a place for me. I was helpful when I was there. And I'm sure there are other things I could do as well. Amina is smart and needs to be in school. Not just sweeping someone else's floors. She got accepted into a fancy one in Shayna. Amina, show her the papers. Baay already gave them money; he wants her to go." He swallowed hard and glanced at his sister. He was sure her lip turned up in a smile as quick as the flap of a butterfly's wing.

"What is this ridiculous talk?" their aunt asked. She leaned forward on the pallet, her hand on her hip. "You cannot run a household. And I'm sure Fallou did not pay all the fees. So now the deposit is probably lost. Amina cannot afford to go to such a school. Besides, that is almost an hour's walk from here. You would not have money for the bus, and you'd never be able to keep up with the fees. No, absolutely not."

"We would do it together," Amina spoke up. "We would help each other. And I do not mind the walk. I have walked farther. I have already been cooking and cleaning since Yaay died. And I have taken care of Tima."

"I can take care of myself now too," Fatima added. "And Jeeg." The family goat lay outside, near the doorway, not allowed inside.

"Baay wants us to stay together. He told me so," Mor said.

"When has he told you this? There was no time," their aunt said, disbelieving.

Mor thought of his promise and his father's words on the wind, knowing she would not believe him. He wished his *baay* would join him.

There is no need to wish, I am here. Look to our flock and find your strength. You are not alone. You have not been abandoned.

Mor sat up taller. His *baay* had really come when he called. Mor squared his shoulders, not giving up. "He is telling me now." His *bàjjan's* eyebrow arched. "We *can* take care of each other."

"That makes no difference anyway," their aunt said. "You

are not staying here. And you will not continue to question my word." Her voice was flat and strong.

"I told you, Auntie, we are not alone," Mor pressed, encouraged by his sisters and his *baay*'s whispers.

"Enough." Their *bàjjan* wagged her finger at him. "I want to hear no more. Besides, I assume you have only a little money from your *baay*. What will you do when that runs out? You truly think Mamadou will pay you a man's wage? What will you eat then? Would you go be beggars in the street, or hope your neighbors would continue to feed you when they have families of their own? What will you do? Will your hand always be out—asking?"

Mor's shoulders sagged, the fight seeping out of him like a deflating balloon. His eyes darted to Amina, but she looked away. Guilt twisted around him. The money was already gone. The last two days he'd felt the weight of the lost pouch in his pocket as if its ghost were nuzzled against his leg.

"He will. I was learning," Mor said. "He, Idy, and Mighty Yacine said I am fast and smart. Even at Baay's burial they told others that when I passed." Mor glanced at the door again, wondering if Tanta Coumba was mad enough at him not to come.

His aunt's laugh was almost a cackle. "But they will not fill your pockets with coins. You will just be scurrying around whenever they have a need. And if not that, what? You have nothing worthy to trade." She puffed out her sleeve. "You are but a little boy no taller than a goat on hind legs."

"I will learn as Baay did," Mor blurted out.

"Hmph." A rush of air left her mouth along with spittle. "It took him years. You do not have such time." A smothered chuckle rested deep in her throat. "How tongues will flap if I allow you to become another wayward boy running in the streets, up to nothing good. No, in the city you will learn the ways of Allah. And that knowledge will last you throughout your life."

Mor did not respond. He looked down at his slender fingers, bare of calluses, unlike his father's heavily weathered hands—a working man's hands. *Baay, I am not enough*, he thought, hoping his father would aid him again.

And as if he'd heard him, help arrived.

DIEYNABA, is that you I hear?" A shadow spread across the doorway.

Everyone turned toward the silhouette as it became more defined. A hand the color of chestnuts pulled the tarp aside.

"Coumba Gueye!" Mor's aunt sprung up in excitement. The closed tin of tea leaves she'd been protecting like a guard over precious jewels rolled off her lap when she stood. She jammed her finger toward it for Amina to pick up; then she beckoned her childhood friend inside. "It has been too long. It should not take death to bring us back together."

"I am where I have always been. You are the one who has become a rolling pebble, my friend, traveling away from your beginnings." Although the words were woven with sweetness, Mor was sure his aunt felt the slight bite by the way her smile tightened. When Tanta Coumba leaned forward to kiss Mor's aunt once on each cheek, baby Zal's head flopped into view. He was strapped against her back in a batik fabric, sleeping peacefully. Little flowers of spit bloomed on his lips as he slept.

"Oh, what a precious child," Mor's aunt said, spying baby Zal over Tanta Coumba's shoulder, "who does not trouble his mother when she visits."

Mor watched the women talking as old friends. His *bàjjan* was quite pretty when she smiled and giggled. Her deep-set eyes sparkled, and her pronounced cheekbones appeared as if they stored cherries when they rose. Getting Tanta Coumba had been a great idea. Her cheerful spirit might help Mor unfreeze his cold, cold aunt. The women's hearty laughter and Tanta Coumba's presence eased some of the anxious grumbling in his belly. It triggered memories of when Mor's mother was alive. When they used to laugh and joke in the vegetable patch, chasing him and Cheikh around.

Tanta Coumba glanced down at Mor and his sisters. A bright smile was on her face. Mor stowed his memory and dipped his head. Amina made room for Tanta Coumba to sit next to their aunt on the raised pallet.

"Again, I am sorry about Fallou," Tanta Coumba said. She cupped their aunt's hands in her own. "He was a kindhearted man and will be greatly missed."

"Yes, a tragedy for sure."

Tanta Coumba let their aunt's hands slip from hers and took the small square of cardboard Mor held out to help fan flies away from her and her son. Baby Zal's head lobbed to the side, trapped in sleep, unconscious of the chatter.

Mor knew it wasn't proper for him and his sisters to remain in the room as Tanta Coumba talked of her childhood friends, including their aunt, so they bowed their heads, but still leaned in close, pretending not to listen.

"Do you remember when your brother took Awa out in that old rowboat?" Tanta Coumba asked their *bàjjan*.

"Yes, yes." Their aunt's scowl lifted. "When they were about eight or so years older than Mor now."

"Mmm-hmmm," Tanta Coumba went on, chuckling before she could get the words out. "And he kissed her. No warning. No permission. And *plop*, she dived straight into the water and swam for shore."

Their *bàjjan* shook her head. "In her beautiful new *boubou*, no less."

"Warning him. Saying: 'These lips are not yours, Fallou Fall. . . .'" Tanta Coumba waved her finger in front of her as Amina, Fatima, and Mor huddled together, trying to hide smiles behind their hands. Even Jeeg had peeked her head under the door tarp to hear.

"'You have not yet shown yourself worthy of them,'" their *bàjjan* continued where Tanta Coumba had left off. "'You will need to do much better than a rickety little rowboat and a few honey-sweetened words to show me that. . . .'"

Mor and his sisters bit their lips not to giggle over the tale they shouldn't have been hearing. Tanta Coumba's words reminded Mor that the painted brand on Jeeg's hip—a red circle over wavy blue lines, his family marking, which everyone in Lat Mata could recognize—had come about because of that day. His father was represented by the passion of the day's setting red sun, while their mother had swum like the feisty blue waves.

Tanta Coumba's memories had Mor's aunt weeping with laughter, each mention of her brother and sister-in-law chipping away at her rough edges somehow. Now Tanta Coumba patted their aunt's thigh. "Your brother was a rare gem."

"Indeed," their *bàjjan* agreed.

"Like their *yaay*," Tanta Coumba added.

"I cannot believe such misfortune has befallen this house again," Mor's aunt said, staring off. "And I do not think the authorities have even caught that dim-witted fool who caused the accident. People say he had at least thirty live chickens strapped to that *moto*." She rocked her head and then refocused on her friend. "Didn't he know some of them were bound to get loose, clucking and carrying on as they do? They say if the truck had been a little farther down the road, all would have been spared. But alas, that was not Allah's will."

Tanta Coumba glanced at Mor and his sisters. "It is a shame. But let us not speak of this now. I'm sure you have happier news from the big city."

Mor's aunt followed Tanta Coumba's gaze. "Yes. You are right, although I'm sure they have heard all of this before."

"Even still, it is better not to pick at a wound that has just begun to heal," Tanta Coumba suggested.

"But we must remember scabs are picked over all the time and they heal just fine. Tougher even."

"But they *do* leave scars," Tanta Coumba said firmly, not backing down. "Besides, you seem well informed. There is little left to say."

Tanta Coumba cradled their aunt's hands in her own, stroking them. Mor wondered if she wanted to shake their aunt's whole body instead. He knew *he* did.

Concern raced through Tanta Coumba's eyes as she watched Mor and his sisters. She leaned forward, handing Mor a tissue for Fatima.

"What will happen now?" Tanta Coumba asked. "To the children, I mean. What are your plans for them?"

Mor's back straightened when his aunt's attention returned to him. He concentrated hard on the time-consuming preparation of the three-round tea service, pouring a little in a glass to test it.

"I am taking them to the city with me in two days."

"So soon?" Tanta Coumba looked between her friend, Mor, and his sisters. "They have not had a moment to grieve."

"They can do that just as well in Dakar." Mor's *bàjjan* shifted her position and ironed out the fabric of her *boubou* with the palms of her hands.

Tanta Coumba stared deep into Mor's eyes. He hoped she could see his hurt, as he had been able to see Fatima's.

She was quiet for a moment, then asked, "Naba, why are you whipping away like the wind? I'm just getting to see you after so many years."

"I am also needed elsewhere. It is a time of great sadness all around. My closest friend has lost her daughter in childbirth, and she cannot seem to find air to breathe."

Mor thought of himself and his sisters. Did she not care about their air?

"I intend to be away for at least three months and need to settle Amina with her host family and Mor at the *daara* before I depart."

Tanta Coumba nodded. "Could they not all go with you? So you can heal together at this sad time?"

Their aunt looked their way. "I am not completely insensitive. I thought of that first. But having three children about might be too much after losing your own. I have made suitable arrangements for Mor and Amina."

"And what of Tima?" Tanta Coumba reached down and tickled Fatima's neck, causing her to cave in her shoulders and smile.

"She will have to come with me," their aunt said. "I have no other choice. She will need to be quiet and out of the way." Their *bàjjan* raised an eyebrow at Fatima.

At this, Fatima's smile vanished. Her focus zipped to her brother. He could read her thoughts once more. Being alone with their aunt probably twisted her insides into knots. She didn't want to go. Even though she would be fed, clothed, and taken care of, Mor knew she would mostly be ignored.

Finding another stitch of courage, he said to Tanta Coumba, "I have told her we can stay here, at least until her return."

Mor's aunt stared at him. The line of her mouth tightened. "I have already told you. That will not happen. I cannot care for two households."

"I told you. I can care for us," Mor added, not backing down. "And Mina and Tima are willing to help."

Their aunt tsked. "Nonsense. I have already said no, and I detest repeating myself. Now stop begging for what will never be." She flicked her fingers back and forth, as if flinging Mor's hopes away.

When she turned her body away from him, signaling the end to the conversation, Mor turned to Tanta Coumba. "You don't mind looking in on us, do you?" Mor said boldly. "We won't be any trouble to you." He held his breath, waiting for her to answer, but his aunt barked at him first.

"How dare you ask her such a thing. Did Fallou never teach you your manners? We were not raised this way."

"He is fine, Dieynaba," Tanta Coumba interjected. "I should be scolding you." Her words were light but firm. "Do you not remember? They will not be alone. There is a village around them."

Now it was their aunt's turn to be silent.

"You've been gone a long time, Dieynaba, but I know you

have not forgotten how we take care of our own." The line of her lips curved up. "I do not have much, with three mouths to feed, but what I do have I can share with Awa's children."

To Mor, the sound of his mother's name was like the warmth of animal hide.

"I cannot ask this of you," Mor's aunt protested. "This is my problem, not yours."

"They are never a problem." Tanta Coumba winked at Mor.

"We will bring you no burdens, Bàjjan, while you are miles away," Mor added. "And you will have no worries about Fatima turning dust under your skirts." He could see the thought spinning behind his aunt's eyes, especially at the mention of not having to tote a mischievous Fatima along. "Tanta Coumba will check on us. And Amina and I will make sure Fatima has all she needs." He felt Amina's steely gaze upon him but did not turn her way.

His aunt sighed and a sliver of hope rose inside him.

"I guess a little less than three months time is not too long if you are looked in on." It was her turn to clasp Tanta Coumba's hands. "You are a true blessing, my friend. I am comforted to know your *barak* is only a stone's throw away."

Even though Fatima squealed at the news, Mor and Amina made no sounds. Calm filled Mor, though he was sure Amina would have plenty to say once their aunt was gone.

Regardless, almost three months was a start.

Tanta Coumba stood. "I'm glad this has all been decided.

And I expect to see you and your sisters, Mor Fall. Do not have me chasing after you, like I do with Zal, and do not let me or your *bàjjan* down," she said. "Awa, Fallou, and your *bàjjan* are entrusting me with their hearts." She placed her hand over her own heart. "I will leave you now."

"Won't you stay and have the tea Mor has prepared?" Mor's aunt reached up to hold Tanta Coumba's hand. "I cannot promise it will be the best that has ever passed your lips, with his careless watch over the pot." Her gaze cut to Mor and then went back to Tanta Coumba. "But it is a special blend I bring from the city. You must try—"

"Of course," Tanta Coumba said, unable to refuse. Her eyes twinkled when she smiled at Mor. "But afterward you need time alone as a family. And by then my daughters will be waiting."

Mor poured tea into the miniature glasses and set them on a plastic tray, offering her the first sips of strong liquid. Tanta Coumba tipped her head at him.

Mor's aunt reached for the second steaming glass, dragging it across the lip of the tray to scrape off the spilled tea and bits of soaked tea leaves. She slurped it, testing the taste, then swallowed.

"*Nekhna.*" Their aunt took a long sip, letting the tea's foam slip into her mouth. "Nice and strong. Not too sweet. But speaking of sweet things, I almost forgot." She reached for her large bag and drew it into her lap. She rummaged through it. "These are for each of you." She pulled out three clear plastic bags, each tied in a knot. They bulged with different-flavored hard candies. "I think some even have a soft chocolate inside."

Fatima smiled at her aunt for the first time. Her one dimple even showed in her right cheek. She looked quickly at Mor, then back at the bags of candy. But she did not move to take one.

"These are from Papa, an old friend of your *baay*'s. I told him it was too much, but he insisted." She shook the bags. "It is ridiculous to give children some of the best *tàngal* in Senegal. One sweet pop each would have been enough."

You deserve more than one sweet pop, my son. You deserve a mound. You have done well.

Mor's smile broke his lips apart. He was keeping his promise.

9

AFTER a night filled with their aunt's snores, Mor and his sisters knelt, quiet as ladybirds, while a stream of their *bàjjan*'s childhood friends and their neighbors chanted *siggilen ndigaale* in their ears, grasping each of their hands and praying they would overcome their grief. Mourners dropped *jaxaal* into a calabash bowl near their aunt's feet. The money would help buy food to prepare a meal for their guests.

"Yes, yes. Fallou and Awa's children are strong."

Mor listened to his aunt say this over and over as each person passed. He wondered if she believed it, or if she was simply happy to have them out of her *meulfeu*'s ruffles for a while longer.

Her bag lay at the edge of the raised pallet, close to the doorway, like it had when she first arrived, as if she wanted it ready for a quick escape.

"Now remember to show respect to this *barak*. And your family name," their *bàjjan* said after all their neighbors had left. "When I leave, you represent the family."

They huddled around a bowl filled with an evening treat of *lakh*, before their aunt's morning departure. Fatima licked every bit of the soured milk, vanilla-flavored sugar, dried coconut, and millet mixture off her knuckles as their *bàjjan* spoke.

"I do not want to hear you've brought any dark shadows to this door. Listen to each other, do right, and keep each other well. Dear Tanta Coumba will keep a steady gaze on you, and I will call from time to time. So do not stray, and do not make Tanta Coumba's temples pulse with worry." She reached into the folds of her *meulfeu* for a purse hung over her arm and pulled franc notes from her pocket. It was more than Mor had ever held, but not more than might be needed to fill a roaring truck with gas. They would have to eat sparingly for it to last. "Oh," she sighed, "I don't know if I'm doing right leaving you children behind."

"We are not alone." Mor got to his feet. He did not want her to change her mind. "Everyone you greeted today will watch over us. We will be fine, Auntie. Baay wanted us to be here." *And Baay and Yaay are here with us still*, he thought, but dared not say.

He gulped down his breath when her eyes pierced his, as if she were trying to reach into his thoughts.

"Here. Keep this well hidden." She folded the notes into his cupped hands, covering them with her own. "Before I change my mind. This should help you buy what you need for a little while. Until you find work. Since you want to grow into a man so soon." She said it as if she were testing him. Like she was waiting for him to change his mind and beg her to take them with her. But he didn't. He was determined to take care of his sisters and stay. He knew their aunt was only thinking of the summer, but he was thinking forever.

"*Jërëjëf*," he and Amina thanked her as Fatima dragged her finger over the tops of her bottom teeth.

Early the next morning their aunt summoned Mor and Amina for morning prayers, even though Amina and Fatima were still not expected to pray. Although Mor was considered young as well, he had risen each morning with his *baay* and wanted to continue the tradition. Once they were done, they set off to meet the *ndiaga ndiaye* that would take their *bàjjan* back to her home. Although they still had a few hours before its arrival, she wanted to leave the *barak* early so as not to take a sliver of a chance that she might miss it. Her need to leave seemed as great as, if not greater than, Mor's desire to stay.

Mor pushed his amulet higher up on his arm, giving thanks to Allah for its protection. He knew he would need it in the coming days and months. Swirls of Wolof floated around them and whizzed past their ears as people chatted loudly about everything from the weather, crops, and fish to soccer. His aunt fanned herself, pacing back and forth across the dirt.

As the *ndiaga ndiaye* bounced down the road in a cloud of dust, two other people waited along with their aunt. One carried a fat bundle on her head tied with cloth, while the other held two squawking chickens under his arms. When a dark hand reached out for his aunt's bag, Mor passed it over to him, saying good-bye to his *bàjjan* as she was hoisted into the rear of the bus after the other woman, since the front held only a door for the driver. As the bus chugged away, their aunt popped her head out one of the long passenger windows and yelled, "Remember, no dark shadows upon our family door."

Within seconds dust and a grunting engine gobbled up her words and she was gone.

They were alone. For the first time in days Mor felt lighthearted and happy to be so.

Back at the *barak* stillness was all around them, and Mor found it strange that he welcomed the silence. He was glad to be rid of their aunt's rustling sleeves, clipped remarks, and sideways glances, which at times were louder in meaning than her words.

Inside their cramped room, however, it did not take long for Mor to grow restless. There were no mourners. There was no chatter. And there was no Baay.

He knew his father did not like idle hands, and neither did Mor at the moment. He hopped up, but before he could even take two steps toward the door, Amina turned to him, peeking out from behind her favorite book. Her only book.

"Are you leaving?"

Mor nodded. "To see Mamadou at Baay's old shop. I want to ask if he has a place for me now."

"I hope it will bring the news you want," Amina said, looking back at her book.

Mor slid into his father's sandals and was about to head for the door, feeling the sun shining bright on him.

"Maybe you should go barefoot or cut off the backs?" Amina added, flipping the page. "There is a knife over there."

"Cut his shoes?" Clouds covered his sunshine. He would never destroy anything of his *baay*'s. He looked down. The sandals were large tan platters under his feet. He could see where constant use and pressure had worn down the rubber soles, while dirt and sweat had created an outline of his father's foot in the darkened leather. Mor's feet were ant prints lost within an elephant's gigantic tread. "I will grow."

"Not fast enough for them to fit today or tomorrow."

Mor ignored her and pushed aside the ragged tarp over the doorway and crossed onto the dirt path. Chickens pecked at spilled grains near his feet, and three girls sang, playing hand games, while two women sat on tires half-buried in the sand. Mor greeted them and others along the path, asking of their families, but everyone kept bringing the conversation to the death of his *baay*. Each time he heard his father's name, new hurt formed like a bruise, too tender to touch. Soon he was ducking down side paths to avoid anyone coming his way. He did not have time to be sad; he had to fulfill part of his plan.

Over him, blackbirds flew in an arrowhead formation, almost as if pointing toward Mamadou's yard. Bits of conversations in the distance wafted past his ears. The air was breezeless, and the dry heat of the summer sun pressed down on him. Mor turned down a tight path between a few of the homes, a shortcut to the main road and the market center of Lat Mata. When he tried to jump a small puddle of morning wash water, he came out of one of his shoes. As he hopped back and bent over to retrieve it, he heard his name.

"Mor Fall, is that you?"

Still leaned over, he peeked between his knees and saw Tanta Coumba framed in a window at the *barak* across the path.

"Why are you sneaking past my door?" Her eyes twinkled as she watched him.

Mor straightened and nestled his foot back into his father's sandal. "I am not sneaking. I am going to Mamadou's."

"But you weren't going to stop. . . ." Her voice trailed off as she disappeared from the window, then reappeared at her front door a second later. Pulling back the curtain, she came onto the path. "Well, you are here now. Can you spare an old mother a few moments?" She was ushering him to her door before he could answer.

Mor glanced in the direction he'd been heading, longing to get started. But knowing it was because of her that he was even still here, he let her lead him inside.

"Did your *bàjjan* get safely away?" she asked and welcomed him into her home.

"Yes, early." He shuffled through the doorway. Aware his feet had a captive audience.

"Where are you going in those shoes?" She chuckled, then fell silent. "Ah, they are Fallou's, aren't they?"

Heat tingled under his cheeks. Standing under her gaze, he felt like a tiny child playing at being grown.

She placed a soft hand on his back and rubbed it in a gentle circle. "I still have my grandmother's old teapot. The handle is missing and it will scorch your hand even through a cloth, but it reminds me of her and I would never think of making my tea in anything else. Sometimes we need these things around."

Since Cheikh had left, Mor had not been inside for quite a while, but it was the same. Their home was larger than his family's, with three small rooms and a slight side garden. It was made from smoothed mud blocks.

When Tanta Coumba dropped the mustard-colored curtain over the door, a golden light replaced the bright morning sun that pushed through the entryway. Incense smoke tumbled in the space. It was the familiar scent of *thiouraye*.

It released a smell that had not perfumed his own home since his *yaay*'s death. In a sea of cloth, on a pallet in the corner, baby Zal slept.

"I've some bread and hazelnut-cocoa spread for you and your sisters," Tanta Coumba said. "I was going to bring it by or have Naza do it, but maybe you could take it, since you are out earlier than I thought."

Mor listened but couldn't hear Naza or Tanta Coumba's other daughter, Oumy, rustling about.

"Ah, but where is my mind?" She tapped the side of her head wrap. "You said you were off to Mamadou's. I don't want to pin you down."

He did not want to be rude after all she had done.

"I can take them."

"Not in those shoes, you can't."

Mor slouched, wishing he could bury the shoes in the sand.

"Don't worry, you will grow into them. But for now I think I might have something more your size. *Kai legui.*" Mor followed, as she'd asked, through another doorway to a smaller area where he had spent a lot of time. It was more of a narrow hallway than an actual room. It was Cheikh's, though. And it looked exactly as it had the day he'd left two years before. "I miss him more each day he is away. But when I come in here, it is like he is home." Her fingers brushed over a pair of his folded jeans. Mor missed his friend too, almost as much as he missed his *baay*.

He looked around at the glossy photos of Herculean

laamb wrestlers that were stuck to the wall next to cutouts of American athletes slamming basketballs into hoops and French rappers posing in sunglasses and baseball caps.

"I can still remember the time my Cheikh fell out of that big baobab and you carried him all the way here on your back, refusing to leave him out in the fields alone. The two of you were like salt and sea. Inseparable."

Mor remembered that day. Cheikh had cried, saying he thought animals were rustling in the branches and that he could not bear to be by himself, even for a second, while Mor went for help. When he was safe at home and his broken leg was bandaged, Cheikh had sworn Mor to secrecy about his tears, and Mor had never told. Cheikh was not only Mor's friend; he was the closest thing he had to a brother.

"I wish it were still so." Tanta Coumba drew her hand under Mor's chin and lifted it to face her. "But it is hard to be so far away." Her hand fell away from his chin, and she picked up a faded pillowcase and hugged it, rocking.

"I hardly hear from him anymore. After two years he's too busy to send word to his mother. And friends in the city have heard nothing of him either. I wish he could have stayed here. Gone to school here with you." She glanced around. Her last words were almost a whisper. Like a secret not meant to tell. Even though Mor already knew it was Cheikh's father who had wanted him to go—to become strong in the city.

After his father had taken his second wife, he had moved

away from Lat Mata instead of keeping his two families close, like most men with more than one wife. On the day Cheikh left, dragging his feet, begging not to be taken, his father had closed his ears to Tanta Coumba's requests to have Cheikh stay.

"His *baay* has no news either. That is what troubles me. Because his father has ties with many people there." She placed her cheek against Cheikh's pillow for the briefest of seconds and sniffed it. "Sometimes I swear I can still smell his scent lingering in the sheets, as if he were just here. It is strongest on Fridays after I have spent a morning at the market. You would think he had just been lying here." She placed the pillow back on his pallet.

Although Mor had not heard from Cheikh either since he left for the *daara*, Mor had heard whispers about how the city could change people, twisting them, and not always for the better. He wondered if that had happened to his friend. The worry etched across Tanta Coumba's face said she might fear something like that too.

"Enough of this sad talk." She clapped her hands together, as if snapping herself out of her sadness. "I'm sure he is busy in prayer and will send word soon. Now let me stitch up my lips and find you what we came here for."

A pair of sneakers and a set of sandals stood in a line at the far end of the floor mat, and Mor wondered, but did not ask, if those were the shoes she was searching for.

"I know he has a pair that are too tight," she said, reaching over the line of shoes to pull up the fuzzy blanket tucked around the pallet. "That boy is like a sprout. His father says we should wrap his feet in cloth instead of paying for something new. But he continues to buy them instead of coming to see his son." Her last words were heavy, weighing her a little. "Here I go again, breaking that stitch." She raised the corner of the bed mat and reached underneath. Mor rushed forward to help her. There were piles of magazines stacked under the pallet, with a pair of gray sneakers wedged in the corner next to them. "Here we go," she said, jerking one free. As she did so, a corner of an unmistakable turquoise-and-ruby-colored cloth with meandering lines of shimmering gold paint peeked from behind the pallet, then slipped out of sight as the pallet shifted. Mor's eyes widened and his fingers reached forward. He nearly dropped the mattress on Tanta Coumba's head as he tried to grab for the cloth.

"Sorry," he said, lifting the cover higher.

"Ah, you are caught." Tanta Coumba snatched the frayed shoelace of the other sneaker. "Here it is. I think these will fit you just fine. Give them a try," she said as Mor's attention was on the space by the wall. Where he was certain he had seen a cloth pouch peeking at him like a field mouse peering out from between blades of grass before it darts back under cover. She held the shoes for Mor, waiting for him to drop the pallet. But he couldn't draw his eyes away from where he'd spied the cloth. Then he felt the mattress and its weight separate from his hands. Tanta Coumba raised it and let it fall. She patted the edge of Cheikh's bed, beckoning Mor to sit next to her.

Even more than feeling strange about being in Cheikh's space or on Cheikh's pallet, Mor felt confused by what he thought he'd seen under his old friend's mattress. Mor found it hard to concentrate. *Maybe it was not . . .* Like him and Cheikh, their mothers had shared everything—pots, seeds, lotions, and folds of cloth. *That's it,* he thought. *It has to be. They shared that cloth. There can be no other expla-nation.* But the thought would not rest, like an overturned beetle trying to right itself. It kicked and kicked at Mor's brain.

He glanced up at Tanta Coumba and paused. Even though her eyes were bright and open, Mor was certain the dark patches under them were caused by a storm of worry. Keeping his thoughts as his own, he sat next to her and pulled on the shoes.

"There," she said once he had them on. "Good, yes?"

Mor nodded. "They fit very well," he said, not letting on that they were a bit big. At least his feet did not swim in them as they had in his father's sandals, which he picked up off the floor mat. "They are perfect. *Jërëjëf.*"

"You are most welcome. I'm glad we had them to give." Patting her hand against the bed mat, she got to her feet. "I won't keep you any longer. I know young men like you and Cheikh do not want to be smothered under their mothers anymore. . . ." Her words dropped off. Then she cupped his chin in her hand. "You are so much like her. With that high, noble forehead and those piercing black eyes. And who could deny the resemblance in your smile? I miss that smile when it disappears." She let go of his face, though she still appeared stuck on her memory. "Have you seen her again?"

Mor shook his head no, though he wished he had.

"I miss her." Tanta Coumba rocked her head as if dislodging the memory, then turned toward the doorway and tucked back the curtain before stepping into the next room.

Mor lingered by the bed. His eyes were fixed on the far corner, where the turquoise-and-ruby-colored cloth with the golden lines was trapped.

"You sure you don't want to pull off a corner of bread or have a cup of powdered milk before you go?" she asked, suddenly reappearing in the doorway.

"No. I'm fine," he said, glancing back at the ruffled corner of the blanket. "I ate, but I'm sure Mina and Tima will come later."

"Very well." She turned back to the front room of her home, waiting for Mor. "I will leave it for them to carry for your afternoon meal."

Mor left Cheikh's room, looking at the bed mat one last time. When he stepped out into the daylight, Tanta Coumba followed behind him. "Do not be a stranger. I expect to see you each day before mosquitos nip at dusk." She scrunched her fingers in his hair for a second, like his mother used to do, then let her hand fall. "It is always a blessing to see the face of one of Awa's children."

"Yes, ma'am," Mor said. "I will see you again tomorrow."

"*Incha'Allah.*" She waved.

Indeed, Mor told himself, hoping it would also be God's will that he should have another chance to take a look behind Cheikh's bed for his mother's *nafa.*

10

MOR'S thoughts were trapped by images of the cloth wedged behind Cheikh's pallet; otherwise, he would have skipped down the dirt road, excited about his new shoes. Although the sneakers were not brand new, they were the first pair Mor had ever owned. He was usually given rubber flip-flops or someone's outgrown sandals.

Never sneakers.

Whenever his *yaay* had taken him to the tables full of people's secondhand clothes and shoes at the market, she'd always tsked when he eyed a pair with gleaming white leather, saying, "What good are those to you? They will be covered with dirt and your feet will be hot in minutes. They are a waste."

Mor had always frowned, thinking of a hundred reasons why they weren't. But now he glanced down at the light-gray running shoes with white racing stripes down each side. Besides a few little scuffs on the front ridges, a frayed shoelace, and a small tear near the little toe of the right shoe, they looked like new. Mor would have to stuff a plastic bag or newspaper in the toes so his feet would not slip around, but they were already a far better fit than his father's sandals. Wearing them, he could hop, jump, and sprint faster and higher than he ever had before. Cheikh's old sneakers were the closest things to perfection Mor had ever worn on his feet. He was sure they were a sign things would work out at the mechanic shop.

As he approached the shop, he squeezed his *baay*'s sandals against his palm. Even though grief now coated most of his memories of the place, Mor's greatest wish at that moment was that the shop where his *baay* had taught him so much still had a place for him under the hoods of the hulking trucks. Being a part of everything there was like how Amina felt about school and books. He used to spend every minute that he didn't have a soccer ball cradled to his foot surrounded by trucks, grease, and tools. For him, learning to fix engines was something he wanted to do forever. He could never imagine saying the same about school. He liked it, and would miss being with his friends all day, but he could always find them on the soccer field. The mechanic shop was where he wanted to be more than anywhere else.

He smoothed down his shirt and glanced at his new sneakers one more time. He was certain they were going to bring him luck.

Before he even reached the stick fence, the heavy beats of *mbalax* gyrated against the air from a radio hung on the side mirror of a rusted truck. Mor stopped and stared as Mamadou, the shop owner, and his two best workers, Idy and Mighty Yacine, a stout woman who could probably lift a full-grown man over her head and throw him a mile, suspended an engine on a sturdy tree branch with a heavy linked chain. A young man Mor did not know steered a 4x4 truck in neutral, with one hand on the wheel, as he walked alongside it, until it was under the branch. The hood of the vehicle stood up, mouth open, waiting for the engine like a crocodile ready to snap at a swooping bird.

The morning sun beat down on their heads, and Mamadou wiped his forehead with a grease-stained rag. When he saw Mor coming, he grinned, a silver cap on his front tooth.

"Ah, what a pleasant sight to see Fallou's shadow." He nodded, shaking hands like Mor was one of the customers who came to his shop. The rippled tin walls were decorated with patches of rust. "What brings you to my door?"

The shop yard didn't actually have a door, only a few tall sticks strung together to act as an entrance. His shop's number was painted in white on one of the makeshift tin walls that rattled with the breeze.

"I came to see if you could use an assistant," Mor said.

Idy and Mighty Yacine held the engine still, mouthing *Alaikum salam* in greeting. They had both worked alongside Mor's *baay*, but another worker thin as a piece of barbed wire, Mor did not recognize. He snickered a bit when he looked in Mor's direction. Mor ignored him, going on to say, "I would not be in the way, and need to work to care for my sisters."

Mamadou's smile faded. His cell phone rang in his pocket. He tossed it to Mighty Yacine. "I'm sorry," he continued, "but I've already hired Khalifa. He could never take your *baay*'s place, but I needed another set of big, strong hands." Looking at Khalifa, Mor didn't think his hands were big or strong. "But even still," Mamadou went on. "I couldn't be responsible for your safety. There are too many heavy machines around. I would hold my breath, worried without my old friend, your *baay*, here watching over you."

Mor wanted to say his father watched over him all the time, but he knew Mamadou well enough to know this would not convince him.

"I understand, but I promise I can be helpful." Mamadou was already shaking his head before Mor could finish. "I've learned a lot here and I am interested in learning more."

"I'm sorry, my boy, but it just won't do."

The one Mamadou called Khalifa eyed Mor up and down, almost as if Mor were competition for his job, but he seemed to dismiss the thought as quickly as he'd had it, rolling his eyes. Khalifa twisted the cap off a bottle of motor oil and poured it into the engine of another truck to the side of Mor. The truck itself towered over Mor, with its thick black tires the size of boulders. The oil gurgled and glugged as it went into the belly of the engine. Mor stared at Khalifa, then at the bottle of oil he used.

"But you said you would always have a place for me. I remember," Mor said, even though he knew Mamadou's mind was decided. He pushed his shoulders back and demanded the tears pushing at his eyes to go away. He refused to show his sadness. If one tear fell, they would all fall.

Mighty Yacine and Idy nodded in agreement.

"You did say that, boss," Mighty Yacine said.

"I know I did," Mamadou said, wiping sweat on his forearm, never taking his eyes off Mor. "But I meant when you were a bit older. When you could manage on your own."

Mor wanted to say he could manage now, but he didn't. Instead he stepped away, straightening his shoulders, and asked, "But isn't that oil much too light for that diesel engine?" He tilted his head toward the truck Khalifa hung over. "If that truck driver motors away with that rumbling in his engine's belly, he will soon hear a rattling noise and be perched on the side of the road." Mor noticed Mighty Yacine and Idy look over at the engine, then grin his way. Mighty Yacine winked. Mor didn't wait for a response, but told Mamadou good-bye. He was almost out of earshot when he heard the thwack of Mamadou's rag against Khalifa's neck.

"You stupid boy. You could have ruined it all with your

careless ways. You better be glad you are my sister's dim-witted son. Otherwise, I would not have you turning my business upside down."

Once Mor had headed down an alley by the back of another business, away from curious eyes, he stopped, his head hung low. That was his only plan and it had failed. It had taken them less than three breaths to cast him aside. How was he going to face Mina and Tima? He had been so sure Mamadou would welcome him as the son of Fallou, but all Mamadou had seen was "Fallou's shadow."

Now what was he going to do?

He did not fight the tear that slipped down his face. Instead he smeared it across his cheek as another fell.

Wandering away from the village center, he headed toward the beach, pulled by the lull of the lapping waves. He had reached a dead end before he had even started. Away from the commotion of the departing and returning *gaals*, Mor sat on a rock and drew his legs up to his chest, hugging them to him. He stared out, wishing a new idea would come.

Your path is not over, and your story is not set. Look to the horizon, my son.

Mor's head sprang up. "Baay?" he called, even though he was sure it was his father. "I have already failed and the sun is hardly in the sky. I'm useless."

One is only useless when he has given up the will to be of use. Do not lose your fight. It should not be plucked as effortlessly as a chicken's feather. My child has a stronger will than that.

Although Mor was disappointed things had not worked out, he was thankful for his *baay*'s words. And suddenly, as he cradled his legs and his father's sandals against his chest, something deep inside him, no bigger than a speck of dirt, told him he'd find another way.

WHEN Mor could make no more excuses, he finally slid off the rock and headed home. Amina and Fatima sat outside their *barak* with Jeeg. Fatima was tucked in between Amina's legs as she rebraided Fatima's hair.

"So did you get the answer you wanted?" Amina asked, making a new part down Fatima's scalp with the comb.

"Not as I expected," he said. His throat felt clogged with marbles. "But I will find another way."

She held the comb in midstroke over Fatima's partially unbraided cornrow. "I told you it would not be easy. Now what are we going to do?"

"I don't know yet," he said honestly. "But I will figure it out."

"And where did you get those?" Amina asked, eyeing his shoes. "You have not already been foolish?"

"Mina, why do you always think the worst of me? Tanta Coumba gave them to me this morning. She didn't want to see me tripping past her window."

Fatima popped one of the candies their *bàjjan* had brought them into her mouth. For the first time Mor noticed all the candy wrappers shoved under her leg.

"How many of those have you eaten? You will make yourself sick," he said, reaching for the bag, but Fatima was quicker.

"These are mine. I can eat as many as I want," she said, hugging the bag. "Get your bag. You will love the coconut ones. I do." She beamed up at her brother. "But the ones with the chocolate in the middle taste funny. I don't like those."

He looked between his little sister and the bag of *tàngal*, then rushed inside for the other bags. "That's it," he said, coming back out with a sack. He dropped the two bags of sealed candy neither he nor Amina had touched into it.

"Hey, you took Mina's, too. That's not fair. Mina, you don't want yours? I'll have it." Fatima twisted toward her sister, only to get whacked by the comb as Amina parted another row of Fatima's hair.

"Sit still, or these braids will go crooked." Amina glanced up at Mor. "What are you about to do with those?"

"Sell them," he said, snatching up Fatima's bag before she had a chance to grab it.

"Give it back," Fatima whined, trying to wiggle away from her sister, but Amina had her locked between her legs, holding her hair like reins, mid-cornrow.

"Stay put, I told you."

"I want my sweeties back. Auntie gave them to me. Go sell your own." Fatima pouted.

"I need to sell them all," Mor said, excited. "This will start us off. Auntie will see, we will be able to take care of each other all summer, and this is a start."

"And what about after that is gone?" Amina asked. "Then what? I know you won't sell Jeeg to the *reykat* like Bàjjan suggested, but what else is there to try? We have nothing else to sell. Surely that money will not last us all summer."

"Aaaahhh." Fatima grabbed for Jeeg. Amina loosened her grip on Fatima's hair.

"Stop, Tima. You know I would never sell her," Mor tried to assure her. "She's family, like you, Mina, and me. She will not be sold like we won't be sold. Don't worry." He glanced at Amina. "Let me start with these today. I haven't forgotten about tomorrow already." He slung the cords of his sack over his shoulder. "The money I get from these will get us started." He tapped the bottom of the burlap.

"I thought you were going to work at Baay's garage," Fatima sniffled, hugging Jeeg's neck as Amina tried to ease her back to finish braiding her hair. "And I saw Auntie give you money. Why are you hiding that? I want my *tàngal* back."

"Tima, stop," Amina said. "You want to stay here? With me and Mor?"

Fatima nodded.

"Then he is right. He needs to sell the sweeties so we can stay. Otherwise, we will have to put you on a *ndiaga ndiaye* to go be with Bàjjan."

"Noooo," Fatima screeched, pulling her legs up, locking herself into a ball.

Jeeg's head flopped off her raised knees, but she didn't let the goat go.

"You can have my *tàngal*," Fatima whispered.

"It will all be okay, you'll see." Mor smiled, spinning toward the path, feeling again like things might just work out.

He shot down a path and turned down another; he walked toward the market, away from the clusters of *baraks* and fencing. A cloud of dust spun up as a tattered makeshift soccer ball rolled in front of him. A stampede of feet soon joined the ball.

Mor's foot crunched down on the plastic to stop it as all his friends from the village raced to reach it first. Looking at their sweaty faces, he realized how much he had missed his friends, whom he'd avoided since the burial. He'd seen pity in their eyes. Pity he had not wanted. But right now he saw excited, determined faces ready to have the ball.

"Hey, Mor, kick it back," one of the older boys said.

"Why don't you get in instead? We could use another

player," Mor's friend Oumar shouted. He wiped his mouth on the shoulder of his green T-shirt. "They have one more than us, and Tapha is already cheating." He pointed behind him.

"Am not," shouted a player standing in the distance between two rusted cans.

"There is no defense down there. You can't just wait in front of our goal," Oumar shouted back. "See?" he said, turning to Mor. "Come in. With you at offense, I can watch him."

Mor saw no pity, only an eagerness to continue playing. He rocked the ball from his heel to his toe and back again. Soccer was his favorite. He really had missed it. The rustling plastic under the sole of his new shoe felt like an extension of him.

Looking at the makeshift soccer field, he thought of his *baay* and one particular game—the old men against the young. The old men had been leading four goals to one. No one could catch Mor's father, who'd scored three of the four goals. He was the most skilled attacker in the game, young or old. Everyone loved to watch his feet when he played. During that match, as fans of both teams cheered him on, he ran straight for Mor, who usually played striker but now was the final defender. A row of white teeth showed when he smiled.

"I see they have finally put in their secret weapon," his *baay* joked over his shoulder to his teammates.

As his *baay* thundered toward him, Mor did not watch his eyes. Instead he stared at his hips. He leveled himself on his toes, ready for any move his father might make, except for the move he did. Within one heartbeat Mor's father scooped Mor up into his arms and threw him over his shoulder. He raced with Mor screaming with laughter and dribbled toward the goal.

Not wasting a second, a horde of young boys ran onto the field, following Mor's giggles. When they caught up to his father, they tugged on his free arm and legs. One boy grabbed for his waist but caught hold of his shorts instead. The shorts pulled away toward his knees as the boy held on tight, but he kept running. Even with two boys pulling on his arm, he managed to snatch the front strings of his shorts before he exposed his whole bottom half to the village.

Women howled and hooted with laughter. Giggles escaped from girls' throats as they pretended to cover their eyes. The men encouraged him to charge for the goal. Mor's *baay* was like a *laamb* wrestler. He was half their gigantic size, but at that instant Mor thought him ten times as mighty. With boys hanging from each arm, Mor flopping over his shoulder, and the small boy tugging on his shorts, his bottom still partially displayed for the sun, Mor's father scored another goal, barefoot.

A wide smile pushed back Mor's cheeks at the thought. He wanted to feel that happy again.

"Get in, man," Oumar urged. "We need you."

Mor glanced around, expecting what, he wasn't sure. It was only him, the ball, and his friends.

Without another thought he dropped the sack and dribbled, faking out his first opponent and then the next. He took off for the goal, like his *baay* had. Determined. He tapped the ball lightly with the outside curve of his foot, prodding it forward. Then he kicked it and a light spray of dirt off the ground. The ball soared past the goalie's hand and just inside the imaginary goal area made by the rusted cans.

A blast of cheers echoed around Mor. A group of boys, led by Oumar, rushed him, while others pounded their fists or flung their arms up, gesturing and shouting at the goalie for missing the ball and to Tapha for being on the wrong side of the field. For a moment it all felt like that day with his *baay*. It was almost as great as it used to be.

Heading the ball to a teammate when it came back into play, he became lost in the game and his memories.

They shouted and yelled, sprinted, dodged, and slide-tackled for hours, not caring about the heat or the time of the day. When they were all panting, tugging at their shirts and shorts, they collapsed in the dirt, and Mor felt happy. Then he froze. His head zoomed in one direction, then whipped in the other. The area was empty.

His sack was gone.

It had happened again.

"What's wrong?" Oumar asked. He lifted his head off the now-squashed plastic-bag ball.

Mor didn't answer. It had been right there. Hadn't it?

"Eh, Mor, what happened?" Oumar asked again.

Mor wasn't listening. He dashed to the spot where he'd dropped his sack. The dirt was tousled with footprints. His pulse pummeled the side of his neck. If there had been a cement wall in front of him, he would have knocked his head against it.

"Are you looking for this?" Oumar walked over, holding the sack out to Mor.

A muddle of brown burlap and military green merged in front of him. Mor blinked rapidly, clearing his eyes of budding tears. "Where was it?" He snatched the sack before his friend could open his mouth.

"Khadim put it under the tree so we wouldn't stomp it."

Mor opened the sack, checking inside. "I thought it was gone."

"No, it was always here," Oumar said. "Come on, let's play."

Oumar mashed the plastic bags back into shape. He bounced the ball off his knee and then trapped it with his chest, letting it roll down the length of his body to the ground. The ball spun at his feet until he stopped it with one tap, then slid it in Mor's direction. This time Mor did not hesitate. He had a job to do and had already ignored it too long. He slung the sack over his shoulder and kicked the ball hard. It whizzed past his friend's elbow, and a few players took off after it.

"I can't, I'll see you later," Mor said as the rest of the boys charged after the ball. He did not watch his friends playing *his* game without him. He loved soccer. His feet didn't seem to have time to meet the ground when he played. But Mor couldn't think about that anymore. He should have been at the market instead of the soccer field. He had lost hours of sales.

Shouts and Tapha's loud voice echoed behind him. It was obvious from the yelling and clipped Wolof phrases that Tapha had snagged the ball and kicked it into an unguarded goal. Mor knocked at pebbles with his foot and tugged hard on the sack cord. He tried to refocus on the market and selling his bags of *tàngal*.

When Mor reached the market area, he halted, mouth hanging open. Fishmongers were packing up empty crates, and shopkeepers were sweeping the last of the dust and rubbish off their mats.

Everything was closing.

How had it gotten so late? Soccer!

Desperate, he rushed toward the first person he saw.

"Excuse me, ma'am. Would you like to buy some sweeties? They are the best ever made. Straight from the city." But the stranger brushed by him, not listening.

He ran up to another, and another, until one man finally stopped, blocked by Mor on the path.

"What is it you are selling?" the man barked. "The sunset will not wait for you."

"*Tàngal*, sir. *Tàngal*. It is the best!" Mor reached into his sack and pulled out the first bag he touched.

It was Fatima's.

Bitten-into pieces of sticky *tàngal* with half-melted chocolate centers oozed from the seams of several pried-open and discarded candies.

"What game are you playing? A fool I am not!" the man shouted, pushing past Mor. "Those are half-eaten."

"Wait, sir. I have more."

When he looked up, a new bag of the hard-shelled sweeties in his hand, the man was already gone.

Mor glanced around the market square.

None of the woman in bright *boubous* still sat under the shade of the gigantic tree that stood in the middle of what was usually a maze of blankets and low-lying tables crammed with everything: bitter tomatoes, mint, soon-to-expire medicine, half-empty bottles of perfume, and anything else vendors thought someone might need.

Everyone had gone home to be with their families and prepare their evening meals.

He had messed things up again.

He was too late.

When you stumble, that is when you rise up and step again. Not all are born walking. Mistakes and missteps are still steps. Do not ignore what they teach.

Mor should have been relieved to hear his father's words, but he wasn't. Shame splashed him like a tossed bucket of water. He felt he could do no right. He hadn't meant to play all afternoon. But he had been happier and felt closer to his *baay* than he had since he went to the clinic. Mor did not tell Baay his excuses. Instead he shoved the *tàngal* back into his sack and headed for home.

Whatever Amina would say, he deserved.

12

WHEN Mor got back to the *barak*, he was surprised to find that Amina had no harsh words.

"Like you said"—she pulled a needle through the fabric of his faded soccer jersey, mending one of its many holes—"there is always tomorrow. Maybe it will be better."

At first worry seeped from his shoulders, but he couldn't quite rest. Her kindness unsettled him, making him feel worse. The failure was now an elephant's foot against his chest.

"I will sell as many as I can tomorrow," he said, watching her. "I promise."

Amina did not look up. She pierced the fabric of his shirt again.

"So, then, can I have some of my sweeties back?" Fatima asked.

Mor dug in his sack. "Only the ones you already opened. I looked like a jackal in a bunny's hide trying to sell those."

"Eck, they were the nasty ones with mint. I don't want those."

"Well, the others have to be sold." He didn't respond when Fatima whined or tried to tug at the bag. He simply sat down and smeared some of the hazelnut-cocoa spread Tanta Coumba had given them onto the end of the bread loaf and lay on his mat, thinking of his father's words, determined not just to walk, but to run.

He was going to sell that *tàngal*.

The next morning when dandelion-yellow light spilled into the window, Mor had already laced up his shoes and tied his protective amulet around his upper arm, ready to face the day.

A better day.

Fatima and Amina had gone down by the river early with Tanta Coumba's daughters to wash clothes. Amina had said nothing more about the *tàngal*, but Mor had seen the disappointment and worry in her face. He also saw the fancy-school pamphlet wedged in the pages of her book.

He pulled it out, looking at the smiling brown faces of the girls on the cover. "Iéna Academy for Girls" was written in green letters across the top, matching the green of the girls' school uniforms. Mor opened it and read: "Iéna Academy for Girls attracts serious-minded girls who are focused and driven to learn." Everything Amina was. Mor scanned the page and found a list of fees. He swallowed hard, realizing how much it would cost. Someone might as well have told him he needed to buy a car in three months' time. He did not see how he would ever have enough, even with their *baay* having paid some of the tuition already.

It cost 15,600 francs per year for tuition, registration, and uniforms.

Add to that 8,500 francs per year for school supplies (ruler, calculator, pens, protractor, paper, colored pencils, etc.).

It was over 24,000 francs, and his father had paid only 14,900.

It was hopeless.

It might as well have been 100,000 francs. How would he ever make that?

But he remembered the day Amina had come back from visiting the school with Baay and Fatima and how happy she had been. Amina loved school the way Mor loved soccer and engines. Mor had never seen her smile so wide. Since the school opened six years before, it had been a dream of their *yaay*'s that Amina would attend. And their *baay* wanted to keep that promise to their *yaay*. He had tried and now it was Mor's turn to do so. He just did not know how.

Staring at the numbers on the paper, he wanted them to rearrange themselves or a few of the zeros to fall away. But they didn't. He needed to come up with a plan. He went over to the shelf and pulled down the Dieg Bou Diar tomato can. The folded franc notes his aunt had given them lay rolled under a rock. He took them out and laid them across the bed and counted.

"One thousand, two thousand, one thousand, one thousand, and one thousand." Their aunt had given them six thousand francs, two thousand to use each month. They could survive on it, but barely. He heard his aunt's words play in his head: *This should help you buy what you need for a little while. Until you find work. Since you want to grow into a man so soon.* Mor tucked the money back into the can. He would show her. He would find a way to get the 9,200 francs Amina needed for school, and they would find a way to make the six thousand francs his aunt had left stretch out for a summer of food. He wanted his *bàjjan* to know they could not just survive but thrive in Lat Mata alone.

After pushing the can far under the bed, he placed Amina's pamphlet back in the pages of her book and left the *barak*. His mind was filled with numbers and days.

He had less than three months. About eighty days.

As he turned down the main roadway, Mor heard the raised voices of his friends again and the scampering of feet, but this time he cut down a side path, ignoring them.

He walked until he heard the commotion of the market. Even though he was still far from the fish area, the stench of drying fish clung to the air. There was almost no escaping it, but a few steps ahead the buttery scent of frying dough rose from a crackling pot of oil that sat on a *barada* burner. Waiting to cross the road, Mor stopped next to the street vendor in her apple-green head wrap and *teybass* dress. She bent over the pot, humming and singing softly to herself while rotating the *tiopatis* in the large fryer. Mor's hand moved over his stomach as it belted out its own song.

The little balls of dough danced in the popping oil, reminding Mor of when his *yaay* used to make them. He'd often sat cross-legged in the dirt, eyes wide, as she'd rolled the hot balls in granules of sugar. He had loved to watch the sugar crystals melt from the heat and oil, creating a sweet glaze. These were slightly different, though. Lying on a yellowing, grease-soaked newspaper, these freshly cooked *tiopatis* were tossed in powdered sugar and coconut flakes. He was not sure how long he'd been staring at them when a white-coated ball that resembled a scoop of shaved ice wavered in front of his eyes. The tips of the vendor's fingers were encrusted with globs of clumped sugar and shaved coconut. Mor wished they were his own, so he could lick off the sugary heaven until his fingers gleamed brown again.

"Take it, and run along," the woman ordered. "I cannot have you drooling over my cooking grease." She clucked her teeth and dropped the *tiopati* into Mor's hand. The powder left a trail of white on his palm, but it quickly disappeared when he gobbled up the fried dough and ran his tongue over the powdered path. Swallowing down the last taste, he smiled at the woman.

"Don't think you are getting another." She shook the dripping spoon at him. "I have hungry mouths of my own, you know." She crouched down and used the spoon to turn the frying dough over in the grease to brown evenly.

"No, ma'am." Mor gave a slight bow. "Thank you for the one you shared. *Jërëjëf.*" After thanking her, he nodded slightly and stepped sideways, away from her mixing bowls, and crossed the street. His stomach gurgled, and he wished he had taken more of the bread or even a few extra sips of the powdered milk Tanta Coumba had given them the day before. But he'd wanted his sisters to have enough.

Knowing he needed to focus and sell the *tàngal*, he tried to push all other thoughts from his mind. The roadways and paths of Lat Mata bustled. No one could ever get lost in the main center of the village. It stretched only as far as a stone's throw in each direction. But enough people passed through that Mor saw many unfamiliar faces. Lat Mata had the largest market area within a day's walk, so many came here to buy and sell their wares. The market was fortunate to be on the main road used by hauling trucks, *car rapides, ndiaga ndiaye*, and tourist vans. There was always plenty going on. Sometimes Mor and his friends used to sit and watch it all, eating a dripping sweet mango in some stitch of shade. But not today. As the streets swelled with people, Mor knew he was at a perfect spot to sell. Opening a bag of sweets, he traipsed up and down the side of the road.

"Sweeties here. Buy your sweeties here. Fresh from the city. Buy your sweeties here," he called in a singsong voice, bumping elbows and shoulders with people as he went.

"Excuse me, miss," he asked one woman with a heart-shaped birthmark over her eye. He had never seen her before, but he thought the heart was a good sign. "Would you like to buy some hard candy? I have pineapple, banana, mango, coconut, cherry, and more. . . ." She shook her head and picked up speed, but smiled as Mor fell in step beside her. "I also have ones with a gooey chocolate or caramel center. Those will probably go quick. You sure you don't want to buy one?" The woman shook her head no again. "Okay, then." Mor's smile slipped a bit. "Thank you," Mor said, letting her pass. He dropped his head a little and was about to turn and slink away when a hand touched his shoulder and he heard a soft voice.

"Whew, all right, I will take one if you regain that beautiful smile."

Mor's head rose as he turned. The young woman with the birthmark held out a coin. His eyebrows lifted, and his cheeks pulled back in a gigantic smile.

"That's better," she teased. "Can I have a coconut one, please?"

His smile began to slide from his lips again when he searched the bags. He'd asked Fatima to take out all the mushed wrappers and all the wasted candies she had already sucked on the night before, but her sticky little fingers had taken all the coconut sweeties, too.

"I'm sorry, but I do not have any left, although the mango and pineapple are very nice. Perfect for this hot, hot day." He shoved his fingers into the bag of sweets, searching for an amber or coral wrapper.

"I guess a pineapple will do."

As she said the words, Mor's fingers found an amber wrapper. "Here you are."

When the woman paid, she said, "Try not to let that smile drop again." Then she strode away.

Encouraged, he called out to everyone he passed, eager to tell them about his wonderful treats, hoping to sell out of the chocolate-centered ones, his most expensive, but no one else listened or cared for what he had to say or sell.

Then a pudgy-cheeked man, scratching a *sothiou* over his teeth, marched toward Mor. Holding the candy bag in front of him, Mor rushed for the man, only slowing his steps when he was about to crash against the man's round belly.

"Would you like to buy some *tàngal*?" Mor asked, trotting backward as the stranger continued forward. "I have many tasty flavors. Would you like to try?" Mor waved the bag under the gentleman's nose. "All the important men of the city select them to eat."

The man leaned forward, smelling the faint mix of flavors. "How much are they?"

"Ten francs apiece, sir."

"Huh, even five francs is too much."

"But they are special *tàngal*. Not what the others sell," Mor added, glancing at the other vendors on the street selling everything from batteries and gum to pots and pans or delicate flowers sprouting in brightly colored fresh-flower hats.

"And what makes yours so special?" The stranger's breath came out in huffs.

"It is the best the city has."

"And how would you know what is best in the city?" The man stared down at Mor, eyeing his freshly scrubbed oversize soccer jersey, which Amina had mended the night before. "You do not look as if you have ever been farther than this path."

It was true Mor had never been in a *ndiaga ndiaye* that traveled to the big city, the far-off places he'd heard about in school, or even the ones closer to home, but it didn't matter. He was certain his *tàngal* was some of the best. Why else would they have such sparkling and crinkly wrapping with wax coating on the inside for when the candy got sticky?

"My *bàjjan* told me," said Mor, wiping a hand across his face to make sure he had no dirt on it. "Try one. You'll see."

The man shoved his chubby fingers into Mor's plastic bag, almost splitting it, giving Mor no chance to snatch it closed. Before Mor had even blinked or noticed what flavor the stranger had popped into his mouth, the man was pushing past him.

Mor scurried backward, then spun to the man's side.

"That will be ten francs, please." Mor stared at the man, hoping he'd pull his coins from his pocket. It was change he sometimes noticed tourists and women in fancy *boubous* discarding at the bottoms of their bags, but he needed every centime.

"I am giving you no money," the man scoffed. "You told me to try, and try I did."

"But, sir, I am selling the candy," Mor said, getting slapped in the arm by the fabric of the man's *boubou* as Mor ran next to him.

"Well, you should have said 'buy' not 'try.'" The man lifted his chin.

Mor could see the candy rolling against the man's cheek.

"Sir," Mor said, stepping in front of him. "You knew I was selling them. They are ten francs apiece."

"Get out of my way. I do not have time for this." The man's hand met Mor's chest, pressing him back. "Next time you will know to say what you mean."

Mor had stumbled again.

An hour later, frustrated at having sold only one *tàngal*, Mor leaned against the corrugated metal over a closed shop's door, watching as a miniature air-conditioned bus pulled off the road in front of him. Within seconds a tide of black bodies in vibrant magenta-, peach-, and indigo-patterned fabrics swarmed the side of the white bus. The young girls thrust their arms forward, trying to be the closest to the glass when the bus driver swung the door open. The girls' excitement rose and their bodies pressed forward as it folded back.

A line of pink-faced tourists, like the other *toubabs* he often saw, exited, smeared head to toe with thick layers of white lotion. The white tourists attempted to push through the determined mob of hawkers but got ensnared instead. Young girls holding out earrings, tissues, tangerines, nuts, and other wares locked around them. When the tourists moved, the girls moved with them. Mor was about to go over and try to sell some of his candy when the bus driver jumped down from the bus.

"Dioggal fi!" He waved his hands through the air, screaming, "I tell you this every time. Get away from my clients and my bus. Stop being pests!"

"We're just trying to make a living like you," a seller shouted back as one of the tourists reached for two rectangular purses she held, made from strips of plastic bags. Mor noticed that even though the bus driver was upset, most of the tourists enjoyed all the attention, and those who didn't reboarded the air-conditioned bus.

"Well, do it away from my bus," the driver countered. He took another step, ushering the girls away as they shouted prices to the *toubabs* that were well over those they would have charged someone from the village.

Reluctantly they scattered, moving aside a few feet, watching the tourists as they glanced around the area or took pictures of things Mor thought were a waste to capture in their fancy cameras. Then he noticed one tourist, separated from the others, crouched down, holding tightly to her bag. She was admiring a bundle of braided and beaded bracelets displayed by color in front of a slender girl with twisted legs who sat on a blanket a ways back from the road. A pair of wooden crutches rested behind her. She smiled up at the woman and nodded when the tourist reached for a stack of bracelets, handing the girl three five-hundred-franc coins, which was over seven hundred times more than what Mor held.

It gave him an idea, though.

He wandered farther down the busy roadway, away from the bus, and stopped at an empty corner. Still in the heart of the traffic, it was ideal. It was a natural stopping point before people crossed the road. He searched a pile of scattered scraps, yanked out a white square of cardboard, and tore away the soggy edges. Then he dragged over an old oil drum crusted with rust and placed the cardboard on top of it.

He unfastened the knots on each plastic bag and watched as candy spilled from their mouths. There were individually wrapped white mints that gleamed like the moon, and others shaped like succulent fruits. Of those, Mor thought the papaya and banana treats would taste the best. From the last bag he grabbed a few *tàngal* with a hard outer shell and a creamy chocolate or caramel center. This bag was the prize of them all, and he could charge a few francs more for one of those. He arranged them into a multicolored line.

Against the white surface of the cardboard, the shiny wrappers of copper and silver stripes shimmered in the sun, and the amber, electric-orange, lime-green, and canary-yellow foils drew the eye of everyone who passed. Mor found a long stick in the dirt and banged it against the side of the drum.

"Sweeties for sale. Get your *tàngal* here."

"How much for one?" a man asked, stopping at the corner.

"They are fifteen francs," Mor said, having raised his own prices.

"How 'bout I trade you a pack of tissues for two?"

"But I don't need tissues, sir." Mor looked from the bag of tissues the man waved in front of his face. The man was swallowing hard and staring at Mor's *tàngal*.

"I don't have anything else." The man rummaged through his pocket and found ten francs and a bit of fuzz clinging to a button. "How 'bout these and the rest of my tissues? Will that do?"

Mor thought a moment, looking at his table full of sweeties. He had sold only one piece in over an hour. "You can have a cherry one." Mor picked a bright-red wrapper off the cardboard, knowing there were many more cherry treats sitting in his bag.

For the next couple of hours, in a blur, a stream of elbows, shoulders, hands, and faces passed by his makeshift stand, but few people stopped to buy.

Mor refused to give up. He continued a steady beat on the old oil drum and slowly managed to sell a handful of the treats. Most went to a man who popped one of the caramel-filled candies into his mouth and turned back around, fishing in his pocket, ready to buy three more.

This lifted Mor's spirits.

But then his energy waned when he looked down at the half-filled table. He still had a whole bag of sweets left in his sack. He looked back up the road and noticed that the young girl selling bracelets was gathering up her blanket. Although the sun had settled lower in the sky, there was still plenty of day left. He wondered if she had sold all her bracelets or if this was the hour she usually stopped. As the parade of people continued their march to and from the surrounding paths, to the beach and market, Mor became determined not to leave until at least half the *tàngal* on the cardboard were gone.

Then he could sell the rest another day. It wasn't a lot, but it was something.

He wanted to bring even a little back to his sisters, who were probably still down by the water's edge, waiting while their clothes lay drying on the rocks.

He wanted them to see he had not stumbled again.

13

LATER, after exhausted shoppers and vendors leaving the paths, eager for something to clear the dust from their throats, had bought all his mints and a few of the chocolate- and caramel-filled treats, he realized his table was much emp- tier. Smiling to himself, he thought it had been a pretty good day. In all he had made 190 francs. Not trusting his pockets, he shoved all his coins into his new sneakers and started gathering up the remaining *tàngal*, dropping it into the last half-full bag of sweets.

Then a clumpy shadow spread in front of him. Mor raised his head as a group of boys approached his table. He was sure he'd seen them before.

"What do we got here?" one of the five boys asked. His

teeth jutted out of his mouth like those of a neighing horse. "It looks like he's brought us some *tàngal*."

"They're not for you. They're mine." Mor swept the bag of sweets into the cradle of his arm. However, he was not quick enough to get all the candies off the cardboard before two of the boys snatched some up. "Give them back."

"I don't think so, man," a different boy, at the back, with an unmistakable gravelly voice, spoke up. The others parted, giving him a path straight to Mor.

Mor nearly choked as he swallowed. It was Papis, the boy with the rock. He hovered over Mor.

Mor clutched his sack to his chest, sure the others huddled around him were more of the Danka Boys. Worry spun in his mind. *What are they doing here? Do they recognize me? Are they here for me?* he wondered. *Didn't the boy on the wall say one of them was from Lat Mata?* Lots of people traveled through Mor's village; it was the largest en route to the city of Saint-Louis. But then Mor stopped wondering. His question was answered. Standing only a few arm lengths away, with a baseball cap low on his head, was his old friend Cheikh.

Excitement danced inside Mor, making him feel like a giddy puppy. Cheikh was home. Mor raced around the cardboard table, charging for his old friend. Forgetting about his candy and the other boys around them.

"Cheikh, you have been gone so long! Have you just come home? Your mother didn't say. I have so much to tell you, and I'm sure you have lots to tell me." Mor beamed as he reached for Cheikh to hug him in greeting.

But Cheikh answered his question with silence, and his greeting with a quick shove and space between them.

"Eh, Cheikh, man, do you know this *khale*?"

Kid, Mor thought. He was more than just some kid. Cheikh had been his best friend since he could crawl.

"Yeah," Cheikh said dismissively. "He's just my mom's friend's kid."

Mor bristled. Cheikh acted as if he were a stranger. He wouldn't look Mor's way. Confused and hurt, Mor stared.

Then Cheikh glanced at him from the corner of his eye. Mor couldn't read the expression etched on his face, shielded by the lip of the cap. "We grew up together. You know. Him following me around." Cheikh gave a half chuckle.

Mor couldn't move, and he couldn't speak. He thought his ears were no longer working right.

"Aww, so then he won't mind if I have some of these candies," Papis said, draping an arm over Mor's shoulder.

"Naw, man, let's just go. I said I didn't want to be around here anyway." Cheikh glanced around as if he expected to see someone else he didn't want to.

"What's the rush?" Papis said. "Your friends are my friends." He snatched Mor's sack from him.

As if his body were on delay, Mor grabbed for it too late, hopping as he reached out. "Hey!"

"Come on, Papis. Let him have it," Cheikh said as if he

could not care either way. "He's nobody."

Mor stopped jumping then. Stopped trying to reach his sack. Stopped everything.

Papis grabbed the remaining bag of *tàngal* out of it, letting it fall.

Mor picked up the sack, pulling it against him. "That's mine," he said halfheartedly as Papis dropped one of the sweeties with a caramel center into his mouth.

Papis strolled over to Cheikh, offering him one. Cheikh pushed away the bag. Side by side, Cheikh stood as Papis's twin, just as tall and just as unknown to Mor as a prowling lion.

When Cheikh's gaze dropped to Mor's feet, Mor shifted self-consciously, trying to hide one foot behind the other. Then the clear image of his mother's cloth wedged behind Cheikh's pallet jabbed at Mor's thoughts.

"It *was* you," Mor said. "You stole it. Just as they steal from me now. How could you do that?" He stared at Cheikh as Cheikh stared at him.

"What is this *khale* yapping about?" Papis asked, snickering. He gripped Mor's shoulder. "No one has stolen anything. We're all friends here."

"Get off me." Mor rotated his shoulder, causing Papis's hand to fall.

Papis held out the bag of candy, and two of the other Danka Boys dived for it, ripping it in two. Candy spilled everywhere, most landing in a shallow puddle. The two boys burrowed their hands in the mucky water like hogs' snouts, nudging each other away, scrapping for the prize.

"You know what you stole," Mor said, turning his attention back to Cheikh. His candy was lost. "How could you? Do you even care that my *baay* has died? You act as if you don't know me. But do you remember him? The one who kicked the football with you late at night when you were upset? The one who showed you how to lace all your fancy shoes. Have you forgotten him, too? The one who was more of a *baay* to you than your own—"

"Enough," Papis said, pushing his hand into Mor's chest. "Your whining is boring me."

"Did you forget him, too?" Mor yelled over Papis's shoulder as Papis bulldozed him back. Tears spilled from Mor's eyes. "Did you?"

Mor did not feel the sting of Papis's elbow against his cheek until he hit the ground.

"I said enough!" Papis stood over him.

"Hey, what's going on there?" a shopkeeper who had tossed Mor a coin for a sweetie earlier yelled. "We don't need your trouble here. Rustle feathers somewhere else."

Papis threw his hand up at the man and made a sucking sound through his teeth. One of the other shopkeepers shook his head but turned from them. No one else seemed to want to get mixed up in the trouble, as if they did not want the problem at their stalls.

"No one wants you here," the shopkeeper shouted again.

But Papis only scowled at him, then turned back to Mor. The shopkeeper rushed into his shop.

"Come on, man, stop," Cheikh urged.

Papis ignored him, too.

Mor pressed his palms in the dirt, trying to push himself up, but a Danka Boy knocked his arms out from under him with a sweep of his foot. Papis grabbed another treat from one of his friends, smearing the wet wrapper across his shirt, then pulled apart the foil with his teeth. He dropped a chocolate-filled sweet onto his tongue, which shot from between his lips like a lizard's.

"*Nekhna*," he approved, smacking his tongue against the roof of his mouth. He plucked all the copper- and silver-striped wrappers out of the other Danka Boys' hands.

"Eh!" one boy complained, staring at the candy disappearing into Papis's pocket. With just a glance from Papis, the boy went silent.

"What else do you have?" Papis's eyes shifted back to Mor and ran down his body, stopping at his waist. "You got something in those pockets?" He did not wait for Mor to respond. "Don't think my boys won't find it."

"Now I told you," the shopkeeper shouted, emerging from his shop with a broom. "I've called the police."

A heavy laugh shook the air. "You think I care?" Papis said. "What can they do? They don't scare me. But you"—he stabbed a finger toward the shopkeeper—"you should feel scared."

If the shopkeeper didn't, Mor did. He wanted to run, but he didn't think he'd make it far before one of the Danka Boys, maybe even Cheikh, stopped him.

The shopkeeper raised his broom again, not backing down. "I told you, git!"

In a flash Papis made for the shopkeeper's door. He swept his hand across the table of goods outside the shop. Cans collided and tumbled across the tabletop. They dropped in the dirt with echoless thuds. The storekeeper charged forward, swinging his broom, as if Papis were a target ball and the broom handle were a cricket bat. The bristles struck Papis against his side. But instead of trying to dodge a second blow, Papis stood there waiting to be hit another time. The man hesitated a moment too long, probably unsure of whether to strike Papis again. Even though Papis was an unruly teenager, he was still a child.

Motion on the still-lively street halted All eyes were on Papis and the shopkeeper. Papis snatched at the broom's bristles and lunged, shoving the broom handle square into the man's chest. The man doubled over, coughing. He slapped against his chest for air. Then his hand balled into a tight fist at the center of his shirt.

That same rumbling laughter launched from Papis's throat again as he threw the broom down. "Stay down, old man. If you know what is wise."

Cheikh pulled for Papis's arm.

People screamed for the police, who still hadn't come. A

couple of those watching offered to help the shopkeeper up, but he waved them back. Even the *tiopati* cook was on her feet, brandishing her glistening spatula like a spear. Papis ignored their outrage. His lip curled and a glob of saliva shot from his mouth. It landed at the shopkeeper's feet. The man's face was still scrunched in pain.

The shopkeeper looked past Papis to Cheikh. "What are you, fourteen?" he said, coughing. "You are old enough to know better than to stand behind such a boy. I know this."

"You know nothing, old man, except to stick your neck where it doesn't belong," Papis said.

Cheikh yanked on Papis's arm again. "Come on. There is nothing here for us."

"Listen to your friend," the shopkeeper said. "These are the first wise words I've heard."

As the other Danka Boys moved toward Papis and the shopkeeper, Mor took his chance to run. He gripped the cords of his sack and took off. Dirt, trash, and pebbles shifted under his feet. He felt as if he were on the beach in Mahktar all over again. His eyes met Cheikh's one last time before he disappeared from sight around a corner.

"Man, let's go," Mor heard Cheikh say.

"Yeah," Papis said. "This place is no fun."

Although Mor wanted to see which way Papis would head next, so he could go the other, his feet didn't want to wait. His legs carried him farther away as if on puppet strings. He obeyed and sprinted down side paths, avoiding the main roadway. When he was sure he heard no one behind him, he slowed. Leaning against a high wall to catch his breath, he looked up and down the alley. Two men sat on a bench up the path where the alley spilled onto a wider road, but there was no one else in sight. Mor picked up his foot and pulled off his sneaker. As he tilted it down, the coins ran to its heel. He grinned. Despite having lost his last sweeties, he had more money than he'd had that morning. He was one tiny step closer to helping Amina and keeping his promise to his *baay*.

Making his way to the other side of the market, far away from the earlier commotion, he kept checking behind him and jumped at every strange or unexpected sound.

The bright orange of ripe mandarins, the vibrant greens and reds of mangoes, and the silvers and browns of fresh fish filled Mor's eyes as he arrived at the vegetable and fish stalls. He held tight to his coins. A stall owner wrapped a package for another customer and paid Mor no mind. The stall owner laughed and swatted flies as she worked. When she finally caught sight of Mor near her table, though, she gave him a stern look.

"Move along. I won't have begging at my business." She hustled over to where he stood next to her loaves of bread, shooing him away, as if he were one of the flies. Or maybe word had reached her about the trouble that had happened at the other end of the market. Mor glanced behind him once more, checking for the hundredth time to see if the Danka Boys were lurking.

"I'm not begging, ma'am." He held out a couple of shining coins. "I've earned this money and I wish to buy a little bread, please."

The woman and her customer both looked at him. He was sure his elbows and knees were ashy, and that he probably had a faint white film around his mouth from lack of lotion, a luxury he could not afford. But he had money for this.

He straightened but did not meet the woman's eyes, showing his elder respect. "Please, could I buy some?"

"Which would you like?" she asked, pointing to the baguettes she had out.

"That one, please." He did not choose the largest or the smallest. He simply chose one that would feed his sisters and him for the next few days.

"Not that one?" She held out a larger loaf.

"No, that one will be fine." He nodded toward the first loaf he had selected.

While she turned away from him and placed the bread in a bag, he quickly retied his shoelace. When he straightened, he put the coins in her hand.

"Thank you." He bowed and smiled at both women and dashed away.

"And *jërëjëf* to you," the stall owner called behind him.

Mor hadn't reached the edge of the fishmongers' tables before he stuck his hand into the bag to break off a tiny piece of the bread. But he pulled on something that did not feel like bread at all. When he looked into the bag and saw a small fried fish, he stopped. After a moment he felt like all the fish's and fishmongers' eyes were on him. He felt like he was back on that beach where Papis had shouted, "Thief!"

He quickly crumpled the top of the bag closed. Should he stay his course, pretending he did not notice, or bring the stall owner's error to her eye?

I know my son will always do what is honorable. . . .

Mor did not need to look around or question his father's words. Slowly he turned and trudged back to the woman, who was talking with her friend.

Their voices boomed with laughter. The stall owner's words rolled from her mouth as if they were tumbling down a hill, picking up speed as they went. Mor wasn't sure he should interrupt.

"Excuse me," he finally said.

"Yes?" The stall owner and her friend glanced down at him.

"I think you made a mistake."

"And what would that be?" The stall owner placed her hands on her hips.

He opened the bag so she could see inside. When she did not say anything immediately, he spoke up. "There is a fish in here that I did not buy." He peeked back into the bag to make sure his touch and sight were not fooling him.

Both women's scrunched lips shifted into slight grins.

"It's for you."

A look Mor did not quite understand passed between the friends.

He got nervous, wondering if they were trying to trick him into giving them more money.

"I cannot take it." Mor raised his voice a little and lifted the bag to her. He did not want to be mistaken for a *saccee* again. "I did not pay for it and have no coins to spare."

The woman leaned down to be eye level with Mor. "Since I've already placed it in your bag, I cannot take it back. Think of it as a gift."

"*Merci waay*," Mor said, thanking her, vowing to pay her back when he could spare the coins. "I can't wait to bring it to my sisters."

In a hurry to get home, Mor darted through the market, keeping alert for any signs of the Danka Boys. It'd been a long day, and even though he had lost the rest of the *tàngal*, he still had food, and a few coins in his sneaker that got him a tiny bit closer to his goal.

14

MOR was unable to pull the door covering all the way back, or plant his foot inside the doorway of his family's *barak*, before Fatima torpedoed into his arms, crushing the bag of bread and fish he had gotten at the market stall.

"You can't . . . you promised. Don't do it," Fatima begged. Her voice was muffled in the folds of Mor's jersey.

"Don't do what, Tima?" Even though she was only six, her grip around his waist was strong, stopping him. "Look at me, what is it?" Mor tried to loosen the knot her tiny fingers had created at his back, but she kept tightening it. Then he tried to lift her head, but she buried it deeper into his shirt.

When she finally raised her head and stared at him, her eyes were swollen and red. Endless streams of tears traveled down her cheeks.

"What happened?" He looked from Fatima to Amina, who sat on the raised pallet with her legs crossed, her face buried deep behind the pages of *La Petite Princesse*, even though she'd read it a hundred times. "What is going on?" Mor demanded. "What has happened to Tima?"

"Nothing," Amina said flatly, and turned a yellowing page in the well-worn novel.

"It is something. She is crying and she can hardly catch her breath."

"When Rama came to play with me," Fatima sniffled, "her *baay* came too." She released her fingers from around Mor's waist long enough to point one at Amina. "And she told him you might sell Jeeg to him. But you can't. . . ."

Mor turned and looked at Jeeg, lying in the corner. She stopped chewing her cud and fixed her eyes on him as if she understood the discussion. "It's all right, Tima. No one is selling Jeeg. I told you that when Auntie left. Jeeg is our family." His worry started to cool. "That would be like us selling you, and we would never do that, would we, Mina?" Mor paused, waiting for Amina to speak. "Mina?" he repeated.

Fatima's eyes were wide and glassy with tears. She watched her big sister carefully.

"It's not that I do not care for Jeeg, because I do," Amina

began. "But we must think ahead. Mor does not have a job yet, and the *tàngal* won't last long. Jeeg would be close. Rama does not live far. I only told him we would remember his kind offer of help."

Mor cradled Fatima's shoulders, which shook from her sobbing. "I will not lie. Money from her sale would be helpful. But Jeeg was a friend to our *yaay*. And she is a friend to us."

"Yaay would understand," added Amina. "She would not have wanted her children to go hungry or not to learn."

"We are not selling her. And we are not going hungry. Allah will provide." The tone of Mor's voice was firm. It softened when he looked back at Fatima. "Dry your eyes. Jeeg is not going anywhere." Mor hadn't thought Fatima could squeeze him any harder, but she did.

"So there is no discussion?" Amina said, putting down her book. Her voice was slightly raised. "Don't think I haven't noticed, money dances in your pockets until it is gone." Her eyes were locked on her brother. "My heart is not coal, but sometimes the hardest ways are all we have. We need to remember that. We can't only depend on you." Her words scorched him. She swung her shoulder in the direction of the goat. "If we need help, our neighbor is offering us help. I did not say for sure we would sell her."

"Jeeg is not going to the *reykat*." Mor's voice lifted.

"Who said anything about the butcher?"

Fatima squeaked and swung her arms protectively around

Jeeg's neck. The goat let out a *m-a-a* and twitched her ears.

"You know that is where Rama's father would take her, just like Auntie wanted to," Mor said. "She is old and can bear no kids to trade or make any milk. What else would he do with her? Let her feed on scraps in the trash heaps or lead her to the trees to nibble on leaves, as we do? What good would that be to him?"

"None," Amina conceded. "I just thought he could help us."

"I know," Mor assured her. "But he would have no need of her alive."

After a moment Amina trudged over to Jeeg, her eyes cast down. "I'm sorry." She stroked the bridge of Jeeg's nose while Fatima eyed her. "I would never want that for you. I was thinking only of francs and not of you. Please forgive me." Jeeg pressed back on Amina's hand and bleated as Amina scratched her. Amina brushed her cheek across Jeeg's shoulder. A dark spot formed on her pink T-shirt.

"I can take care of us," Mor said, still stung by her earlier words. "I know you don't think so—"

"How?" Amina paused. She sniffled, then slapped at another tear. "You've lost our coins, or won't tell us how you've spent them. Where is Yaay's pouch? And where is the money Auntie left?"

Mor was quiet long enough for the outside sounds to creep back into the small space of their home. His concern for Fatima had blocked them all out, but now the laughter of a child, the wail of a baby, and the whistling of a man all trickled inside.

"The pouch fell from my pocket." Cheikh flickered through his mind. "But I have hidden Bàjjan's money and have brought home a little more."

"Why didn't you tell me?" The words shook as they left her throat.

Mor knew instantly that she was hurt. "I thought I could find it and get it back."

"Did you?"

He heard a tinge of hope. He did not want to crush it, like Cheikh had crushed his, but he could not lie to her. "No."

"You have convinced our *bàjjan* to let us stay, and you have no plan. What happens if you fail?"

Mor heard her fear.

"I won't," he said, with more certainty than he felt. "I have already sold some of the *tàngal*."

"And you think that matches what was lost? A few sweeties sold could not come close to three thousand francs."

"No, but it is a start."

"And what will you sell next if it is not Jeeg?" Her voice turned hard. "Bàjjan has not given us much. And for the next few months we will be alone. We have no extra for anything else but food. What exactly do you have of value that can help us? I want to stay as much as you. To go to school and not clean some stranger's house all day and night, but maybe we are not meant to dream and want something better. I don't think dreams are for us." On the pallet behind her the edge of the Iéna Academy pamphlet was visible, tucked under the corner of her book.

Her doubt pierced, but it was an emotion Mor could handle. Not like her loss of hope, which swallowed him whole. It showed his failure.

He gazed down at his sneakers, thinking of Cheikh. Hurt seemed to stab him from every direction. He was exhausted. It had been less than a week since he had been trying to do more than play at being a man. And so far he was still just a boy in his *baay*'s sandals.

He was about to try to explain further when their *yaay* appeared by the window. Her fuchsia *teybass* swirled at her ankles from a breeze Mor could not feel. His hands fumbled with the bag of bread and fish he'd forgotten he held, then stopped rustling when she smiled down at him. He felt his face washing over with warmth. His heart nearly catapulted out of his chest with each beat. He wanted to rush into her arms but knew he would probably pass right through her.

Gliding over to her children on delicate feet, Mor's *yaay* sat by Amina' side. One of her hands settled on her thigh. Amina didn't move. She couldn't see or feel their *yaay*. But the tight clinch of her jaw softened. She almost looked like her lips might break a smile. Mor was sure if happiness could have been poured, it was poured over Amina right then, spilling across her thigh. That was how the touch of his mother's *spirit* had first felt to him. It was like having a thousand more games of *le foot* with his *baay*.

"I want to trust that you will find a way," Amina said, calmer now. "We all will try."

Turning to Mor, their mother withdrew her hand and settled it in her lap. Mor looked down at where her hand had left Amina; her skin was as brown as it had always been. There was no outward change. But inside, he was certain, there had been one. Their mother's touch had absorbed some of his fears the last time she appeared to him, outside their home, when he was unsure and afraid. And he believed it had done the same for Amina now.

"What's in here?" Fatima asked, no longer worried about Jeeg's fate. She reached for the bag Mor held.

Mor's eyes were still locked with those of their *yaay*.

"Let me see," Fatima said. She tugged it, quickly ripping the bag from his grip, and opened it.

"Bread and fish." She reached for it hungrily.

"I thought this could be a celebration for the first coins I have made us." His eyes traveled between his sisters and their mother. "I cannot take all the praise, though. A nice lady at the market gave the fish as a gift."

Amina placed a platter under the grease-soaked bag on the dirt floor. She had no idea how close she was to their *yaay*, and how her movements made the shoulder ruffles of their mother's *teybass* flutter. Her eyebrows made a rippled line when she glanced at the empty space that captivated her brother.

While they ate, their mother stayed with them. Mor wanted to ask Amina if she felt anything near her side as she knelt next to their *yaay*, her elbow brushing against their mother's skin. But he said nothing. He and his *yaay* simply watched Amina and Fatima enjoying the fish and bread, licking every drop of fish juice and oil off their fingers as they went. Mor stared at the meat of the fish as it was pulled away, leaving clean white bones. When Amina offered him some, he told her to eat her fill, like his *baay* always used to.

"But there is enough to share," Amina said, taking another nibble.

To most, the small fish that sat in front of them would hardly be a meal for one, let alone three.

"No, I am fine," he protested, thinking some of it needed to last for breakfast. He prayed his stomach wouldn't rumble.

His *yaay* shook her head. She reached out for the fish and mimicked the act of eating, by bringing her pinched finger-tips to her lips. Still, Mor did not reach for the food until her hand rested over his, sending tingles and pops through him. He let her guide his arm toward the platter.

"Just a little," he said to Amina. He never wanted his mother's hand to leave his.

"I love fish," Fatima cooed, pulling more meat from the bones.

Then, from that little spark, a thought burst into Mor's head.

"I should become a fisherman. Go out in the mornings with the fishermen and bring home a big, tasty fish for us each night," he blurted out, excited.

"But you do not know how to fish," Amina chuckled, tearing off a tiny piece of bread. She knew to save it too. The skin around her lips glistened with oil. "How will you do it?"

"Our *baay* did not always know how to fix motors, but he became one of the best at it in the village. I will go and learn. I will become a fisherman." He smiled at Amina, liking his sudden idea. Then his smile faltered. He realized his *yaay*'s hand no longer touched his and that she was gone.

"Are you okay?" Amina asked.

"Yes," he said, convincing himself he was. He turned from the empty space. "I'm fine." Although his mother was no longer by his side, he felt her presence in the room, as if her scent lingered. He inhaled, dreaming of her jasmine and rose lotion. "Don't worry," he said, looking back at Amina. "I will learn the sea. And we will soon have more fish then we will ever need."

Amina nodded, one eyebrow raised. Mor ignored the look of doubt on her face.

"So did you sell all the *tàngal*?" she asked a moment later.

"It is all gone," Mor said weakly.

"All of it?" Fatima looked up from dragging her finger across the grease-stained bag.

Amina tilted her head slightly, reading Mor's face like it

was a page from her book. A page that was out of order.

"I did not get all that I wanted. But I will find another way. Tomorrow will be better, *Incha'Allah*," he said with more confidence than he was certain of, but he knew they needed to believe it to be true. Even him.

15

THE next day Mor left his bed mat as the purplish pinks of dawn split the night sky. Braving the early-morning chill, he pulled his arms inside the folds of his T-shirt to keep warm and headed across the village to Lat Mata's beach. Halfway to the short mud wall that separated the beach from the roadway, lavishly painted boats came into view, sitting in a haphazard line. Their bows were bird beaks pointed to the coming sun, and their flags ruffled like feathers whipping in the wind. A group of older teenagers sloshed through the surf and loaded empty buckets onto a gigantic *gaal* as water splashed against the boat's sides. A man in blue flip-flops and a shirt with cutoff sleeves untangled netting that lay like a coiled pangolin at his feet.

Mor jumped the wall, excitement coursing through him. Then he stopped. He did not know where to begin. He looked around at all the men but was unsure whom to speak with about a position on one of the boats. Determined not to turn back, he trudged through the sand until he came to a group of men hoisting a massive heap of netting into a *gaal*.

"*Balma*, but does anyone need help?" Mor gazed up at the men's faces. No one glanced his way. "Excuse me," he said again, his voice as loud and strong as he could make it. "I am a hard worker and it will not cost you much to employ me."

The fishermen laughed at this.

"We can hardly support ourselves and our families. How are we to take on another?" a man with a face as round as a soccer ball asked. He tugged in the part of net he was gathering.

"You are a little boy," another fisherman said, spitting bark from his lips, some tangling in the hairs of his hennaed beard. He shoved his *sothiou* in the back corner of his mouth and pulled his beard once before reaching for the net again. "And you would get yourself hurt." He yanked on the netting. "Or worse, get in our way."

Why did everyone think he couldn't help? "I'm small. I don't take up much space. Everyone always says I'm a fast learner," Mor said. His voice got swallowed in the roar of the foaming white waves.

"You are already in our way." The fishermen pushed by him, no longer willing to delay their work. As they readied themselves to leave, Mor sprang to avoid the last of the netting being whipped into a boat. His head collided with the hip of one of the men. As he turned to apologize, he stepped on another fisherman's bare foot. Even though he didn't think he'd be in the way, he found that he was.

Along the beach everywhere he stepped was the wrong place to be. Either a net was being dragged by his feet and he needed to leap aside, or a *gaal* was being launched into the water, sliding off enormous rolling logs. When he thought he was finally a safe distance away, a fisherman touched his arm. He leaped back, thinking he was about to be squashed by a boat.

"Calm yourself." The fisherman leaned forward and gripped his shoulder. "You are fine." His hair was a field of tight graying curls. "I'm sorry we cannot help you, but you see those fishing vessels in the distance?" Mor looked out to where the man was pointing. Large boats rested on the horizon, with massive nets held out like wings. "They come from far and wide to catch our fish, and there is hardly any to spare." The man patted Mor on the back. "I'm sorry, but I doubt you will find work here." He turned from Mor, then raced for one of the huge *gaals* rocking in the morning tide.

Soon Mor was left alone on the beach with broken boats and old retired fishermen sitting back, talking, and watching the change of light on the horizon. Mor stared at the departing boats. He was about to turn for home when he spotted a man with thick dark-reddish-brown dreadlocks hunched on the edge of a boat, mending a fraying net. Mor headed toward him.

"*Biddééw bi leer gi lëpp-lëpp bi yoon wi. . . .*" The words left the man's lips like a song, but it wasn't a song. Mor wasn't exactly certain what it was, though. The man spoke his native Wolof, but the words fell together funny. Mor thought he'd heard him say something about starlight, and a butterfly on a path, yet together they made no sense. As Mor approached, the deep drone of the man's voice became a tumbling ramble of sounds. It was Mor's mother tongue, but the meaning was a mystery. "Honey-watered moon"? What could that possibly be? Was that even what he'd said? The words were whispers. Sweet and soothing, almost like his father's riddle of words.

"Pardon me, sir?" Mor stood before the man. "Are you going out on the water today?"

The man continued to whisper to himself, not looking up.

"Sir?" Mor took a timid step forward. "I'm sorry to bother you, but I wondered if you needed help out on the water?"

The man still did not glance up.

Digging his foot in the sand, Mor flicked a little of it in the air. He craned his head forward, staring at the man. The whites of the man's eyes raced back and forth under their half-lowered lids. Then the man's lids snapped back. Between his hanging dreadlocks two piercing brown eyes

155

stared at Mor. The fisherman's eyes ran over Mor as if memorizing every inch of him. Mor did not allow a muscle to flex, but he suddenly recognized the man from the path where his *baay*'s accident and his run-in with the Danka Boys had happened. He'd been the one muttering as he pedaled by on a rickety bicycle with a clanging bell and screeching wheels, with a bird as company. Then the man's eyes lowered as quickly as they had risen. His hands never stopped working on the tattered netting. Mor let out a tiny huff. A part of him wanted to move forward, but he backed away.

He trudged up the beach to its bordering wall. He heaved himself onto it and dangled his legs over the edge. His heels banged the crumbling mud bricks, knocking away chunks of hard-packed dirt, as he watched the man. Now what was he to do? Drop his own string in the water? His ankles as bait?

The lone fisherman dumped his netting into his boat and moved to push the *gaal* out to the water. Then he paused. With a jerk of his head, his dreadlocks whipped over his shoulder. His eyes stayed trained on Mor. The two stared at each other for what seemed like forever. Confused, Mor broke their eye contact and turned to see if something or someone was behind him. But there was no one there. The strange man with dreadlocks that hung down his back like slumbering snakes still stared at him.

Unsure what to do, Mor climbed down off the wall and waited. The man made no signal for him to come closer, but Mor took a few half steps forward anyway. As he got nearer, the man motioned toward the other side of the boat. He placed his hands on the splintering wood and waited for Mor to do the same. Mor copied him, balancing on his tiptoes. The man gave the boat a hard shove, dislodging it from its berth in the sand. It lurched forward and Mor almost fell face-first onto the beach. Getting his bearings and his balance, he quickly pushed the *gaal* as well. When the boat was in the grip of the waves, the fisherman climbed in and extended his hand to Mor, who was almost completely submerged in the surf.

After Mor was seated inside the small *gaal* on one of two wooden planks nailed down at either end of the boat, the man yanked at the engine cord. It puttered but did not start. He tugged again but nothing happened. Then he took out a wrench and let it slam against the dented motor casing. It collided with the shell in a rattling bang. Mor leaped, alarmed.

"It will only get worse if you keep doing that," Mor blurted out as the wrench crashed against the cover once more. "I might be able to do something. My father taught me a lot about engines before he . . ."

Agitated, the man muttered to himself as if he had not heard, then threw the wrench down and stared at the engine. Mor slid off the plank where he sat and, on unsteady legs because of the shifting waves, made his way to the engine, kneeling in front of it.

"May I?" he asked. Without waiting for an answer, Mor grabbed hold of the wrench and leaned in to inspect the engine. "Here is the problem," he said, taking a yellow covered wire between his fingers. "It has come undone. This isn't a truck engine, but they are mostly all the same." He respun the yellow-coated wire around its bolt and checked that the other wires were secured. "There," he said, getting up and brushing off his knees.

He handed the man back his wrench.

"I don't think we will be needing this."

The man tilted his head, examining the engine. Then he glanced at Mor. When he dropped the wrench and yanked the cord, nothing happened. Mor was anxious. The man pulled it a second time, and the engine rattled and came alive. A bluish translucent cloud of smoke swirled into the air. The scent of burning fuel was strong.

"*Jërëjëf.*" The man steered the boat deeper into the ocean.

Mor gripped the rotting wood plank across from the man and smiled as the tiny boat hurtled forward across the water, slicing through the waves, cool wind against Mor's face.

Mor swallowed hard. A shallow puddle lapped at his feet in the bottom of the boat, soaking his sneakers even more. With everything happening so fast, he'd forgotten to take them off. "I have never been on a boat this far out before," he offered as the breeze tried to cut off his breath. He squinted at the man, who still spoke only to himself. "I am Mor Fall. Thank you for giving me this chance."

The man still said nothing to him. And Mor wondered if the fisherman would even pay him, or if he'd cheat him like the rude villager who'd taken one of his *tàngal*. "Excuse me, sir, but how much will I get paid for my work today?"

The fisherman kept his eyes trained on the horizon.

"Sir?" Mor gripped the seat tighter when they bounced through choppy waves. He wished he'd remembered to ask about money or fish before he got into the boat. Now it would probably be another day with nothing.

As they approached a cluster of *gaals*, the engine's roar died down and the man maneuvered through the idle boats. Fishermen jeered and pointed when they saw Mor in the boat.

"He's gone out with *doff* Demba." A fisherman in a yellow jacket pointed. "Now we know we'll catch some fish. Fish jump into our boats just to get away from him."

"I don't know why he even bothers to bring that rickety junk out here," a young fisherman shouted across the water, cupping his hands over his mouth. "One day that engine will find a way to scurry away and drop into the sea. Leaving him stranded."

Mor couldn't understand why they were being this way. Their jokes were not funny. The man they called "crazy Demba" had a boat that looked much like theirs. The colors were more faded, and it was evident he had patched up holes with flimsy pieces of wood and tarp, but it was still floating, and the way that a little bit of water pooled in the hull was no different from many other *gaals*. Somehow he found money to keep it fueled, and Mor had fixed the engine. So Mor tried to ignore the taunts and jokes, as Demba did.

Demba revved the engine. As they moved past the fishermen, Mor could see the large fishing vessels in the distance coming closer. Soon the other *gaals* behind them looked like specks in the sand. Mor's nerves pulsed, getting quicker with the rocky sway of the boat. His eyes darted between the open sea and the beach. The boat thumped along as it picked up speed. Part of him wished he had not fixed the roaring motor.

The waves are a mother's rocking arms, and the gaal *a restless child. Ease your fear, for you are cradled. She means you no harm.*

Although he always welcomed his father's words, they brought him little comfort as Demba pressed the boat even farther out to sea. "Are you sure we should be going out this far?" Mor looked nervously over his shoulder at the shore, and then around him at the endless span of salt water. Large birds circled close by.

Settle your heartbeat and unclench your fist. The water will not claim you as its own.

Demba turned the engine off, and Mor remained silent, holding to his father's words. They sat for a long time, staring at the glassy surface of the water. Demba watched the birds clustering over their heads, eyeing what Mor hoped were schools of fish in the deep waters. He motioned for

Mor to take one end of the netting and stand next to him. Demba rocked his body back and forth, nodding for Mor to mimic him. Mor followed everything he did. When they had built up some momentum, the sides of the boat teetered, touching the cresting waves. Demba nodded and let the netting fly onto the water as Mor did the same. They watched the mesh of electric blue, sun-washed green, and fraying black sink into the sea. Before Mor could get his balance, Demba pulled on the cord wrapped around his hand with a quick jerk to yank the netting closed. But Mor stumbled and tripped on it. He was over the lip of the boat before anything could be done to stop it.

At first the water was refreshing and cool against his skin, pressing his clothes to him. Then the current pulled him down, quicker than the netting that was sailing beside him. He reached out for it, but it moved away on the wave of water created from the thrust of his hand. Fish swam frantically inside the net as he reached out again. As he held his breath, his cheeks puffed out on each side. He kicked his legs behind him. Panic strangled his bones. Not being a strong swimmer, he had never been deep in the water alone. Cheikh or his father had always been at his side.

Mor's arms flailed, dragging him deeper. A stinging burn shot through his lungs. He squeezed his eyes shut; then they flew open. The salt water was a flame against them.

You are a cuttlefish, my son. . . . His *baay*'s voice joined him, a distant echo in the water. *You have almost a dozen arms with tentacles that stretch around the world. If you cannot reach the sky with one, try another.*

Mor threw his hand in front of him, sweeping it through the water, clutching nothing. *Reach out again. She will not claim you.* Mor listened, and tried his other arm. He felt the coarse plastic netting graze his palm as it moved through his fingers. He closed his hand tight around it, and his body launched through the water as Demba pulled the net.

When Mor's head broke the surface, Demba released the net and reached for Mor. Most of the trapped fish sprang to freedom, wiggling out of the parting net, slipping by Mor's legs. Demba did not try to grab any; instead he dragged Mor inside the boat. Mor's sneakers squeaked against the starboard lip of the *gaal*. Demba hit him high on his back, dislodging most of the water Mor had swallowed. It stung as it raced up his throat. He coughed and spit up what felt like a river. Demba hauled the netting into the boat next to Mor. Drenched from head to toe, Mor created more of a puddle in the bottom of the *gaal* than the caught fish that flapped around, trapped in the net. A third of the fish that had traveled through the water with him had escaped. Now there was barely enough to layer the bottom of the hull. Mor knew from watching fishermen so many times when they came into shore that a full hull was the sign of a prosperous day.

Demba stared at him hard before turning away. He struck a match and used the flame to heat coals sitting in a makeshift burner secured by a thin wire to an inside corner of the boat. After blowing on the coals until they glowed a dazzling orangey red, he wedged a kettle on top of the pile. He crammed tea leaves inside the kettle and filled it with water from a plastic bottle. Leaving it to heat, Demba divided the fish evenly among two net bags and hung them over either side of the boat. The fish's tails slapped at the water.

When the water in the kettle bubbled, Demba filled a tin cup with tea and offered it to Mor. He puffed out his cheeks and blew at the steam rising in front of Mor's face.

"*Jërëjëf*," Mor thanked him through chattering teeth and numb lips. The metal scorched his wet fingers, but the heat felt good. He wrapped the bottom of his soaked T-shirt around the cup and blew over the rising steam. His mother had always said green tea was the cure for everything: a fever, a chill, or even a tummy ache. So Mor sat gratefully sipping the hot liquid. It calmed his still-thumping heart.

The boat swayed with the waves as they lingered. Birds squawked overhead, eyeing the fish, and fishing trawlers' horns bellowed in the distance. Demba gathered the netting back into his hands. Mor's legs sprang up to his chest as the netting slithered past his feet. He was about to hurriedly finish his tea and help Demba, but Demba's intense gaze pressed him down. Mor obeyed, his body mimicking the rock of the boat as Demba threw out the netting again. It disappeared like sugar dissolving in liquid as the ocean consumed it. Mor huddled in his seat, away from the edge, and clung tightly to the warmth of the empty cup. When Demba snatched at the cord around his wrist, Mor made sure one of his hands had a firm grip on the plank below him. Demba dragged the net up over the lip of the boat, but the belly of the netting held far fewer fish than it had the first time it was submerged. Mor could not bear to look. It was his fault Demba had lost his fish.

The fish flopped at Mor's feet as Demba sorted them. Mor ducked his head in shame. He felt useless in this boat, drinking this man's tea.

After a time he felt Demba's eyes on him and realized he was shaking. Squeezing his fists in his lap, he tensed all his muscles, hoping to stop his shivers. But it was no use. Soon Demba started the engine and directed the boat toward the shore. The other boats were still casting their nets as Demba and Mor motored by. The hulls of their *gaals* were filled with jerking fish.

"Why do you not stay and continue to catch?" Mor asked. His teeth chattered as the wind whipped against his wet skin.

Demba stared at the approaching shoreline.

"I'm fine," Mor continued, biting down to stop his teeth from rattling against each other. "The sun has dried me. Look." Mor set the metal teacup down and held out his hands, wiping away visible beads of water. "The tea has warmed me and settled my nerves." Mor's eyes turned from the beach back to the water and then up to the sky. "There is still a full day of light. I can work," he rambled.

Demba stared past him and did not change the course of the boat.

Mor felt sick to admit it, but the fishermen were right. He had gotten in the way.

And he didn't deserve a coin or a fish.

16

WHEN Demba's boat butted the nearly deserted shore, he shut off the motor and jumped down to the wet sand. No other fishermen were in sight, only children smeared in soap bubbles bathing in the tide. Demba motioned for Mor to stay seated, and without help he pulled his *gaal* back on land to the very spot it had been that morning. He lobbed the three net bags of fish into three buckets of shallow water and set them in the sand. Then he hoisted Mor out of the boat as if he were a baby. Mor wanted to squirm out of his grip and get down himself, but his body felt as malleable as one of his sisters' rag dolls. Even still, when his feet touched the sand, Mor reached for one of the heavy pails, ready to lug it up to the market area.

Demba's dreadlocks swung as he shook his head in refusal. Mor let the handle drop. Part of him wanted to run home and never look back at the beach again, and another part of him wanted to drop in the sand where he stood. However, when Demba grabbed the buckets and ambled up toward the roadway, water droplets plopping in the sand behind him, Mor trekked in the line of splotches, turning where Demba turned. Oddly, they headed away from the beach and the fish stalls.

"Shouldn't we go that way?" Mor pointed beyond a cluster of women sitting and standing along the roadside, hoping to grab shoppers before they reached the chaotic market. Big plastic tubs, each a color of the rainbow, sat on the ground in front of them, filled with fish to sell. "I know you don't have much, but I am sure you could get something for them."

Demba kept moving away from the women and turned down a path hidden by high white walls.

"Did you hear me, sir?" Mor asked, almost jogging to keep up with Demba's strides. "You may not get much, but even a little—"

Demba dropped one of the buckets next to Mor's foot, causing Mor to hop back. About eight fish sucked at the water inside the pail. Then Demba grabbed the handlebar of a rusty old bicycle that leaned against the wall. It was the same bicycle Mor had seen him riding on the path to Mahktar. A tiny bell looped around the center bar jingled, and a hefty man came out of an open door across the path.

"Ah, it's you, Demba. You are back early, no?" The man rubbed his thick hands together. Sprouts of hair grew from the backs of them. "I thought someone was out here messing with your bike. As always, I was ready to chase them off for you." The man chuckled, his plump belly bouncing up and down.

Mor couldn't see him chasing anything, except perhaps a fish across his plate. The man rubbed his engorged stomach and stepped out on the path. "Not many fish today, I see. But I suppose you find it enough." The man shook his head and turned back toward his door, kicking at a tiny swatch of fabric that blew out of his shop. Peeking inside, Mor saw three men at sewing machines with yards of cloth stacked around them. The hum of Demba's voice melded with the noise of the churning machines.

When Mor turned back around, Demba had secured a pail handle to each end of the handbar, and one was strapped tight with cord to the middle bar of the frame. To Mor it looked as if it all would topple over at any minute. Demba pointed to him, then to the handlebar. Mor stepped away, unsure. The man looked at Mor and smiled in surprise. "Found yourself some help, have you, Demba?" Demba didn't respond, but the man didn't seem to want, or expect, an answer.

Then Demba glanced back at Mor.

"Go ahead, get on," the man from the clothing shop said,

coming out of the doorway with a blue plastic bundle. "The day does not wait."

Feeling guilty about losing him a full day on the water already, Mor stepped on the front tire and climbed up on the handlebar. The cold metal pressed into the backs of his legs.

"Don't forget this." The man shuffled forward in his slippers, holding out the package. "These are the dresses Yvette Maal requested for her eldest daughter's wedding. Each of her girls will catch the eyes of all when they wear them."

When Demba took the bundle of wrapped cloth, Mor flung his hands to his sides and clenched the bar beneath him. Demba seemed unconcerned with the wobble of the bike as he secured the package to the back rack. Mor watched him closely. Although his lips rumbled every second with words piled in strange ways, Mor noticed that Demba hardly spoke them to others. So far his conversations had seemed to be meant for him and the air. His flowery words of "honey-watered moon" were like the poems and songs Mor's *yaay* used to whisper late in the night as he and his sisters fell asleep. But like he did with some of his father's riddles, he wondered what they meant.

"Oh, and grab more roots for the pain in my knee. . . ." The man winced, cupping his kneecap with pudgy fingers. He lifted his head to the sky. "I can feel rain coming."

Mor looked up, but there were no clouds overhead. With a stream of mumbles and nods, Demba pedaled away.

The buckets were covered with mesh screen lids, and on every bump water splashed through the slits in the wire veils. As Demba followed the main road out of the village, Mor did not ask where they were headed. He knew he would not get an answer anyway. Or if he did, probably not one he would fully understand. Instead he let the breeze and sun warm his damp clothes.

Demba whispered, "Sun knows the notes to play with its golden heat."

The rhythm of his mumbling mimicked the sway of the bike and the churn of the pedals. It grew louder when they hit a pebble and quieted to a murmur when they rode through the tall grasses.

On their ride they passed a fruit vendor, a roadside barber, and a tire stall. When they reached a butcher stand with a skinned goat hanging from an iron hook tied to a tree, Mor looked away, thinking of Jeeg and Fatima's tears. He settled into the rhythm of the bike, ignoring his nausea. Flecks of dirt flinging into his eyes and nose pestered him, but after a while, to his surprise, Demba's rambles about fish, skies, muddy water, and moon slivers started to relax him. He found them as natural as the birds tweeting in the trees and as expected as the buzzing of a fly.

As the bike traversed yet more uneven dirt paths out into dusty fields, Mor began to think it was a never-ending journey. The backs of his legs were getting bruised and sore from being jostled against the bar, and soon the intense heat made him light-headed and sluggish. He squinted, trying to ease the motion in his head. Demba, however, did not seem to mind the scorching sun or the constant juggling act of teetering buckets as they went farther and farther away from the water and Lat Mata.

Just when Mor thought the little bit he had eaten for breakfast was going to launch up his throat and greet the afternoon, Demba slowed the bike. Mor did not need to figure out Demba's gestures this time. He flung his body off as soon as Demba put his foot on the ground.

Mor wasn't sure where they were. It seemed like they'd ridden for days, though judging from the height of the sun in the sky, it had been only a few hours. Dry, hot air pressed against him. The smell of the sea had all but vanished, unless he stood over the buckets of fish. And with his stomach churning, he decided not to breathe in the fish too deeply. They had traveled inland in a direction he had never gone. It made no sense that Demba would go so far when he could easily sell his fish closer to home. Even though Mor thanked Allah for the chance to be on the water, he didn't understand.

He tried to ignore his confusion and hoped his head would just stop rocking. He could barely hold it up or keep his eyes open. In the distance four circular mud-constructed houses poked their heads above the high grass and the bundles of branch fencing around them. Off to the side was a wooden stand with clear yellow, green, and orange glass bottles resting on its shelves. The light bounced off them, throwing sparkles of color across the ground. The man seated on a wooden stool next to the makeshift gasoline fill-up stall bowed his head hello.

Three boys in T-shirts that reached their knees rushed toward them, each prodding a rolling hoop with a hooked stick. Demba untied the center bucket and propped the bike against the gasoline stall.

"The wheels rest their spinning."

The attendant nodded. "Fine, fine."

Heading toward the children and the homes, Demba whipped his head back, and his dreadlocks wrapped around his neck and shoulders like a scarf, then slipped back down. The children giggled and hid behind the tallest boy, letting their hoops collapse in the dirt. Their eyes focused on Demba as if he shone; then they moved their attention to Mor, who stood right behind him. For no reason Mor could explain, he felt proud to be with Demba, who strode across the dirt like a lion hunter.

"You ride with him?" the oldest boy asked Mor, jutting his chin toward Demba's back.

Mor nodded, feeling more important with each step. He ignored the ache and chills running through him.

"He just let you?" The inquisitive boy fell in beside Mor, the smaller boys acting as his tail.

Mor shrugged, wishing the boy would stop talking. He was loud and his words pecked at Mor's temples.

"Do you go on the water, too?"

As Mor nodded, the boy added, "Can you ask to bring me? I want to be out at sea, not here farming this dry dirt. My family has lived here so long that my father and grandfather know no other way, but this is no life for me. They will not see reason. I am the oldest son." The younger boys still peeked from behind him.

Mor stared at the boy. He had both his father and grandfather with him, and they wanted him with them, to teach him. Mor could not understand why the boy would want different than that.

He rocked his head, about to speak, but it throbbed. His head felt like it was still in the boat. Mor found it hard to listen.

"You all right?" the boy asked, leaning too close to Mor's face, making him go cross-eyed.

Mor stepped back and wiped his hand across his upper lip and brow; they were covered in sweat.

"You don't look okay," the boy continued. His head weaved in and out of Mor's focus.

"I am," Mor said, though he wasn't completely sure. He quickened his pace to catch up to Demba but soon slowed, unable to catch a breath.

The other boys helped Demba with the buckets of fish.

"Maybe you should have Demba make you a tea or something. He knows all the plants and berries to use. My grandmother has shown him everything since he was young."

Mor was curious about Demba and these people who seemed to know him so well, but right then his head demanded more attention than his curiosity.

A woman with skin as smooth as a pebble rushed from one of the small mud-walled houses, swinging a small pouch. The boys resembled her in every way, from their long, slender faces to their deep dark-brown eyes. She clutched the ample fabric of her yellow *boubou* in her hand as she shuffled across the dirt, stopping only to eye the fish the smaller boys carted away in the buckets.

"Aww, my friend, you are here." She took Demba's hand in hers and pressed her cheek to his shoulder before pulling away. Demba stood still, letting her. "Do you have my daughters' dresses?" she asked. "They're restless like lion cubs, eager to see."

He gestured for Mor to retrieve their bundle from the bike. Then a girl whose face looked as if it could have been chiseled from the same piece of wood as the boys' and the woman's ran up beside them. She grabbed the bundle as soon as Mor freed it, and raced away, smiling. The woman grinned as the girl giggled, yanking the plastic from around the fabric, a group of girls around her.

"My daughter's manners have run away with her. Forgive Bintou," the woman said. Then she glanced at Mor and seemed to forget her next thought. "Idrissa?" The name hung in the air; then she brushed it away with the shake of her head wrap. "Of course he is not. Idrissa went with Allah many sunsets ago. But he looks so much like him."

"*Guèlew lii yobouna lepp*," Demba said.

"Yes, yes, I know," she said, looking at Demba. "The breeze does carry all things. Even what we do not want to let go of." She stared at Mor then. "Since we know you are not Idrissa, what is your name, young one?"

"Mor Fall," he spoke up, though his throat felt like he had not had a sip of water in days.

"It is a pleasure. I am Yvette." She rested her hand over her heart and smiled. Then she patted Demba on the shoulder. "Come, come. You know she waits for you." She and Demba started back toward the gathering of houses. "Come, Mor. You are most welcome as well."

Mor followed behind, even more curious. But the more he thought, the more his head felt pressed between two rocks. When they got to the houses, Mor wobbled, and leaned on the wall for support. A woman with wrinkles like folds in a dress sat on a large stump. A cloth was draped over her lap. Bark and leaves lay in piles as she plucked petals from a light-green stem. Her face brightened when she saw Demba. Taking her hand, Demba closed his eyes and bent forward, pressing it to his forehead in greeting.

When he released it, she tapped his cheek, then her gaze fell on Mor. Without her having to speak, Mor was certain he knew what she was thinking, and so did Yvette.

"I know, Mother. It is like Idrissa came to smile on us for another afternoon."

Demba shifted from one foot to the other.

"Rest easy," the old woman said to him. "We are not trying to trouble you with these words. I've known you since before you were his age." She nodded toward Mor, then turned back to Demba. "I know how things are unsettled within you."

Even though her speech was more simple, Mor was just as confused as when Demba spoke. Who was Idrissa? And why did the thought of him make Demba sad? He wanted to ask but decided he'd better not.

The longer he stood on his feet under the screaming sun, the harder it was to focus on what Demba and the woman were discussing. Mor dared not tell Demba he wasn't feeling well after all he'd put him through on the water. He blinked as a dribble of sweat caught in his eyelash. He was silent, swaying as the old woman picked up one of the leaves.

"You see this vein along the edge?" Her finger traced a line in the leaf she held. "That is what you must—"

Mor's head slammed against the dirt before she could finish her thought. He was conscious only of the weightlessness of his body as it fell.

"He is all bones . . . ," he heard Yvette say. A soft hand was nestled behind his head. "A grasshopper has more meat."

"You have worked this boy too hard." The older woman's voice grew stern. "He is too young for this work."

Mor wanted to jump in to protest, but he could barely open his eyes or lift his finger.

"The breeze rattles the covered windows," Demba mumbled, as rapid as darting fish. "It is not allowed."

"He will be fine, Demba. He will be fine." The edge was off the old woman's words. "You and I will make it so."

"Bintou, fetch water," Yvette called.

As Mor heard feet run away, he tried to form words. Then his head was tilted back and his mouth pressed open to allow warm liquid to trickle down his throat.

Coughing it up, his body surged violently forward. Yvette, who held his head, switched between thumping and rubbing his back until he had spit out all the unsettled broth.

He felt like even more of a burden sitting in his own spit with a huddle of brown eyes fixed on him. Demba alone did not stare. He busied himself with a mortar and pestle, grinding some of the leaves the old woman had spread in front of her. Mor tilted his head and noticed a gathering of berries by Demba's feet. A fire slapped at the bottom of a boiling pot of liquid.

Demba scraped the paste he had made into the pot and stirred, muttering to himself again. Mor closed his eyes, unable to make out any of the words. He simply wanted to lie still. He hoped the constant sloshing feeling in his head would stop.

Mor didn't know how much time had passed, but he felt the heated water coating his closed lips and he opened them.

"That is it," the old woman said as Mor drank. "Take it down slow. It will make you strong." After a few more sips his head was laid back down. A cool cloth pressed against his forehead. "You have mixed well, Demba. He will be fine." Soon the sun would slip out of the sky. Demba scooped Mor into his arms again like a newborn babe, but Mor made no complaints. He rested his head on Demba's arm as he was carried to the bike. Demba situated him on the bike bar between his arms, not the handlebar. Mor wanted to say he could manage, but knew it wasn't altogether true. He was definitely better than he had been when they first arrived, but all he wanted was more sleep. The boy Mor had spoken with earlier stacked the empty buckets; then Yvette wrapped two loaves of bread and some kola nuts in cloth. Touching Mor's forehead one last time, the old woman added the bundle that had rested in her lap to the bucket. His eyelids flickered open and closed as the boy placed two bottles, strong with the stench of gasoline, in the bucket, fastening it all to the back of the bicycle. Instead of getting on the bike himself, Demba held the handlebars.

"Be well," the women called as Demba guided the bicycle down a pebble-laden path.

Even though Mor wanted to plod beside him, showing that he was strong, he was grateful for the support Demba's body gave as Demba maneuvered the bike over the rough terrain, mumbling.

"Bane bou gnou làkhas gnou boleko booko guisse dagaye khi khat."

Soon the rhythm of Demba's thoughts about "rolling rocks" joining "broken breaths," the crunch of Demba's sandals, the wheels against the dirt, the never-ending rustling of trees, and the conversations of birds rocked Mor back to sleep.

DEMBA and Mor were halfway back to Lat Mata when Mor was able to sit up and look around, balancing on his own. But each time he did, Demba pressed him back down.

"I am okay now. See?" He shook his head from side to side, only becoming mildly dizzy again. "You don't have to walk anymore, we can ride."

"My winged feet are our slippered wheels."

Between his rambles Demba kept walking. As they neared Lat Mata, Mor felt worse about all that had happened. He was an added burden to a man to whom most of the fishermen had not shown an ounce of kindness. With each step Demba helped Mor. But how could he help Demba? All he had was a churning belly and a spinning head. He thought of his sisters, his promises, and a nearly empty tomato can tucked under his parents' old pallet. Empty ideas of how to repay this stranger whirled in his head along with wonderings about the boy they had called Idrissa, whom he seemed to look so much like.

When they returned to the beach, the other fishermen had already brought in their catch. Wet, turned-over sand and a few fish were the only evidence that the *gaals* had gone out. Birds pecked at the fish being spoiled in the sun.

Mor stretched and yawned, surprised to have fallen asleep again in the crook of Demba's arm. The turbulent sea inside his head had stopped rocking, and his nausea had all but gone away. He took the buckets Demba untied and was surprised to see three fish still swimming in one.

"What are you doing with these?" he asked. "Do you sell them too? Or are they for you?" Mor would have loved to have just one for him and his sisters. But feeling like a burden already, he would never ask.

Instead of answering, Demba gestured for Mor to follow him. He led him to a bright-blue shack with a low-lying, rippling tin roof. It was tucked along the beach wall under the shade of a large palm tree across from the fish stalls. A rusted orange soda pop sign hung from a nail on one of its three walls. Under the cover of the roof, a man lounged on a chair with his face hidden by a wet handkerchief. His legs were crossed and stretched in front of him. He wiggled his toes as if keeping the beat to a good song.

Demba stopped in front of him, blocking the man from the sun.

"We are out of soda for the day," the man said, not taking off the cloth. "But I do have a few juices left." When Demba did not speak or move, the man finally stirred and removed his handkerchief from his face.

"Demba, my friend, I heard you went home early with no fish. Most of the other fishermen have caught almost nothing today as well. So I thought I would not see you."

Demba dropped the bucket of swimming fish.

The man shook his head. "You are fortunate," he laughed. "I should not have thought your hands would be empty. They are never so. A man who shares with others is always rich." The man got to his feet and mopped his sweat-speckled brow with his handkerchief. "What do you have for us? Red-fish, *bonga*, *thiof*, or capitaine?" The man grinned, displaying a wide gap between his front teeth. He peered into the bucket Demba held out to him. "Nice, nice. And there are three."

Demba stepped to the side, revealing Mor.

"Now, who is this?" the man asked. His eyes squinted when he grinned.

Mor moved forward, expecting him to say something about the Idrissa the women had kept speaking of, but he didn't.

"Speak, son, speak. Or has a golden jackal run away with your tongue?"

Mor found the man's smile infectious. "No, sir."

"I see, I see. And do you have a name?"

"Mor, sir."

"Well, Mor, I'm Amadou, the best fish fryer in all of *Sunugaal*." He poked a finger at his chest proudly. "You'll see. It will only take a moment to fry these up."

He took the bucket and went into the interior of the shack; Mor followed. Lighting a match over a squat kerosene drum, Amadou rotated a knob to lower the energetic flame. A deep black-crusted pan sat on top of it. The liquid inside started to pop and snap almost instantly. Amadou rinsed the fish in a large basin, then sliced through them with a knife, leaving all their entrails on a chopping board. He sprinkled the fish with spice from a dented tin shaker and dropped them into the sizzling pan.

Mor lingered near his side while Demba placed the loaves of bread he'd received on a square table covered with a sun-bleached plastic table cover. Amadou followed the direction of Mor's gaze.

"Did you like it on the water with Demba?"

"Yes, very much," Mor said, then dropped his head. "But I don't think he liked it very much. I might have been more trouble than help."

"I doubt that. You were his company when he was alone."

Mor knew Amadou was only trying to make him feel better. Demba did not seem like he ever minded being alone. He always had himself to talk to.

"Though next time," Amadou continued—Mor wanted

to believe there'd be a next time, but he wasn't so sure—"be watchful and listen to Demba's words. Learn from them and him. He will make you more than just a sound fisherman."

"But how come they don't always make sense?"

Amadou threw his head back and gave a silent laugh. "He is a man of complex thought, but if you watch him, you will understand more than words can ever explain."

Mor glanced back at Demba, sitting at the table. Mor promised himself that if Demba let him come back, he would watch and listen to everything.

Amadou moved the fish to a tray covered with a sheet of newspaper and brought them to the table. The smells were dizzying, but this time in a good way. Mor's stomach talked to him as he slid into a plastic chair. "Okay." Amadou clapped his hands together. "Now you will taste the best fish you have ever tasted."

When Demba placed a whole fish in front of Mor, Mor's eyes raced between his, Amadou's, and Demba's plates. His jaw lay open. Even though the fish was only inches away from his mouth, with its tail lopped over the edge of his metal dish, Mor could not believe it was all for him. He had never had an entire fish to himself before. While Demba and Amadou pinched at chunks of meat, devouring their meals, Mor kept to a small section of the spiced fish.

"I cannot believe you do not like my cooking. Your taste has gone missing." Amadou eyed the uneaten portion of fish. He pushed his metal plate, which held only the glassy eyes and sucked-clean skeleton of the fish, to the center of the table.

"No, sir, it is very good." Mor gave a half smile and wiped his hand across his mouth. "But I want to bring some to my sisters. They are waiting for me at home. And they will like it too."

Amadou nodded. "You are a good brother."

"I'm not sure," Mor whispered.

He licked his fingers before wrapping the rest of the fish in a piece of newspaper Amadou handed him. He took a last bite of meat before he closed the paper. Demba pushed the remaining half loaf across to him. Mor grinned and tucked it under his arm. Demba had done more for Mor in a day than many might do in a lifetime. When he stood to say thank you and good-bye, Demba caught him by the wrist. Mor stiffened. Had he done something else wrong? Demba's grip was firm, but it didn't hurt. Mor's heart tripled its beat. He looked to Amadou for help.

Then Demba turned over Mor's hand and placed a few shiny coins in it.

Mor stared at his open palm. Although at the start of the day he had hoped he'd be paid, now he didn't feel that he deserved it, as relieved as he was. "Are you sure?" He glanced down. He had been given three hundred francs. Much more than he had gained for selling his bags of *tàngal* for most of a day. His hands were filled with fish and bread and then coins, which danced in his hand under the eye of the late-afternoon sun. "Thank you, sir. You have been so kind to me."

Demba's dreadlocks fell forward when he nodded.

Amadou smiled.

Just as quickly as Demba had grabbed Mor's arm, he released it. Then his attention turned to the waves. After thanking Amadou, Mor paused, then stood in front of Demba.

"I know I was not the best fisherman today, but could I come back tomorrow?" Mor scrunched his hands and toes tight, hoping. "I will be much better than today."

Demba said nothing.

"I promise I will try harder not to get in your way," Mor pleaded.

"Waves are not my captive. Fish are not marked with my name. A catch decides that fate."

Mor flipped the words over and over in his head, trying to make sense of them. "I'm sorry, but I don't understand," he finally admitted. He looked again to Amadou for help, but he was busy clearing the plates. Mor stared at Demba, who was already looking back at the sea.

Mor bit at the corner of his lip. *I have to try.* "I will be here tomorrow. *Incha'Allah.* And if you want me to, I will get in your boat. And if you have left without me, I will understand." And with that he was off, hoping for another day on the water with Demba.

18

FULL with fish and bread, Mor's stomach felt as if a million moths' wings flapped inside him as he turned for home.

I know your mind is light and your hands are full, but haven't you left someone else's empty?

Mor stopped, not sure whose riddle of words was harder to understand, Demba's or his *baay*'s.

"Why can't you just say what you mean?" Mor whispered to the sky, wanting and not wanting his father to hear him. "Whose hands?" he asked the air, wishing he could see his *baay*.

Your pocket holds a coin that is owed to another. Do not forget your debt. Make good on your promise.

It was true, Mor had forgotten all about the kind woman in the market.

Turning, he ran toward the village center, hoping she had not packed up for the day.

"Eh, Mor, wait up," his friend Oumar called to him as he raced down the path. Oumar dribbled his plastic-bag soccer ball toward Mor, weaving through the thinning crowd. "Where have you been?"

"Around," Mor said once Oumar had reached him. Oumar nudged the ball his way. Mor happily passed it between his feet before tapping it back.

"You're never around." Oumar rolled the ball up his foot, popping it to his knee.

"I am." Mor balanced the ball on his head when Oumar launched it through the air. "I just have things I have to do now."

"Like what?"

"I have to take care of my family."

"Don't you have a *bàjjan* for that?"

"She's not here." Mor bounced the ball from one knee to the other.

"Where'd she go?" Oumar stole the ball from Mor when he dropped it to his foot.

Mor stole it back. "Away."

"She just left you?" Oumar shot his leg out, trying to snag the ball, but Mor was too quick.

"I wanted her to go."

"Why?"

"Because I want to take care of my family."

"I don't get why." Oumar raced in front of Mor, trying to get in position to snatch the ball again. "It means you can never play."

"I'm playing now," Mor said, spinning around Oumar with the ball under his toe.

"You know what I mean." Oumar stopped in the dirt, his hands on his hips in frustration as Mor sailed by him again.

"I play when I can and work when I have to." Mor kicked the ball back to Oumar. "It's not so bad."

"It sounds bad to me," Oumar said, waiting for the rolling ball.

"It's not," Mor said, stopping. "We will all have to do it sometime."

"For what? You think one day you're going to become some big, important man around here?" He stuck out his chin and raised his chest, strutting around the dirt.

"No," Mor laughed. "I've become a fisherman."

"Who'd let you in their boat?"

"Demba."

Oumar stopped knocking the ball between his feet. "Now I know he's *doff*, letting you go near his boat. I'm sure you're both scaring the fish away now," Oumar chortled.

"Whatever," Mor said, glancing behind him down the road. He was just able to see the first stalls of the fish market. Some were already empty.

"I have to go," Mor said, thinking of his *baay* and his promises.

"Where are you going now? You're always going the other way."

Mor glanced at the oil-soaked newspaper and the bread for his sisters and the coin he owed. Would he ever be able to think just about himself again? Eat all his fish and play soccer till he couldn't stand? "I have to go before everyone leaves the *marse*," he called back, moving away from his friend, not wanting to think about the things he could do and have anymore.

"Next time, then." Oumar rocked the ball under the sole of his foot again.

"Next time." Mor waved and dashed off.

"Slow down, slow down," an elderly woman in an baggy *boubou* said. Her arms thrust forward, stopping Mor before he stepped on her feet. "There is no crocodile snapping at your ankles to reach here first. What you miss today will be here tomorrow." She continued talking as she strolled past him. "There have always been fish here . . . every day of my life."

"Sorry." He shuffled a few steps, then picked up speed again. When he reached the stall owner who had given him the fish, his breathing was heavy.

"Ah, my little friend, you are back?" She fanned herself as she leaned on her table full of mandarins, orangey-reddish brown *sidèmes*, lettuce, tomatoes, and smoked fish. Her loaves of bread were hidden under a cloth. Though it was not enough camouflage to fool the flies that swarmed over them.

Mor opened his hand to her. Three polished one-hundred-franc coins sat in it. "This is for the fish."

"And where did you find money so soon?" She dropped two of the coins in a drawstring pouch dangling from her wrist and rooted around for his change.

"I am a fisherman now," he said, beaming, when she gave him fifty francs back.

She held a mandarin out to him and he paused. He was not sure he should spend more of his money so soon. The smell of citrus rose from its skin. It had been weeks since he had bitten into anything smelling so sweet. When he offered her the change back, she quickly waved him away.

"No, no. The first coins were plenty. Save the rest of your money." She pushed his hand back toward his pocket. "So, a fisherman, you say? And with whom do you fish?"

He took the mandarin from her hand and bowed his head in thanks. "Demba. Do you know him?"

"Ah, yes, I know him well. We all do." She grinned down at Mor, then glanced around. "He brings me herbs for my gout." Then her brow became crinkled rows of lines. "You are not frightened of him? Many older than you are."

Mor raised his shoulders and then quickly shook his head. He was a little afraid, but not much. "He has been nice to me and very patient. I can't be afraid of someone like that."

"He's a good man and knows many things. You would do well to listen."

"His words are confusing, though," Mor said.

"Though they appear a tangle, when unwoven, they are a sturdy string."

"Someone else said they are important. But I just don't understand. My *yaay* used to sing songs with words like those. And I never understood that, either."

She tapped at his chest with her finger. "You be a good friend to him. And he will be a good friend to you."

"Yes, ma'am." That, Mor could understand and do.

He was about to turn and go, when she asked, "Does your mother need any of this wonderful lettuce?" She picked at a few of the leaves. "They are fresh today." Water beads trickled off the greens.

"I don't have a *yaay* anymore." He stared at the leaves, thinking of his mother's spirit.

"I'm sorry. Maybe your grandmother?"

Mor shook his head.

"An older sister?"

"My sisters are both young."

"Your father?"

Mor hung his head. "He is gone now too."

"Then who do you have caring for you?" She reached out her hand and cupped his elbow, drawing him closer to her.

"I care for us." He stuck out his chest the same way Oumar had done.

"And what of your family?" she asked. He read the concern on her face. "No uncles or aunts to take you in?"

"Our aunt has let us stay here for the summer."

"Let you?" The stall owner stepped back, her mouth open. "What type of neglect is this?" Her voice rose, causing a few heads to turn. "We do not do this. You are but a child."

The word "child" hammered against his head. "I asked her to."

"Tah. She is supposed to look after you, as her elders once did for her. That is how it is done. You do not make the decisions."

"She's coming back," Mor rushed to add, worried he'd already said too much. "Our mother's friend is watching over us while she's gone, and our neighbors check in too. Most days my sisters are with them playing and doing chores together. We are fine."

"I will trust your words, but know that from now on my eyes are also on you."

Mor let out a heavy breath, relieved their conversation was coming to an end.

"Take these," the woman said. She dropped three egg-size *ditakh* fruit and another mandarin into a bag. She left it open for Mor to throw in the mandarin, the fish wrapped in oil-stained paper, and the bread he clutched. "It has been a slow fruit day," she said before Mor could protest. "It would be a shame for their sweetness to be wasted. They will sour tomorrow."

Mor knew what she said was not a complete truth, but

he did not refuse. Instead he cradled the heavy plastic bag, excited to have gifts again for his sisters.

His smile pushed up the corners of his mouth. He had coins in his pocket, fish in his belly, and a feast for his sisters. Even with being sick, it had been a long time since he'd had such a happy day.

"Bring me some of that fish when you catch it. I can sell it at my stall." She put one hand on her hip and swept the other in front of her face to catch the breeze.

"I will, I will," Mor agreed. He stepped out of the way of a fishmonger lifting a stack of wet crates and headed away from the stalls.

When he got on the main road again, he saw Oumar and their friend Khadim across the street. He waved, but Oumar didn't see him. As he was about to cross the road, calling out to them, he stopped. In the shadows cast by one of the cement-walled buildings, beady black eyes tracked him. Papis and two other Danka Boys stepped out. Papis raised an eyebrow, watching Mor. Mor didn't want to wait to see what he would do next; he just ran as far away from the market and Papis as he could get. He was not going to let the Danka Boys spoil another day.

19

BY the time Mor found himself on the path outside his door, he was tired, excited, and relieved to have escaped the Danka Boys.

"Mor!" Fatima rushed out of the *barak* to greet him. "We missed you. But I played with Rama and Oumy, and helped Amina at the well. I danced as she pounded maize. Amina pretended she was beating a drum. It was fun! We ate lunch with Tanta Coumba, and I played with baby Zal. He's funny. He can make little bubbles come out of his mouth like this." She tried to make bubbles, but spit ran down her chin instead. She wiped it away as she continued to ramble on. "So did you become a fisherman like you said you would? Or did you play football *aaaalllll* day? Mina thinks you played. But I think you fished." Fatima joined her fingers with Mor's. "What's in there?" she asked, noticing the bag in his other hand.

"It's a treat for all of us. A way to celebrate today."

"Is it *tàngal*?"

"Nope." Mor held the plastic bag high as she tried to jump for it.

"Is it papaya?"

Mor shook his head as Fatima giggled, skipping around him. Jeeg came out from inside the *barak*, craning her nose up. "*M-a-a, m-a-a,*" she bleated as she sniffed the air.

"Uh-uh," Mor joked, leaning toward Jeeg as if in conversation. "It's not orange peels, either."

"You're silly." Fatima covered her mouth, laughing. "She didn't say that. She said 'rusted cans.' She loves rusted cans."

Mor shook his head. "It's not those, either."

"Let me see, let me see, let me see." Fatima hopped, trying to pull his arm down.

"Okay, okay," he said, dropping his arm. "But let's go find Mina first and celebrate together."

Before he could finish, Fatima released her hold on him and went tearing into the *barak*. "Mina, Mina," she shouted. "Mor has a surprise."

When Mor stepped inside, Amina was sitting, legs crossed, on their parents' pallet, folding the day's laundry. When she looked up, her eyes went from Fatima to Mor, a question present in them.

"Mina." Fatima jumped on the pallet next to her sister, her

knees in one of the folded fabrics. Amina shooed her and Fatima leaped up again, dashing back to her brother's side. "Mor has a surprise."

"I know. I heard you outside," Amina said. "I think everyone in the village heard you."

Fatima pulled on her bottom teeth with her finger. Then she looked at Mor. "Can you show us now?"

"Yes," Amina said a little lighter. "Can we see this great surprise?"

Mor opened the bag for Fatima and let her peek inside.

"He brought mandarins. We haven't had mandarins since Yaay died. She loved them. . . ." She trailed off for a second, still searching the bag. "What's this?" She dug inside the bag, poking at the oil-stained newspaper.

"Fried fish," Mor said, and smiled. "We got it on the sea today."

"We?" Amina asked, sliding to the edge of the pallet.

"Yes. Demba and me. I think I might be a fisherman now." He would deal with tomorrow when it came. Right then he just wanted to have fun with his sisters, like they used to when their *baay* was alive.

"Mor is a fisherman. Mor is a fisherman." Fatima spun around him, the mandarin in her hand.

"*Duhgu . . . duhgu . . . duhgu,*" Mor grunted as he moved his hips in his favorite dance. "Come on, Mina. Tonight is a party." He ticked his hips in a box, then lifted his leg and jumped.

Fatima danced over to Jeeg, swinging the goat's ears to the beat of a song in her head.

"*Duhgu . . . duhgu . . .* ," Mor said again, rocking toward Amina, grinning, lifting his eyebrows to his beat. He tapped out his foot in front of him.

"Oh," she said, sliding off the pallet. A smirk across her lips. She laid the half-folded T-shirt down. "Out of the way. Let me show you what you're supposed to do." She lifted her *sër* to her calves so she had room in it to dance. The sarong flapped in front of her, mimicking her movements. She batted her elbow forward then back, leaping off the ground.

The widest smile Mor had seen in a while brightened her face. He hadn't realized how much he missed that smile, which was so much like their mother's. Her hand flew up and down as she slapped her bare feet against the dirt floor, then leaped over and over, faster and faster.

Mor grabbed the empty water bowl under the shelf and beat his hand against it to the rhythm of Amina's dance. The beat of the makeshift drum caused Amina to move even faster, taunting Mor to keep up.

She stomped. He banged. She hopped. He tapped.

Fatima bounced along, clapping and hugging Jeeg around the neck all at once.

Amina's feet kicked up dust, while Mor's hand pounded the metal bowl, a tinny sound vibrating through the space. When Amina fell back on the pallet, her breath flying out of her, Mor crashed to the floor. Fatima dropped down too. Jeeg stood over them all, staring.

Amina was the first to laugh. A laugh that was light and free of worry. Mor couldn't stop smiling. This was the Amina he wanted to stay.

"Can we eat this now?" Fatima said, picking up the mandarin again. "Please."

"All you do is think of food." Mor shook his head, grinning. He placed the bowl back under his parents' photograph. His parents smiled on him from their picture.

"I want to hear about you being a fisherman," Fatima said, biting into the peel. "And I'll tell you how Amina slipped in the mud at the river." She giggled, glancing at her sister, who dabbed her T-shirt across her forehead.

"I didn't slip," Amina said. "I meant to slide down that hill." A chuckle escaped her throat. "It was quicker than walking to wash the pots."

Mor laughed, wishing he had been there to see it.

"It was funny." Fatima crammed some of the fruit into her mouth. "She had mud all over her bottom. Everybody laughed. Then she pulled Naza and her friend Tening in, and they started splashing, so Oumy and I jumped in too. It was so much fun!" Fatima stopped talking long enough to shove another piece of mandarin into her mouth. "Then Oumy and I made mud pies until Tanta Coumba came and called us back. She needed her clean pots to make dinner." Fatima held her belly and laughed, her cheeks full of mandarin. "Oumy had mud on the side of her face, and we smeared it on Jeeg. But she didn't like that too much, though." Fatima popped another slice of tangerine into her mouth, even though she hadn't finished eating the first three pieces she'd shoved inside.

"So tell us about your fishing," Amina said, tucking the folds of her *sër* into her lap. "We want to hear everything, don't we, Tima?"

Fatima got up off the floor, letting the mandarin peels fall to the ground. Jeeg was quick to nibble them up. Fatima crawled across the pallet and tucked herself next to Amina.

Mor sprang to his feet, ready to tell them everything. They stared at him like they were the audience and he was on a stage, like they'd done when their parents were still alive. Amina took a slice of mandarin from Fatima's hand as Mor became an actor, playing the mighty Demba. He grabbed a T-shirt and pulled it onto his head, then whipped it back and forth like Demba's dreadlocks.

Amina and Fatima cried with laughter as he flung the T-shirt off and pretended to fall overboard as his extra-clumsy self.

Their giggles and his impression of Demba's jumble of words sailed out the door and into the air past their *yaay*'s spirit and their *baay*'s breath.

20

AS Mor slept, he dreamed of happier times. He'd gone to bed smiling, Fatima's and Amina's laughter tickling his ears. But when he turned onto his side, curling on his mat for a bit longer, a new sound greeted him. A faint yet close whistling.

He narrowed his eyes, letting them adjust to the dark, but nothing was out of place. Everything was as they had left it. His sisters still snuggled close to each other on their parents' pallet. Then he noticed Jeeg was not in her usual spot by the door, but her tether rope snaked outside under the door flap. He was about to lay his head back on his elbow when the whistling started again. Soft at first, then a little louder, as if it were coming from right outside his door. Wiping the sleep from his eyes, he slipped into his *baay*'s sandals.

Weet-wooh-wooh . . . weet-wooh-wooh led him to the door.

When he pulled back the door cover, he wasn't sure what he expected to see, but his eyes were not ready for what he saw—his old friend sitting on an overturned crate, whittling and whistling at his door in the middle of the night.

"What are you doing over here like a mongoose at a termite mound? You are not welcome here anymore." Mor rubbed his eyes again, making sure they weren't deceiving him. "Go away."

"I miss this." Cheikh smiled as if he had not heard what Mor had said. "Jeeg warming my feet in the night air as I carve. Remember when we used to sit out here with your *baay* and talk like men?"

"Do not mention my *baay*. Don't let thoughts of you, him, and me pass your mind anymore. You didn't come . . ." Mor trailed off, angry.

"He used to make the best tea those nights. Strong and sweet. With the right amount of spearmint."

"Did you hear me?" Mor knocked Cheikh's shoulder, causing him to carve extra deep in his wood.

"I remember the time—"

"Stop, stop it now. You are lying. You remember nothing." Mor pushed him again. "Especially not how to be a friend."

Cheikh rocked off balance and Jeeg jumped back. She nudged the door cover with her nose and went back inside.

Mor lowered his voice to almost a whisper, remembering his sisters. "How could you be so mean in the market? Let your friends steal from me as if you didn't know me. I hate you." Mor kicked at the crate. "I wish you never came home."

Cheikh did nothing.

"Does your *yaay* know who you've become?"

Cheikh spun on Mor. He pointed the knife tip at his childhood friend. "My *yaay* knows nothing. And you better forget any thoughts you have of telling her. It would not serve you well if you do."

"Now you threaten? It's me. The one who was there when your *baay* dragged you screaming from your mother's arms to send you to that *daara*. Remember? You didn't want to leave Lat Mata for anything. You cried then the tears of a *liir*, no older than your baby brother. Your father let me walk with you then so you would stop. I have not forgotten that day. Why are you now acting as if you're not my brother?" Mor studied Cheikh closely. Straggly threads dangled from the armpit of Cheikh's basketball jersey. The red dye from his shirt had bled into the yellow-banded collar.

"Don't speak of things you do not understand," Cheikh said.

"Then explain. I am here. I am listening."

Cheikh went back to whittling his wood. "I am here to offer you a chance."

"A chance at what?"

"Safety." Cheikh rose to his feet. "You will need it if someone catches your scent."

Cheikh dusted off his jeans. Curls of wood fell to the

ground like Mor imagined snow would. He stared at the curls against the dark earth for a long time.

"Safety? What do I need to fear?"

"You're alone now. Not everyone is out to help you."

"Like you?"

Cheikh's eyelid twitched. Mor hoped his words had had some effect.

"Just know I warned you," Cheikh said. He pushed the back of the knife blade against his thigh, folding it into the hilt, and shoved it into his pocket. *Weet-wooh-wooh. Weet-wooh-wooh. Weet-wooh-wooh.* He whistled, strolling away from Mor. The conversation over.

The chilled air brushed against Mor as nighttime insects were awake with chatter. Mor swept his hand across his eyes and went back inside. Amina craned her head to look toward the doorway.

"Mor?"

"Yes," he whispered. "Go back to sleep. There are still hours before the sun greets us again."

As if already in a dream, Amina rubbed her cheek against her arm, smacking her lips and tongue together. Then she smiled in her sleep. Mor tried to hold on to that smile as he lay down again for the night.

Safety? What from? he thought, tossing Cheikh's words around in his head until he rose hours later. Cheikh had said them like a warning. Were the Danka Boys coming for him? If so, why? He had nothing.

Mor tore off a piece of bread and bit into it as he pulled the door cover back.

"Good luck on the water today," Amina said before she turned over.

He stared at her and Fatima for a long while, holding on to their laughter from the night before. Trying to block out Cheikh's threats.

Every step he walked toward the beach that morning, his worry about Cheikh became less and his hope became stronger that Demba would be there waiting for him, so he could have more funny tales to act out for his sisters. As he came close to the beach wall, he held his breath.

He didn't let it go until he saw Demba there.

Waiting for him.

21

AFTER a week on the water Mor was used to waking up with the sun. But it was earlier than that when he squinted and wondered why the predawn light and a damp breeze were seeping in through the doorway. The plastic door covering should have defended against them. Blinking rapidly, he tried to wash the sleep from his eyes. Then he stopped. He heard more than just the usual light snores and heavy breathing of his sisters.

Someone was at their door.

He squinched his eyelids and tried to focus but couldn't make out the features of the person who filled most of the doorway. He thought it was Cheikh again. And even though he was hurt by so much his old friend had done, he was curious about his return. He thought maybe what had been broken could be fixed. But when his eyes focused, and the face in shadow became clear, he almost choked on the air.

It was Papis.

Mor's optimism plummeted, replaced by worry. "What are you doing here?"

"You and I share a brother."

Mor threw back his cover and jumped to his feet. He hated that he'd been ready to forgive Cheikh just seconds before. "He is no brother of mine," Mor whispered, hoping not to wake his sisters.

Papis threw his head back in silent laughter. "He says you want to join the Danka Boys. I told him to stay behind so I could see for myself. Is that true, my friend, do you want to be my brother?"

"He lies. I do not want to join you."

Papis glanced at the pallet where Mor's sisters slept. But he didn't leave the doorway. "You have a lot to protect. Are you strong enough to do it alone?"

Mor stared at Papis, clenching his fists at his sides.

Don't be lured by threats. For they are only bait. Their aim is still to ensnare you. Be mindful. Your strength is not the question. It is your will. Is it made of a tortoise's shell?

Mor stood taller knowing his *baay* was with him.

"I don't hear you." Papis smirked, cupping his hand around his ear.

"Leave us alone." Mor took a step forward. "I will never want to be like you."

"Tut-tut-tut, don't be so quick to say 'never.'" Papis shook his head, pushing out his lips. "There may come a day when you crawl to us, begging to be a Danka Boy, and then you would be a liar."

Mor turned to make sure his sisters still slept. Fatima's arms were spread wide, while Amina's were pressed to her sides, her book, with its stained red-cloth cover, under her thigh.

"What do you want?" he whispered.

"What do you have?"

Someone laughed outside.

"Nothing."

"I don't believe that." Papis looked around. He kicked a pebble. It tumbled toward Jeeg, resting by the wall. She raised her head, then tucked it back over her legs when she saw he held nothing for her to nibble. "Don't be a *fene kat* already."

"I am not a liar," Mor bit back "Just get out!" Mor charged forward, trying to push Papis onto the path, but Papis didn't budge.

He was a stump. And with a shove he knocked Mor to the dirt.

"Be warned." Papis held up one finger. "Because of our shared brother, one touch is all you get. Nothing else will be ignored."

Stand your ground, my son. Even the mighty have fallen.

Amina murmured in her sleep as Mor got back to his feet.

"Don't think I haven't watched you all these days," Papis said, "with that *doff* Demba carting you and fish around the village on that rickety bike of his." His hand slapped hard against his own neck, and the buzz of a mosquito vanished. He flicked it off his skin. "I know you have more than you need. Especially when you sell to that market woman. That should be shared with your new brothers, no?" His eyes shifted from Mor to a green pot in the corner with a dishcloth draped over it.

"I told you. We have nothing."

"And I told you, I don't believe you." Papis stepped forward, letting the door covering fall behind him. "So I guess I will see for myself."

Mor blinked, readjusting his sight to the dim light that came through the cloth-covered window. Amina grumbled and opened her eyes. Then they flashed wide when she saw a boy standing in the center of their floor.

"Mor?" Amina pulled Fatima back.

"Mina, stop," Fatima whined. "I don't want to wake up. . . ." She tried to snuggle against the back of Amina's shoulder.

"Shhh," Amina warned. She stretched her arm behind her, cradling her sister. She looked at her brother and then at the boy hovering inches away.

"Get out," Mor demanded.

Instead Papis bent down and snatched the cloth off the dented pot.

It was empty.

His eyes swept around the room. Within three long strides he was at the far wall of the *barak*. He searched its only shelf and knocked over the picture of Mor's parents that rested between a box of matches and a burned-out candle.

"Leave our things alone. You've already stolen enough." Mor glared at Papis and snatched the picture off the floor before it got stepped on. Mor's bed mat covered most of the open floor. Papis traipsed across it, tracking dirt.

"I don't have time for hiding games." Papis's eyes locked on something white under the raised platform Amina and Fatima slept on. "You do not want me to leave here empty-handed."

"Come on, man," the person outside whined, impatient.

"*Nopil*" shot from Papis's mouth. The voice went quiet. Papis reached Mor's sisters before Mor could stop him. He crouched and yanked at the cloth covering the partially hidden plastic bowl, causing Fatima to jump. Awake.

In a panic she kicked out, knocking Amina's red book against Papis's shoulder. Amina scrabbled to reach it. But as if Papis sensed her love for it, he tossed it carelessly out the doorway.

The boys outside scoffed. "What are we supposed to do with this?"

Mor heard a rip and the scratch of paper. He glanced at his sister, whose jaw was set and whose face was as hard as the floor he slept on.

"No." Mor ran to the doorway and snatched the door cover back. The pages of Amina's book littered the ground like ash from a fire. He spun and ran over. "Leave us alone!" His voice vibrated and his fists collided with Papis's back as Papis remained hunched by the uncovered bowl.

Papis jumped up. The back of his hand slammed into Mor's cheek, knocking him away. "I warned you."

But Mor didn't give up. He ran for Papis again. This time the boys outside rushed in to hold him back.

"You stupid *khale*. I warned you. One touch was all you get." He shoved Mor to the ground, kicking his foot. Mor tucked himself into a ball as the two boys held him down, one slapping the back of his head.

"*M-a-a*," Jeeg bleated, and then ran outside, still tethered.

Fatima cried and Amina pulled her little sister closer. "Get off my brother!" she screamed.

"Ahh." Papis knelt, ignoring her. His hand went under the pallet. "I knew something was here."

He had no clue of the silent storm Mor could see erupting inside Amina's eyes. Papis had discovered a chunk of bread, two small salted fish, a mandarin, and two brown speckled bananas rumbling inside a bowl. With one swoop of his arm he snatched up the food. When one of the bananas dropped onto the dirt floor, he did not bother to pick it up.

"That's breakfast, lunch, and dinner." He winked, tucking the bread under his arm and cramming the other food into his pocket. "Check the rest." Papis nodded to one of the boys, who let go of Mor and dived under the pallet. "What other treats are under there?"

And like an obedient puppy, the boy scrounged around, pushing aside bags and tossing out tin cups.

Then once he reached behind the last box, Mor's heart froze. The boy's legs stopped flailing. He'd found something.

He crawled out and handed a bundle wrapped in cloth to Papis.

"Don't touch that." Mor bucked against the dirt and the other boy, struggling. He'd almost made it to his feet when the boy who'd rooted around under the pallet crashed into his legs, sending him to the ground again.

"Stop it!" Amina screamed as Fatima cried.

"Nice," Papis said, ignoring them as he removed the cloth from around the Dieg Bou Diar tomato can. "Ah, I think I will hold on to this." He scooped out the folded notes their *bàjjan* had given them, then tilted the can, letting all the coins Mor had earned run into his palm. They sounded like pebbles hitting tin.

It was everything they had.

Don't let your fight leave you, his father encouraged. *You must still be strong.*

Mor squirmed, but he couldn't break free. He kicked and clawed, watching Papis shove all he and his sisters had into his pocket.

"You are a thief!" Amina shouted, still cradling a crying Fatima.

212

But as quickly as Papis had slunk into their *barak*, he was gone. The other Danka Boys released Mor with one final kick to his side.

You will need your strength and a plan. This fight will not soon be over, his *baay* warned as Mor rushed for the doorway, ready to chase the Danka Boys.

When he smashed the door cover back, he saw the pages of Amina's book flying in the wind like eggshell-colored birds.

He paused only for a moment. The Iéna Academy pamphlet was balled on the ground. Mor jumped over all of it and sprinted across the dirt. He ran down the path after the boys, his bare feet slamming against their footprints.

"Eh," one of the Danka Boys said, looking back. "You want some more?" He raised his fist.

Then Papis turned, smirking, walking backward, chomping on Mor's banana. "See you again when you have our fish."

Mor halted, heaving. He knew it was no use. His *baay* was right. He would need his strength and a plan. There was only one of him against a cete of badgers. He watched, helpless, as they strolled down the path, laughing, with his family's money and their food.

Before he even reached his family's *barak*, he heard Fatima's cries against the silence of the early morning. He was surprised none of his neighbors heard her as well. The sound, and the sight of Amina crouched in the dirt, gathering the pages of her torn book, shattered him. As he neared their door, he reached down and picked up the pages that were drifting away.

"I'm sorry." He could hardly get the words out as he handed her the shredded pieces of her book. He went to pick up her crumpled pamphlet.

"Leave it" was all she said, turning away.

"We will be all right, Mina. I will make this better. . . ." Mor wanted to promise it, but he didn't. He was already breaking enough promises after less than two weeks on their own.

"How?" She spun around to face him. "They have turned it so the sun is in the dirt and the dirt is in the sky. No. We will not be all right." She snatched another page up from the ground. The fire in her eyes raged. "You need to watch yourself." She batted the pages in her hand toward him. "Why have they singled you out? Where have they come from? Maybe they heard we were alone, I don't know, but I do know this will not end today. Bananas and two small fish will never be enough to satisfy boys like that. With them you are either friend or the innards of a fish, and today you are the guts being yanked out and tossed aside."

Mor didn't dare tell her about Cheikh's return or that he might have brought the boys to their door. Nothing he could say would bring her comfort. She had spoken a truth he was just beginning to realize. There was a divide in the road he traveled, and now he had to choose a side.

22

THE Danka Boys had caught Mor's scent and were on his trail. Like a cackle of hyenas, they circled around him. For some reason they weren't going to leave him alone.

And his friend Cheikh had led them right to him and his sisters. They had taken everything from them. Even Amina's book.

Mor remembered when Ms. Renée, a volunteer from an aid organization, had given it to her. It had been Ms. Renée's favorite book when she was Amina's age, and she'd carried it to West Africa for company. But when she'd seen how much Amina loved to read, she'd given it to her as a present. Although Amina couldn't make out all the words back then, Ms. Renée had assured her she'd grow into them, like she would grow into herself. And every day Amina had sat on the stump at the front of the *barak* while the light was bright, between her chores, and read, her face buried in the pages. She'd even read as she walked from school, lost to the days, her eyes racing across the black ink on each cream-colored page.

Their *baay* had often teased her that she'd miss the world going on around her because of that book, and Amina had always said, "But there are worlds in here I would never know." Their *baay* had smiled then and joked, "Then I will let you be lost for now, but there will always be a *lampe tempête* in Lat Mata to guide you back home." She would smile absently and turn her page.

But now her book was in tatters.

She sat on the floor, the pages and pieces spread in front of her. Fatima was curled on the pallet, her thumb in her mouth, having finally cried herself back to sleep. The orange light of morning pushed through the window covering as Mor readied to leave. Silence lay between him and Amina. He placed his *téere*, his protection, up on his arm, knowing he needed it more than ever, and turned just as his *yaay*'s spirit became clear beside Jeeg, a blur of brightness coming into focus. The light around her was a dim golden halo. Jeeg cooed as Yaay stroked behind her ears. How Mor wished she would stroke behind his, too. She reached out a hand to his cheek. He closed his eyes and remained still for the briefest of moments, trying not to miss a second of her touch. When he opened them, her eyes were resting on Amina and all the torn and crinkled pages around her. She glided away from Mor and stroked Amina's back as Amina stacked page after page in order. Little mounds of the torn pages grew in the dirt next to Fatima's rock dolls, which lay in a circle on floor.

The dolls were nothing but misshapen rocks Fatima had collected and imagined were her real friends, having them talk and dance around the yard. Though when Mor moved to get nearer to their *yaay*, he realized the rocks had been carefully painted with faces. Some smiling, some not. Scraps of cloth covered their little bodies. When he peered even closer, he saw there were two male rocks and three female rocks, one draped in a mini *boubou* and a head wrap, made from an old *sër* of their mother's that had ripped. Then it hit him like a crashing wave. The rocks depicted his family. Two of the rocks were bigger than the others, while yet another was a slumbering goat.

Mor turned toward Amina, breaking the silence. "When did you make these for Tima?"

Amina looked up, pages in her hand. "When you were not around." Her tone poked at him. He tried to ignore it.

"I didn't know you painted."

"You don't know a lot about me."

That time her words left a bruise. "I'm sorry."

She watched him for a moment, then returned to her book. Her finger hovered over the page numbers. Mor looked to where their mother's spirit had been, but it was gone. No bright light. No good-bye.

All Mor wanted was to curl into a ball on the floor and never straighten again.

Do not slump in a sludge of pity. It does not shake from your skin so easy. Use that energy to step forward on your path.

Mor wanted to ignore his *baay*. He wanted his *yaay* back.

We are both here for you, my son. But now is not the time for coddling and softening gestures. Now is a time to knock off fear.

Mor glanced at Amina, seeing if there was any hint that she heard their *baay*.

You see your sister is ready to charge like a ram, but I want you to stand for them. Step from the shelter into the heat and the light.

As he moved to the doorway to leave, he felt Amina's eyes on him and turned.

"When the sun is fully out and more people are in the streets, take Fatima to the market. There is a nice woman there, near the last stall, named Basmah. She will give you bread and beans. Tell her I will bring her coins and fish. I'd go myself, but I don't want to keep Demba waiting. Please stay in the eye of the market today."

"We'll just go to Tanta Coumba."

"Tanta Coumba is not taking care of us. I am. Think, Mina. She might call Auntie to come get us if you worry her with this."

Amina cut her eyes at her brother. Mor could tell by the way she swished her lips from side to side that she had more to say—but she didn't. She busied herself with the stacks of pages covering the floor.

"Bring Jeeg with you. I do not trust having her here alone." And with that he stepped out of the *barak* to whatever awaited him.

With each step he searched the nearly empty path. The shadows played with his mind all the way to the beach and Demba. No Danka Boys in sight. Only chickens clucking around a yard, and a couple of the village men setting off for the beach ahead of him. Some nodded a good morning, but most kept their distance because of Demba. Those who had known Mor's father tried to warn him to stay away from "that *doff* fool."

Mor ignored their talk.

Demba was slowly becoming a friend.

When Mor approached the beach, many of the other *gaals* had already pushed off, but Demba sat waiting for him, breaking sticks in the sand. Since that first day Demba had never said anything about Mor joining him out on the water, but each morning he was always there waiting, not leaving until Mor arrived.

Every time Mor saw him, he let out a relieved sigh. "*Assalamu alaikum*," Mor greeted him, nodding. As Demba's lips moved, Mor was sure some of the garble of words was "and upon you the peace."

When they had pushed the *gaal* far enough out to sea, Mor climbed in as Demba revved the engine. Demba didn't use the wrench anymore to bang the stubborn motor, since he had Mor. Like Demba, the bullheaded engine had also become Mor's friend, puttering and stuttering most days.

As usual, they motored past the other *gaals* and the quiet snickers in search of swarming birds. Mor sat at the front, holding tight, welcoming the cool spray on his face, trying to forget his earlier morning visit. Fear gurgled inside his belly, and he wished he could shake it off like he had his fear of the open sea, and Demba.

Without having to be told, Mor turned and started readying the netting when Demba slowed the engine, turning in the direction of a cloud of birds diving into the water.

Once the boat had settled, rocking with the waves, they swung their bodies in unison, releasing the net. It floated on the water, soon disappearing as schools of fish frantically swam this way and that. And then together, in one joined heave, they tugged the netting closed, trapping the squirming fish. Ever since the first time overboard, Mor had been careful to brace his bare foot on the edge of the *gaal* for leverage as they hauled the catch onboard.

Demba watched Mor with eyes of a hawk.

"Storm clouds circle," Demba muttered as they separated the fish, whose blush-colored scales mirrored the rays of the sun as their mouths puckered at the foreign air, hoping for salted water.

There wasn't a cloud in the sky, but Demba was right. Storm clouds did circle Mor.

With each day Mor understood more and more of what Demba said and meant. As his *baay* had asked him when his voice first came to him, he was listening.

"Rain dances your spirit wet."

"But I'll be fine," Mor said. "I have to be. I will find a way to dry." Mor whispered the last words, still shaken and bruised by the morning.

He did not want to burden his friend with it. His cuts and reddening skin were his own, well hidden by his shirt and shorts. There was nothing Demba could do anyway.

Demba's eyes surveyed Mor's body, lingering on his hands and then his head, as if he could see through the fabric to Mor's forming bruises. Mor looked down at his own small hands, wishing they were powerful like Demba's, and like his *baay*'s had been. Once he'd thrown the last of the fish into the buckets, Demba poured in salt water, to the relief of the twitching fish. The engine came to life again with a chugging cough as Demba turned the boat toward the shore.

Mor glanced down into the half-full buckets. "Are we going to another spot? There are plenty more fish out there to catch." He thought of the extra money he needed to make and the crumpled school pamphlet, with the girls in their bright-green uniforms, left in the dirt.

Demba shook his head and kept on his course. When they

were closer to the shore, away from all the boats, he turned off his engine. Mor looked around. They had never fished so close to land before. They would be lucky to bring in a handful.

"Are you sure?" Mor asked. "This seems an unlikely spot to catch anything." But before Mor could ready the netting, Demba dived into the water.

Mor stared over the lip of the boat, disbelieving. When Demba rocketed up out of the sea like a whale, a spray of water left his lips. His dreadlocks bobbed around him like an octopus's tentacles. Mor smiled down at him. Then in a flash Demba's arms came up and grabbed Mor's, flipping him over the boat's edge. Mor screamed as he crashed into the water, flopping about. His smile disappeared as he tried to keep his head above the frothing liquid.

"Demba, this isn't . . ." He took in a mouthful of water. "*Khak! Khak!* I . . . can't swim." As he flailed, he was certain he saw the makings of a smile cross Demba's lips, but as quickly as he saw it, it disappeared.

His feet jerked and his hands thrashed the water. He was going to sink. Demba treaded calmly beside him, as if he had sprouted gills and a fin. "*Ndokh mi niak la ci sa soufou tankayi,*" Demba muttered. This time Mor couldn't put it all together. It made no sense. The sea wasn't grass under his feet, and the waves weren't flowers at his fingertips. He didn't have time to figure it out before his head dropped underwater again.

Like the first time over a week before, Mor panicked as the water locked over his head. His eyes burned in the sting of salt. Water filled his open mouth.

Mor couldn't calm himself. He couldn't break the surface of the water, no matter how he tried. Then two strong arms propelled him up like a jumping fish. Demba held on to the back of Mor's shorts and did not let go as Mor splashed about, regaining his breath.

"That wasn't funny," Mor yelled. "Let me back on the *gaal*." But when he looked at where he thought the boat should be, either it had moved or he had. Panic filled him again, until he saw it floating on the waves a little ways away. "We need to get back before it gets too far," Mor said, worried.

Demba made no move to hurry. He continued to float on his back, still holding Mor's shorts. Suddenly Mor realized he was free to push with his arms and kick with his legs without worry of sinking. It was much like he had started to learn to do with Cheikh so many summers before. But unlike Cheikh, Demba was still there, by his side, helping him swim.

He swam in circles for a while as Demba held him, remembering some of the strokes Cheikh had taught him. When they turned to swim for the *gaal*, Mor noticed both of Demba's arms cutting through the water, one after the other. He was no longer holding Mor up. At first Mor almost faltered, but Demba flipped onto his back, arm raised, ready if Mor needed him. At that moment Mor could do it himself, but knowing help was beside him made the journey a little less scary. He did not have to do it all on his own.

23

MOR twisted in his sleep, smiling. His head was pressed into his *yaay*'s old cloth, and he was thinking of Demba's words from a week before: "Fridays are castles for kings, adventures with brother, kicking games and resting waves."

At first he hadn't realized what Demba meant by it all, but now, after his second week on the water with him, Mor welcomed the free day to go to the mosque early like he had always done with his *baay* and to play *le foot* with his friends late into the afternoon.

The first Friday, when he had reached the beach and found no trace of Demba or his bike, he had wandered around lost. Demba's boat was there, but there was no Demba. Mor went to the dressmaker, asking after his friend.

"Ahh, today is his day with Idrissa," the man said. Again it was the name those women had called Mor.

"But who is Idrissa? Where does he live?"

The man glanced down at Mor, slowly rubbing his belly as if he didn't realize it. A toothpick swung up and down between his teeth.

"You do not know of Idrissa? Of course you wouldn't. Demba would never say anything to you of the one you favor. He is down that way under the crosses. Besides Demba and the scraggly grasses, they are all that rest out there."

Mor looked where the man pointed. The only thing he knew to be at the end of the road was the cemetery, shared by both Muslims and Christians. His *baay* and *yaay* were buried there. It overlooked the water.

"When did he die?" Mor tried to ignore thoughts of his father's burial and the dirt closing over him. He didn't want to be sad, but sadness never waited for anyone to be ready.

"Allah took him long ago," the dressmaker said. "He was just about your age, a few years younger than Demba. Fridays are for Idrissa. Demba and his birds sit with Idrissa every Friday morning, telling him of the week they would have had together. Idrissa died on a Friday morning."

"How did he die?" Mor asked, grateful to finally be learning something about his friend.

"Sickness touched his young brother's heart, and there were no medicines, barks, leaves, or brews that could cure him. That time left a scar on Demba. After that he journeyed far and wide to learn all he could about the herbs and the plants around him."

"He lost his little brother?" Mor said, more to himself than to the dressmaker. He couldn't imagine how he'd feel if he lost either Fatima or Amina. He was doing everything in his power to keep them with him now. "He's still sad?"

"There are days," the dressmaker said. "But since you've come onto his path, they come less and less. I suspect you are good for Demba, and he is good for you."

"Yes, sir," Mor had said, walking away from the man's shop and the whir of the sewing machines.

When Mor opened his eyes this Friday, his sisters' pallet was empty. He flung himself up, searching, frantic. Then as he watched Jeeg riffle in a bowl of orange peels, he remembered they were joining Tanta Coumba and her daughters for a trip to the market. Together. They were safe. Relief poured through him, but so did guilt. Keeping the news of Cheikh's being home left him feeling miserable. Tanta Coumba had helped them to stay, and holding on to this secret was an awful way to repay her. But he had no choice. Telling wasn't a chance he could afford to take.

"*Lahilaha IlAllah . . . ,*" intoned the imam.

Mor lowered his head and whispered, "Mohamed is his messenger."

The other men around him in the mosque did the same.

Following the prayer as his *baay* had shown him, Mor

bowed, bent, and rose with the tide of faithful bodies. Since the Danka Boys had come to his door, he had been so worried about where he would find the money that he and his sisters needed just to survive, along with the money for Amina's school. He had promised her, and it was that and the hope of keeping his promise to his father that kept him going. And as he gave his problems over to Allah, he felt better. When his doubts were fierce, he would often forget that. Then in a reflective moment, when he was alone, he would call on him, no longer turning away.

After he finished his prayers and left the mosque, he headed farther away from the noise of the market. He was excited to spend the rest of the day with Oumar and his other friends, kicking the soccer ball and forgetting all he had to do—at least for a couple of hours.

Mor dragged his hand along a high wall as he ambled along the path. A crooked smile set on his lips when he realized he hadn't seen the Danka Boys in a week. Not trusting that they wouldn't appear at their home again, he'd found new hiding places for the little bit of coins he'd started to save again.

But even when they weren't around, they still filled his thoughts. He did not trust they would stay quiet forever, yet he still welcomed the break. He picked up his speed down the road, ready to get to his friends. There was silence all around him on the empty path, with most people still praying in the mosque or bartering in the market.

Then Mor heard breathy whispers.

"Let's bring them down to the pit," someone said. The voice was gruff and forceful, but that of a boy, not a man. It carried in the hush of the day.

"Why don't we take them back to Mahktar?" another boy asked. His voice was a little higher in pitch.

Mor stopped running.

"Because you don't just bring someone else's goats to your front door, *badola*."

Mor blocked out all other sound. He knew those voices.

"Who you calling a dummy? Dummy." The pitch of the boy's voice rose and cracked. Then something banged against the wall and his words got muffled.

Mor rushed forward, nearer to the entrance of the alley. As he moved closer, shuffling feet and heavy grunts met his ears. He tilted his head and peeked. A frail-looking boy with knobby elbows and knees with dark scabs was sandwiched between another boy and the wall. Three goats were pressed together beside them, trying to avoid being crushed or fallen on as the boys wrestled. Mor sprang back as one of the boys stumbled toward the corner where he hid.

"Shut up," one hissed.

"No, you," the other countered. "You started it."

"Get off me, Abou." The boy's bristly roar grew strained. The scuffling stopped.

Mor knew if he glanced around the wall right then, he would come face-to-face with them. "Come on. We need to get them out of here."

Mor crouched low against the wall and took a chance. When he peeked, the boys' backs were to him. One of them yanked at the ropes knotted around three goats' necks, while the other, scruffier boy, with dust coating the side of his face and hair, shoved against their haunches. The goats didn't budge. No matter how hard the boys pushed and tugged, the animals stayed locked in place, moving only an inch when their necks were in danger of snapping.

"Diallo, they don't want to move," Abou observed.

Diallo hustled forward. His open plaid shirt whipped behind him, revealing a yellow T-shirt almost brown with grime. He was shorter and sturdier than his accomplice. "Just stop yapping and push."

They yanked and prodded at the goats some more, but the animals stayed rooted to the path.

"Hold up." Diallo waved his hand.

"What for?" Abou slackened his grip on the ropes hanging over his shoulder. His arms and legs were covered in healed-over scabs and picked-at blemishes.

"This one needs more mud." Diallo thrust his finger toward one of the goats as he squatted to grab a clump of pasty dirt. Mor's eyes followed the direction of Diallo's hand, smearing mud over the goat's white fur, to the painted blue waves under a red setting sun.

Jeeg.

Mor surged to his feet, ready to bolt around the corner. Then he froze. Diallo had withdrawn a long silver blade.

Mor feared the thief would cut Jeeg's neck right there in the alley, or his for trying to save her. But then another thought seized hold of him. Where were his sisters? His panic multiplied.

He prayed they were still with Tanta Coumba and her daughters, Oumy and Naza, around plenty of people.

He tried to calm his racing heart. His gaze flew between the gleaming blade and the path to his home. He wanted to rush to their *barak*, but he knew if he did, Jeeg would be gone. *Think*, he demanded silently, *think*.

He told himself his sisters weren't home yet. That they were safe. He held tight to this thought, although a pinprick of worry still stabbed at his chest. *They are fine*, he told himself again. *They are fine.*

"Why did you tie these knots so tight?" Diallo cut the rope, separating Jeeg from the other two goats. "This one is the problem." Diallo nudged Jeeg. "It doesn't want to move, but I bet I can make it." He poked her just enough with the tip of his knife to get her attention. She started and kicked her hooves out, taking a step. A trickle of blood trailed down her white fur. "See?" he said, nudging her with the knife again.

Mor's teeth dug into his bottom lip and he jerked forward, wanting to snatch the blade from Diallo's hand, but he stopped himself. He had to wait for the best moment.

"You take those two"—Diallo motioned to the goats near Abou—"and I'll deal with this one."

"Why do I have to take two?" Abou whined. "Who put you in charge?"

"Just move before someone sees us." Diallo wrapped Jeeg's rope around his fist and shoved her forward, knocking his knee into her gashes. Her blood smeared his shorts.

Mor wasn't sure what to do. Should he try to snatch her back? Or run for help? There were two of them, a knife, and endless places for them to go.

Intelligence and calm are the mightiest weapons of a warrior. Not a gun or a blade. His father's voice rested in the air next to his ear. *Yes, they can draw blood in an instant; however, an unrushed and capable mind can battle any man. Patience will reveal the opportunity. Wait for your moment to strike.*

Mor's breathing was erratic. He had to settle himself and think, but there was no time, for when he peered around the wall again, the boys and goats were gone.

Mor darted past where they had stood. He halted at the opening of the next crossing path. He took a quick look around the wall and found no one there, but the goats' hoofprints and the boys' footprints glared up at him from the dirt like bread crumbs. He followed them onto another path and then another. When he came to a wider street, with paving bricks stretching across the road, he seemed to have lost them. Looking left and then right, he almost missed them as they scampered around another corner. He took up the chase, keeping a safe distance. Every time they trotted down a deserted path, Mor waited until they turned down another before racing after them. Mor did not pass any adults on the paths that he could reach out to. Diallo and Abou made sure to keep to deserted back roads, though at times there were gaggles of small children busy with their games while teenage girls, giggling and gossiping, watched over them.

When there were no more corners to turn and no more walls to hide behind, Mor stopped. They had reached the dusty road and flat plains leading out of Lat Mata. He watched as the boys stumbled across the grasses, dragging the reluctant goats behind them. Defeat squirmed up his toes. The thieves had made it. There was no one left to stop them.

No one except Mor.

WHEN the boys became slender stick figures running in the distance, Mor chased after them. He followed them far out of Lat Mata, ducking behind the mammoth trunks of looming baobab trees dotting the open plain. His eyes never left Jeeg. The Danka Boys had strayed far off the main path when they stopped at a junk heap of a car, rusted and tilted in the dirt. Diallo thrust Jeeg's rope to Abou, and soon she was hidden behind the vehicle with the other two goats.

"Tie one down with this," Diallo ordered. He threw a thin cord he had taken from inside the trunk to Abou.

"We will feast like kings tonight," Abou said. "Papis will thank us for our finds. We'll be big men for the night."

"You'll never be a big man," Diallo teased.

A rock went flying through the air.

Diallo ducked, laughing. He bent behind the car, and all was out of view: the boys, Jeeg, and the knife. Not wasting a second, Mor bolted across the dirt, his concentration fixed on a huge baobab tree close to the car. He let out a heavy breath when his back was safely pressed against the grooves of the tree's bark. The boys and goats were still blocked by the car when he sneaked a peek around the tree. Rocks circled a large fire pit, enclosing charred firewood, off to the side of the wreck. The seats from the dismantled vehicle ringed it. The car's tires were submerged in the dirt.

Mor moved along the tree. The base of its trunk twisted itself like heavy rope deep into the dirt. Its roots looped and crossed one another into the soil. Wiggling his body, he wedged himself between the roots, hoping to remain out of sight but still able to see. When he focused back on the car, he saw Diallo standing near the fire pit over a smooth, flat rock.

He dragged the knife blade across it, and the hilt caught a ray of sunlight. Mor's body tensed.

One of the goats wailed a steady *m-a-a*.

"Hold it down," Diallo shouted as they disappeared behind the car again.

In the sliver of space between the car and the ground, Mor could barely make out the whitish-pink belly of a goat with its legs strapped together. There was no way to tell if it was Jeeg, though. Two goats' tails twitched above the car's hood, and Mor lay helpless and panicked as he heard the trapped goat buck and *m-a-a*.

Then there was silence.

"That's not how you do it." Abou's voice broke through the quiet.

"You think you know better than me?" Diallo snapped. "I've been doing this since you were still in Yaay's belly."

"Liar," Abou retorted. "You're only eight minutes older than me."

"And those eight minutes show that you were too stupid to know it was time to come out," Diallo snarled. "That's why your head is like a pear. They had to tug you out."

"Not true," Abou shouted. "It shows how ready Yaay was to push you out. She didn't want you then, and she doesn't want—"

Something crashed against the car.

Then Mor saw legs together, flailing and churning up dust. The brothers tumbled into view, grabbing at each other. Diallo tried to press the knife toward Abou's face, but his elbow was trapped under the weight of Abou's body. They jammed together, making it hard for either of them to throw a punch or even move. They were a knot rolling across the dirt, away from the goats.

Strike, my son.

Mor did not need to be told.

Dashing away from the protection of the trunk, he hurried around to the back of the rusted car. His heart thudded, blocking out all else. Through the open space where the car doors had been, he watched as the two Danka Boys continued to pummel each other in the dirt. Nothing but the next punch, slap, or scrape seemed important to them. Mor scrabbled to the side of the car, stealing a glance around the broken headlight. Sensing a presence, the goats scooted out of his reach, scared.

"Shh, it's okay," he whispered.

He crawled closer, reaching for their ropes, which were tied to a stake in the ground. Then he stopped. A limp goat lay in front of him. He hoped its chest would rise. Then he saw it. A trail of blood stained the fur at its neck. It dripped into the reddish-brown dirt, turning it black. Scrambling to the goat's side, he brushed away the cracking, caked-on mud over its flank. There was blue paint, but no rolling waves. And no red sun.

It wasn't Jeeg.

Mor hustled to the knots, frantic to untie them. The goats shielded him, but for how long? The boys could look up at any moment. The knots wouldn't budge.

He turned to the two goats, thinking he could loosen the knots at their necks. One of them instantly butted against him. It was Jeeg. Mor wanted to rub the hair at the bridge of her nose like she liked, but there was no time. Working on the knot, he glanced up every few seconds.

The boys still wrestled in the low grass. A string of insults trailed them.

By the time Mor finally got Jeeg free, the skin of his finger-tips was scratched and peeled and freckled with pricks of blood. Ignoring it, he pushed Jeeg toward the back of the car.

"Go," he urged.

But she wouldn't leave his side.

He knew he needed to take off running with her, but he couldn't leave the trapped goat. He tried with all his might to unfasten the knot at its neck, but it wasn't coming loose. He yanked on it, then tugged on it, and the trapped goat let out a *m-a-a* that could have woken any hibernating beast.

Mor didn't think, he flew, diving behind the car with Jeeg, then peeking around it.

Diallo flung Abou to the side. Dust clouded the air. Mor heard his own heart pound in his ears.

"Shut up," Diallo shouted, looking toward the car and the left-behind goat.

"Who are you telling to shut up?" Abou kicked at his brother.

"Who are you kicking? I was talking about the goat." He slapped his brother on the side of his head.

And they were fighting again.

Grunts and huffs signaled Mor's chance to run. He and Jeeg streaked away from the car, leaving the other goat behind. They sprinted toward another baobab tree, farther away. This one was even more enormous than the first, with a hollowed-out space in the trunk. Mor squeezed Jeeg inside, then shimmied in beside her, glad that the area made for sacrifices held no bones, beads, or pot offerings to the spirits, only streams of melted white candle wax. Mor pulled at the grasses around the mouth of the tree and piled them high. As he grabbed for more, Jeeg nibbled their camouflage.

"No." Mor jerked her head back.

Her little bites had made a perfect spy hole. He had a concealed view of everything around him. But if he and Jeeg moved too much, the boys would have a perfect view of them. There was no way they could get away together unseen across such a barren landscape.

They would have to wait.

25

DO *not burden your shoulders with the blame of that slaughtered animal. Or wring your hands, ashamed of the one left tangled. Casualties are birthed in war. And there is no cowardice in waiting for the enemy to retreat. . . .*

The words of Mor's father helped settle his breathing and his guilt as the Danka Boys continued whirling insults at each other.

As Mor hunkered down, ready for a long wait, Jeeg let out a low *m-a-a* and dug her hooves into the dirt, attempting to get out of the hollowed tree trunk. Desperate to quiet her, Mor clamped his hand over her mouth and used his body to press her down. The more he tried to restrain her, the louder her cries grew. So he let her go.

Then, in a slow, casual chomping, she started eating their grass wall again. This time Mor didn't stop her. As the grass cleared, Mor glanced around the area just beyond their hideout.

Suddenly Abou bounded in Mor and Jeeg's direction, his red T-shirt ballooning at his back. Diallo took up the chase. Neither of the boys slowed long enough to notice the missing goat.

They were so close to the tree, the dust sailed into Mor's eyes. All they had to do was turn, and Mor and Jeeg's hiding place would be revealed. "Eh!" a voice rang out. Alarm straightened Mor's spine. A new fear grabbed him.

"Get up, you fools." In a few gaping strides Cheikh was in front of the tree. He pried the brothers apart. "Enough, before my foot jumps in to end this for good."

Cheikh shoved the brothers away from the opening of the tree, but Mor did not relax.

Even though Cheikh was only one person, Mor was certain he could've taken on the two thieves and won.

A pleading *m-a-a* sounded from behind the car, and Cheikh stopped. Then he dragged the boys toward the rusted vehicle.

"Where'd these come from?" Cheikh insisted.

He stared at Abou.

Abou shrugged, shrinking under Cheikh's stare. "We just grabbed 'em."

"It's no big deal, man," Diallo added. "One of them is from that *khale*'s place. He has no parents to tell."

Mor scrunched up his lips and balled his fists.

"It was easy," Diallo snickered. "No one was there."

His sisters were safe.

"Wait." Diallo whirled around. "Where's that other goat?"

Both Cheikh and Abou scanned the area. Mor slunk back, pulling Jeeg with him.

"I told you to tie it tight." Diallo glared at Abou.

"Who cares," Cheikh interjected, shoving the brothers. "You should be glad it ran off. That's one less owner coming after your necks." He untied the knot around the other goat's neck and kicked it into running as it bleated at the air.

"Hey," Abou whined.

Cheikh shot a sideways look at him. "Now do something with this one."

"You're not the boss of me." Diallo scrunched up his lips.

"Nor do I want to be." Cheikh stepped inches from Diallo's face. Neither blinked.

"Skin it, and cook it here. And hurry up before someone comes," Cheikh said, turning away.

"No one would dare come to our fire pit unless they want trouble." Diallo raised a fist. "Besides, no one knows this place but us and a few girls." He smirked.

For the first time Mor saw letters painted in red on the side of the rusted white car. They read Danka Boys, with trails of dry paint running down from each letter.

"Just hurry up." Cheikh nodded toward the ground. "And

make sure you burn away the branding before you go carrying off the skin."

"I know," Diallo snapped.

"I'm not so sure about that," Cheikh said, turning away. "We don't want your mess to follow you back to Mahktar." He shook his head and pounded across the dirt. He strode right by the tree Mor and Jeeg hid in, not slowing his pace.

Mor finally exhaled.

26

AFTER Cheikh left, Mor and Jeeg lay hidden, soon growing tired of Abou's and Diallo's constant insults. They couldn't talk to each other without a jab, a kick, or an unkind word being thrown. Finally, after what felt like another endless hour crammed in the hollow of a tree, Mor and Jeeg found their chance to run. While Abou and Diallo fought over how to build a fire, Mor pushed Jeeg from their hiding place, tugging at her neck until she followed.

"Go, girl. Let's go," he urged Jeeg as he picked up the pace, trying to put as much distance between him and the Danka Boys as he could. He knew Amina and Fatima must be frantic with worry. It was long past the time he usually got home, and Jeeg wasn't there either. He was also certain Amina would weigh him down with questions when she saw him.

The late afternoon sun got lost behind heavy gray clouds, causing it to grow dark. There were no homes around them, only the thatched peaks and rippling roofs in the distance near Lat Mata. Mor listened and searched the land for any signs of other Danka Boys.

Jeeg trotted close at his side as rain started to fall. By the time they reached the path near their family home, they were soaked and mud splotches covered their legs. Mor stepped into the tiny clearing outside his house, out of breath, then halted in the mud. Demba sat drenched in the rain, swaying back and forth, mumbling to himself. When he glanced up, raindrops webbed his lashes. He rubbed his thumb across something in his hand.

"Demba," Mor shouted, thankful to see a friend. "You'll never believe what happened to Jeeg and me." He rushed forward as Demba got to his feet. The rain pressed Demba's knee-length shirt to his skin. The legs of his gray *toubëy* were also soaked through.

"Beauty's worry tramples the mud." His words competed with the pouring rain, but Mor had heard them.

Demba said nothing else. Instead he pressed what he held into Mor's palm. It was a flat, elongated stone. Then he lifted his bike, which rested against the *barak*, turned onto the path, and left.

Mor watched him go.

"Mor, is that you?" Amina yanked back the door covering,

drawing his attention. She ran out in bare feet. "Where have you been? Have you seen Jeeg? How could you leave us to worry like this?"

"Amina, Amina. Stop assaulting him," Tanta Coumba called from inside over Fatima's sniffles and cries. "Both of you come inside before the rain takes your health."

When Mor and Amina stepped inside, Tanta Coumba threw up her arms. "Thanks be to Allah. You are safe."

"Mor," Fatima heaved, still crying. She bolted out of Tanta Coumba's lap to hug her brother. "Jeeg is missing too."

But before he could respond, Jeeg bounded through the doorway, wet fur slicked to her body.

"Jeeg!" Fatima let go of her brother and clasped her arms around Jeeg's neck. Jeeg bleated.

"Where have you been?" Amina asked again, then sneezed. "We have been worrying." She nodded toward Tanta Coumba's daughter, her best friend, who knelt on the floor with Fatima's rocks. "Naza and I have been everywhere in this rain looking for you. First we went to the market, then to the lot where you play. No one saw you all day. Then we went back to the market and to Tanta Basmah. She brought us to Demba. He searched for you too and told us to wait here with Tanta Coumba."

"He didn't want to stop searching," Tanta Coumba added. "I demanded he come out of the rain for a bit, but he refused. Instead he paced and sat outside, scanning each path to your yard."

"He has waited with us for hours." Amina looked her brother up and down, her hands on her hips.

Tanta Coumba agreed, nodding. "This is not like a child of Awa's, causing others so much worry."

"It wasn't my fault," Mor began. "Two boys stole Jeeg this afternoon."

"Why not go for help? Thieves do not care who they hurt."

"There wasn't time," Mor said. "I would've lost them."

Remembering how Papis had reacted to the first threat of the police, Mor worried that telling her any more might bring added trouble to his family if all the Danka Boys weren't caught. Papis had threatened the shopkeeper in view of so many and had not been scared.

"Jeeg is back and I am fine. We'll be okay."

Amina and Fatima stayed quiet, though Amina twisted and squirmed like she wanted to speak.

Mor rubbed his thumb against the long, smooth rock Demba had given him.

Tanta Coumba frowned. "I will not sleep easy tonight knowing this. Collect dry clothes. You will be spreading your pallets under my roof."

"But we're fine," Mor objected. "We can stay here."

She shook her head. "No. I will not hear of it. You will at least stay the night with me. I couldn't face Dieynaba if something happened to you."

Mor nodded, ready to end the conversation before it led to having to name the Danka Boys.

❖ ❖ ❖

When Mor woke the following morning, achy and sore, he felt something hard pressing into his spine and tensed. Where was Jeeg? Were they still trapped in the gut of the mighty baobab? But when he opened his eyes, he saw Jeeg tucked by a wall and remembered.

They were all at Tanta Coumba's.

Relieved, he flicked at what pressed into his back. It was the flat rock Demba had given him. He turned it over in his hand, wondering what it was for. He twisted to see Fatima close behind him, her bony knees poking him too. From where he lay, he could see Amina on the pallet in Cheikh's room, alone. She was turned toward the wall near where he'd seen his mother's *nafa*. But there was no way to search without waking her.

Although he wanted to stay and try, he knew the fish were not asleep and neither probably was Demba. His body still ached from being crammed in the hollow of the tree. He ignored it and got up to pray. At the doorway he glanced back as a sleepy Fatima got off the floor, eyes barely open, and went into the room with Amina. She crawled onto the raised pallet and was soon fast asleep again. On the floor by Mor's mat was their rock family. He went back and placed the one Demba had given him on the floor with them.

Walking out the door, he did not worry about his sisters' safety for the first time in a long time. Once outside, he made his way past scrawny goats, and a few loose chickens pecking at tiny stones. Small green tomatoes grew on vines in Tanta Coumba's tiny garden. As he turned down the deserted path that led to the beach, he felt someone join him.

He turned to find Cheikh.

Tired, and worried, Mor almost sounded like he was begging when he spoke. "What do you want? Why won't you just leave me alone?"

"I've told you what I want. What I think you need. Join us."

"Why do you even pretend to care?" Mor stepped back toward Cheikh. In his exhaustion he seemed to find strength. "Are you the one who put my home under his nose? There are so many others who have more than me."

"None that are so easy to pluck from," Cheikh said. "It's simple. He's seen you are alone now and is restless."

"And he's your friend?"

"It's not that simple," Cheikh said, looking past Mor at two men heading up the path. Mor followed Cheikh's gaze. When he turned back, Cheikh had slipped into the shadow cast by the nearest *barak*. They didn't know the men, so Cheikh stepped back out. "He has done a lot for me."

"But you are sneaking past your mother's house like a fox after chickens? Why haven't you gone home? Are you ashamed?"

"Stop talking about things you don't understand." He lowered his voice as the men passed, nodding good morning.

"Then tell me. I want to understand," Mor pleaded. He really did want to know why his friend had chosen this boy over him and his own family.

Cheikh was quiet for a long time. "My mother will have no choice. My father will send me back. Even though he has moved away and has little time for us, she is still his wife. He wants me at that *daara*. But I will not go back." Cheikh shook his head, as if trying to wipe away a memory. "Never."

"But why? What was so wrong?"

"I never had enough."

"Enough what?" Mor almost felt as if he were standing in the sand with his old friend again.

"Enough of everything. Rice, money, whatever they asked me to get. I never had enough. But Papis always did. He had enough food. Enough money. But more than that, enough will to take the blows for me."

"I don't understand."

Cheikh glanced around again, then slowly lifted his shirt. Healed-over slices crisscrossed his back.

"What happened to you?" Mor rushed forward, about to touch his friend's skin, but Cheikh lowered his shirt before he could.

"That slash over Papis's eye is for me. He stepped in front of the whip when I'd had enough. Then he helped me escape with him. I can never go back to that."

Mor wanted to say maybe Cheikh's dad would under-stand, but he knew he wouldn't. He was a man who did not tolerate weakness, and Cheikh running would be considered weak. Cheikh was right. His father would send him back.

"But why do you take what doesn't belong to you? Why do you now inflict pain yourself?" Mor asked instead.

Cheikh shook his head. "*I* have never taken what doesn't belong to me or what hasn't been given."

"Your friends do. They took all we had. And you took my *yaay*'s *nafa*."

"Before you accuse, be certain," Cheikh warned. "I stole nothing. I found it."

"Then where is it?" Mor raised his voice, not caring who heard, but Cheikh glanced around.

"It is in the safest place I knew to put it."

"The safest place is with me." Mor tapped his own chest. "It's my *yaay*'s."

"There hasn't been an opportunity to get it back." Cheikh slipped to the side of a fence when someone else came into view, passing down the roadway.

"Cheikh," Mor said when the person was gone, "you can't keep hiding. There is no life without family."

"Papis is part of my family now." Cheikh said it with a certainty Mor couldn't understand. "He would give anything for me, and I for him."

"You would even hurt me and my sisters?" Mor whispered, stepping away. "You are my brother."

"That's why you should join us. A brother to me would

then be a brother to him. Your scent would become his and you would all be safe."

"I don't want that scent." Mor thought of all the things the Danka Boys had done.

Cheikh stared at Mor. "As you protect Jeeg and your sisters, we would protect you. We remember what it was first like to be own our own—making sure there was enough food, and being careful that others didn't take all we had."

"But you're the reason I have to worry. You are the ones taking from us."

"I've warned you; now it's up to you to decide if you really wish to take care of Mina and Tima."

Cheikh said their names like he truly knew them, like they were his family. But Mor knew that wasn't true, because that Cheikh was gone.

Cheikh shrugged, backing away, as another group of men started toward them on the path. "You may not have a better choice."

Mor watched his friend duck down another path as the men neared where they had been standing. The men glanced in the direction Cheikh had gone, but kept walking. Mor turned Cheikh's words over in his mind.

Should he really join the Danka Boys?

WHEN Mor reached the beach, his thoughts were full. Cheikh's words and the marks sliced across his back blocked out everything else. Mor couldn't believe someone had done that to his friend. Tanta Coumba would never want to send Cheikh back if she knew. But Mor also knew that Cheikh's *baay*, who was nothing like his own, would have told him there was no time for a boy's tears. Mor thought about that day Cheikh had left and how his tears had disgusted his father. His *baay* had yelled that the *daara* would make him into a man.

Mor wondered about the *daara* his *bàjjan* wanted to send him to in two months. Would it be the same?

When he reached the beach, most of the *gaals* were already

on the water, and hardly any fishermen stood about the shore. There was no sign of Demba or his bike, but his boat was on the sand just as he'd left it. Mor wandered over to the mud wall and sat, wondering if Demba had kept his eyes closed to the morning.

But like Demba had waited for him, he was willing to wait for Demba.

As the sky changed from the pale orange of daybreak to a brilliant blue, bright with light, he continued to wait. Thoughts of Cheikh and the Danka Boys ate away at the minutes. The more Mor thought, the more he got confused, dreading any decision he might make. He had to prove to his aunt that he could take care of his sisters well beyond the summer. He needed money and food, but the Danka Boys were a constant threat to that, and he had less now than he had started with. They had all but wiped away Amina's dream of going to that fancy school. And now Mor couldn't even think of attending the local village school if he wanted to try to make the money back. He'd have to work.

But what if he did join them? What would they expect of him?

Mor looked around, wishing Demba were there. Where was he? Even though he had no right to be, Mor started to get annoyed. He jumped down off the wall and paced back and forth in the sand.

Then Demba pedaled into view. A strange, misshapen straw hat with an opening at the top of it rested on his head.

His dreadlocks sprouted through the hole. As he rode closer, Mor saw that a new bird clung to a piece of the hat's raggedy edge. He didn't think it was real until it craned its tiny head in his direction. He had never seen a bird so at home on a man's head before. This bird was no bigger than Mor's fist and was the color of lemons, with black flecks on its wings.

It chirped at Demba's ear. As if they spoke the same language, Demba raised his palm and the bird hopped onto it. It pecked at the seeds he held there.

"Where have you been?" Mor asked as Demba propped his bicycle against the wall and sat in the sand next to where Mor stood. Mor looked to Demba's boat and then at Demba.

"Are we not going out?" Mor asked. "I'm ready." But Demba didn't appear to be in any rush to move.

Mor sloshed back and forth across the sand in front of him. He stopped and faced Demba. "Are you going to talk to me? Are you angry?" Mor huffed when Demba didn't answer. He flopped in the sand next to him. After a few minutes he jumped up, pacing again. The Danka Boys and Cheikh did not let his thoughts rest, so neither could his body.

Demba did not seem to mind, though. He simply fed the bird every few minutes, staring out at the water. The waves crashed against the shore, and the salt air lay heavy around them. Mor's hands were sticky with perspiration. "I'm sorry you spent the night waiting for me," he mumbled. "I did not mean to cause any of you worry."

For the first time that day Demba looked in Mor's

direction. The little bird took flight, then settled in another of Demba's deadlocks. Demba gave a slight nod, then looked back out to sea.

Moments later, without explanation, Demba got up and headed to the boat.

Out on the water the air was cool, smelling of the sea. Usually fishing was a bright spot for Mor, no matter how overcast the sky, but this morning was different. He was too bothered by all the things standing in his way. The sky reflected his mood, turning from a radiant clear blue to a gloomy gray.

Demba ignored the changing colors and sped away from the shore. He headed toward the other boats in the distance.

"Why don't we go over there?" Mor asked, pointing a distance away from the other boats. He did not want to be around anyone, especially people he knew could turn unkind.

But Demba didn't listen.

"Demba, I know you hear me," Mor said. Water lapped at the sides of the *gaal*, and seagulls soared overhead. Mor could just make out the voices of the fishermen as they approached. As usual, some of them snickered as Demba's boat glided through an open path between them. "Why don't you ever listen to me?" Mor added. "We should've gone the other way."

Boats ringed them off their starboard and port sides. Some of the fishermen kept to what they were doing, while a few laughed and pointed at Demba's peculiar hat with the bird flying around his head. For the first time Mor was embarrassed by the taunts and jeers. He crouched deeper into the boat. He wanted to be invisible.

"Why are you wearing that stupid hat?" he asked in frustration. "Do you want everyone to think you're strange?" The words launched out of his mouth before he could trap them.

"Did you hear that?" a middle-aged fisherman from the nearest boat chuckled, and pointed at Demba. "The boy finally realizes how *doff* Demba is."

Mor was shocked his words had traveled so far.

"Son," the man called. "Don't you know it is not a hat at all? He wears a weaverbird nest upon his head, and I think the weaverbird wants it back." The man gave a hearty laugh.

Mor stared at Demba's head and realized where he had seen that makeshift hat before. Hoards of them hung in the trees around the village. Occasionally a nest would fall and crash against the ground, but Mor had never seen one on someone's head. Suddenly the sky, which had quickly piled with storm clouds, sent a sweeping wind sailing on the waves. Out of nowhere a lightning bolt sliced the air. The engine of the mocking fisherman's *gaal* rattled.

Then, without warning, it burst into flames.

Fishermen from the boat dived into the water. From other *gaals* people shouted and motioned for someone to douse water on the engine. The man who'd teased Demba frantically scooped water into a pail, hanging over the side, and flung it on the fire. When the liquid hit the flames, the engine sizzled and the fire went out. Men splashed in the ocean close to the smoking boat but dared not climb back inside until they were sure the flames would not reignite. All at once heads and pointing fingers turned toward Demba, who sat calmly, mumbling to himself, his dreadlocks camouflaging his face as the bird circled its nest.

"It was him," a fisherman bobbing in the current accused. "He is responsible."

"Hush, before he sends a wave to drown us all," another fisherman cautioned, treading water near the smoking *gaal*.

Mor knew superstitions surrounding water and mystical beliefs wove together with his people's Islamic faith; however, he'd never seen grown men so scared. He had seen people rush to consult *serigne*, giving these religious teachers money and other alms to ward off evil spirits, or bring wealth and prosperity to a family, but he was still startled by the certainty of the accusing fingers pointing at Demba even though he'd hardly stirred.

"I told you it is evil he practices with his muttering," the first fisherman retorted. "Now you all have seen it."

Mor swung around to face Demba, causing the boat to rock. He was fearful of what the fishermen believed Demba had done.

Is it true? Mor wondered. Did his friend bring evil spirits? Mor had never seen Demba pray or recite a verse from the Koran, but whatever Demba believed or whoever he prayed to, Mor just didn't want to accept that his friend could be capable of such harm. Then he halted. Was this because of what he'd said? Had his words somehow angered Demba and he'd lost control? Mor didn't want to believe it.

He touched his tiny amulet on his arm.

Uncertainty crept into his thoughts. And as if Demba had read Mor's mind, he focused on Mor's eyes.

"Misfortune's stamp desires blame. A bright-red bird imprisoned in their colorless cage." His voice was steady and clear. Mor even understood.

The more time he spent with Demba and watched and listened to him, the more he began to understand how he thought and sometimes how he saw the world. Even though his words were always a puzzle, Mor knew Demba was the bright-red bird that was trapped in a colorless cage, because he was different from those around him. But in no way was Demba *doff*.

Mor studied his friend. "I am sorry for being mean. You've never been the cause of my problems, and I have messed up and become the cause of yours."

Demba watched the lone fisherman.

He blinked slowly and Mor knew he had accepted his apology.

The smoking boat across from them continued to sway in the wake of the outboards that had puttered far away, bringing more distance between themselves and the bright-red bird that was Demba. Only three vessels remained by the stricken *gaal*.

Smoke blew away with the wind. The clouds started to break, as if the sun's rays had muscled them aside. The winds died down, and the owner of the damaged *gaal* slumped down in his boat.

"I'm ruined." He rubbed his hand over his balding head. Then he turned his attention to Demba and jutted out his chin. "Because of him."

"That's not true," Mor shouted in defense of his friend. "Demba would never do anything to hurt anyone. Tell them, Demba." Mor looked back. But he could tell by the set of Demba's shoulders and how he held his head high that he was not going to say a word in his own defense.

Even though some of the other fishermen did not seem to want to listen, Mor thought Demba should at least try to convince them they were wrong.

Mor noted that the remaining fishing vessels gave Demba's boat a wide berth. The bows of their *gaals* were painted with the owners' names, or the words "Allah's Blessing " in Arabic, French, or Wolof. Mor could not understand how untrusting of Allah they all were at that moment, believing instead that the work of menacing spirits was afoot.

"We need to cast them out," someone urged. "Or they will do us all harm."

One fisherman in a knit cap pulled hard on the string of his motor. "If you're to do that, it will be without me," he said. "I want no part in this. They are fishermen just like us. If he has powers, why doesn't his hull spill over with fish?" The eyes of the fisherman and his crew stayed fixed on Demba as they motored away.

An older man with a *sothiou* dangling from his mouth cupped his hands and shouted, "Souleymane, come in our boat. Fish with us before the morning is over."

"I cannot leave my vessel. It is all my family has."

"What good is it for any of you if you sit out here in the baking sun when there are fish to be caught?"

The men in the other boat chattered among themselves like birds on wires. Mor couldn't hear their words, but it was clear a few of them wanted to stay and help him, while it was obvious by others' gestures that they wanted to get out and collect a morning's worth of fish.

The fisherman pulled the motor string and revved the engine. "We cannot waste petrol bringing you in now. Come with us."

Souleymane shook his head. He watched the last of his men climb into the other fisherman's *gaal*.

The words "You stubborn ox" were carried on the water as the last *gaal* fled.

Souleymane's boat tilted back and forth. The lip of each side kissed the waves. Birds fluttered nearby, signaling the location of a school of fish. But Demba did not steer his boat away.

He and Mor kept their distance from Souleymane, watching and waiting.

❖ ❖ ❖

Before the sun's midmorning heat strangled the air, Souleymane looked around, desperate. He glanced at Mor and Demba, sitting off in the distance. Mor was sure a blend of pride, embarrassment, and stubbornness tied by fear kept him from asking for their help. The hum of the other motors had long since been cut off in the distance. Frustrated, Souleymane kicked his engine with his sandaled foot and then leaped back, holding his toe.

"Why do all fishermen think banging an engine is the way to fix it?" Mor grinned for the first time all morning. He jumped into the water, no longer afraid of the waves, and swam with Demba's wrench in his mouth before Demba could react. Mor's head did not break the surface until he emerged at the bow of the fire-scorched *gaal*. He swam as if he'd been swimming his whole life out in the middle of the sea.

"I am done." Souleymane's head drooped between his hands. "My fishing day is over even before it has begun." He wallowed. "I've no fish in my hull, no money in my pocket, and no food in my children's bowls. How will I ever pay for a new engine?" He shook his head, then catapulted backward when Mor grabbed hold of the boat's edge.

Mor pulled the wrench from his mouth and tossed it into the boat. Then he grabbed hold of the side of the *gaal* and swung himself inside.

"Stay away from me." Souleymane scooted away from Mor. "You and that crazy Demba have done this to me."

"Sir, we did nothing. Please let me try and help." Mor wiped beads of salt water from his face.

"What can you do that all those men could not?" He opened his arms wide toward the fishermen in the scattered boats.

"They did not spare the time to try," Mor said.

"You have a lot to learn of these seas," Souleymane retorted. "If they don't bring fish back, there will be someone else ready to sell to their usual buyers. They will come back for me."

"So you will sit here sizzling instead of letting me help you?"

"If you say you do not have the power to destroy my engine, then how will you, a little boy, have the power to repair it?"

"It is not power. My *baay* taught me." Mor moved toward the distraught man. "I might be able to fix it."

"Fix it? It cannot be fixed."

"My *baay* said anything can be fixed with time and tools." Mor grinned, thinking of his father's words. He picked up Demba's wrench from the hull and held it at his side. "Please let me try."

The fisherman finally gestured toward the sagging engine.

Mor dried his hands on an old rag in the boat, then unlatched the hooks securing the cracked hood and sat back on his heels. He examined the wires and plugs inside. The motor was different from Demba's and any other he had seen, but he did not let on.

Follow the wires, my son. His father's words were a welcome guide. *Like any well-trodden path, they will lead you where you need to go.*

Mor did as his father advised. Going to work on the engine, he peeled away the melted plastic so he could get to the wires. He traced the meandering trails of yellow, blue, and red, concentrating hard. Then his face broke into a smile. He recognized the spark plugs.

Some of the wires were badly singed, and it took a while to peel back the casings. The smoldering Senegalese sun beat down on his head and back as he hunkered over the engine, but he ignored the heat. Instead, he concentrated on the skills his *baay* had taught him.

When he finished twisting and reattaching the wires, he peeked over the side of the boat at the back of the charred engine.

"Do you have a sturdy piece of wire?" Mor squinted as the sun shimmered off the surface of the water.

"What I have is what you see." Souleymane swept his open palms around his empty hull.

Mor's gaze landed on the netting, which would do him no good, then on the teakettle in the corner. It was secured much like Demba's, with a long, wound piece of thick wire.

"Demba, *kai fii*," Mor called, motioning for Demba to bring his boat closer.

Souleymane jumped to his feet, almost falling over. "Why are you beckoning him? I don't want him near my boat."

"But what if he can help?" Mor asked.

"*Doff* Demba? What can he do for me?" Souleymane scoffed. "He brings trouble wherever he goes."

Demba's words came back to Mor.

"I'm sometimes scared of things that are different too, but I would never understand them if I did not try." He thought about the first time he heard Demba's words and how they were like a knot to him, or a language he could not unscramble. "Demba has waited by you when no other fisherman has. Even when you blame him, he is here to help. He is my friend."

Souleymane went silent. Mor could tell he was deciding among trusting him, staying stranded until the other fishermen returned, or paddling back to shore with his hands as the sun rose higher in the sky.

"Very well." He threw up his arms.

Demba revved his engine and guided his *gaal* through the water, pulling even with the other vessel. The little bird that had been fluttering around him all morning was nestled in his dreadlocks. The fisherman clutched the far side of the boat. Mor thought he might fling himself into the water if Demba got any closer.

Mor took a step away from the engine and dived back into the ocean himself. His body cooled instantly when the water wrapped around his skin.

"Where are you going?" Souleymane's voice shook. He leaned over the side of the boat, talking to Mor, but his attention was on Demba.

Mor bobbed near the engine. "This burned wood is barely holding the engine up. I'm going to try and hold it in place with this wire while you both lift it back up."

"What? You want him in my boat?" Souleymane shook his head like a wobbling top and rubbed his hands over each other. "I can do it myself."

Mor looked between his friend and the fisherman. "It's heavy. Let Demba help you."

Demba rose and Souleymane stared. He opened his mouth, about to protest, but Demba was already getting into his *gaal*. The little bird hopped from one lock of Demba's hair to another like they were tree branches.

Souleymane blinked rapidly. Sweat beads clung to his eyelashes. He took a timid half step forward and then another until he was at one side of the engine. Demba's long, slender fingers, with lines resembling burrowed tunnels in his black skin, reached for the engine as well.

"*Benna . . . ñaar . . . ñett . . . ,*" Mor counted, and dived underwater.

His cheeks puffed out as if a thousand grains of sand were crammed into his mouth. When Demba and Souleymane lifted the outboard motor, he inspected the back of the *gaal* to make sure it had not been charred too badly and that the engine would not speed away and sink once

Souleymane started it. He emerged from the sea, saltwater droplets tumbling over his eyes. He fastened wire around the tiller and the base of the engine for extra security, leaving a little slack so the tiller could still move. Then he took in a huge gulp of air, went back under, and tapped the side of the boat, signaling for them to ease the propeller back into the water. He jostled the engine back and forth to make sure it was secure.

"All done," he said, panting, after breaking through the surface of the water.

Souleymane's face held a blank stare. "It looks no different than it did before." He was sweaty and the skin of his forehead lay in tight folds.

"Try it." Mor swam away from the motor and held the side of Demba's boat. "Twist the handle."

"This will never work," Souleymane said as he rotated the ignition handle. A faint breath of smoke coughed from the engine, but it didn't start.

"Try again," Mor encouraged.

On the second try the motor rumbled and sputtered, singing an erratic but present hum. Then it puttered but didn't stop. Water churned under the boat. "*Alhamdoulilah*, thanks be to God." Souleymane motioned upward.

Once Demba had climbed back into his own *gaal*, he helped Mor in as well.

Souleymane turned to Mor, holding out Demba's wrench. "Why are you not hanging around the motor shops?"

Mor thought about how his *baay* used to hoist him up to peer down into the truck engines. Although he loved fishing with Demba, his fingers seemed so much more at home tinkering with wires and tools rather than nets and scaly fish. "They think I am too young."

"Well, they are ignorant, as I have been." Souleymane patted his brow with the oil-stained cloth Mor had used. He grinned, shaking his head. "I've been a stubborn *yëkk*." While he spoke, Mor envisioned him as a feisty bull in a busy roadway, blocking traffic.

Mor smiled. "It will still need repair, but it'll last for today."

Souleymane waved his hand at the air. "I need to repay you," he added. "Both of you."

"*Juróom*," Demba said, his attention on the water.

"Can't he bring us more? The more fish we have, the more money we can make."

"*Juróom*," Demba said again.

"But—"

"*Juróom.*" Demba's mind was made up.

"Just five fish, sir," Mor grumbled. He wanted to agree with Demba, but unlike him, he could use more fish. After all he had lost, he needed to find ways to get more money for Amina's school fees. But like Demba, he was beginning to understand that he should not take just because he could. He wasn't a Danka Boy. He sighed. "You can bring them to Amadou's. Demba always finishes his day there." He brushed the dripping water off his face with a corner of his damp T-shirt. "That will be thanks enough."

"Only five? Why so few?" Souleymane showed a smile full of crooked teeth, one of which was capped in shining sliver.

Mor glanced Demba's way, but his friend made no outward gestures, and Mor took this to mean that his part in the conversation was done. "He only takes what *he* needs." Mor held the last words longer than he needed to. He glanced at Demba, but his expression hadn't changed. Mor was struck at how he was beginning to understand Demba's nonverbal language, as if the movement of Demba's hands, eyes, body, and dreadlocks were writing his meanings in the sky.

28

THE rest of the day on the water was perhaps their best yet, and with a hull loaded with buckets full of fish, Mor dared to smile. Souleymane repaid them, and Mor feasted on an entire fried fish by himself with bread and *frittes*. Before working with Demba on the water, Mor and his family would have been lucky to have fresh fish a few times a month. They usually had small smoked ones with their millet and leaf sauces. Now he was eating french fries and an entire *bonga* fish on his own. Of the five fish Demba had asked Souleymane to bring, two were left, and Demba gave those to Mor, insisting he bring them home to his sisters after he sold the remaining *bonga* fish they had caught to Basmah. Although he had lost all the money his family had a few weeks ago, fishing was slowly starting to replace it. With each day out on the water a few more francs were added to their tomato can.

But now for every few coins he received from Demba, only one went into the can, while the others went into a hole Mor had dug near his bed mat in case the Danka Boys returned. With a little over seven weeks until their aunt's return, he had managed to save over 1,900 francs again and still keep them fed. It was a long way away from what Amina needed, but it was a start. He had to stay optimistic.

There had also been no sign of the Danka Boys. He'd been lucky to avoid them each day and at night by staying near Tanta Coumba, but he knew his luck would probably run out soon. Cheikh's warning had told him that.

Mor shook off these thoughts and hurried across the dirt in the market, lugging the big blue bucket.

"I'm here," Mor said, rushing over to Basmah's stall as water sloshed around him.

"Take a breath. I'm in no rush." Basmah took the bucket from him. "Now tell me all about your day."

"I can't stay long. I have two gigantic fish for my sisters." He lifted the newspaper that contained the fish. "Souley-mane's best catch." Then he dropped his arms hastily, looking for Papis's spies.

He gulped down a rush of air and went into his tale of the fishing day. When he came to the end, he knew he had left little out.

"Well, you've had quite a full day." Basmah placed a

bulging clear plastic pouch filled with ripe *sidèmes* and a wedge of bread into a paper bag. Mor remembered when he used to pluck the fruit off the tree with his *yaay*, ready to nibble the small, orangey-reddish-brown globes before he'd even gathered a handful. "I didn't know you could fix *gaal* motors. Can you fix refrigerators, too?"

Mor shrugged and grinned. "I can always try."

"You're full of surprises," she chuckled, taking a few coins out of her drawstring bag to give to Mor. "The next time mine goes kaput, I'll be calling you. Bring these *sidèmes* to your sisters." She patted the bag. "They are sweeter than the oranges they picked this morning. And tuck this money somewhere safe. You and Demba have given me some fine fish to salt this week."

Mor scanned the area. "Could you keep it for tonight? I will come for it tomorrow." She glanced around as well before slipping it back in her bag.

"*Jërëjëf,*" he said, then hesitated, having an idea. He grabbed a few coins from his pocket. "Can I have two of your smaller dried fish, please?"

"My, aren't you hungry today." Grinning, Basmah picked two medium-size fish out of the packing crate.

"The smaller ones will do." Mor pointed to the tiniest dried fish on the table. They looked like peanuts compared with the larger ones.

"You still have room for even these after all you've eaten today?"

"Maybe." Mor lowered his eyes. He hated misleading her but knew he should keep the real reason for the fish a secret. He felt her watching him and would not meet her stare.

"I guess you are a growing boy." Basmah packaged up the fish. "Is everything okay, my new handyman?" she asked, a note of concern in her voice. "Your face has clouded."

Mor tried to smile, despite the anxious turn of his belly. Feeling uncomfortable under her gaze, he blurted out, "Yes, I am fine, but it's getting late. My sisters—"

"Okay then." Basmah waved him away.

"Thank you again for the fruit and the bread," he said, and dashed through the market.

Mor sprinted around the corner, then stopped abruptly, peeking back around the wall. Although he was on the lookout, he wanted to make sure no one was headed his way. The Danka Boys had the ability to find whatever they searched for, and Mor hoped they'd changed their minds about searching for him. He wished more than anything that Cheikh was wrong about everything. He stuffed his earnings from Demba into his shoe, then ripped open the bag of *sidèmes*, and a couple of them rolled to the dirt before he could catch them. The rest he dropped into his back pockets, leaving a few in the bag. His cutoff shorts had been a grown man's jeans, so the pockets were deep and spacious. He tore off a large piece of bread, took it from the bag, and wrapped it in the newspaper along with Souleymane's fried fish and the remaining french fries.

Grease instantly soaked through the paper. He lifted his oversize T-shirt and slid the newspaper into the band at the back of his pants, and tugged his belt cord tighter, securing it against his skin. Then he pulled his shirt back down. The bread was ridged and the fish were oily against his bare back.

Leaving the tiny dried fish, the rest of the bread, and the last of the *sidèmes* in the paper bag, Mor crumpled it closed and started toward home.

He shuffled two steps and felt ridiculous. He was about to remove the fish and bread, but then he thought it was better to be a little slicked with grease than to have his sisters hungry if he ran into trouble.

Every few steps he glanced over his shoulder, sure someone was following him. But no one paid him any attention. When he reached his path, his shoulders relaxed a bit, but they shouldn't have. Papis, Diallo, and another Danka Boy he didn't recognize strolled onto the path in front of him, blocking his way. Mor fiddled with the sides of his T-shirt, pulling it down, even though it was already below his knees.

"So, you thought I had forgotten about you?" Papis did not pause for an answer. "Or did you think I would get tired of waiting?"

Mor focused on the scar running over Papis's eye. The first few times Mor had seen it, he'd thought it just made Papis look tougher, scarier, but now Mor saw it differently. Papis had knowingly taken the slice of a whip to protect a friend. Even though Mor stared at the healed-over gash, it was still hard to believe Papis had gotten it trying to protect someone, not because he was the cause of a fight.

"Eh, grab his bag," Diallo said, nudging the other Danka Boy.

Papis's hand lashed out, slapping the air to silence him. Neither of the boys reached for the bag.

Mor glanced around, wondering if Cheikh watched from a distance.

Suddenly Papis snatched the bag himself and opened it. He took out a *sidème* and bit at its skin, popping it in his mouth. Then he spit out the nibbled-around pit like a bullet. "This is all you have?" He shoved the bag in Mor's face. Mor stood perfectly still. "How do you not have more fish than this?"

Mor cleared his throat. "I already ate my piece with Demba." A wad of saliva slid down his throat. "That's for my sisters. Can I have it back?" He held his hand out but was careful not to move too much for fear the greasy paper from the fried fish would slide down his back and out the bottom of his shorts.

"This isn't for them," Papis said, and smirked.

"That isn't enough for anyone," Diallo blurted out, looking over Papis's shoulder.

"Shut up," Papis snapped, sending Diallo a frosty scowl. He shoved his hand back into the bag. "You know this snack is for me." Papis bit a chunk out of one of the dried fish, then chased it down with a corner of bread. "And when I come back"—a mash of half-chewed food was visible when he spoke—"you better have more. I want my fish if you are not joining us."

"This is a waste, man," the Danka Boy next to Diallo said. "I told you we should've grabbed him on the beach when he still had those buckets with the *doff* dread."

"*Nopil*, Laye."

Wait, they'd watched him and Demba? Even though he'd sensed they had, hearing it was true unsettled him even more.

"Papis was too busy with that girl selling flowers, weren't you, Papis?" Diallo laughed, as if sharing a joke.

Papis snarled. Diallo's smirk vanished.

Papis turned back to Mor, his expression menacing. "Your ears seem to have been filled with wax. Or you were still sleeping. . . ." Papis took a step closer to Mor. The heat of his breath hit Mor's cheek. "But I know I told you to bring those fish to me."

"They weren't for you," Mor said, standing his ground. "I need to feed my sisters. Why do you keep bothering me?"

Papis smiled. "Why not?" He stared at Mor, his smile growing. "From now on do as I say. You will not go to the market. You will come to me. Got that?" He nudged Mor in the chest, seeing if he understood. The greasy newspaper crinkled and Mor hoped it would not slip down his back. "I can be a friend or an enemy. You must choose who you wish to see. It could all go so much easier if you listen to your brother and stomp the paths with us. You would get a share."

You are a clever player in this game. With a magician's sleight of hand, you are outwitting your opponent. But is that enough?

This time his father's observation did not help Mor feel better. It actually confused him further. Did his *baay* want him to join the Danka Boys? Or did he want him to find a better way to defeat them?

"Eh." Papis snapped his fingers in Mor's face, knocking his father's words away. "Make a choice." He dropped the head of the dried fish into his mouth. The tail rested on his lip for a split second, then disappeared.

"Look," Diallo snorted, pointing at Mor's thigh.

Mor glanced down.

A trail of fish grease ran down his leg like an army of ants. Mor slammed his legs together, mashing the oily trail against his inner thighs.

"Don't stand there dampening the earth." Papis raised an eyebrow. "Go find a tree to shield you."

The other Danka Boys shook with laughter.

In the distance Fatima appeared at the door of their home. Then she raced for her brother. "You're that mean boy. Get away from him," she shouted, pushing through the gap between the Danka Boys' elbows before Mor could grab her. Her hands were balled tight. Their target: Papis.

"No, Tima," Mor said as her little fists collided against Papis's hip.

"You ruined Mina's book. And you hurt my brother," she yelled. "I don't like you."

The Danka Boys laughed harder.

Mor rushed forward, grabbing at Fatima's hand, worried the fish would fall out. He could imagine how angry Papis would be if he knew Mor had tried to deceive him, but he had to protect Tima.

"You better stop her before I grow tired and squash the bug that buzzes around me," Papis warned.

Fatima's little fists flew wildly, slipping from Mor's grip.

Then Amina's voice broke through the laughter. "*Yamal*, Tima. *Yamal!*" Amina barreled across the dirt. The stick she held tipped with paint dropped from her hand. She shoved past Diallo to reach for her sister, pushing against Papis's chest. He didn't budge. Her eyes darted to Mor, then back to Papis.

"You better get control of these two." Papis knocked past Amina and Fatima, dropping another *sidème* into his mouth. "We'll see each other again, Mor Fall." Turning, Papis flicked his fingers above his head, and the other Danka Boys trotted behind him like obedient dogs.

"Stay away from my brother," Fatima yelled again. Tears ran down her cheeks.

Amina's eyes, which were rimmed with dark circles, stayed trained on Mor. "She could've been hurt."

Fatima's tiny fists were still clenched at her sides.

Mor stood very still. Again. There would be no more breaks. And no certainty of when the Danka Boys would come. They were like worm lizards slithering out of burrowed holes whenever it suited them.

"Mor." Amina elbowed him. "Did you hear me? She could have been hurt."

"But she wasn't." Mor blinked, knowing that wasn't what Amina wanted to hear, but it was all he could think to say. "I'm sorry." He looked around the path, surprised only a few children had come to their doorways to see what the commotion was.

Amina sulked, holding Fatima close to her as Mor turned for home. He felt her eyes locked on his back. When he and his sisters went inside their home, their shadows danced on the walls behind the light of the oil lantern. Amina didn't stop to take a breath as Mor stepped over a pile of rocks, sharpened sticks, and two bottle caps of paint.

"I think we should tell Tanta Coumba."

"We can't," Mor said. He thought of Cheikh and the other Danka Boys. "It would bring more trouble. There are too many of them. They seem to multiply each day. If it's not one, it'll be another. We have to find a different way. She might tell our *bàjjan* to come get us."

"First he took our money, then our breakfast and lunch. And now he has taken our dinner, too, and still he wants more. He will not stop. What did you do to make him act this way?" Amina's voice filled the space.

"Why do you think I'm the cause?" Mor was hurt. "Maybe I'm just unlucky."

"Maybe you are," she said under her breath. "But now so are Tima and me." She sat on the floor by a pile of rocks with painted faces.

Mor wanted to ask about them, but he didn't. "Don't worry," he said, lowering his voice as if Papis could hear. "He hasn't gotten our dinner today." Despite everything, a small grin lifted the edges of his lips.

He raised his shirt and took the grease-soaked newspaper from his back. He laid it on the floor and opened it. The bread had absorbed most of the oil from the french fries and the fish, but it still looked delicious to Fatima, whose eyes grew. Even Amina stopped her shouting long enough to watch Fatima kneel before the food. They hadn't had french fries in a long, long time.

Amina stared at the food.

"You tricked them, you tricked them." Fatima bounced on her knees. "You fooled those bad boys." She pulled one of the smushed fries from the others. "Mmmm."

Mor could see the anger softening in Amina's eyes.

"Come on, Mina." Fatima pulled on her sister's arm, chomping on the french fry. "Mor brought *frittes*."

Fatima fed Jeeg a fry.

"Clever trick," Amina said with a smirk, pulling off a piece of the grease-soaked bread.

Mor started to sit, then sprang up, rolling onto his side.

Amina lifted the newspaper before he smashed the food.

"I almost forgot," he said, pulling the *sidèmes* from his back pockets.

Amina actually laughed first. Though in the back of his mind Mor couldn't help but think of the Danka Boys.

29

BUT I can do it," Mor said several days later when he and Demba returned from their bike ride. Demba was insisting that Mor go home early, but Mor knew it wasn't right not to finish his job. "I *always* go. I'll see my sisters after."

Mor wasn't sure if he'd run into the Danka Boys, but he didn't want Demba to have to either. They were his problem, and they were expecting their fish. He just hadn't figured out how he'd handle it.

Demba held the bucket of fish for Basmah at his side. Mor went to reach for it and Demba did not pull away.

"Hours are uncertain. And days hold no promises."

Mor let his hand fall. He wasn't sure, but he thought

Demba was talking about not having enough time with Idrissa. Mor had nothing else to say.

He slunk away, glancing back, wanting to warn Demba to look out for the Danka Boys, but he didn't. Watching Demba go, he tried to reassure himself that the Danka Boys would never cross him.

His aunt's return was almost six weeks away, and he'd been so busy trying to get the coins he and his sisters needed to show her they could build a life on their own that they hadn't had much time together. And as the summer days ticked by, Mor agreed with Demba: Days didn't hold any promises, and he wanted to make sure he and his sisters spent as much time as they could as a family, in case there were not many chances left.

When he got back to his sisters, the salt-touched air in the *barak* felt light. Amina sang under her breath while Fatima talked to her rock dolls. Cut fabric lay on the floor in piles.

"Let's go to the market and get a papaya. I have a taste for a juicy papaya, don't you?" He tickled Fatima until she squirmed. "Tomorrow is Friday, let's start my time to relax early."

"Really? I want one." Fatima dropped the piece of cloth she held and jumped to her feet, pulling Jeeg. "You can have some too," she said into her ear.

Mor went over to the sleeping mats and pulled them from the corner. Dug out low in the wall was a sliver of a hole. Squirreling his fingers inside, he yanked out a plain brown pouch that blended with the dirt floor. He sat cross-legged, with his back to his sisters, and poured all the coins onto the floor in front of him. Every day he did the same thing when he returned home with new coins in his pocket; he counted them up—2,560 francs in all. He still had a ways to go before he reached the 9,200 francs Amina needed, plus what they required for food. But he refused to give up, even though it all seemed impossible. And he wouldn't stop trying, not even on the day their *bàjjan* returned.

"What are you doing?" Fatima peeked over his shoulder.

"Nothing, Tima." He scooped the coins back into the pouch and added the 300 francs he'd just received from Demba to the rest.

"We won't have any money in that ditch if you keep spending it on such luxuries." Amina coughed. She did not look up from the fabric she was cutting when Mor turned around after placing the mats back in front of his hiding place. A tiny piece of crinkled paper that was once a candy bar wrapper rested near her knee. It had a list written in Amina's careful hand.

barak-brown and yellow yellow, red, blue-brown
grass-green yellow and blue-green
goats-white red and white-pink
people-brown and pink yellow and red-orange
sky and sea-blue
flowers-every color

When she noticed Mor staring at it, she carefully folded it over. The logo for a chocolate bar, one Mor was sure Amina had never tasted, showed. Then she slipped it into her pocket.

"What's that?" Mor asked.

"Just some notes for myself. Nothing important to you." She coughed again, pulling at a thread in the fabric she stitched. Then she looked up at her brother. "What you should be concerned with is spending our coins on a papaya."

"I am saving," he said. He crawled under the pallet behind her and dragged out the Dieg Bou Diar tomato can. "And I get a little more every day. If there are fish in the sea, we will have more." Mor smiled, dropping thirty francs into the decoy can. "Every day we get closer to getting you in that fancy green uniform."

Mor could tell Amina was trying not to smile at the idea, but her cheeks lifted even though she looked a little tired.

The Danka Boys hadn't been back inside their *barak* since stealing Jeeg, but Mor wasn't willing to risk it. He rewrapped the tomato can and hid it back under the pallet. He'd learned it was better not to let his guard down, but it had been a good morning on the water, and he wanted to enjoy the rest of the day with his sisters. They'd just have to stick to the busiest paths and hope the Danka Boys had other things occupying their attention.

"Come on, Mina. We will just get one to share," he said, coming out of his own thoughts.

Amina looked around at the piles of fabric cutouts all over

the floor. "All right. All right," she said, and stretched. "I guess I am done for the day." She packed her materials in the plastic bag and followed Mor and Fatima outside.

On the way to the market they laughed and joked about all the stories Mor had heard from the other fishermen that week on the water and the ones Amina and Fatima knew from being at the village well. Some of the other fishermen had begun to greet Demba like a friend. And one had even had Mor check a pesky problem with his engine. Although Mor had not been completely sure how to fix it, he'd known exactly what the problem was, when the fisherman's mechanic had not.

"Hey. What's so funny?" Mor jumped, then turned and saw Oumar coming up beside them. His soccer ball was tucked under one arm.

"Hey," Mor still laughed. "I was telling them about something Demba said."

"Oh, that *doff* fisherman." Oumar's smile dropped. "You're always with him now."

"He's not crazy," Mor shot back, his smile gone as well. "He's my friend."

Oumar shook his head as if he pitied Mor. "You want to go play *le foot*?"

Mor hesitated for a second. He glanced at Amina and Fatima. He knew that look of disappointment on their faces all too well. "No," he finally said. "We're going to the market."

Fatima's face instantly lit up again.

"You'd rather do that than play?" Oumar held up his ball and looked at Mor as if he'd grown two fish heads from his neck.

Fatima pushed closer to her brother and brushed her cheek against his arm.

"Yep," Mor said, and meant it. "Another time, Oumar."

Oumar stopped in the street, watching them go.

Mor continued his story about Demba as they walked on, Fatima giggling the whole way. But when they got to the stall at the end of Basmah's row, all their laughter stopped.

"Oh no," Mor said, sprinting across the market to Basmah's stall. He reached her ahead of his sisters.

A trickling of juice and seeds from squashed tomatoes and split melons dribbled over the lip of her table onto the ground. Basmah crouched down, shoveling the destroyed fruit into a plastic bag with two pieces of cardboard, while the vendor next to her stall swept up a scattering of spilled dried beans.

Mor held open the plastic bag as she dumped the soppy chunks of food inside. Soon his sisters were close at his side to help.

"What happened?" he asked. Though he knew he hadn't been clever or lucky. He hadn't escaped the Danka Boys.

"Street boys, that's what." She braced her hand on the corner of her table for leverage and got up. "Those runaway *talibés* are getting more and more out of hand. They ignore their *serigne*'s teachings and become reckless and a danger."

She patted Mor on the shoulder after he tied the stuffed bag closed. "Why can't every child be more like you and your sisters?"

He and Amina flung each other looks of worry. He tried to smile, but a sickening feeling lodged inside him. He and his sisters continued to clear away the damaged fruits and vegetables as Basmah spoke.

"One minute they are little boys running around with tomato cans, asking for bits of food and donations for their *daaras*, then the next a few bad seeds have sprouted and are robbing me of all my fish." She fanned herself with her hand.

"They took all of them?" Mor surveyed the mess. He hoped it was a bad coincidence her stall had been rifled only days after Papis's warning, but he didn't think so. "Did they take anything from anyone else?" He nodded toward the vendor still picking up handfuls of beans.

"No. Sidy reached out to grab one, but the boy was too quick. He knocked Sidy's table as they escaped." She tilted her head at the empty spot where her salted fish had been. "They came with buckets of their own."

Before Basmah had even finished her sentence, Fatima tugged Mor's arm.

"Tell her about the mean boys," she said, cupping her hands around her mouth as she tried to whisper. Though her hushed words sounded louder than the howl of a jackal.

"Shh." Mor put his finger to his lips. "That's our secret."

"Why? You should show her how you tricked them.

Maybe she can put all the fish in her *boubou*." Fatima giggled, probably envisioning Basmah with a tableful of fish stuffed in her dress.

Basmah came up beside them. "Don't have such a long face. It will not happen again," she said with a confidence Mor wished he shared. "There are only a few of them against all of us." She swept her arms around her, and the vendors near her nodded, as if hanging on her every word. "They caught me asleep once, but they never will again. Besides, you will bring me more fish to stock my table tomorrow. *Incha'Allah.*"

"But—" Mor began.

"But nothing." Basmah took the undamaged oranges Amina held out to her and placed them with the other salvaged fruit on her table. She scooped up a handful of *sidèmes* and gave them to Fatima.

Fatima bit into a plump one. "Thank you," she managed between bites. "It is so sweet. Even better than the ones Mor stuffed in his pockets." She offered Mor one.

"Pockets?" Basmah searched Mor's face. "I gave you a perfectly good bag."

"He almost sat on them too," Fatima laughed, her mouth crammed with two more.

Basmah looked between Mor and his sisters, confused. Mor wished Fatima would shovel all the *sidèmes* into her mouth.

"That's enough, Tima." Amina stepped toward their sister. "Save some for when we get home."

"But what if those boys come back and take them?" Fatima

asked, shoving another one into her mouth, spitting the little pit on the ground. "I want to finish them now."

Mor rummaged through his pocket and pulled out a couple of coins, offering them to Basmah.

She glanced at them, then back at Mor.

"For the *sidèmes*." He knew she would not take the money, but he truly wished he could pay her for all her stolen fish.

"Put your money away. It's no good here today." She unfolded a handkerchief she had tucked up her sleeve and wiped her forehead and under the front of her head wrap. "I think I may close for the day. I don't have much left. Besides, my spirit is dampened."

Mor lowered his eyes. "We can help," he offered, pulling one of the packing crates from under her table.

"No, I won't hear of it. You've already done enough. Go enjoy your evening. I'm sure we've all had a long day in the sun."

"But we didn't get the papaya." Fatima swallowed down the last of the *sidèmes* in her mouth.

Mor nudged her, and Amina pulled her into her arms. Fatima twisted, pulling away. Basmah, with her back to the commotion, grabbed another crate and set it on the edge of the table. Then she took the one Mor held as well, before hugging him to her chest. He stiffened, then relaxed. She hugged like his mother. Strong and suffocating, yet warm and cozy all at once, smelling of the same jasmine-scented lotion his *yaay* used to buy in the market.

"Sorry," he whispered into the crook of her arm, the words getting caught in the folds of her dress.

"Now go, I insist," she said.

When she dropped her hands, Mor moved away quickly, shielding his face. He raked the backs of his hands across his cheeks and over his eyes. There were too many tears to go unnoticed, so he pressed his shirt against his cheeks.

"Dust," he said. Although no one had asked.

After his sisters had each hugged Basmah, she picked up an undamaged papaya off her table and dropped it into a bag, winking at Fatima.

"Sorry," Mor whispered again.

When they left her, neither he nor Amina felt like going anywhere but home. Mor waited for Amina to say something, but she never did. She focused on the dirt as she held Fatima's hand. He knew her silence meant she was truly worried but that she did not want to frighten Fatima.

As they plodded home, a chain of girls with linked arms skipped down the street ahead of them. Fatima's friend Rama was leading the march.

"Let me go," Fatima whined, struggling to pull loose of Amina's hand.

"We need to get home," Amina answered.

"Why? There is nothing there but you and Mor. I want to go with my friends." With her free hand, Fatima tried to peel Amina's fingers from around her own.

"She'll be fine, Amina." Mor glanced around. "At least one

of us should enjoy this night." He understood Fatima's need to play with her friends. With his days full of fishing and worrying after his sisters and Jeeg, he had not laughed freely with his own friends over a soccer ball for a while. And he missed it. He thought of how he had dismissed Oumar and felt guilty. Sometimes he wondered if all his sacrifice was worth it. He wanted to have fun too.

"Go," Amina said, sounding tired. Beads of sweat dotted her upper lip and hairline. "Stay near. And only for a little while. On your way home untie Jeeg from the post by Tanta Coumba's door."

Fatima flitted down the street after her friends.

Once Fatima was gone, Amina wasted no time.

"You know it was those boys," she said, watching Fatima run, then skip, then run, dancing with Rama in the street. "They did that to Basmah." Her long, reedy arms hung at her sides. "You should have told her."

"It might not have been them." He knew he told a lie. He shoved his hand deep in his pocket. Besides the few coins he'd brought out to pay for the papaya, he felt lint and the hole that had started out the size of a pea. "We don't know."

Amina stepped in front of him, halting his steps. "Your lies will not make it so. You know it was them. It is unfair not to tell her. They stole in a crowded market. They can do more."

Mor kicked the dirt; then he stopped, gawking past her.

"You have nothing to say?" Amina continued, wiping her lip with the back of her hand. Then she turned, following her brother's gaze. In the shadow of a path Diallo stood grinning next to the Danka Boy they called Laye. Amina went still as a stone, like her brother.

The Danka Boys watched them, as lions observe their prey. Neither Mor nor Amina took a breath.

When Diallo's hand flung something from his side, they jumped and he snickered.

A salted fish landed at their feet. "Tomorrow." He bucked his chin toward the fish, then elbowed Laye, signaling for them to leave. They backed away, keeping an eye on Mor and Amina until the path curved and they were gone behind a woven fence.

Amina and Mor stared after them. The bag of fruit rustled as Amina squeezed her hand tighter around it. The happy voices of women coming up the road behind them pushed against their fear.

"Ah," Tanta Coumba said as they turned. "The lovely faces of Awa's children." Her smile slipped a bit once she reached them. "My goodness. Why such sagging expressions?"

Out of the corner of his eye Mor saw how ashen Amina looked. He hadn't really noticed it before. The usual dark circles under her eyes were even darker. Sweat sat on her hairline.

"You do not look at all well." The other women with Tanta Coumba gazed with concern.

Mor stared down at the salted fish, covered in dirt, that had landed near the front of Cheikh's old shoe.

Tanta Coumba noticed the fish too. "Is that what troubles you? A little fish? I'm sure we can find you something else to eat."

She rubbed Amina's back. "No fish should get you this down."

"We should get home," Mor whispered. "We have more to eat." He pointed to the bag in Amina's hand.

"Yes, yes. That would be good, I think. Go and rest. And if you need anything, you know where I am." She looked back at Amina. "It will all be fine, child."

As they left Tanta Coumba and her friends, Mor hoped her words were true, but hardly anything had been fine in the last few minutes.

30

MOR thought he was falling and tried to flap his arms like a bird, but they were somehow glued to his sides. Choking on air as a surge of salt water launched from his throat, he realized with a fright that he was drowning. But the sea was not just rushing in around him; it was coming out of him. He was choking, sprawled across the sand. He hacked and hacked, but the salty water did not stop flowing. When he tried to stand, he kept slipping. He had no feet. Instead there was a long, slippery tail, with iridescent scales stretching up his torso.

"It's ready for the skillet," someone spoke with a voice as gravelly as sandals grinding seashells.

Before Mor could turn his head, something grasped his

tail. Finding himself swinging upside down, hovering over a snapping pan of oil, he tried to scream. But all he could do was suck as water spilled from his mouth.

"Look at this *dieune*," the person laughed. "It thinks it will get away."

"All fish do. Just gut it and stuff it and let its eyes pop in the grease," a deeper voice said.

Mor wiggled and waggled, trying to break free. The voices kept laughing. Then, when he thought he had swung loose, he realized too late that the person had released his grip and that he was headed straight for the sparking pot. . . .

"Ahhh," Mor screamed, and leaped from his mat. His face was bathed in sweat. The last image he remembered before flinging open his eyes was that of the dark-brown faces of Cheikh and Papis cackling as he splashed, tail twitching, scales burning, into a pool of scorching oil.

Mor glanced around in a panic. Fatima sucked her thumb, something she hadn't done much of since their *yaay* had smeared a bitter berry paste on it while she slept. He envied her peaceful slumber when his was a churning storm. He glanced over at Amina, expecting to see her curled with the pages of her book that she'd tried to mend with string and a needle, but instead she tossed back and forth, sweat covering her face and shoulders. She seemed to be faring far worse than him in her own nightmare.

"Mina, wake up. You're having an unhappy dream." Mor

reached to nudge her, but when he touched her skin, he drew his hand back as if he'd touched hot coals. Her arm was a flame. And her forehead was no better. "Mina, get up."

Worry flooded through him as his sister continued to toss across the pallet, her hair spiking in every direction. Something was wrong.

Shaking her, he tried again to wake her, but all she did was mumble words he couldn't understand. He rushed over to the water bowl and scooped some into a cup. Fatima kicked out and grumbled, not wanting to budge from her sleep as Mor moved her aside. Lifting Amina's head, Mor tried to get her to drink, but water pooled at her closed lips. It spilled down her cheeks.

"Wake up, Mina. Wake up," Mor shouted. His voice disturbed Fatima's sleep.

"Leave Mina alone," Fatima whined. "We want to sleep." Her head flopped back down next to her sister's.

"Get up, Tima, and go get Tanta Coumba. Something is wrong with Mina."

Fatima rolled onto her side, falling back to sleep.

"Tima, go get Tanta Coumba. Mina is sick."

Fatima's eyes sprang open then and she turned to her sister. "Mina?" She nudged her sister, then looked at Mor, worried when Amina didn't wake up. Amina always woke before Fatima. "What's wrong with her?"

"I don't know. Just go."

"Is she going to be okay? She has to be okay. Wake up, Mina." Amina's head jerked as Fatima continued to yank her.

And again Amina muttered something neither of them understood.

"Go." Mor pushed Fatima. She scrabbled off the pallet and ran out the door.

He kept touching Amina. Her skin was hot like a flame. "Wake up, Mina," he begged. "Wake up."

He had seen this before when his *yaay* first got sick so many years before. There was nothing they could do for her then, but he hoped there was something he could do for Amina now. He ran and pulled a cloth from the folded stack on the shelf and poured water into a bowl, like his *baay* had done all those years ago for his *yaay*. He soaked the cloth in it. When he turned to race back to his sister, their *yaay* was sitting on the pallet, Amina's head in her lap. Even though Amina still twisted and groaned, she seemed almost calmer.

"Yaay," Mor breathed. He knelt at their side. The cloth dripped on the dirt floor. "What's wrong with her? Does she have the same sickness as you?" He asked questions he knew he would not hear answers for. "Please don't let her go away too." As he laid the damp cloth over his sister's forehead, he heard two sets of hurried footsteps rushing for their door.

"Mina's not going to die, is she?" Fatima cried. "Oh

please, oh please don't let her. She promised she would always stay with me." Fatima's crying entered the *barak* before she or Tanta Coumba did.

Tanta Coumba swept in, no head wrap on her head. "What has happened to our dear, feisty Mina?" she asked Mor while rushing toward a restless Amina. "Does she not wake?"

Mor shook his head, not wanting to move from Amina's or his *yaay*'s side.

Tanta Coumba eased him over but did not make him get up.

"Fetch me some fresh water from the well, and that bowl so I can soak more cloths in it. Spark a fire and boil me some hot, hot water." Tanta Coumba barked orders as, thankfully, Naza and Oumy rushed in after her. Naza held baby Zal against her hip as she grabbed the bucket for the well and was off.

Mor knelt, paralyzed, not sure what to do first. He kept staring at his sister, who looked so much like their *yaay* had when she had lain on that same pallet, sick. He had to look away. Worry nibbled at his insides.

"Grab me those cloths." Tanta Coumba snapped him to attention, her fingers clicking in his face. "Be quick. I will need some roots to make a strong tea."

"But what is wrong with her?" Mor asked, still not moving.

"It looks as if a fever has taken hold of her. The stress has been too much."

Mor instantly felt ashamed and wanted to run from the *barak*, knowing he was the cause of her suffering. He had drawn the Danka Boys' attention, and it had been at his pleading that they'd told their aunt to go. He stared at his sister, their mother's shimmering hand cradling her face. "The rags," Tanta Coumba asked again, holding her hand out.

As Mor reached up to grab all the cloths from the shelf, small misshapen pieces of fabric in every color sailed to the ground. They mashed into the dirt as he stepped on them, handing Tanta Coumba a few cloths.

Naza, who was a year younger than Mor, stepped back into the room, the well water balanced in a bucket on her head, while her little brother lay sleeping tucked on her hip. Mor rushed to help her take the bucket off her head, nearly tripping on his mat, which almost sent the water crashing to the dirt. Naza quickly steadied it. Only a few drops made splotches across the floor. She laid Zal down in the corner next to Jeeg, wrapping Mor's bedsheet around him.

Every inch of the *barak* was being used. Mor felt in the way. He tried to hold Fatima in his arms, but she pushed away from him, wanting to be near Amina.

"Go care for Jeeg," Tanta Coumba whispered. She guided Fatima toward the goat. "She is worried too."

Still crying, Fatima dashed to snuggle with Jeeg, leaving Mor standing alone. He stared at everyone around him. What could he do for them?

He stepped into the yard and saw that Oumy, who was Fatima's age, had built a fire, heating water to boil. She looked up at Mor, then continued breaking sticks to place on the fire. He turned back to the doorway but knew he just took up space in the small *barak*. Slumping to the ground on the outside wall, he pushed his feet against the dirt.

Some of Fatima's rock dolls lay before him. He noticed more rocks had been added to her collection. She didn't just have their family, now she had stones painted with grass, flowers, fish, and the sea. There was even a little *gaal*. Then he noticed the flat reddish-brown stone Demba had given him that night in the rain. A dark-green cloth was wrapped around its middle, and when Mor picked it up and turned it in his hand, the face of Demba stared up at him. Amina had even glued straw to make his long, thick dreadlocks. A weaverbird nest was on his head. She had paid attention to all the stories Mor had told. Most of the time, he thought she hadn't been listening.

"Demba," he said out loud, holding the rock in his hand. He jumped up, still cradling it, and ran. "I will be back," he yelled to Oumy as she dropped leaves into the pot. His bare feet crushed against pebbles and trash as he ran, but he didn't care. He had to find Demba.

The only problem was Mor did not know where Demba lived. He ran to the beach, knowing he wouldn't find him at such a late hour, but he didn't know where else to go. The shore was deserted, filled with waiting *gaals*. He sprinted across the sand to Amadou's shack, but it was boarded up tight.

The market area was empty and so were the roadways. There was no one around. He spun in the middle of the path, searching. Which way could Demba be?

The last time he couldn't find him, he'd run to the dressmaker's shop, but when he reached it now, all the lights were off. He pulled on the gate, but it was bolted. Then he glanced down the path, remembering Demba's little brother, Idrissa, and the cemetery by the edge of the village. Hadn't the dressmaker said that only Demba and the cemetery lay down that way? Did that mean Demba lived out there too?

Mor raced up the road and cut down a narrow path through the trees to the cemetery.

A ramshackle cabin he'd never paid attention to before, made from secondhand boards, with chipping paint of every color, stood in the distance. The planks were nailed together, camouflaged by brown and green netting and a thatched roof. Demba's black bike, with its box on the back, leaned against the wall with another that was missing a wheel. Mor bolted to the door and banged against the wood.

"Demba, Demba. Are you there?" he shouted. "Wake up. Demba, wa—" As he was about to hammer his fist against the door again, it swung open.

Demba squinted at Mor.

"Mina is sick. You have to come." Mor tugged at Demba's

arm. "Demba, please, Mina needs you. Something is wrong."

Demba freed himself from Mor's grip and backed away from the door.

"I will not be able to take another breath if Mina cannot," Mor pleaded.

Demba had crossed the darkened room in an instant. He stuffed bundles of roots and plants wrapped in cloth into a sack. The shelves around him were crammed with everything from jars of liquid to leafy plants, tweeting uncaged birds, fading magazine pictures of blue skies, and a collection of bottle caps. Photographs of stern-looking people dangled from the makeshift roof on string as well as drooping vines and ribbon. There was even a neat row of worn books off to the side. Tucked at the end, a slim, well-worn book called *Le Petit Prince* caught Mor's eye. Part of the cover was missing.

Demba took the book from the shelf and slipped it inside his bag. A faded red pallet lay on the floor, and Demba reached over it to grab a knife. A golden flower sat in a soda bottle beside it, along with an image of two smiling boys, one in a bright-blue shirt, wet from the sea. It was nailed to the wall where Demba could see it each time he woke. Mor wondered if it was a young Demba in it, with his arm around his little brother, Idrissa, but there was no time to ask. They had to get back to Amina.

Demba took a small mortar and pestle from the wooden table in the corner. On the way out he whistled to the birds flapping around, settling on anything to be closer to him as he passed. When he latched the door closed behind them, the birds came to sit on the open window, then spread their wings and flew as Mor and Demba dashed back to Amina.

31

AS Mor and Demba raced across the night, a cloud-covered moon was their only light. When they reached Mor's family's home, Amina looked no better. Tanta Coumba sat over her, patting a damp cloth to her head. Yaay stroked her hair, while Naza sat with her knees up at the end of the pallet, reading bits and pieces from the ripped pages of Amina's book aloud to her. They each looked up when Mor and Demba entered.

Tanta Coumba gave a weak smile.

Mor glanced around for Fatima, and as if Tanta Coumba read his thoughts and worry, she said, "She is with Oumy at my home. She has cried a river of tears and now needs to rest." Tanta Coumba stood up to greet Demba.

Demba paused for a minute, staring into her eyes like he sometimes did with Mor, as if he could see through to someone's soul. Sometimes Mor felt that he could. Demba bowed his head deep and whispered something Mor couldn't make out, though Tanta Coumba smiled. Demba sat on the wooden stool Tanta Coumba had vacated. He held Amina's limp hand in his. For a second Mor even thought Demba had glanced at the space where his *yaay* rested, as if asking her permission to take care of Amina. He shook the thought from his mind as Demba lifted the damp cloth off her forehead and put the back of his hand against her skin.

"Can you help her?" Mor rushed forward. "Can you make her better?"

Demba did not look his way as he concentrated on Amina.

"What's wrong with her?" Mor asked, hoping one of his questions might get an answer out of his friend. "Will you give her the same root you gave me when I was sick? Is that what she needs? Please make her better." Mor thought if he stopped talking, he might start to cry.

"Easy now," Tanta Coumba said, coming up to him, taking him in her arms. "Give him time. He has only just arrived."

Demba looked around the *barak*, but it was clear from his searching that he couldn't find what he required. Mor spoke up again.

"I can get anything you need," Mor said, breathless, as if he had sprinted two kilometers.

Demba glanced at Tanta Coumba and then at Mor. It was Tanta Coumba's turn to read thoughts.

"Why don't you go and comfort Tima? I am sure what she needs is a brother's hug." She held Mor's face in her hands.

"But you said she cried herself to sleep. I want to stay here with Demba."

"No," Tanta Coumba said firmly. "You will go to Tima. She also needs you now."

Dragging his feet, Mor moped out the door again, wishing there were more he could do. When he got to Tanta Coumba's home, he hovered at the entrance, sweeping away intruding tears. He peeked through the window beside the door. Oumy slept next to baby Zal on a floor mat. But Fatima wasn't sleeping. Her back was to Mor. She was sitting up, her legs pulled close to her chest, with Jeeg next to her. Rock dolls lay around her feet. She held one in her hand and was speaking to it.

"You better get better," she said to the rock, sniffling. "And finish my pebble village. You promised you would. And Oumy is waiting for hers. We collected all the rocks you told us to. So you promise you will wake up and finish?" She made the little rock doll nod its head. "You have to be okay." She held the doll against her chest, tucking up her toes under her *ser* for warmth. She lay back on Jeeg, closing her eyes.

Mor knew she'd have questions as soon as he stepped in the doorway. But he knew he had no answers that would comfort either one of them. So instead he walked away, down a path leading away from Tanta Coumba's house and his. Then he heard the unmistakable scratchy voice of Papis coming from behind another *barak*. Mor pressed himself against the nearest wall. A burly baobab tree could not have stood any stiller than him.

"Why are you trying to stop me?" Papis said. "I thought you didn't want to be seen around here."

"I don't," Cheikh whispered. "And neither should you. He is not worth your trouble. He has no more use than a flea."

The words bit like a thousand red ants at once.

"Why are you trying to keep me away?" Papis asked. His voice drew closer. "Even in your insults, you seem to protect."

Cheikh was silent for a moment. "I just don't think he's worth our time."

"He thinks he can refuse me. Aren't you the one who said you would never again let someone get the best of you?"

Mor strained to hear Cheikh's response. "This is not the same. He's done nothing to us."

"He has refused us. He thinks he is too good for the Danka Boys. This *badola* must learn. He cannot think he has gotten the better of me."

Mor slipped around the back of a *barak* as they approached, shielded by a line of drying *boubous*. He peeked between the stiff fabrics as Cheikh scanned the area. He and Papis continued down the path directly toward Mor's hiding place.

"We are not back at the *daara*, Papis. Let it go." He

stopped, yanking back his friend's shoulder. "Not every turn needs your revenge."

"How can you say that after the cut I took for you?" He thrust his finger at the split but healed-over skin around his eye.

"I will never forget it," Cheikh said flatly. "But he is not one of us. You've taken his fish. It's done."

"I will say when I'm done, not you." Papis was inches away from Cheikh's face. "And I am not."

Mor recognized the threat for what it was, and knew he had to do something before it was too late. Part of him wanted to go back to Amina to protect her, and part of him wanted to charge after them for the worry they had caused her. His feet turned left and right on the path like the beetle he'd pestered so many weeks before.

Your predator is ready to strike; have you assembled your shields? Do you trust that you can defend your castle?

Mor didn't care anymore if he was ready or not. Amina was sick and it was partly their fault. He torpedoed out of the shadow and straight for Papis, arms raised. "Aghhhhhh," he screamed.

At first Papis and Cheikh were startled to see a blur of fists and legs coming at them, but after Mor landed his first blow to Papis's stomach, Papis's fist sent him to the ground. Mor jumped back to his feet, lunging for Papis again.

Papis shoved him down like he was a piece of paper in the wind.

"Aww," Papis chuckled, crouching down, his hand around Mor's throat. "It looks like the worm has come to save us the trouble of finding his hole."

"Leave my family alone!" Mor swung his arms wildly, but Papis easily dodged each of his punches.

Papis laughed at his efforts.

"Come on, man. Let's just go." Cheikh glanced around as he tugged on his friend. But Papis yanked his shoulder forward, freeing himself.

"No." Papis smiled, releasing Mor's throat. Mor was relieved he hadn't squeezed. "The *badola* has come to fight. So fight we will." He stood, mashing his sandal into Mor's chest, grinding it against his shirt. Mor bucked and flailed, trying to get up. He swatted at Papis's leg, but Papis was too strong.

"Get off of me," Mor yelled. "My family has nothing for you. You are a coward for always coming after me. Someone tough does not charge for someone small."

"Ah, so you admit you are nothing but a *liir*."

"You are the baby. But you think I won't fight back? I will." Mor tried to pry Papis's foot off his chest with his hands. "You've hurt my sister." Tears mixed with snot as it trailed into his open mouth. He clawed at Papis's leg, while Cheikh yanked at Papis from behind.

Papis scooped up a handful of dirt, letting it fall into Mor's face and open mouth. "Shut up. I'm getting tired of your yapping."

Mor spit and hacked.

"That's enough," Cheikh demanded, his voice low and firm. Suddenly the pressure of Papis's foot was off Mor's chest. He rolled to his side, gasping.

"Stay down!" Papis kicked him one last time as Cheikh dragged him back. "Let me go!" Papis twisted in Cheikh's arms, knocking Cheikh back.

Cheikh stumbled in the dirt. But he met Papis eye to eye. "Enough."

Papis paused for a moment, staring at Cheikh. Then he hitched up his pants. "Aww, come on. I was just having a little fun with the *khale*."

"I mean it," Cheikh said. "I will go, and I won't come back."

"You will not leave me. Where will you go?" Papis said. "To your mother? To him?" He pointed to Mor, still crumpled in the sand. "They were not there for you when you were sent away. I was. Only me." Papis jabbed at his own chest. "They will not make sure you aren't sent back."

"Enough" was all Cheikh said again before he headed down the path away from Mor, Papis staring after him. Cheikh glanced back as Mor got to his feet. "Go home. There is nothing more for you to do here."

Mor batted at the dirt and tears mingling on his cheeks as he watched the Danka Boys walk away.

32

THE night after Amina fell ill was sleepless for everyone, including Jeeg, who could normally snore through anything. They each watched every twitch Amina made, thinking it was a sign of something: She was getting better; she was getting worse; she needed another cloth under her head; she didn't want a cloth at all. Tanta Coumba and Naza stayed at her bedside, wiping the sweat from her forehead and neck every few hours. They fed her small sips of the broth Demba had made whenever her eyes fluttered under her eyelids. They did not open, but her lips would part a little, taking in the warm liquid. Mor watched as it traveled down her throat, hoping it would instantly make her better.

Tanta Coumba had thought it best for Fatima to stay at her

barak with Oumy and baby Zal, but Mor had refused to be away any longer.

"I have to be with Amina," he had said, and Tanta Coumba had not demanded that he go.

Throughout the day and the next night Amina twisted, mumbled, and moaned. Mor worried it was a song for the dead. She reminded him so much of their mother that he often had to look away or run outside for a moment of air.

Their *yaay* appeared throughout the day, each time a bit dimmer, a bit less sparkly, as if her spirit were not strong enough to stay for every moment. When she wasn't there, Mor paced and waited on Amina as best he could, which meant being faster than Naza to bring the kettle, or racing to Tanta Coumba's house to fetch something she needed for Amina.

He wanted to help his sister. He felt that so much of the blame for her fever was his. If he had not badgered her and their *bàjjan* to stay, she might have been well in the city. Her worry here had become a sickness. They did not have enough money, and he could never seem to defeat the Danka Boys. And even if he did, he imagined they might be like a headless snake that still bit.

There was no escaping them.

"Sit still, child. Sit," Tanta Coumba said to him hours later. "Weaving a path in the floor does no one any good. Why don't you go over and rest at my house, or go and sit by the sea. Fresh air will do you good."

"I can't leave her," Mor said again. He feared that if he took his eyes off her for more than a moment, she would somehow not be there when he returned.

"Very well," Tanta Coumba sighed, turning back to Amina.

When Demba or Yaay's spirit was there, Mor didn't feel as hopeless. Demba brought in the smell of the sea and medicine, and Mor's mother a calm. Resting her daughter's head in her lap when Amina thrashed across the bed the most, Yaay would stroke her fingers against her daughter's cheek, Amina's muscles would relax, and she'd fall back into a deep sleep.

"A waterfall of sleep, wet with strength," Demba said as he stepped into the *barak* on the third morning. "Strength splashes will; will stretches us awake."

"Do you think she will wake today?" Mor asked, hopeful.

"Dews of golden morning alit her palm."

Demba smiled, Mor thought. *Demba never smiles.* Then Mor spun around, following Demba's gaze. "Mina!" He rushed to the bed, where his sister looked around, her hand outstretched, catching a beam of sunlight coming through the window where their *yaay* had been. Her forehead crinkled, beaded with sweat. "You're awake. I knew you would. I knew you wouldn't leave me." He hugged his sister close and she hugged back.

"*Alhamdoulilah!* It is so nice to see you back with us." Tanta Coumba dabbed at the sweat on Amina's forehead. "Your brother has not left your side. He is a good *caameñ.*"

Tanta Coumba rubbed Mor's back. "He has been so worried. As have all of us. How are you feeling, child?"

Amina tried to swallow, but they could tell it was difficult for her. Naza reached the pitcher and cup before Mor could get off bended knee. She handed the cup to him, so he could help Amina. He sat on the edge of the bed where his mother had sat and helped tilt Amina's head so she could drink.

He was so relieved. His sister was still with him.

When the light of morning crept in their door the day after Amina woke, and baby chicks pip-pip-pipped in their neighbor's yard, Demba filled the doorway. Crinkles formed at the corners of his eyes as he watched Amina laughing, busy listening to Naza whisper about news down at the well. He stepped inside, nodded, and held out a small covered pot to Tanta Coumba. She dipped her head slightly as if she already understood.

"Get me some of that steaming water so we can wash her down with these herbs." She waved her hand toward the pot outside on the fire.

Naza scurried off the pallet. She was faster than Mor every time.

"Breeze of butterflies." Demba turned to leave.

"Give me those sheets I have brought from my house." Tanta Coumba pointed at a folded pile in front of Mor.

Mor passed them to her, then he raced after Demba.

"Wait," he called as Demba trotted down the path, his weaverbird swooping in, circling his head.

Demba slowed as Mor caught up to him. "Sweet waves curl from you," he said, then stopped. "Freedom cycles joy. Your day, an open gate."

"But I want to go on the water with you," Mor said, crestfallen. "Amina is busy with Naza. She brings her laughter. And that is what she needs." He dropped his head a little. "Naza is better at it right now than me. I'm the one who's brought her so much worry. Made her sick."

Demba shook his head. "Petals blossom under rock and sun. Beams of sun are you."

He nodded at Mor and continued toward the beach. Mor watched him go. "*Jërëjëf* for making her better," he called after him.

When Mor slumped back to his *barak*, Tanta Coumba and Naza were busy adding Demba's herbs to a pot of water to help Amina bathe. Even though her eyes were open and her strength was coming back, they wanted her to rest.

"Go breathe the fresh air. Your eyes were the first Amina saw when she woke. She knows you are here for her. Now go do something for you," Tanta Coumba said to Mor. "You have too much energy to stay cooped up among us women." She drew the cover over the door closed.

Mor didn't have a chance to protest.

He stepped back from the doorway, a little hurt, but understood Amina needed her rest. He was just happy she had not died. He stood, staring at his home and his freshly swept yard, and wondered what things would have been like if Amina hadn't been okay. But as soon as the thought formed, he shook it out of his mind. Amina was going to get strong again. He knew it.

He was about to turn away from his door when his eyes settled on a bicycle propped up at the side of his *barak*. The same wobbly old bike he'd seen at Demba's the day Amina got sick.

Freedom cycles joy. Your day, an open gate. He remembered Demba's words, taking in every inch of the bike. More rust than paint covered it, but Mor didn't care. He glanced behind him, hoping to see Demba, but he knew he was already gone. Mor bolted for the bike, with its curved handlebar and wide, chestnut-colored seat, a gaping rip splitting its center, exposing yellowed foam.

He grabbed the handgrips, rolling the bike back and forth across the dirt. The bent front wheel had been replaced, and a slightly dented yellow bell had been fastened on the bar. A stick at the back held a triangular cloth that flapped against the air. Green, yellow, and red bands sewn together, with a green star drawn in the middle. His country's flag.

Mor wanted to rush inside and show Amina but wasn't sure if she was already bathing.

"Demba brought me a bike," he yelled at the tarp.

"Ah, so you've found it," Tanta Coumba called. "He left it while you slept by your sister's side. Now go pedal off and tell me how the wheels work." Tanta Coumba poked her head around the door cover, smiling. "And don't come back until your legs wobble like the sea." She flicked her hand through the air, shooing him away. "Be careful," she pleaded before tucking back inside the *barak*.

Mor rushed back to the bike and pushed his foot against the pedal, climbing onto the seat as he always watched Demba do when there were no buckets of fish weighing him down. The bike didn't teeter. Demba had been letting him practice on their long journeys back from outside the village, and now Mor knew why. Demba had held the back of his bike for Mor, giving him lessons. It had become one of Mor's favorite parts of their trips, pedaling around with Demba jogging after him, watching. But this bike was even better than Demba's. Mor could touch the pedals and sit on the seat.

Now he could ride on his own.

The wheels spun across the dirt as he rode away from his home, down the path leading to the beach, and hopefully Demba's *gaal*, to thank him. As he rode, loose pebbles took all his concentration so he wouldn't fall, but by the time he reached the beach, his heart had stopped racing every time one found his wheel. When he got there, though, the beach was deserted. All the fishing boats were gone, including Demba's. The water was sprinkled with vibrant-colored *gaals* and dark-skinned men. Pushing off again, Mor pedaled away from the beach and the market area in search of his friends.

When he rolled up to the clearing where he often played soccer, he saw his friends Oumar and Tapha and another boy sitting under a tree. A cageful of birds rustled at the feet of the boy Mor didn't know. He used to know everyone who came to play.

"Hey," Mor said, bringing his bike to a stop in front of them. "You want to play *le foot*?"

"Where'd you get that?" Oumar said, staring at Mor's rusted bicycle. He tossed his makeshift ball between his hands.

"From Demba." Mor grinned. He wanted to ring the bell but didn't.

"I don't know why you're so happy," Oumar said. "It looks like a piece of junk to me."

"Yeah," Tapha said, "like he found it in a rubbish heap."

Their words hurt.

"It's not so bad," the new boy added before Mor could defend his bike. "I'd take one."

Mor smiled at him.

"Can I try it?" the boy asked.

"Sure," Mor said. "Just be careful."

Oumar smirked. "Like it matters." Then he cupped his hands, calling after the boy who rode it away, "It's a pile of junk, Alassane. Beware it doesn't fall apart as you ride."

Mor couldn't understand why Oumar was being so cold.

"Why are you here, anyway?" Oumar continued. "You never have time for us anymore. You are always rushing off to your sisters or that *doff* Demba." His eyes followed Alassane on Mor's bike.

"Don't call him that," Mor demanded.

"That's his name." Oumar and Tapha laughed.

But before Mor could say another word in Demba's defense, they heard a scream.

Mor whipped around, expecting to see the little boy in the dirt, his bike on top of him, but instead Alassane was being yanked off the bike.

It was the Danka Boys. Papis held on to the handlebar as Alassane scrambled across the dirt, getting up.

Alassane stepped sideways, gaining his balance. The Danka Boys surrounded him.

"Give that back. It's not mine," Alassane said, trying to reach for Mor's bike.

Mor was shocked by Alassane's courage, or his stupidity. It was hard to tell. Or maybe he hadn't met the Danka Boys before. A glimpse of that first day on the beach sprang into Mor's thoughts. Maybe if he hadn't been there, Papis wouldn't be bothering him now.

Diallo pushed Alassane to the ground again, as Laye, Abou, and Cheikh came up beside Papis.

"I'm just going to take it for a little spin," Papis said, climbing on. "Our *kharit* won't mind." The word "friend" took a long time coming off his tongue. His eyes flashed to Mor.

How had he known whose bike it was? Cheikh had said

Papis had spying eyes and ears all over Lat Mata, and he believed him.

"Don't worry, he is a good *kharit* to me. We shared a laugh just the other night." Alassane's eyes zipped to Mor, scared, then back to Papis, who straddled the seat.

Papis took off down the path, and it wasn't long before a sandy-colored dog darted across the dirt after him, barking at his heels as he pedaled. The dog kept in step with the bike, at times jumping on its hind legs, as Papis rode away.

Mor wasn't sure if he'd ever see his new bike again. He stared back at Cheikh, who met his gaze. Mor thought he saw him shrug, but then Papis was back, slowing the bike with his foot, since it had no brakes. A dust cloud and the dog trailed along beside him. The dog's pink tongue hung from its mouth. A rope tied around its neck had a small tag hanging from it, made from the aluminum of a soda can folded around an oval of cardboard. Painted on the front were the words **LOKHO NDEYDIOR DANKA DOG.**

"So, you've brought me a bike," Papis said. "How thoughtful of you." He held the bike out, looking it over. "It won't get noticed in a junk heap, but I think I'll keep it."

"That's mine." Mor clinched his jaw. "You can't have it." He went to lunge for the handlebar, but a tight grip held him back.

It was Cheikh. He grabbed Mor like he had Papis a few nights before. Mor yanked his arm free.

"Let go. I want my bike back."

"Uh-uh," Papis warned, wagging a finger in Mor's face.

"It's mine, not yours. You want me to have it, remember?"

"No I don't," Mor said. He pulled on the handlebar. Papis didn't loosen his grip. Neither did Mor. "It belongs to me. It was a gift."

"Some gift," Papis chuckled.

Mor looked around him for help, though he knew he wasn't going to get it from Oumar and Tapha, who stared, mouths wide. Or from Alassane, because he was still being strong-armed by Diallo. Cheikh did not even bother glancing his way a second time.

Mor tugged the handlebar again. This time Lokho snarled and growled, baring the tip of a sharpened tooth. Mor pulled his hand back quick as Papis smirked.

"Why do you make your life so hard?" Papis asked Mor. "It doesn't have to be. You could have the peace you're looking for. We can always use someone tough."

He is a chameleon, changing his guise. Do not be fooled by his sugar. Though his words weave sense, they are really coils to ensnare you. Be stronger than him, my son.

Mor wanted to listen to his father, and believed his words to be true, but he thought of Amina and Fatima and of how tired he was: tired of running, tired of fighting, tired of worry. He just wanted it all to be over.

Mor hesitated as Papis and the others stared at him.

Don't, my son. Have the will of a lion.

But right then Mor felt more like a sheep, following behind a herd of five.

"Okay," Mor sighed, as if finally releasing a boulder he'd spent too much time trying to push uphill. But as the word left his throat, it tasted of bile.

Papis's lip curled up at the corner, and the eyebrow with the healed-over gash lifted. He glanced at Cheikh, who did nothing, then he let go of Mor's handlebar. Mor caught the bike before it fell. Then Papis turned his attention toward Oumar and Tapha, who froze, but his gaze went past them, landing on the birdcage. The birds tried to flap their wings, wishing to be free.

He strode past them to the cage and unlatched it, whistling almost exactly as the *pithis* inside did. "Come out," he said gentler than Mor ever thought Papis could be. Though Mor worried that at any minute Papis would pull one out and squeeze it to death, or worse, stomp on its head. However, all he did was call them out one by one, chirping to each as he flung it toward the sky to fly.

"Hey!" Tapha started to rush over, but Laye stepped in his way.

Papis cut him a look. "Nothing should be caged."

Mor thought of Cheikh and the other Danka Boys but kept silent.

When the last *pithi* had flown from the cage, Papis stood. "And don't you dare call them back," he warned Tapha, before eyeing Oumar. "Now give me that ball." Papis nodded to the bundle of smushed plastic bags wrapped with twine Oumar held in his hand.

Before Oumar could do anything, Laye knocked it loose, trapped it with his foot, and popped it into the air. Papis let it roll down his chest to his knees, where he juggled it off both his thighs, and then from foot to foot. Everyone watched as he moved, controlling the ball in a tight space, until it got a little ahead of him. Cheikh reached out for it with his own foot. They lobbed the ball back and forth, until Papis kicked it high and far. All the Danka Boys charged after it, including Lokho.

Mor, Oumar, Tapha, and Alassane stood watching.

"Are you just going to stand there?" Cheikh called over his shoulder. It was the first smile Mor had seen on his face in a long time. "You're one of us now."

Tapha and Oumar exchanged looks. Mor hesitated, then rested his bike on the tree next to the empty *pithi* cage. He wandered onto the field. Screams and shouts and jokes echoed around him. Light laughter, breezy and free, walled him in on all sides. It unsettled him to think that soon he would be passing the ball to boys who'd caused him so much trouble. That they would be his teammates. But he had no other choice.

The teams naturally fell into place with Papis and Cheikh on one side, and Diallo, Abou, and Laye on the other.

"Mor, you're here." Cheikh tapped the ball with the side of his foot, sending it to Mor like he always had when they were younger. The ball stayed cradled against Mor's foot as if on a short string. He charged for the cement wall, rolling it against the sole of his shoe as he spun past Abou. Only Laye stood between him and the goal. But instead of kicking the ball to bend around him, a move Mor could've done in his sleep, he passed it to Cheikh, who was also waiting to score. The ball sailed through the air, slammed off the wall, and bounced to a stop.

"Yes!" Cheikh pumped his fist in the air.

Mor smiled, remembering the way it used to be, until Diallo started shouting.

"Naw. That wasn't a goal. The goal is over here, not there."

"What kind of field are you making?" Cheikh asked. "Goals aren't in the corner."

"Papis, man." Diallo looked at Papis. "Come on. . . ." But as if he already knew the answer, he turned and stomped away, yelling at Laye instead for not defending the goal better.

"Eh, where are you going?" Papis asked Alassane as he walked down the side of the field, away from the game. "Get over here. And you, too," he called to Oumar and Tapha. "Now!" he ordered when they each hesitated. "You're our posts, now go stand like trees and do not move."

Like tree trunks, they didn't sway, just cupped their hands in front of them. Oumar and Tapha were on either side of Laye, while Alassane and a rock marked off Papis's team's goal.

Suddenly the bright-blue plastic bag wound with twine arced through the air, landing near Mor's feet.

"Why don't you just hand it to him?" Diallo slapped his

twin on the back of his neck. "Go get in our goal. You are no use to us on the field. Laye, come up here with me."

"Oh, shut up," Abou yelled. "You're no better with that stump of a foot."

"Better than you," Diallo shouted, trying to slide-tackle as Mor passed him, but Mor was too quick, leaping over his leg.

A group of small boys playing in the dirt at the side of a *barak* ran over to the field to watch.

After leaving Diallo in the dust, Mor passed to Cheikh, who lobbed it to Papis, who was clearly offside, standing by the goal. He knocked it in with his head. No one complained.

He raised his arms high, screaming, "Gooooaaaal!" Then he tugged at the front of his shirt, running around the field like a professional player after scoring at the World Cup. Mor was surprised he didn't slide to his knees in the dirt.

They continued playing, and Papis continued cheating. Everyone ignored it until he drilled the ball at Oumar and it grazed the outside of his shoe. Papis started jumping around again, arms lifted. Mor wasn't sure if it was the intense heat from the sun or standing still watching others play for over an hour that did it, but Oumar spoke out.

"That wasn't a goal," he grumbled.

"What was that?" Papis rushed him and grabbed up the front of his shirt. "What did you say?"

As if just realizing he'd opened his mouth at all, Oumar tried to take it back. "Nothing. It was nothing. Goal. You scored. Gooooooaaaaaalllll!"

But it was too late.

Papis's hand flew through the air and latched on to Oumar's neck like a serpent, shoving him to his knees, then against the dirt. "No. I think maybe you need a better view. Stay down here so next time you'll know my aim is good." He pushed off Oumar and stood, slapping his hands together. "Let's play."

Mor wanted to say something or do something to help Oumar, but like Oumar had stayed silent earlier, Mor stayed silent then. He had to think of himself and his sisters. He was done crossing the Danka Boys.

Oumar dared not move as Laye and Diallo kicked dirt in his face. "You better not let another ball through!" Diallo warned. Oumar was trapped whatever he did.

As they played, Abou tripped over Oumar again and again. Sometimes on purpose. Sometimes acting like he'd forgotten Oumar was even there. He squished Oumar's hand twice and knocked into his head, laughing. "Oops."

Oumar didn't make a sound, but a tear rolled down his cheek.

Mor tried to ignore it and play the game he loved, but every time he dribbled toward the goal, he felt Oumar's eyes on him, pleading. Instead of charging forward, and easily spinning the ball under his foot, circling around one of the other Danka Boys, he would pass it off to Papis or Cheikh and drop back to defend their goal.

He was miserable. Papis had even found a way to ruin his favorite sport.

Mor watched Cheikh pivot and move. Cheikh lifted the ball on the lap of his shoe and hopped it over Diallo's lunging foot. Diallo punched the dirt when Cheikh scored, then blamed the goal on his brother. Diallo and Abou ran for each other, fighting, and Cheikh had to pull them apart. Mor was actually surprised they had lasted that long before taking a swing at each other.

There was nothing fun about this game.

"Knock it off, you two!" Papis shouted, then pointed at Mor. "You, get over there. Abou, over here. If you are going to fight, I want it for me."

Abou smirked at his brother, who Mor could tell was envious. Diallo bucked at the air, ready for another fight.

On the first play the ball landed at Mor's feet. He knocked it to Laye, who was open, but Cheikh quickly blocked it. Mor raced after his old friend, watching his hips as he dribbled, certain of his fakes and remembering all his old moves. Once Cheikh had left Diallo in the dirt, Mor was able to catch up and face him. When Cheikh went left, so did Mor, swiping the ball from his foot. Mor was off again in the opposite direction. He could hear Cheikh's laugh behind him. Not evil or bitter, but happy, like it used to be when they challenged each other and the better fake-out had won. But Mor had to push the memory to the back of his mind because after he easily slipped around Abou, it was just him, Papis, and open space.

Mor tried to tilt to the right and move to the left, but Papis followed. He pulled the ball back under the sole of his shoe, changing directions, but still Papis was locked to him. He thrust his head one way and swung his body another, but Papis was there. Like with everything else, Papis was an unrelenting opponent.

But at this Mor was better.

He slowed his dribble to a crawl, watching as Papis's shoulders relaxed, ready at any moment to strike out his leg to try to capture the ball. But a second before Papis moved, Mor acted, knocking the ball with the outside of his foot. He dodged Papis and sent the ball sailing ahead between Alassane and the rock that marked the other goalpost.

Mor's teammates and the little boys gathered at the side of the field cheered, teeth gleaming. Mor was about to smile as well, when Papis butted Alassane in the head.

"You are a goalpost. My goalpost. Nothing should pass you. Nothing." He dug his finger into Alassane's forehead and pushed him back. Alassane stumbled and fell.

Mor rushed to help him up.

"Leave him," Papis snapped as he turned his back and walked away.

Mor quickly gave Alassane a hand up. Tears ballooned in Alassane's eyes.

"Sorry."

Alassane shook his head. "You better get away," he whispered. "For both of us."

Mor glanced over his shoulder and saw Papis scowling. From then on Mor avoided scoring a goal, like everyone else on his team.

This was life as a Danka Boy.

33

AFTER three more days of constant bed rest, Demba's broth, and Tanta Coumba and Naza wrapping her in steaming-hot cloths soaked in Demba's herbs, Amina was doing better. She even bossed Mor about.

"You've already lost another button? Do you think we have bags full?" she asked.

Mor smiled with relief as she fussed. She was back to her old self.

"Aren't you late for Demba?" Amina got up and laid the book Demba had given her on the pallet. Mor also noticed she had smoothed out the balled-up Iéna Academy pamphlet and had slipped it inside like a bookmark.

"Out, out," she teased like their *yaay* used to, pushing Mor toward the door. "You have fish to catch, and I have my own things to do."

"Mina, you still need to rest, you know," Mor started. "Tanta Coumba and Naza have taken care of everything. You don't need to start housework again so soon. Tima and I need nothing."

"Not everything I do is chores. Maybe there are things I want to do for myself."

Mor thought about the wrinkled chocolate bar wrapper he'd found with all the lists on it, and about him becoming a Danka Boy. He wanted to tell her, but he knew she wouldn't be any less worried. She actually might just get mad.

"Demba and I have sold many fish, and another fisherman asked me to look at his *gaal*'s motor. He said he will pay me a few francs. We still have a few weeks before Bàjjan's return. I know I don't have all you need for school, but I think I might be able to show her we can care for ourselves. What do you think? Would you be upset if you couldn't start school as soon as the year begins? Maybe soon after instead? They might hold you a place with Baay's money until then."

"If that is the way it has to be, then that is the way it will be." She sat on the floor and pulled out a plastic bag stuffed with what looked like mini cloth outfits. When she caught him staring, she pushed it closed behind her. "I wish we could pick coins from trees," she said lightheartedly.

So did Mor. He wished it were that simple. He wanted to

say more, but Amina looked away. Then she glanced back up at him as he stepped out the door.

"Thank you for trying. And *jërëjëf* for looking out for me when I was sick."

"I didn't do much," Mor said, suddenly bashful. "Tanta Coumba, Naza, and Demba did everything."

"No," Amina said, a hint of seriousness in her voice. She held a white-faced rock doll. "You watched over me. And that is the most important."

Before Mor realized it, she hopped off the ground and hugged him, whispering against his neck.

"Thank you for trying to help me with school. You keep the dream alive in me, like Baay did. You are a good brother. I am proud of you." As he blinked, she released him and was back kneeling on the floor, dressing another doll, before he could find the right words to say.

When he stepped out of the *barak*, he didn't think he could feel any better.

He got on his bike and steered onto the lane, passing by Tanta Coumba's door to say his greetings and to check in on Fatima and Jeeg.

When he pulled his bike up alongside Tanta Coumba's window, he heard Fatima's little voice. "Let's pile all the small, smooth ones here. Mina likes those best."

"And we can put this on here like this," Oumy said.

Mor peeked in the window, but Fatima's and Oumy's backs were to him. Jeeg popped her head up, looking at him.

"Morning, Tima," he called through the open window.

Fatima jumped to her feet. "When can I go be with Mina?" she asked before he'd made it to the door. "She is better now."

"Not yet, Tima. She still needs her rest."

"But she's fine. She's up and doing stuff."

"You'll see her this afternoon when Tanta Coumba and Naza go over."

"But she is my sister. Why can't I see her now?" Fatima whined.

"If you want her well, you can't."

She plopped back down next to Oumy and Jeeg. Her bottom lip stuck out as she pouted. A pile of rock dolls lay between them.

"They are so wrapped up in their rocks," Tanta Coumba laughed.

Mor's shoulders lifted in surprise. He hadn't seen her hunched in her garden at the side of the *barak*. Baby Zal crawled in the dirt, putting fistfuls of it into his mouth. She tapped his hand away from his lips.

"You might as well go and fulfill the day Allah has planned for you. They will be busy all morning. As you can see, they have risen almost before the roosters."

Mor nodded, happy to see that Fatima had found something to busy herself. But a part of him felt as if he was being left out of something. He couldn't help feeling that Amina was keeping a secret from him.

But wasn't he keeping a secret from her, too?

❖ ❖ ❖

"Mor brought us a chicken. Mor brought us a chicken." The words found their way down the path to Mor's ears even before he saw Fatima and Oumy singing and dancing around the yard in front of the *barak*. At first he wasn't sure he'd heard them right. Then his focus landed on Tanta Coumba dropping chicken parts into a large black pot of sizzling oil, while Naza chopped up onions against her palm, a half-full bowl beside her feet.

Where had a chicken come from?

Mor remembered the last time they'd had one. It was on Amina's birthday, a year before. Her teachers had given her a certificate saying she had the highest marks in the entire village school. They came to the *barak* to ask if she and Baay might speak with other girls and their parents at a meeting about the importance of girls getting an education. Mor remembered how proud they'd all been, but their *baay* especially. He'd held Amina close and whispered: "Your *yaay* always believed this of you." He had hugged all of them then, saying the chicken wasn't just to celebrate Amina's birthday and the certificate. "It is to celebrate our family and how we've done it together." Late nights with Baay going over numbers in the dirt, Mor testing her on spelling words when Baay was working, and Fatima helping with chores when Amina needed to study. "We've all done our part," their *baay* had said. And now Mor watched as Amina giggled again, rinsing rice in a metal bowl filled with water.

They all looked so happy.

"Aw, Mor," Tanta Coumba called when she looked up. "Why are you rooted to the road? *Kai fii.*" She called him over with her hand.

"Mor!" Fatima and Oumy rushed him, squeezing his waist tight. "You brought us a chicken," Fatima said, her chin digging into his stomach as she smiled up at him. She and Oumy hugged him again and then skipped off laughing, still singing.

"Thank you," Amina said. She glanced at him and continued letting rice fall through her fingers.

"Yes, *jërëjëf.* It is a very nice surprise. And a wonderful way to celebrate your sister's returning health. You must be doing quite well out on that water with Demba, even though many do not have a catch every day. You are both blessed. We all are. Chicken is a rare feast for any of us," Tanta Coumba said. "Such a thoughtful boy to invite my daughters and me to share it."

Mor wanted to tell them they were wrong, that he hadn't bought the chicken. But he couldn't.

"Laye was very nice this time. Not like before," Amina added. "I think he even tried to say sorry."

"Laye?" Mor hoped she didn't notice the surprise in his voice.

"Yes. Didn't you send him?" Amina searched his face.

Mor hesitated.

"Well, it was very thoughtful," Tanta Coumba said. Her

back was to Mor and Amina as she flipped over the frying chicken. "Sending him has given us more time to prepare. This *yassa* will be tasty."

Mor couldn't believe it. Another Danka Boy had come to his home, but this time it was to give, not to take. It was going to take a while before Mor would ever be able to believe it. Even still, for him, a day like this almost made every bad day worth it.

A few days later, on his day off, the Danka Boys waited for Mor on the path.

"Come on," Papis said, draping his arm over Mor's shoulder as if they were old friends. All the kids they passed stepped out of their way, staring as though they walked on gold. It was a strange feeling to be part of a group that every other kid watched and noticed. Each second he was with the Danka Boys, he saw more and more how they looked out for one another. In a strange way it felt nice not to be alone. Not to turn with worry whenever he heard an approaching footstep. They also understood what it was like to take care of themselves. But he still needed to get used to the fact that Papis was at the head of it.

"Where are we going?" Mor asked as they stomped down the center of the road, no one bothering them.

"We have a game," Papis said. "You're going to score. And score a lot. You're not too bad with a ball, you know."

The edge of Mor's lip lifted.

"We're going to put those skills of yours to use. Salif and his boys aren't going to win today."

"Who's Salif?" Mor asked.

"You'll see." Papis patted Mor's shoulder and strutted ahead of all the Danka Boys, Lokho prancing at his side, tail wagging.

"See?" Cheikh whispered, coming up beside Mor. "He's not so bad."

"I guess." Mor shrugged. He still had a couple of healing bruises to prove otherwise.

"That's it," Papis shouted after the ball had sailed through the goal for the sixth time. The game was finally over after a lot of pushing, shoving, offsides, and underhanded tricks, like holding shirts and tripping, and the Danka Boys had won mainly because of Mor's five goals. "We are the champions." Papis held up an imaginary Africa Cup trophy, pumping his fist in the air.

Salif's shining soccer ball, with a few black and white patches missing, spun in the dirt until Papis swooped in and snatched it off the ground without complaint from Salif, except for his flaring nostrils and a flexing jaw. Papis also grabbed the handful of money he and Salif had dropped in the dirt before the game. He slipped most of it into his pocket, then strolled over to Mor with a wide smile on his face. Mor tensed.

"Here." Papis pushed the ball against Mor's chest and

slapped two five-hundred-franc coins into his hand. "If you do that every game," he chortled, "I'll be rich. Not bad, *khale*. Not bad."

This time when Papis said "kid," it didn't sound like a slop of fish guts smeared on the bottom of his shoe. Mor was part of the group, and he had a new ball and money to prove it. Although he smiled, its brightness didn't reach all the way down to his belly. He had always thought he would feel happier when he got his first real soccer ball.

34

BEFORE the chickens in a neighbor's yard had started rustling their feathers, when the sun still only peeked in the sky, Mor pedaled down to the beach. He found Demba lying under a palm tree. His dreadlocks sheltered his face. As Mor approached, he couldn't tell if Demba was awake or asleep. The little weaverbird hopped on and off Demba's clasped fingers as his chest rose and fell under his hands.

As quietly as he could, Mor eased his bike onto the sand, not wanting to wake Demba if he slept. For so many days and nights he had been at Mor's home, checking on and helping Amina. Mor was sure Demba was tired. But as soon as Mor went to sit next to his friend, Demba got up and headed toward his boat.

As Mor started to follow him, someone cleared his throat behind him. Mor turned to see Papis standing at a rock, his foot resting on it. Although he no longer flinched when he saw Papis, Mor's good mood vanished.

"What are you doing here?" he asked, glancing back at Demba readying the boat.

"Eh," Papis said with pretend shock. "You are a Danka now. I will always be around. And you will always have our fish when we ask, won't you, brother?"

Mor wanted to tell him to cast his own net, but he didn't. He just stared as Papis rubbed his *sothiou* across his teeth, cleaning them.

"Make sure they are big." Papis held his hands apart.

As Mor turned away, Lokho and Diallo trotted up the path to their master, eyeing Mor as he went to Demba's *gaal*.

"Remember," Papis yelled at his back, "if I don't get my fish, no one gets any. You hear me, *khale*?"

Mor gulped. This time "kid" sounded like a warning, closer to the slop of fish guts again.

"We are your brothers first."

Mor walked like an inching snail back to Demba as Demba stared past Mor at the other Danka Boys. Mor was one of them now, and he had to get them fish. He also needed more fish to sell to help Amina.

When he and Demba were on the water, his every thought was consumed with bringing Papis what he wanted. And finding a way to get more money for Amina. Should he just ask Demba to catch more? Could he manage to get a few on his own? He wondered if Demba would be disappointed in him for joining the Danka Boys.

"Demba . . ." Mor's voice battled with the grunt of the engine. "Could we put a few more fish in the bucket today? That is, if we are lucky enough to catch more."

At first Mor wasn't sure Demba heard him. Then Demba said, "Golden skies again and again. Fish too."

Mor had been getting so good with Demba's coded messages, but this one made him wonder. Did he mean there would always be plenty of fish, or something else? Then, as if he had read Mor's thoughts once again, he said, "Greed chases the horizon but never catches the golden sky."

Demba knew, like Amina had, that no amount of fish would ever be enough for Papis. That nothing would ever be enough for him. That he would always want more. Mor had been excited about the francs Papis put in his hand, but he knew it all might come with an even higher price.

When they got to shore, they had the same three buckets full of fish they always had. There were no more in them and no less. Mor had asked Demba over and over if they could catch a few more, but after the first time he had not replied. As usual, Mor headed to Basmah's table, while Demba waited with the bikes at the edge of the market. When Mor rounded the corner near her stall, he noticed Lokho sniffing the ground before he saw Papis. He stopped and cast a glance back toward where Demba had been, but he couldn't see him or the bikes.

"I know you weren't going to that market lady before you found me?" Papis asked.

"I didn't know where you were," Mor said.

"Well, you do now." Papis gestured for Diallo, who hopped off a crumbling wall to take the bucket from Mor.

Mor held the handle back. "These are for Basmah."

"Have you already forgotten? You're a Danka Boy now. You share everything with us and we share with you. Chickens, balls, a cut of our winnings."

"I didn't ask you to."

"You don't get it. You don't have to. And there could be more. Just tell me what you need"—he snapped his fingers—"and I can have it."

Papis stared at Mor, his eyes shifting back and forth, as Diallo hovered over the bucket, waiting.

Mor didn't want to know how, but he was sure Papis could probably find the money to pay for Amina's school in a second. *How easy it could be.* He looked down at the fish, deciding whether to hand Diallo a few. What would that hurt? He would find some way to make it up to Demba.

"You know what," Papis said. "Go on, sell the fish."

Mor exhaled. He rushed to walk away before Papis changed his mind.

"The money would be better anyway."

Mor stopped. Water splashed out of the bucket.

"Eh, what goes on over there?" Basmah yelled, her hand on one hip, a machete for hacking fresh coconuts in the other.

Papis came close to Mor, his breath a blanket on the side of Mor's neck. "Remember, we come first now, brother."

Papis and Diallo sauntered away as if they had only stopped to say hello.

Mor's heart pounded against his chest. Then he caught sight of Demba staring from a distance and hurriedly looked away.

"What were those boys wanting of you?" Basmah asked when Mor reached her. "There is nothing good there, especially for a boy like you. Don't let them rob you of your goodness." She took the fish from Mor, and like each day, she was about to pay him for them, when he stopped her.

His eyes quickly searched the space around them. "Um, could you hold it for Demba? For tomorrow?"

As if no explanation was needed, she scanned the area herself, then nodded. He would find another way to give the Danka Boys what they wanted without involving Demba or his other friends. Or at least he hoped he could, even though he had no clue how just yet.

When Mor got back to Demba and their bicycles, Demba said nothing about what he'd seen. They simply rode out of town in silence and rode back after their deliveries in the same way. They passed down the main road, as they always did. And as usual, the street was alive with activity. Vendors were selling, tourist buses spit smoke, *toubabs* took pictures of everything with their fancy cameras, and village girls hawked their wares from baskets, buckets, and tarps at the roadway's edge.

Off to the side a small group of tourists crowded over something or someone. Mor paid little attention as he passed, but when he heard the unmistakable giggle of Fatima, he dug his heels into the dirt. Demba kept pedaling, but after a few seconds he slowed, looking back. Mor jumped off his bike, maneuvering to the crowd. When he peeked past the arms of two tourists, he was surprised to see Fatima posing with three of her rocks dolls as a woman took her photograph.

"This is me." She held out one rock. "And this is my sister, Mina, and this is Jeeg. See, doesn't it look just like her?" She held the rock next to Jeeg, who stood by her side. The woman gave a delayed laugh as a black man with them translated Fatima's words into a language Mor could not understand. She and another woman nodded at the man, then one crouched down to have her picture taken with Fatima and Jeeg.

"What are you doing here alone?" Mor pushed through the crowd, about to snatch Fatima from where she stood, not caring about interrupting the woman's picture. Then he saw Amina, Naza, and Oumy kneeling on a tarp, a cluster of travelers around them as well.

"Oh," Fatima said, excited. "This is my big brother, Mor." She rooted around in the dirt to find the stone Amina had made of him in a yellow fabric soccer jersey with a tiny green star painted on the front of it. Fatima held it up and then giggled, picking up another. "And this is Demba," she said. "Our friend." She pointed to Demba, standing in the road with the bikes.

The tourists turned, cameras flashing.

"He even has a little bird that flies around his head. Can you see it?" Fatima asked the *toubabs*, her finger outstretched. "Everybody thinks he is scary, but he is very nice. He plays with me and my rocks whenever he comes over." She beamed.

The interpreter translated and the tourists laughed. They talked rapidly to one another.

Mor just stared.

Amina sat on the square blue tarp, surrounded by baskets of rock dolls of all shapes and sizes. Some rocks had clothing and some did not, some showed flowers, while others showed baskets of fish or *tàngal* or a horse and cart. There were even pale-faced ones with bright-pink cheeks, blue eyes, and a stripe of white lotion down some of their noses.

"Did you paint all these?" Mor asked, not believing what he saw. "How? When?"

"With these," Amina said, lifting her hands. Then she turned her palm up, taking money from one of the travelers, who held a set of five stones in her hand. "When you were out."

"She is buying them for her grandson," the interpreter told Amina with a smile. "She thinks he will like the *car rapide* bus most."

Amina nodded her thanks, putting the money she'd received into a green tin box that sat in Naza's lap. Naza had a stick and was writing numbers in the sand for another woman, who held up six fingers.

Mor's eyes bulged as he looked in the tin and saw a couple of folded bills and coins before Naza closed the lid. A flat basket held a needle and thread and a couple of little outfits, which a tourist was picking through.

How had he not realized? She hadn't been making all those rock dolls for just Tima and Oumy. She'd been making them to sell.

"Why did you not tell me?" he asked his sister as another traveler reached in front of him to take the small wooden *gaal* Oumy held out to him.

Mor watched as the familiar toy passed by his face. It looked like the ones Cheikh had always whittled, but it was painted. A handful of other painted wooden toys sat before Oumy. Mor looked at her closely. Did she know Cheikh was here? Had he made these for them to sell?

He wanted to ask so many more questions but didn't want to be in the way. "They are trying to raise money for their schooling," Mor heard Fatima say. "Then when I get older, we will need to make even more rock dolls for me and Oumy to go too."

At first Mor was ashamed he couldn't provide all the money for them, then, stepping back, he smiled watching Fatima pose with her rock dolls and Jeeg. He was proud of both of his sisters.

When he stepped back to Demba's side, he looked up at his friend. "Did you know?"

Demba held Mor's bike out to him, then pulled a rock

doll out of his pocket. It didn't look like Demba.

Mor stared closer. "Is that me?" he asked. Then he realized where he'd seen a shirt that blue. In a picture of Demba as a boy. He scanned his friend's face. "Idrissa." Demba pushed the rock doll back into his pocket.

"Idrissa built rock castles."

Mor stopped. Those were the most untangled words Demba had ever spoken.

"What was he like? Can you tell me?" Mor asked.

Demba waited for Mor to take his bike.

"Please."

"He was the sea, the sand, and the sunshine." Demba's eyes were bright and clear, staring off. "He was life, and giggles, light."

Mor didn't want to move as Demba spoke, but Demba still held Mor's bike out to him. He took it, and they meandered through the flow of people, away from the main road. Mor hoped Demba would say more. But he didn't. Instead he got back on his bike, and they rode away from the noises of the village center.

"Your light is not far."

"What do you mean?" Mor asked. He pedaled fast to keep up with Demba's easy pushes against his own pedals.

Then Demba turned down a path they didn't usually travel but Mor knew well. It was the road his *baay* had taken each week to the mechanic shop. When they slowed by the familiar stick fence, Mor rushed forward.

"Why are we here?"

"Your light."

Mor glanced at the yard. Old *motos* and parts lay everywhere. "They don't want me." Then he turned back to Demba. "And now you don't want me anymore?" He bit at his bottom lip. "Why have you brought me here? Do you want to get rid of me?"

Demba stared at Mor. "Roots remain for a thousand years." Then he looked at the entrance to the shop. Mor didn't want to go in again. He'd really be thought of as a restless gnat. Demba waited. Unable to stall, Mor slid off his bike, letting it settle in the dirt.

When he walked into the yard, Mamadou, Mighty Yacine, and Idy were peering under the hood of a hulking truck. There was no sign of Khalifa. Mamadou had climbed on top of an oil drum to get higher over the engine.

"*Assalamu alaikum,*" Mor called out.

"And upon you be peace," the three mechanics responded in unison, turning from the engine. Smiles broke across their lips as they realized who stood before them. Mor smiled back.

"Ah, my young friend," Mamadou said, jumping down off the drum. "And Fallou's twin. It is good to see you again. Your *bàjjan* has called twice asking after you. I have relayed all the messages Coumba Gueye has given. So you are a fisherman now?"

Mor shifted his feet in the dirt. He wondered what his aunt was thinking when she made those calls. He didn't bother asking if she'd wanted to speak with him or his sisters; he thought he already knew the answer. He glanced around the yard, so many memories present there, and then his gaze landed on neat rows of small parts laid across a hammered-out metal tabletop. He'd missed Mamadou's "table of toys," as Mamadou always called it.

This is where your heart beats like mine, my dome. *Where your fingers are energized and your mind shines.*

Mor was relieved to hear his father's words. Since ignoring his last cautions, he'd worried his *baay* was gone.

"I don't mean to be a bother," Mor began. "But I wanted to see if you could change your mind. I'm happiest here, where you and my *baay* taught me about engines. I'll listen and do what you tell me. I know I still have too much to learn, but fishermen have trusted me to look at their engines after I helped another out at sea. I am getting better. And if you taught me, I know I could be really good. I could bring you new business, because sometimes I know the days can be slow. The fishermen would come."

Mamadou cut him off. "Mighty Yacine and Idy have been after me for days to come to your yard." The other two mechanics nodded. "We've missed you here as well. You are a fresh and shining metal among all our rust. Besides, your presence would never be as much of a bother as my trouble-some nephew was to me."

"Yaa . . . yaa . . . yaa." Mighty Yacine slapped her hand against her forehead, shaking it.

"He ruined everything he touched. I had to toss him back to my sister before he ruined my business," Mamadou continued. "Even though you still can't reach the steering wheel and pedals all at once, you already know more than he ever will. I can't pay you much, because I don't have much to pay, but my true wealth is in here." He tapped the side of his head with his grease-stained finger. "And I'll share it with you."

Mor bounced, excited. How had Demba known? His smile broadened. *I shouldn't be surprised*, he thought. *Demba knows everything.* Mighty Yacine and Idy shook his hand and patted his back.

"We will do the heavy lifting," Mighty Yacine added.

"And you'll be our eyes," said Idy, pushing up his glasses, as Mighty Yacine and Mamadou nodded in agreement.

Is it that easy? Mor wondered, not trusting that he could have one of his most heartfelt wishes come true.

"We are ready to have you back whenever you want to come," Mamadou said. Then he held up his palm at Mor. "But I still want you in school. You cannot run a business if you have bolts and piston rings rattling around in your head instead of sense. I learned that from Khalifa."

"School?"

"Yes," Mamadou said, smirking. "The place with books and pencils."

Since the day his *bàjjan* left, Amina's schooling had been his focus, not his own. He had thought that was over for him, telling himself that it wasn't important to him. But now Mamadou was telling him he didn't have to choose—school or work. He could have both.

"Your *baay* would come down from the heavens and rattle my life if I took that away from you. He always bragged that all his children were going to be a hundred times smarter than him."

"Yes, I will go to school," Mor said. "I promise. Thank you, sir."

After saying good-bye, he rushed out of the shop, eager to tell Demba the news. Then he paused. When would he fish with Demba?

As if Demba heard Mor's thoughts again, he said, "Fish welcome dawn."

He was right. He wouldn't be able to go to the market, but dawn would be their time together. Then village school. Then Mamadou's shop.

Mor's smile spread wide. After so many bends and turns, he thought he could finally take a breath, if he could just figure out what to do about the Danka Boys.

35

WHEN Mor got down to the shore the next morning, a crowd of fishermen were circled around where Demba's *gaal* rested on the shore.

Mor dropped his bike in the sand and raced forward toward the tops of Demba's dreadlocks and the weaverbird peeking over everyone else's heads.

"Excuse me. Let me through, please," Mor said, pushing past elbows and hips to get to Demba, who stood at the center of it all. "What's going on . . . ," he started to say, then saw the answer.

A perfectly charred hole marred the side of Demba's boat, big enough to kick a soccer ball through, but not large enough to pass one of their buckets.

"It was the Danka Boys," Mor yelled. "They did this." The accusation was out of his mouth before he even thought it through. He didn't care, though. They had gone too far. They had messed with too many people he cared about. He had thought everyone was safe now. "They did it because of me," Mor said under his breath. "I don't want to be a Danka Boy."

"I don't know who the Danka Boys are, young man," Souleymane piped up, "but I do know we have enough supplies around here to fix this. Babacar, Adama, Seydou, grab your tools. Issa, Daning, and Aziz, pull off some of the wood planks on the old Diop *gaal*. A friend I owe a debt to in more than five fish needs our help. We are fishermen together."

Souleymane barked orders to the others, and everyone fell in line helping fix Demba's boat, as if a harsh word had never fallen on the waters between them. Demba stared at his *gaal* as a few of the men broke off the burned wood, ready to replace it.

"Demba, did you hear me?" Mor said again, scooting out of the way when the ruined planks were thrown in the sand by his feet. "The Danka Boys have done this. I thought if I joined them, we would all be okay. But we won't be, will we? I'm sorry they've done this. I'm sorry I've brought them here, too."

"Storms fall where they choose." Demba stared at Mor as men leaned over Demba's *gaal*, stuffing and hammering wads of palm fiber in between the newly fastened planks to make sure the boat was watertight.

Mor listened to the banging around him, wishing the Danka Boys would find somewhere far away for their thunder. He'd thought he could protect everyone on his own, but now he wasn't sure. Had he made a mistake in trying to stay? In trying to keep his *baay*'s promise?

Within three hours Demba's *gaal* was back on the water and all the fishermen were casting out their nets again. The boat's swaying made Mor feel like a novice on the water. The Danka Boys' faces invaded his every thought. He could think of nothing but silly, childish threats, which would never scare them. Or worse, things that would give them more reason to torment him, his friends, and his family. Being with them seemed no better.

Demba had watched him all morning, staying silent except for a mutter or two when it was time to cast out or drag in the nets. But his eyes followed every movement of his boatmate. Mor sat with his knees locked at his chest, as if his thoughts were a thousand people crowding the *gaal*. The breeze sliced across the choppy ocean waters. He dipped his finger into the water and brought it to his lips, which were parched and scaly. Absentmindedly, he ran his tongue over the chapped grooves. The salty liquid tickled his tongue and stung his broken skin.

Giving no warning, Demba swatted Mor's hand from his lips. Startled, Mor hopped back, sending the boat into a wobble.

"A sea of fire will twist your insides." Demba motioned toward the water and then shook his hand. He hunched over, holding his stomach, and rocked more vigorously than the boat on the waves. He crinkled up his face as if in pain.

Mor would have laughed at Demba's acting if he hadn't been so worried.

"I wish I could make Papis's belly ache like that," Mor mumbled. "And Cheikh's, too."

He wished for anything that would stop them from wanting to eat for a while. He could not knock their teeth out with one punch, as Papis had once threatened to do, or frighten them in their own *barak*, but maybe, just maybe, he could figure out a way to make their stomachs fold over in pain so they would no longer trust his fish. Without much thought, he sorted the fish into the tie-dye-patterned buckets, flinging them this way and that. Then, when he tossed a fish and it missed the bucket, landing in the mucky water at the bottom of the boat, Mor flung his head back as if receiving an electric jolt. He had an idea.

"Could we catch a few more?" He gestured to the fish when Demba started the motor.

Mor's question was met with a blank stare.

"Just a couple," he asked. "We might need them, since Basmah and my sisters are eating with us today."

Demba peered into each bucket, studying the contents as if he had special vision that allowed him to see and count each fish in the tangle of tails. He reached for the motor's throttle.

"Wait . . . ," Mor began. He knew in order for his plan to work, he needed a lot more fish. "I need them, Demba." He swallowed, his throat still scratchy from the salt water. "Please."

The hull of the *gaal* was full for Demba, even though there were only three or four plastic buckets alive with flopping fish splashing in water. Demba had told Mor once that to lure even one more fish into his net at that point would be selfish, because four buckets gave everyone what they needed—no more, no less.

Right now Mor disagreed. He needed more.

Demba glanced into the buckets again and then at Mor. Demba's eyes seemed to drill a tunnel into Mor's brain. Mor wanted him to see that he was determined to prove he could take care of himself and his sisters. He was ready to show he could be a man. When the netting under his feet was yanked, Mor jumped.

Demba stood, clutching a handful of net. He leaned near the side of the boat and waited for Mor to pick up his end. They cast the net out one last time. It sank quickly, unlike the nervous anxiety at the bottom of Mor's stomach.

He watched the net submerge, and then they quickly snatched it up, pulling it in. Mor always marveled when there was something inside. So many times fishermen's nets came back empty. They hoisted the net out of the water, and after they sorted the fish into the already-full buckets, Demba waited for Mor to speak.

"Jërëjëf." Mor couldn't meet his gaze. He didn't want him to see in his eyes the desperation that he felt.

He didn't know what else to do.

As Demba started the engine for home, Mor let his plan play out in his head. Nervous adrenaline churned inside him like the propeller blades spun the water. His every thought was on the fish and what to do with them. He craned his head up to the cloudless sky, hoping his idea would work.

It had to.

36

ONCE on shore, Mor and Demba threw the extra fish into a fifth bucket Demba usually used for random things they pulled from the sea: old sandals, plastic, rubber, or anything else that didn't belong. Then they hauled the heavy buckets up to the roadway. Demba fastened four to his bicycle, since Mor still couldn't completely balance with more than one. Then as he climbed on his bike, he reached out to Mor for the last bucket. Mor hesitated, hugging the pail close to his chest. Demba patted the top of the handlebar, ready to secure the bucket.

Mor hesitated. "I was hoping to take this one."

"To Amadou."

"No." Mor tried again. "For me. I was hoping to keep it for me."

Demba took the bucket from Mor's hand and rested it on the middle bar, wrapping a cloth around it and his waist as a belt. Then he pushed off.

Disappointed, Mor watched him go. He glanced back at the *gaal*, wishing he could push the heavy boat out to sea on his own. Knowing it was a hopeless thought, he climbed on his bike and tried to think of another solution.

When Mor pedaled up to Chez Amadou's, Demba was waiting, holding out the fifth bucket. Mor slid his feet to the dirt to stop beside him.

"This isn't for him?" Mor glanced at the shack.

Demba thrust the bucket at Mor's chest. Water splashed up, coating Mor's shirt.

"Your battle."

The word "battle" sat heavy in Mor's ears. Now that he had the fish again, he didn't know what to do with them. He didn't want to battle anyone. He just wanted to protect everyone. He left the fish in a corner by Amadou's for safe-keeping, then hustled back to his bike and a waiting Demba. Once out in the plains, they bumped along past where Demba picked berries and leaves. Mor swung his head to the side, almost causing his bike to topple over. As they rushed by plants, he wondered what they were all for. But before he could ask, doubt filled him. He didn't think he could go through with it. Or that his plan would even work.

Courage is your strongest weapon, my son. And opportunity your ally. Do what you must in these hours of war.

Another fighting word. Mor wanted no battle and he wanted no war, but his *baay*'s voice mixed with his own frustrations and was the welcome push he needed.

"Demba," he began. "What berries would I need to bring fire to someone's belly?"

Demba did not answer. He just continued to pedal.

Mor raced to catch up to him; even with all the buckets, he was still faster than Mor, as if buckets of fish and water were strings tied to his bicycle.

"Demba, I need your help," Mor said as he caught up to him. "Will you help me?"

In answer, Demba turned down a new path. Letting his foot drag along the gravel road, Demba slowed his bike, and Mor did the same.

"Fire cannot settle all things."

Demba climbed off his bike and left Mor in charge of keeping it and the buckets upright. Demba squatted in the grasses, pulling back branches and bushes. He tore leaves off a few plants and put them in his small satchel, the same one he had brought to help Amina. Then he tramped deeper into the thicket. The trees snapped behind him, curtaining him from view. Mor held tight to the handlebars, wishing he had the neck of a giraffe as he strained to see.

The bushes shook and parted. Then Demba came back into view. The pouch he held had swelled. He swung his leg over his bike and settled in, waiting for Mor to climb back on his own.

Mor kept his eyes on the road ahead, but his focus was on the leaves Demba had collected. Were they for him?

The dread in his stomach leaded Mor down with knots.

His thighs ached and sweat littered his forehead by the time they reached the first outcropping of homes they always went to. He tried to push his thoughts away as he followed behind Demba, wanting to ask another question about the plants he'd picked, but Demba was immediately swallowed by hugs from Yvette, as if she hadn't seen him three days before. Water spilled from the buckets on his bike.

"Ah, it is always nice to see you again, mirror of Idrissa." Yvette always greeted Mor the same way. He liked it. It seemed to bring light to Demba's eyes when she said it, in the same way that Amina stood a little taller when people called her "Awa's little double." "It always does our hearts well to see you."

She patted Mor's arm and led the way to the old woman's home. As usual, Mor sat on the stump under the window and waited.

"Why do you need those? They are a step away from poison if not handled right," Mor heard Yvette say.

He peeked through the window and saw Demba taking a jar of dark berries off a shelf lined with other jars, much like the shelf in Demba's own home.

"They will not hurt a thing," the old woman said to her

daughter. "They bring heat when heat is needed. Demba knows more about these things than any of us do now. He is even my brain at times."

A few moments later Demba came back outside, the little jar concealed in his sack. When they got back to the bikes, two buckets were loaded down with handwoven reed baskets, animal skins, and bananas. Like every time they had come before, three young girls took the remaining fish to smoke, so they could sell them to people even farther from the water. Yvette's daughters always left things behind in the buckets that people had traded for the fish instead of coins.

As they waved good-bye, Mor couldn't wait to ask Demba about the jar.

When they reached Chez Amadou's, Demba placed the buckets in the sand and leaned their bikes against the wall.

"Ah, there you are," Amadou said, appearing around the side of the eatery. His sandals were covered with granules of sand. "I wondered how much longer you would be." He wiped his hands on a cloth, then slung it over his shoulder. "Come, come. The ladies will be here soon," he said to Mor.

Mor glanced at Demba, wanting to see if any of the plants, berries, and roots were for him. But he joined Amadou instead.

"Why do you look as though you've eaten something sour?" Amadou's booming voice was full of mirth. "You don't want to be my sous-chef and help make my famous *ceebu jën*?"

"No. I do," Mor said, giving Demba a last look.

"Don't worry about him." Amadou's eyes rested on Demba. "He enjoys watching the waves."

Tomato broth bubbled in an enormous pot. Yams, onions, carrots, cassava, and a tiny dried herring added for flavor bobbed to the surface. The smells were dizzying, gnawing at Mor's concentration. He inhaled deeply.

"Wash your hands, then, and scoop out the vegetables while I drain the soaking rice."

Mor scrubbed his hands in a bowl of sudsy water, then took the spoon, finding it hard not to grab small pieces of steaming cassava or carrot as he pulled them out, placing them in a covered bowl.

"Go on, taste it." Amadou nudged Mor's shoulder. "Do we need more flavor?"

Mor tapped the spoon against his palm like his *yaay* and Amina always did. Broth dripped down his hand, but he caught it with his tongue. Smacking his lips, he wanted another taste.

"It's perfect. But I can try it again to be sure," he offered.

"Ha ha . . . ," Amadou chuckled. "Yes, why don't you. We can never be too certain."

Four clear glass jars with screw-on lids were huddled on a shelf nailed near the fire. One contained salt; another, black pepper; a third, gold-and-red-checkered seasoning cubes; while the last was filled with chili peppers soaked in oil.

Mor stared at the farthest jar.

"Ah, you think it could use more spice. A cook after my own heart. Spice makes it dance." Amadou covered two freshly fried fish with a tin platter to keep them warm, then pricked a habanero pepper with a fork and dropped it into the pot. After it boiled a bit, he scooped it out with a cup of broth and set it to the side, then poured in soaked rice by the handful until it was barely covered with broth. "We don't want it too hot for your young sisters' palates. Basmah always says how lovely they are when I go to her stall for my supplies."

Mor dug his toe into the sand and dragged his attention away from the jar as Amadou spoke.

"I am excited to have them all join us, aren't you?" Amadou leaned into the steam. His nostrils flared as he smelled the food. "You will love my fish and rice. It cannot be beat."

"Could I have some of those peppers?" Mor pointed to the jar, too preoccupied to really listen to Amadou talk of his prizewinning recipe.

"Ah, the true sign of a strong man." Amadou clapped his hand hard against Mor's back and chuckled. "You like it hot, eh?" Nodding in approval, he took down the jar of oiled peppers and handed it to Mor. "It's all yours. But I warn you. They are *saf*." Amadou's smile was broad. The gap between his front teeth was almost as wide as Mor's pinky. "Only use a few drops."

Mor dug into his pocket for a couple of coins.

"Oh, you want the whole jar?" Amadou chuckled, waving

his hand. "Put your money away. The fish you and Demba bring are payment enough. Just be careful with that. It can make even the toughest fall."

Mor hoped that was true. He thanked him and pushed the jar into his pocket. He noticed it was wet, as if the jar were sweating from what it contained.

"Now we just need to wait for our guests and our rice." Amadou took a seat across from Demba at the table, while Mor stood, anxious to get the fish he'd set aside.

He wondered how many chili pepper seeds he'd need to stuff into each fish to give someone a stomachache, even someone with the strongest of stomachs—something Mor suspected both Cheikh and Papis had. He pulled the small jar out of his pocket, doubting he had enough. His eyes fell to Demba, who still watched the waves.

Demba turned to him.

Everything about Mor's expression said, *Demba, I need your help.*

And Demba understood. He got out of the chair and walked to the side of the shack. Mor was right behind him.

"Hey," Amadou called. "Where are you two going? They will be here soon."

"Um, we'll be back," Mor said, rushing to join Demba.

"If you must." Amadou clasped his hands over his stomach and closed his eyes, getting comfortable in his seat.

Mor hauled the bucket of fish and seawater over to where Demba was, out of view of the tables. The fish lay in a heap, thrashing their fins in the shallow water. Mor's rippled reflection wavered as he stared till his eyes glossed over. The shadow of Demba's dreadlocks was visible in the sand when he stood over Mor. His well-used mortar and pestle were in one hand, while he held the little jar Mor had seen in the old woman's home and his bulging bag in the other.

"I just want them to leave me alone," Mor confessed. "To leave us alone. Our fish, you, me, Basmah, my sisters. I don't really want them to hurt. But I want it to all stop." He eyed the jar.

Demba bent down and handed Mor the bowl and grinding tool, and then pulled a few leaves from his bag, tore them into pieces, and dropped them and some berries into the mortar. "Grind." He motioned toward the pestle. Soon a juicy paste emerged. Demba scooped up a handful of salt water from the bucket of fish and dumped it into the mortar. Then he tore up a few more leaves. They were a waxy, dark green with thorny points and floated on the surface of Demba's liquid concoction.

"What are those?" Mor sniffed the mixture and crinkled his nose. It smelled of warm cow dung. He buried his face in the fabric of his T-shirt.

He kept his nose and mouth tucked in the crook of his arm and scraped the paste into the bucket as Demba instructed. Then he used a stick to stir the water and paste, careful not to jab the fish. The water had an iridescent film, and a few of the squashed leaves that had not settled to the bottom of the bucket floated on top.

Mor tapped his finger on the surface of the water, then brought it to his nose. The smell almost curdled his stomach. He pulled it away from his face and wiped his finger in the sand. Then he stared at Demba in wonder. "How do you always know exactly what I want? What I need?"

"My eyes are not clouded."

"This won't harm them really, will it? Just keep them away? I only want them to stay away." Mor felt his *khalat* stirring. His conscience was on guard.

"Wants are gifts we do not always receive."

"But will it work this time?" Mor asked. He heard the desperation in his own voice. He just wanted Demba to tell him it would all be okay, even if it wouldn't. He just needed to hear that.

Fatima's laughter suddenly bounced in the air from the front of the shack.

"It has to work," Mor whispered.

Demba pointed at a ramshackle outhouse under a tree, then back at the bucket. The skin at his eyes crinkled in the corners. The amusement that was stamped there helped ease Mor's worries at least for the moment.

"Let's eat," Amadou called as Fatima and Amina poked their heads around the corner. Mor was grateful Amadou steered his sisters back to the table with Basmah.

As he grabbed the bucket to move it farther into the

shade, water sloshed and a smell like rotten eggs and feces commanded all attention. Mor prayed the stench would die down. Otherwise, Papis and his friends would back away before he could even hand them the fish. For a split second he thought smearing himself in cow dung might be a better solution.

He placed the bucket a safe distance away from Amadou's table but still within sight. Fewer fish flinched and flapped as Demba's concoction saturated the salt water. Mor's stomach jumbled with anxiety again as he wished for the moment this could all be over.

37

WATER sloshed around, wetting the side of Mor's shorts and trickling down his leg, as he lugged the bucket home. The overpowering smell of Demba's mixture had lessened, camouflaged by the heavy scent of fish and waste from the market. Nothing about the water looked different from any other seawater except for the tiny pieces of leaves and berry skins that had fallen to the bottom of the bucket along with sand.

Fatima skipped in front of her brother and Amina, who steered Mor's bike beside her. Fatima's smile took up half her face, and Mor was sure her full stomach lay happy under the fabric of her dress. Unlike Mor, she had been able to enjoy the wonderful feast Amadou had prepared, while Mor had gone through the motions of nibbling his food but tasted nothing.

"What are you going to do with those?" Fatima hopped in front of him. She stuck her head close to the water and poked at the fish.

"Don't," he shouted louder than intended. He swung the bucket away from her, water slopping. But not before she'd submerged her finger in it.

Amina pulled Fatima close to her with one arm, glaring at their brother. He dropped the bucket and took Fatima's tiny finger in his hand and wiped it dry with a corner of his shirt. "When we get home, wash it good."

"Why?" Fatima asked. "I can lick it clean." She brought her finger up to her lips and opened her mouth to suck it.

Mor snatched it away. The force of his hand caused Fatima to scratch her cheek with her nail, close to her eye. She yelped and smashed her face into Amina's dress, crying.

"Mor, what are you doing?" Amina said, holding her sister close.

"Sorry. I'm sorry, Tima." He knelt in front of Fatima and tried to get her to face him, but she wouldn't budge from the fold of Amina's *sër*. "Tima, please don't lick your finger or rub your eyes until your finger is clean."

"Why?" Amina cut in. "You are a fool if you have done something to those fish."

"I'm not." Mor straightened. "Why can you never trust that I'll do all I can for us?"

"I do," she said. "I have, but my place in our family is not always to trust with blindfolded eyes," she said flatly. "Yaay always told me to never stop questioning, because that will keep us safe."

"I will keep us safe," Mor added.

"You are trying, yes. But what have you done to those fish, then?" she asked, glaring at the bucket. "Why have you given Tima a scare?"

"It's nothing," Mor said, heaving the bucket up again. "Just make sure she washes her hand."

Amina stopped in the middle of the path, blocking him. Her hands were in fists against her waist. She was just out of earshot of a cluster of women sitting on cement bricks and plastic chairs in the shade of a tree, but she still whispered. "You think I don't know you're giving those fish to that boy and his friends?" Her eyebrows rose as she spoke. "Even if you give them some today, they will be back tomorrow. And if there is something wrong with the fish, it will be even worse. Then what will you do?"

"I have to try. I can't sit and do nothing. Maybe they will leave my fish alone after this. Maybe they will think it is no longer worth the risk."

"Or maybe they will find another way to harm you. Us. Have you thought of that?"

"Stop, Mina." He drew back his shoulders. "I have to try. And if you have no better suggestion, leave me alone. I don't need your doubt kicking me right now."

Amina opened her mouth, then closed it again. She and Mor stared at each other, Fatima looking between both of them.

"Mor Fall." He turned away from Amina and squinted toward the multicolored *boubous* and head scarves of the women sitting under the tree. "I was telling my cousins that you are doing good things out on that water." He searched Tanta Coumba out among the women. She sat at the center of the group, baby Zal snuggled at her breast, eating hungrily. "Why is it that these last few days I only see you when you are passing down the road or I am on my way to market? You are not like your sisters, who I see at least three times a day. Haven't you learned the way to a woman's heart?" she teased. Her head tilted back, and her laugh seemed to spring off the shoulders of the other women, making them laugh as well.

Mor was not sure how to respond with so many eyes on him.

She adjusted her son in her arms. "Going to see a woman is what captures her heart." She leaned in and whispered, as if giving the code to a secret combination. "You need to stop at my door. Not because I catch you sneaking by, but because you want to come to it. Understand?"

Mor nodded. But he found it harder and harder to greet her, knowing he was keeping Cheikh a secret from her. She talked of her son every time Mor saw her.

"The water keeps me busy." He lowered his head in apology. "And I haven't wanted to disturb you."

"Nonsense. You must come. I love your company, especially with Cheikh so long away."

Even though dark rings pressed under them, Tanta Coumba's eyes were bright. Her face was set in a relaxed grin. He noticed her gaze and the other women's rested on his bucket of fish. He wished the dirt under his feet would open and swallow it whole.

It was expected of him to offer her some. Though he knew she would always turn it down unless it came directly from Demba, Mor couldn't take a risk that she would say yes today. His grip tightened on the handle. All the women looked from him to the full bucket. Their expressions were changing. "I know you sell those to Basmah in the market," Tanta Coumba began. "You better get to her before they spoil."

Mor's heart burned with thanks. They both knew Basmah and the market were behind him, but she had given him a way out.

"Get on your way, Mor Fall. But remember a woman's heart. . . ." She grinned at Amina and Fatima.

"*Incha'Allah.*" Mor did not meet her eyes. He did not know how he would face her if Cheikh became very sick from eating his fish.

"Go now," she said again, as if giving his feet a gentle push forward in the dirt. "You are making your parents proud."

But was he? The weight of the fish doubled in his hand. How would his parents feel about the tainted fish he carried? Looking up into the clouds, he thought, *Am I doing right?*

A leader does not falter on the path he has chosen. Go forward with confidence. Camouflage your worry and doubts. For they are what will cripple you before your enemy even takes aim.

But have I chosen the right way? Mor wondered.

Only time can reveal the reward of your choice.

"But what do you think?" he asked aloud, wanting more than anything to hear his father say that what he planned to do was okay. "Baay? Are you there?"

It no longer matters what I think. As a man it is your choice and your consequence.

Mor stared up at the sky, and when he looked back ahead, Amina's eyes were trained on him, full of questions and concern, but she said nothing.

He truly wished she could hear their *baay* too.

As Amina and Fatima stepped into their home, Mor searched the road around him; there was no sign of the Danka Boys or anyone else. He sighed. His arms and shoulders ached from carrying the bucket. Splotches of water freckled the path like bread crumbs to his door. Glancing around once more, he hoisted the bucket up and trudged inside his home.

He and Amina sat in opposite corners, while Fatima lay on her belly in the center of the floor, kicking her feet and playing with her rock toys as Jeeg watched. Mor stared at his youngest sister for a while, a war battling out in his head. He did not know whether to go out, stay and wait, or hide.

He tried to lie down, but his muscles twitched, not letting him relax.

Soon he paced the floor, creating a carpet of footprints.

"Why don't you sit down?" Amina snapped, shifting on the pallet. "You're going to wear the dirt down to the middle of the earth."

Mor stood still for a second, then treaded in a different direction. *What if they don't come?* Then his plan would be for naught, and his courage would surely seep away like the water if he dumped out the fish. He eyed the wrinkled picture of his *yaay* and *baay* sitting on the shelf.

"I have to go." He spoke hurriedly, glancing out the open window.

In a panic-free second, with all his restlessness and frustration propelling him forward, he made a decision. He was going to find the Danka Boys.

38

ONCE outside, Mor made it only two paths away from his home before he heard Papis's taunting voice.

"Eh, where have you been? Don't you have something for your boys?" Diallo, Abou, Laye, Lokho, and even Cheikh were around him. "Where's our money?"

"I don't have any," Mor said. "I have fish."

"I see that. But that isn't what I asked for. Don't tell me you can't listen." Papis stepped forward. So did Diallo and Abou. He scraped the end of a *sothiou* across his teeth. The chew stick left pieces of bark sticking to his lips and tongue. He made a ticking sound.

"Here," Mor said, raising the bucket. His arms shook, but he wasn't sure if it was from the weight of the bucket or his nerves.

"I don't want rotting fish anymore—I want money."

Mor wondered if he could smell the concoction. "I told you. I don't have any."

"Why do you keep lying to us? We see you getting money in the market. That lady is always slipping it out of her little pouch. You are one of us now. We come before everyone else."

"I don't want to be one of you anymore," Mor said. "I never really was." He glared at Cheikh, surprised he was so close to home in the middle of the day.

Papis scoffed. "You disappoint me. But you aren't the only one." He cut his eyes toward Cheikh. "Sometimes the word of a brother isn't as strong as it used to be. But that is no matter." His voice dropped a bit and turned menacing. "But you will still bring me what I want. You have not seen me at my best. Things for you could get much, much worse." He poked Mor's chest. Water spilled on his Conforce sneakers, knockoffs of the famous American brand. "Hey, watch it." He leaped back. "Handle this boy," he ordered. "I am growing tired of talking." He yanked the *sothiou* out of his mouth and swung it like a conductor's wand, ordering Cheikh and the others to play his tune.

Diallo stepped forward first, his chest puffed out. "There better be a lot of fish in that bucket for me."

"For you?" Papis yanked Diallo by the collar of his shirt, choking him. Diallo's eyes bulged. Papis spit yellow splinters of bark out of his mouth like sparks of dragon fire. "Don't forget yourself. Everything you get is for me first. You get my scraps . . . after Lokho." Papis snickered and turned toward his mangy dog, who was scratching himself.

Diallo slunk back. Mor watched as one of his own bullies got bullied himself. When Papis reached for the bucket, Mor tugged the handle back. His courage and determination were growing. "It's not for you anymore."

"Don't play with me, boy," Papis warned. "I'll cut you."

It is now or never, Mor thought. He knew just the fish would not be enough. Superstitions played heavily in his thoughts. He remembered the fishermen's reactions that day on the water with Demba. He himself did not believe almost anything could be a sign of evil, but he hoped the Danka Boys felt differently.

He inhaled deeply and whispered to his father's spirit for strength. Then he jerked his body, muttering. At first it was just a low hiss, but then his lips shook, a rapid stream of words flying from his throat. Cheikh's brow made one line, and Papis and the other Danka Boys took cautious steps backward, staring. They concentrated on Mor, their focus as steady as that of an antelope tracking danger. Mor felt ridiculous, but he knew this was the only way. He closed his eyes, squeezing his eyelids tight.

"Hey, man, what is he doing?" Laye asked. The ground crunched under his feet as he backed away even farther. "I've seen people doing stuff like this before. He's crazy."

"He's as *doff* as that Demba," Cheikh pointed out.

"Yeah, man," Papis laughed. Then he choked on his laughter when Mor's eyes shot open, staring directly at him. Papis sprang backward, startled. But realizing all eyes were on him now, he stopped and tried to snatch the handle from Mor again. This time Papis underestimated the strength of Mor's grip. Papis had to yank up, bringing the bucket close to his body. A wave of water rose from it. Droplets flew—splashing against his chest and into his eye. The chew stick fell from his lips. "Ahh!" Papis yelled. He wiped his wet hands across his face. "My eyes are burning." He tripped over his own feet, blinking. "What did you do to me?"

Mor took a deep breath. His plan was working better than he'd imagined. If pretending to be a *téere sorcièr* was what it took to get Papis to leave him alone, he was up for the challenge. He continued mumbling and muttering; even a frothing bubble of spit piled at the corner of his lips.

Lokho snarled, baring teeth.

"Those who harm me will be harmed," Mor professed in a garble of words.

The Danka Boys pushed at one another, seeing who could put the most distance between themselves and Mor.

"Eh . . . I wouldn't mess with him," Cheikh warned. He shook his finger in Mor's direction. "You heard what Demba did to that fisherman's boat when he laughed at him?"

"Yeah," Abou agreed. "This *khale* can probably do the same. Let's get out of here." Abou shuffled back a few more steps.

Laye joined him.

Cheikh, Diallo, and Papis remained.

Papis stumbled in Cheikh's direction, pushing him out of his way. Papis's arms stretched in front of him. His eyes were pressed shut, water webbing in his lashes.

"Where you at, you *badola*?" Papis balled his hands and swung at the air, searching for Mor.

Mor dipped and swayed, dodging the frantic blows that came his way. Cheikh and Diallo had to do the same. Rubbing his eyes, Papis swore under his breath. "You better not let me find you. . . ."

"I would get out of here, if I were you," Cheikh whispered close to Mor's ear. "If he catches you—" But before he could get the next word out, Papis lunged for Mor.

He caught hold of Mor's shirtsleeve and whirled him around, causing Mor to lose his balance a bit. When the first punch made contact with Mor's jaw, his head flopped to the side. The pressure of Papis's fist mashed the jellylike flesh of Mor's inner cheek against his teeth, cutting the inside of his mouth. He tasted blood. Then another blow whizzed past his ear, followed quickly by another that slid off his cheek.

The force of the swing knocked them both into the bucket. It crashed in the dirt. Mor could hardly make out the fish squirming at his feet. The next punch grazed him below his eye. The skin instantly swelled. Then *pop*—he was struck square in the eye.

Then the nose.

"That's enough, Papis. That's enough." Cheikh tried to get between Papis and Mor but found only Papis's fist instead, right against his ear. He grabbed at it, hunching over.

Lokho barked and clawed at the dirt.

Papis snatched at Mor's shirt again. His grip was like cement, holding Mor in place. Mor tried to duck and dodge, but as if in slow motion; the punches were coming too quick. Each came faster, harder, stronger.

Mor tripped over the overturned bucket, landing on his hands and knees. Though he was grateful it had dislodged him from Papis's fist. He hacked, spitting up saliva. His skin burned where Papis had slugged him. Then Mor felt every rib come to life as Papis kicked him. Dust danced around him, landing in his eyes. While Papis rubbed his own eyes, Mor hastened to his knees. He knew if he gave in, Papis would be back tomorrow, the following day, and the next.

"Every punch you send me, you will feel in the pit of your belly," Mor wheezed. He spit blood. "Every time you spit on me, your throat will crave liquid."

"Shut up," Papis yelled, shoving him. His eyes were watery and inflamed.

Mor swayed backward but stayed on his feet. Papis smacked him again and again.

Mor fell.

"Stay down. . . ." Mor heard Cheikh's voice.

"I can't," Mor said, scrambling to his feet only to have the

382

rubber sole of Papis's sneaker collide with the groove behind his knee.

Mor's legs buckled and he collapsed to the ground again. He groaned. When Mor looked up, his eyes locked with Cheikh's for only a moment. His old friend stood an arm's length away. Mor tried to call to him, but the words wouldn't rise in his throat. He gave a halfhearted reach for Cheikh. But instead of Cheikh grabbing hold of his arm, Papis did. Mor yelped in pain as Papis twisted his hand behind his back. Mor was certain it was only a matter of seconds before he heard the snap of his bone.

"*Bayiko*, man." Cheikh bounded forward. "Let him go." He struggled to pull Papis off Mor.

Mor blinked rapidly. He thought he was dreaming. Groups of children crowded him from each end of the road. The bucket lay next to him in the dirt. Water dribbled over the lip. And a fish's protruding eye stared at him. Its mouth was open, gasping for water. Its tail gave a listless swing. It acted as Mor felt.

I know you are tired, but you are also strong.

"Baay." Mor pressed his ear against the cool dirt, wanting to close his eyes.

It is not your time to rest. You still have work to do.

"I can't."

You can, and you will. . . .

39

MOR did not rise. He did not even grumble. His breathing was shallow and his thoughts slept. His eyelids were sandbags over his eyes. When he hoped he would finally see darkness, he saw an image of his family instead. They were all together, but they were apart. Each member was framed in a bubble. As if each one had floated from a different corner of the village to come home.

His mother was outside the door of their *barak*, pounding maize. The steady thump of the wood against the grain matched the drumming of Mor's heartbeat. Amina sat crossed-legged on her bed mat in a brand-new green uniform, reading aloud to everyone. Fatima played with rock dolls near the door as Jeeg nibbled on an orange peel.

Mor's *baay* tinkered with a handmade music box, pieces spread across the pallet. Mor remembered the melody that box made. But where was he?

Then his eyes flew open and he looked around, panicked. Where was he? Faces came into focus, and he saw Cheikh pulling at Papis. He remembered.

When your enemy falters, or is tangled in the reeds, it is your time to act. Strike now! The resounding thunder of his father's voice rocked his body. The words swooped into Mor's ears with the rush of an ocean wave. And as if echoing his *baay*'s command, the wind rumbled through the paths. It sent sand hurtling off the ground like a mob of attacking bees.

Mor tried to squeeze his fingers into balls, but the energy needed to lift his hands seeped from his muscles and every pore.

Your fists are not your mightiest weapons; your will is.

Mor wanted to believe him, yet his arms refused to move. The ground underneath them shook as Papis's towering frame careened toward him, most likely propelling his and Cheikh's weight with his rage. Mor needed to find his own rage. He remembered Amina's worry and sickness, Tima's fear, the near loss of Jeeg, Basmah's ruined table, and Demba's charred *gaal*. He thought of his own sleepless nights, and his fingers began to ball up in the dirt. His nails dug into his palms.

"You are mine, *badola*," Papis roared. His elbow landed

square in Cheikh's chest as he tried to knock him off. But Cheikh did not moan or cower. He held tight to Papis.

Lokho barked, clapping his teeth together, a meter from Cheikh's leg.

You are fierce, my son. In this forest you are not the rhinoceros that plows ahead with a mind only filled with destruction. You are a beetle by the same name, carrying almost nine hundred times your weight. You are indomitable. Capture your strength. Unleash your will. And fight.

Mor felt the twitch of every muscle and the blood coursing through each vein. The rasp of his own breathing grew stronger. He pulled his arms in tight and blocked out the distractions of pain. He concentrated, steeling himself to move.

You need to rise, hiss, and chatter. This is your war.

Rolling onto his stomach, Mor felt the tearing in his side but ignored it. He had to be strong for his family. For his friends. For him, there was no other choice.

The bucket rocked before him on the ground. Fish lay limp around it in the dirt. There was a shallow pool of water, leaves and berries left inside it. Mor hoped it would be enough. He scrambled to his feet and grabbed the bucket. The water slapped against the sides. Leaves and berries clung to the wet edge. This was his chance. Cheikh blocked Papis long enough for Mor to gain ground. He had to hurry or the opportunity would be gone.

"Cut it out, man," Cheikh pleaded with Papis, whose fist

was cocked, ready to strike. "Can't you see he can't take much more?"

"What is that to me?" Papis slipped loose of Cheikh's grasp and bulldozed straight for Mor.

Mor was ready. Concentrating with every bone and muscle of his body, he swung the bucket forward. A wave of water arced through the air. When Papis charged, mouth open wide slinging threats, he met the wall of water full on. The water exploded against his skin, spraying everywhere. Mor closed his eyes as droplets hit his face. When he opened them again, Papis was soaked. Clumps of mushed leaves and berries clung to his cheek, then dropped to the dirt. He froze, his shoulders lifting, shocked. But he didn't stop for long. His arm launched forward, his fingers clawing for Mor's throat. But Mor was able to swerve out of his grasp like he did in *le foot*, dodging opponents. As he moved, the momentum of the bucket caused it to crash hard against Papis's side.

Papis stumbled back on his heels, not expecting the blow. Demba's concoction dripped from his face. Pieces of berry and leaves shot from his mouth as he spit. Tiny flecks clung to his tongue. The ball in his throat slid down and then back up again. Mor hoped it had taken some of the tainted water with it. Papis stared at Mor. His eyes, clouds of red. He raked his shirtsleeve across them vigorously.

Lokho raced for Papis, but Papis tripped over him, pushing him away. Lokho tucked his tail and whimpered.

A number of the village children leaned in, staring.

Mor couldn't stop now. He was sure Papis wasn't done. "Heat will burn your eyes worse than a thousand grains of salt. Flames will rise in your throat and shoot through your belly." Mor didn't know where he was finding the words, but he was. A glimmer of him and his father acting out stories for his family rippled through his thoughts.

"You won't be talking so tough when I reach you," Papis sneered, righting himself. He blinked rapidly, squinting.

Mor was sure everyone and everything was a blur around him. Papis yanked the arm of one of the children watching. The girl screamed, scratching at Papis's fingers. Papis threw her to the ground when he realized it wasn't Mor.

The kids moved back and forth like the tide, depending on where Papis stumbled or swung. Mor made sure to stay out of his reach as well. He also avoided Diallo, who stood at the edge of the mash of kids, focus targeted on Mor. His eyes locked to Mor's movements. He had not raised a finger to help his fellow Danka Boy.

Then, without warning, Papis doubled over and clutched his stomach, moaning. He pulled at his shirt.

All the children gasped.

Then the sky cried. Large splotches of rain assaulted the bright day. Darkened blots multiplied around them, until the rain fell in a heavy sheet. The water made everything hard to see. Wiping frantically at his eyes, Mor kept his head trained on Papis, in case he surged forward under the cover of rain.

Papis swayed.

"The sky has opened, spitting on your venom," Mor said, using the sun-shower as his prop. "You cannot conquer me when I have the sun, wind, and rain on my side. You are not that strong." Mor swallowed down the blood in his throat. The flesh on the inside of his cheek had ripped open.

A wave of whispers rippled around him from the growing crowd. Although the ones in the front wanted to take a cautious step away, the latecomers pressed at their shoulders, pushing them forward. The looks on everyone's faces began to change as they watched Mor. Some grew clouded by doubt, many by surprise, and others lifted in pure enjoyment.

"Stop your childish ramblings." Papis wheezed and tromped forward. "You can do nothing to me," he blustered. However, he didn't sound as menacing as Mor knew he could be. When Papis tried to stand upright, his head dropped and he crouched over again, grasping at his stomach. The crowd sucked in a collective breath, pointing. Rain washed over their faces and drenched their clothes. Papis squared his shoulders. Even though his arms still clutched his middle, Mor knew he was determined not to lose.

He barreled forward, like a charging water buffalo on attack.

At first Papis's feet sloshed across the mud. Then his shoulders drooped and his breathing became raspy. It no longer seemed as if he had the strength to reach Mor at full force. Mor hoped the concoction was taking full effect as he easily sidestepped Papis's advance, sending Papis careening into the outstretched palms of the gawking children.

"Get offa me," he yelled, pushing against the arms in the crowd. He slobbered as he spoke. A mixture of rain and saliva glopped onto his words.

When he turned to face Mor, every muscle connecting his forehead, cheeks, and mouth was scrunched taut. He staggered forward like a drunk after too many cans of La Gazelle. His feet lost traction in the fast-forming mud, and his legs splayed out like those of a baby giraffe leaning down to a watering hole.

He scrambled to his feet again, but Mor could see the fight had left him. He was in pain. He glanced at Mor, eyes filled with rage, frustration, and something else. Could it be a speck of fear? Mor doubted it, but as he took a step forward, Papis took a half step back. No one else might have noticed, but Mor did. He kept his eyes trained on Papis just in case he was wrong.

The crowd even seemed to sense Papis had lost some of his fight. A small boy in a long, dirt-painted shirt dared to reach for one of the motionless fish. But Papis snapped, groaning. Still selfish, he yanked the tainted fish from the little boy's hands, shoving him. The boy skidded to the ground.

"These are mine," Papis growled.

The boy instantly wailed, rattling the air with ear-piercing screeches. Papis ignored him, and no one else dared move to help. Papis snatched the bucket off the ground and filled it with the mud-caked fish. Torn pieces of leaf and berry lay across the ground with them. Papis did not leave a single fish behind.

Mor hunched over and clutched his knees to steady his balance. Saliva pooling in his mouth had the taste of metal. He couldn't believe Papis's greed. He wanted it to all be over. Driven by thoughts of his family and friends, Mor found his last breaths of strength. "When you take from me," he said, wiping his face of rain, "your belly will stir with *safara*." Letting the image of a blaze play in his mind, he hoped Papis's stomach would spasm with fire. "In each scale and in each chunk of meat is my curse."

Papis stopped and squinted at him, snarling. But when he opened his mouth to speak, a howl escaped his throat. He needed every bit of his strength to remain standing.

Although Demba's concoction was not meant to make Papis deathly ill, Mor knew if Papis believed Mor had the power to place a *gris-gris* on him, his mind would take over. A mild stomachache would become much more. Even though Papis said he did not believe Mor's riddles, Mor knew the sheer pain might weaken him and change his mind.

And as if the sun-shower knew it was its time to stop, the sky closed up and the last drops of rain fell.

"Water leaves you." Mor pointed up, thankful for all of Demba's mutterings and the now-clear sky. "The fire will be left to burn." Out of his nonswollen eye Mor watched Papis's eyes widen a bit as he traipsed across the dirt, aimless. Any second he was going to topple over. Cheikh reached out to help him.

"*May ma jaam!*" Papis snarled. He rotated his shoulder and Cheikh's hand dropped. "I don't need you," he snapped. The last of the rain cascaded down his face, but still, tears were visible on the rims of his dark-pink lids. He cradled the bucket to his chest and pushed through the crowd. He didn't look back. Diallo chased after him, torpedoing a wad of spit at Cheikh's feet as he passed.

Mor's old friend halted. Rain had pressed his white T-shirt against him like a second skin. Cheikh watched the other two Danka Boys go.

Mor didn't notice Fatima until she rammed past the shoulders of their neighbors.

"Brother," she cried, hurtling toward Mor. She hugged his waist tight.

He grimaced but hugged her back. Pain ripped through every part of his body.

She tilted her chin up, studying his features as if she had never seen him before. "You made him cry."

Mor didn't have the energy to correct her. Papis wasn't crying because of him; he was crying because of the concoction.

"Even in the rain I saw it," she added as if he were going to deny it. "You're strong." She crushed herself against his wet T-shirt.

You have done well, my son. The road is trampled and bloody, but you still stand.

Relief and exhaustion suddenly pummeled him. He wasn't sure how much longer he could stand. He wanted to fall in the dirt and sleep, but everyone's eyes shifted back to him when Papis disappeared around the corner, Diallo and Lokho close behind.

Cheikh was the last to look away.

Turning from the path Papis had taken, Cheikh watched Mor and his sister. He did not wipe away the rain that shellacked his skin. He ambled toward them, then faltered. He and Mor stared at each other. So many emotions swept past Cheikh's eyes. Mor was sure some of them even mirrored his own. Hurt. Frustration. Hope. Worry. Then he offered Mor his arm and his body as a crutch. Mor hesitated, even though he was about to slip to the ground, carrying Fatima with him. Searching Cheikh's face, he found that the flash of his old friend that he'd seen glimpses of since his return had pushed the other Cheikh aside. Mor clutched Cheikh's offered hand. Sensing the support, he felt his legs buckle, and Cheikh bore most of Mor's weight. With Fatima close at her brother's side, Cheikh half carried, half dragged Mor through the parting crowd as the light grew golden in the late-afternoon sky.

40

AMINA stood in the doorway of their *barak*. The door covering swung up in the breeze, hitting the backs of her legs. She remained motionless as her fingers gripped the doorframe. She stared at her brother, worry lines crowding her face. When Mor gave a weak smile, she catapulted toward him.

"What happened to you?" she asked, staring at his face. Jeeg poked her head out the doorway too. "I was just going to call Tima back home when I heard all this commotion. Was that you? Did that boy do this to you?"

"Mor made him cry," Fatima giggled, all worry gone. "He was tough." She balled up her little fists and spun around, punching.

Cheikh eased past her and helped Mor onto the pallet when they got inside.

Amina turned on Cheikh, just recognizing him. "What are you doing here?" she asked, surprised. "When did you get home? I knew Oumy and Naza were keeping secrets. Were you with my brother? Did you let that boy do this to him?"

Cheikh held up his palms at the assault. "I see you haven't changed much," he said, smirking at her. "My sisters kept my secrets because I asked them to. You are not the only good sister around."

Fatima had stopped mimicking a boxing match and ducked under Cheikh's arm, pushing between him and Amina, breaking up their staring contest. "Move," she demanded. "I have to help my brother." She brought over a shredded cloth and a bowl of water, half of which she spilled on the floor.

They all turned back to Mor.

A surge of pride skated through him as he noticed some of the kids on the path peeking through their window. He had finally done something. He had finally taken a stand. He had not given up. And although the throbbing pressure in his head kept a steady beat, he felt pretty good. His brow had split open, and drops of blood and water dripped over his lump of an eye. Fatima dabbed at it with a corner of the cloth she'd grabbed, then she pressed the material against his jaw. The pain was immediate, as if she'd punched him. It spread through his body, pounding against his temples and throat and coursing through his veins. He could feel every bruise forming and knew his body would have crumbled if he had been struck even one more time.

"Go outside, Tima." Amina tried to take the cloth from her sister as Mor winced.

Fatima held tight to it. She looked determined to nurse her big brother herself. When Amina backed away, Fatima dipped the cloth in the water again and started to clean off the dirt and blood around Mor's knuckles. Mor did not protest. Her touch had turned lighter. Then Jeeg came behind her, licking Mor's wet fingers as if making sure Fatima had not missed a spot.

"Jeeg," Fatima said, but neither she nor Mor pushed Jeeg away.

When Fatima had cleaned each cut, scrape, and scratch she could see, she wrung out the cloth and dropped it into the murky pink water, then moved to kneel at Mor's feet.

"Let's go outside for a bit, Tima." Amina stepped through the doorway, looking back inside. "Give Mor a minute to breathe."

"No." Fatima snuggled close to her brother's leg. "I want to stay with him. Everyone always makes me leave."

Mor raised his foot and wiggled it playfully near her ribs, tickling her. His face cinched up as he held back a moan. "Just for one minute," he mumbled, holding up a dirty finger.

Fatima giggled, pushing away her brother's foot. She studied his face. Then she slowly got up and left his side, glancing back with each step. Jeeg's tail twitched as she followed Fatima.

"Git." Amina shooed the nosy children away. "There is nothing more to see. Go home."

When Mor could no longer see or hear the children or his sisters, he let out a low, slow groan.

"I never knew getting kicked could hurt so much. It never does in football." He sounded as if his mouth were stuffed with rags.

"Well, it's nothing to get used to." Cheikh leaned against the wall. His foot rested flat against it. "You're full of surprises, you know that?"

Wincing, Mor quickly retracted a smile that split his lower lip deeper. He grabbed the cloth Fatima had discarded and wiped at his mouth, patting a new stream of blood.

"Clever trick." Cheikh took out his pocketknife and the wood he had been whittling the last time Mor had seen him. Cheikh carved whenever he was nervous, bored, or passing time, or now any moment he wasn't using his knife to threaten or chase people away.

"What are you making?" The balled-up cloth was pressed against Mor's jaw. He was anxious to take his mind off the pain.

"It's for Naza. She's been selling them." Cheikh ran his fingers across the smooth edge. He held it out to Mor.

"I know." He studied his friend. "So they know you're here?"

"They're my sisters," Cheikh said. "Like you, I want to make sure they are safe and have all they need. Besides, they seem to be better at keeping secrets than you or me. For the longest time Oumy just kept begging me to make more *gaals*, and buses, and *motos*. I didn't understand until I saw all the rocks. They are a better kind of sneaky."

Mor turned the little boat over in his hand, admiring Cheikh's skill. Mor couldn't believe Cheikh had whittled down a branch to what Mor held. Long grooves in the wood resembled the individually bent planks that made up real boats.

Mor handed it back to him, and Cheikh slipped it into his pocket.

After a while Cheikh dropped his foot and pushed off the wall, about to leave. Mor shifted. Pain awakened his body.

"You cannot hide from your *yaay* forever," Mor said as Cheikh turned to go.

"And you cannot play clever tricks every time. He'll be back, you know," he warned, as if he hadn't heard a word Mor said.

Mor stopped. He rubbed the cut on the inside of his cheek with his tongue. "Not tonight."

Cheikh cast the cover aside and turned. "Maybe not . . ."

Mor noticed part of Cheikh's body lay in the glow of the light outside, while half of it lay in shadow. Mor wondered what side Cheikh would choose.

Then, as if answering Mor's question, Cheikh stepped into

the light. Mor slipped off the pallet and followed him. He smiled, ignoring the biting sting at his lip.

"What?" Cheikh asked.

Mor shook his head, looking around the empty yard. "Nothing."

"I don't want to knock away your smile, but he'll come soon. I'm sure of it. And I may not be there to be a bump in the road to slow him. I'm sure he thinks I've betrayed him, and he will never forget what you did to him in front of so many."

"I hope he doesn't." Mor hawked up a gob of bloody saliva. It sat like a marble in the dirt outside the doorway.

"You escaped once," Cheikh said. "But I can't promise you will again. You are a brave *khale*. I only hope your bravery and wit don't tire. I know him."

"I hope I will have another trick by then. *Incha'Allah.*"

"We both may need a trick or two." Cheikh started walking toward the path.

"Are you going to your mother's? You can't go back to Mahktar," Mor said. Cheikh had put himself in danger for him. "You can stay here if you want. We can figure out something so your *baay* won't send you back. I know we can." Mor reached for Cheikh's arm to slow him. "You cannot go back to Papis. He was not born with a heart."

Cheikh shook his head, stopping. "What he did was wrong. Many things he has done are wrong. And I would defend you again tomorrow if I had to make that choice, but I'll also never forget whips have sliced him, scorching cigarettes have seared him, and those supposed to care for him have tossed him in the rubbish heap too many times. A heart was rarely shown to him. I won't forgive him, but I won't forget, either. He saved me when I was broken."

Mor stared. "Don't go back. He'll hurt you. They'll hurt you."

"I won't just slink away. We've been through too much for that. He hardens more each day, and I have hardened beside him. But don't worry, I won't do it anymore."

"Don't go right away. Wait for him to calm."

"He's a prideful lion, pacing a cage, he will never calm. His rage will only build toward me. I have to do it now. Besides, like you have seen, nothing is safe when your scent runs under his nose."

Then he grinned. A dimple appeared in his left cheek, but his smile was not enough to camouflage his worry. "I'll be fine. Now worry about yourself, Mor Fall." Cheikh said Mor's full name, sounding like his mother. He moved away, then spun, traipsing backward. "Remember to twist like the head of an owl, so you can see behind you. You can never know where he will be."

Taking the toy *gaal* from his pocket again, he placed the blade of the knife against it, striking the wood.

Mor watched him go, his rain-drenched clothes clinging to his tall, slender frame. "Go to your *yaay*," Mor called again. Cheikh raised his hand in a dismissive wave as

Amina and Fatima returned on a different path.

"When did he come back?" Amina asked. "I'm sure you are so happy to see him."

Mor kept watching his friend walk away.

"I am," he finally said, and meant it.

When they went back inside, the glimmer of his mother's *djiné* sat at the corner of the pallet where she had been when she cradled Amina's head in her lap each day while Amina was sick. She smiled at Mor, tilting her head slightly. He wanted to rush toward her, but before he could, Fatima, Amina, and Jeeg crushed against him. They pushed against his ribs and side, squishing him. At first he flinched as they pressed against his bruises, but he soon realized he felt no pain. As the setting sun's amber light flooded through the window and doorway, he saw that holding on like this, they were one shadow on the wall, one family. And no matter what tomorrow would bring, they had survived another day together.

WHEN Mor swallowed, it was as if a ball of hard-packed sand were trying to pass down his throat. All he could think of was water. He grimaced and rolled onto his side. His ribs felt crushed by an elephant's foot. All too quickly he became aware of bones and muscles he had never known until then. His body screamed out for his attention, but the ache just under his lungs was the loudest. Then a soothing humming blocked out all other sound. It was a familiar song. His favorite. He tried to open his right eyelid, but it was swollen shut, as if sewn together with Amina's needle and thread. Squinting out of his left eye, he looked around the still-dark room. Jeeg was in her usual corner, and his sisters were snuggled close to each other on his mat. The night before, Amina had ordered him to take the raised cot for more comfort. And now he was relieved to be on the softer padding that cradled his body instead of the unyielding dirt.

Next to them was the small metal bowl filled with water and a rag. Even in the dark Mor could tell the rag was soaked in his blood. The humming was still there, but it was not coming from his sisters. Turning his head, he focused on the shelf that held his parents' photograph. His eyelids fluttered. He ran his hand over his eye, trying to wipe away the sleep. Humming was coming from somewhere. He held his breath and propped himself up on his elbows and stayed perfectly still and listened.

It cannot be, he thought a moment later as his mother glittered into focus. Even though he saw her with his own eyes and heard her with his own ears, he couldn't believe his ears weren't playing a trick of their own. The familiar melody was coming from his *yaay*. He had never heard her spirit before. She was crouched down under the shelf, humming. The sound was what he imagined paradise to be. She smiled when she turned his way. She picked up the water pitcher and poured him a cup of water as if it were just another day. She stood and handed the cup to him. Before the water even touched his lips, he felt its coolness through the plastic mug. The water trickled over the cup's edge as he tilted it back, swallowing every drop. It was the sweetest, coldest water he had ever tasted.

When he lowered the mug, she held out the pitcher, offering him more. She had stopped humming.

He tried to speak, but his *yaay* placed a finger over her lips to quiet him as she refilled his mug. Then she put her hand to her heart and began to hum again. He relaxed. After he finished the water, he settled back onto the pallet and listened. His whole body loosened, as if freed from a belt that was cinched too tight. He tried to keep his eye open, but it grew heavy and he fell back asleep.

"Can I have his *thièrè* now?" Fatima asked. "He hasn't moved and it is almost noon. The cow's milk in it will stink, sitting in the heat."

"It will be fine," Amina whispered. "Now leave him alone. He needs his rest."

"But he won't eat it. He didn't eat last night, either."

Mor could feel Fatima standing over him. Her body blocked out the light that had been hitting his face all morning.

"You can have it," he said. His voice was heavy with sleep. He didn't want to open his one good eye, because he knew his *yaay* would be gone. Instead he wanted to lie balled up with the memory of her fresh in his mind, easing the sting of his aches.

"You need it," Amina said. "Your stomach cannot stay empty. The millet and cow's milk will give you strength."

"I can't." Mor wrapped his arms around himself and carefully curled his legs a little. His eyes were still closed. "I would probably throw it up."

"You have to eat," insisted Amina.

"Later," he said, and slipped back into a welcome sleep.

Demba's imposing figure hovered over Mor, much like he'd hovered over Amina.

"Demba?" Mor whispered, about to rise on his elbows, but Demba pressed his shoulder down.

The air smelled of steam and a piney licorice. Clumps of boiled-down grasses, leaves, and what looked like berry skins covered Mor's chest. The mixture was hot against his skin as Demba applied it to his cuts and gashes, but it soon cooled.

"Stop moving so much," Amina snapped. "You keep knocking everything off."

As Mor relaxed back into the pallet, Demba smeared a dusty-smelling orangey paste over his swollen eye.

"How long has he been here?"

"A few hours," Amina said, softening. "He hasn't left your side except to play rock dolls with Tima as he brewed leaves on the fire. He can make really funny voices for the rocks." She gave a light laugh.

Mor was about to say thank you to Demba, when Demba's large, calloused hand lifted his head, pressing a cup of warm broth against Mor's lips. Although it was nothing like the water his *yaay* had given him, he drank it down, eased by the warm liquid running through him. When Demba placed his head back on the pallet, Mor wasn't certain if he'd whispered "*jërëjëf*" out loud or in his dreams.

❖ ❖ ❖

A little later, as Mor rose, still a bit achy, he realized the sun was already sliding out of the sky to make room for the moon. His sisters were gone and so was Demba. But he heard hushed voices outside the doorway.

"You'd rather run with demons than come home for shelter? I still do not understand that." It was Amina's voice Mor heard.

"Well, I'm not running with them now," Cheikh said. "I'm here, aren't I?"

"Well, you should have been here all along. If Naza hadn't been keeping secrets, I would have told her that." Amina actually sounded a little hurt that her best friend had kept something from her.

"Don't blame her. She was doing it for me." Cheikh paused. "Wouldn't you have done the same for Mor?"

"Yes," Amina agreed. "But—"

"There are no buts."

Mor could hear a smile behind Cheikh's words.

"Do you think they will send you back?"

Cheikh went quiet.

"I mean, your *yaay* can't let him."

"She will try her best, *Incha'Allah*," Cheikh said. "That is all she can do."

"Was it really that bad?"

"It was," he said flatly.

"Do you think the one my *bàjjan* wanted to send Mor to is the same?"

"We can only hope it isn't. They are not all bad."

Cheikh turned toward the door as Mor reached it.

"Ah, so he rises," Cheikh said, getting off the little stump he was on to greet Mor. Amina rose as well.

Mor tried not to show how much pain he was in when he absently bent to drag over another smoothed stump. He clutched his side. It was still very tender.

"Where's Tima and Jeeg?" Mor was nearly hoarse. He glanced up and down the street before taking another step. There was no sign of Demba, either.

"*Malikoum Salam* to you, too," Cheikh said. "They are with Oumy."

Mor was about to apologize for not saying hello, but stopped. He was not the only one with a split lip. The skin around one corner of Cheikh's mouth bulged, and a long gash ran over his mouth. A purplish-black bruise visible against Cheikh's dark skin haloed it. "What happened to you?"

"Nothing." Cheikh shrugged the question off.

Amina sucked her teeth but didn't share her thoughts for once. "Are you hungry? Thirsty?" she asked instead.

Mor shook his head, then regretted it. He leaned against the outside wall. "No food, but maybe water." He glanced inside the window to where their mother had sat through the night with him, humming. The corners of his mouth turned up despite the sting. Amina handed him a mug of water. He sipped the lukewarm water, heated by the daylong sun. It was nothing like the cool, honeyed water his mother's *djiné* had given him.

"Here," Cheikh said, thrusting a turquoise pouch with globes of red and strings of gold crossing it. "Sorry it has taken so long for me to get it back to you."

"Yaay's pouch." Amina reached for it before Mor had a chance to react. "You had it?" She stared between her brother and Cheikh.

Mor noticed coins didn't clank inside it as Amina fiddled with it in her hand.

"Diallo and Laye got to it before I saw it." Cheikh looked at Mor. "They took whatever *khaliss* you had, but dumped everything else in the sand."

Amina open the *nafa*. An old seashell, a baby tooth, a curl of hair, and a button fell into her hand. They had it all back.

Amina walked inside, staring down at the treasures, forgetting both Mor and Cheikh were there.

Mor turned to Cheikh, unsure of what to say.

"Remember when we crept under the pallet when our *yaays* were chattering—" Cheikh started.

"And took out the coins and filled the *nafa* with stones," Mor finished for him. "My *yaay* was ready to skin a lion when she got to the market and only had pebbles to pay the fish man with." Mor let out a small laugh. "She tried to take a switch to me for that."

"Mine did," Cheikh laughed. He winced as if he remembered the punishment, but it was probably just because of his split lip.

When they both looked up, Tanta Coumba was standing before them. She smiled. "Oh, how it does my heart good to see you two laughing as you always should." Then her eyes narrowed and she looked at Mor. "But I am not finished with you. Only these bruises keep me from taking a switch to you. How could you keep such a truth from me? How could you let my boy have even one more day of hurt? I thought you were better, Mor Fall."

Mor couldn't look at her. She was right. There were not enough ways for him to say that he was sorry so that she might believe it. Whatever she wanted to do to him, he would deserve.

"Stop," Cheikh said to Tanta Coumba, standing up and holding her shoulders. He towered over her. "I told you, it wasn't his fault, or Naza's or Oumy's. If you want to be mad, be mad at me. Mor was being the friend that you have always believed him to be. Every time he saw me, he begged me to come home."

Mor felt her glance his way, but he didn't look up.

"Hmph," she sighed. "I will speak no more of it now. You are both my children, and I love that you are here with me and safe." She rose on her toes and kissed Cheikh on the cheek, closing her eyes and hugging him as she did so.

Then she pressed her lips to Mor's forehead and stepped inside the *barak*, greeting Amina, who still stared at the little treasures from their mother's *nafa*. Mor knew tears streamed from her eyes as she sniffled. Tanta Coumba did not bother her; she simply tied the door tarp in a knot to let the breeze in and pulled Mor's sheet off the bed.

She balled it up and tucked it under her arm. Then she spread a freshly washed one in its place. When she stepped back outside, she tilted Mor's head toward the sky to examine his swollen eye.

"It's healing well." She picked up the metal bowl filled with used rags. "Demba should be back soon." Then she turned to Cheikh. "When you leave here, the only path you know is to our door. You hear me?" She stared at her son, her hennaed finger pointing at him. "Our door," she said again, as if he might not have understood the first time. Then she bid Mor good-bye and walked away, the sheet and the bowl of bloody, rung-out rags in her hand.

"So are you going to tell me what happened?" Mor asked after she left. The skin around his jaw was still swollen and sore.

"I did." Cheikh looked up. "I found it tossed aside in the sand."

Mor just stared at his friend. At his busted lip.

Cheikh smiled but flinched. The cut in his lip was in charge. "It's nothing, really." He pressed his hand to it. "It seems we met the same fist, that's all. I think we both knew it would happen."

"What else happened?"

"Not much. Diallo had the pleasure of shoving me out. He's always wanted to be at Papis's side."

"Are they going to leave you alone?" Mor was frustrated by how calm Cheikh was.

"Who knows."

Mor wasn't sure what else to say. His friend sounded almost sad that he would no longer be a Danka Boy.

"You and my *yaay* can never understand the hell we were mixed in together. We will always be brothers, even when we disagree. He just needs to find a better way. He hasn't yet. And I realize I cannot find that way for him. He has to want to find it himself. He has so much anger, and I see it now. I was just so grateful. I guess all this time I ignored it." He took a new piece of wood and his knife from his pocket. "Shouldn't you be resting anyway?"

"I have been." Mor studied the bruises on Cheikh's face. "So will your *yaay* tell your *baay* you're here?"

Cheikh stared straight ahead. "She has to. But she says she'll give me time."

"Maybe she will think of some way you can stay. Or we can." Hope rose in Mor's voice. Even though he wasn't certain of his own future, he was hopeful for his friend. "How are you with bigger ones?" Mor nodded to the wood Cheikh carved. It was another little *gaal*.

"What do you mean?" Cheikh stopped pushing his knife against the stick.

"Demba needs the rotted boards taken out of his boat

411

before it sinks. It's holding up, but it could use work." Mor ignored the urge to blame Cheikh and the Danka Boys for the fire. "He would pay."

"I don't need your charity."

"It's not," Mor said. "You'd be repairing his boat."

Cheikh didn't say anything.

"Souleymane also needs help. His boat is the one that caught fire. He might give you a chance."

"Why would you do this?" Cheikh asked.

"Why would you let me remain hidden under that netting on the beach?" Mor kicked at the dirt. He and Cheikh watched each other.

A small smile crept across Cheikh's mouth, reaching his eyes. "So you did know it was me."

"Not at first."

The two friends were silent. An unspoken understanding passed between them.

"This might be how you get your *baay* to let you stay."

"Maybe."

"Maybe?" Mor wanted Cheikh to be as excited as he was about the idea. If Cheikh brought money into the family, his father could no longer say he just took up space. He might actually look forward to the coins coming through his door. "If that doesn't work, we will find another way. I promise." For Mor, this promise was as weighty as the one he'd made to his *baay* and his sisters.

"*Incha'Allah*," was all Cheikh whispered.

42

FIVE hundred francs, five hundred, five hundred, two hundred francs, two hundred, five hundred, and five hundred more," Mor said as he and Amina sat on the dirt floor of their *barak*, a stack of coins and notes between them.

Fatima sat at the door as lookout, though none of the Danka Boys had been seen since Mor scared them away.

"Don't forget the trick can." Mor wiggled under the bed and pulled out the tomato can wrapped in cloth. Inside a handful of coins jingled. They clinked and tumbled on one another as he poured them onto the floor.

"Five, five, five, ten, ten, ten, twenty, twenty, twenty-five, twenty-five, twenty-five, fifty, one hundred, one hundred, one hundred, two hundred, two hundred, two hundred, two hundred, five hundred, five hundred francs." He added the coins with the others. "So how much do we have?" he asked Amina, who wrote down the numbers on a torn piece of cardboard.

"Um." Amina pointed her pencil at each number, mumbling to herself as she added. "That makes five thousand two hundred ten francs."

"That's all?" Mor asked, sounding deflated. He was sure he had made more. "But that is not enough. I only got you halfway. I checked the paper." He shook his head, crestfallen. He had tried all he could try, but it wasn't enough.

"Don't be sad yet, brother. We still must add this." Amina pulled her own pouch out of a secret hiding place under a pile of rocks not yet turned into dolls. She opened it and let coins and a few folded notes fall on the floor.

Mor's eyes bulged as he leaned forward. "How much is here?"

"Enough," Amina said, smiling.

Mor poked through the bills with his finger. "Is this all from your dolls?"

"There was more. But Naza did a lot of work too. She sewed most of the dresses."

Mor couldn't believe how much she had made off her rock dolls. Then he thought of all the *toubabs*, who he knew would always pay more than the villagers.

"It's exactly two thousand nine hundred ninety francs," she said. "So that makes—"

"Eight thousand two hundred francs," Mor cut in. "I can do that math."

She looked down at her paper. Her face fell a little. "But it is still not enough."

"It isn't?" Mor tried to add again quickly in his head. She was right.

Amina placed the cardboard on the floor by her feet and stared at the coins. With each passing second she seemed to shrink in front of Mor's eyes, collapsing in on herself.

He wished there were something he could do, but they had run out of time. He thought of the *tàngal* he hadn't had the chance to sell because of the Danka Boys. Then he thought of his soccer ball and wondered if he could sell it. As much as he wanted one, he did not want anything from the Danka Boys.

Then he remembered.

He jumped up and ran outside. Amina barely looked up when he raced off. He went around the back of their *barak*, tossing aside the soccer ball, and dug deep. Right where he'd left them sat the two five-hundred-franc coins like seeds in the dirt. They had been his reward for helping Papis win the soccer match when he was a Danka Boy. He hadn't wanted the money then, but now, after all they had put him through, finally some good could come out of crossing paths with the Danka Boys. A money tree hadn't bloomed, but these would do.

Mor squeezed the coins in his palm and sprinted back to Amina. "Mina, Mina, we did it."

He placed the two coins on the ground in front of her. At first she stared past them, almost gazing through the dirt. "Look, Amina. Look." Mor shook her. "We did it. We did it! We have enough. You are going to school."

"What?" Amina said, her head bobbing back and forth as he shook her. "What did you say?"

"I said you have enough for school."

"But how?" She stared at the coins.

"It doesn't matter, just know we did it. We really did it, Mina."

Amina reached over and hugged her brother, knocking over all the coins. Fatima bolted back inside, colliding with both of them.

"Mina's going to get the green uniform?" Fatima asked.

"And the cream blouse," Amina said, wiping her eyes. "We did it."

"We did it!" Fatima echoed. "Now we can stay."

Amina pried her sister's arm from around her neck and gathered the money together to put back into the pouches. "Maybe," she said. "We still have to convince Auntie."

"She has to say yes," Mor said, not letting the thought of their *bàjjan* dampen his spirit even a little bit. "She can never say we're a bother to anyone now. We have done it on our own."

"We have done it, Baay. We have made it through the summer together. That is what you wanted. Auntie will have to let us stay now, won't she?" Mor craned his head back, searching the brilliant blue sky. Light, airy clouds rushed across it, as if in a race with the finches and buntings flying by.

"Who are you talking to?"

Mor jerked his head down. He stumbled, missing a step.

Right in front of him, Papis leaned against a mud wall, picking something from his teeth with his finger. No one else was around. At first Mor was ready to run, but even his healing bruises weren't reason enough to make him scatter. He wouldn't roll back down a hill he'd spent so much time climbing when he was so close to reaching the top.

"What do you want?" he asked.

"What do you think?" Papis got off the wall and flicked away whatever he had found wedged in between his teeth.

He watched Mor closely but stayed off the path, as if wanting to keep distance between them.

It was the first time Mor had seen him without any other Danka Boys. Papis didn't look as intimidating without his herd.

Then, in the distance, the faintest of whistles boomeranged off an alley wall.

Papis looked toward the sound, and Mor stepped toward him. When Papis turned back, Mor saw a faint flicker of unease in his eyes. He remembered that same look during their fight. His closeness unnerved Papis. But Papis was too proud to show it.

Mor studied Papis's face and his beady black eyes, which

stared back at him. The gash over his eye reminded Mor he was human. Mor found he was no longer scared of him. "I know your fear," Mor said suddenly.

"Fear?" scoffed Papis. "I have no fear."

"You are afraid of me," Mor said. "Afraid of what I can do. Afraid of what Demba has taught me." Mor's voice was as calm as the ocean on a breezeless dawn. He spoke as if he and Papis were relaxing on a beach wall, sharing an engorged plastic bag of *bissap* juice. "Afraid that I am not afraid of you anymore. That is your fear." Mor went silent and let his words settle on Papis. "Because if I, a boy no taller than your elbow, am not afraid . . . why should anyone else be?"

Mor felt the heat rising off Papis's skin. A thin vein pulsed in his neck. Papis did not blink or speak. Neither did Mor.

"You are a tough little *khale*, I will give you that." Papis wiped at his mouth. "You could have been a fierce Danka Boy behind me."

"My *baay* taught me to stand behind no one." Mor took another step forward.

Papis stepped back before he could stop himself.

The corner of Mor's lip pushed up. "If I wanted to hurt you, I could, but that is not my—"

"Tah, you could never hurt me," Papis jeered.

"Are you so sure?" Mor crossed his arms, finding confidence and strength. He didn't have any tainted fish or scary words, but he didn't need them. He just needed Papis to believe.

After a silence that stretched like an eternity, Papis smiled a crooked smile and widened the distance between himself and Mor. "You are an interesting one, like that coward you believe to be your brother, seeing good where there is only filth." He jutted out his chin. "But one day both of you will see the world is no better than the sludge I was born in."

"We'll never see that," Mor said.

Papis hawked up phlegm in his throat and let it launch across the dirt. "You know nothing." His voice grew bitter. "And neither does that traitor Cheikh. You will both see!"

The set of Papis's jaw, the narrowing of his eyes, and the return of the boy Mor had first seen on the beach came upon him like a sandstorm.

"Do not get comfortable. Neither of you are completely out of my netting." Papis leaned forward. "I will still squash you if you cross me."

"And I will still come at you with fire," Mor warned, surprised by his own force. "Remember, I am not scared of you, and neither is Cheikh."

Papis bared his teeth like Lokho often did.

But Mor didn't back down. "Come for me." He poked at the air. "And you will see all I can do." He slapped his hand against his chest.

Papis's foot hovered behind him, ready to move back again. "You aren't worth the trouble," he said, puffing out his own chest. "I have more important things to take my time. You are nothing and you have nothing I want." He hopped back, picking up his pace with each step until he was almost running.

"Stay out of my way, *khale*."

"No," Mor warned. "You stay out of mine."

Papis batted the air with his hand, and from a safe distance away he cupped his hands over his mouth and shouted, "You better run when you see me."

But Mor was the one who watched him run away instead.

43

"SO much has happened since I left on that bus bound for Dakar," Mor heard his aunt say two days later on a bench outside Amadou's shack with Tanta Coumba. "I hardly recognize these children. How the summer sun has changed them."

"That is what happens when children are left to blossom," Tanta Coumba told her. "They grow."

"Yes, though sometimes they can twist and be ensnared by weeds," Mor's *bàjjan* cautioned.

"They can indeed . . . ," Tanta Coumba whispered. She glanced her son's way. It was only a quick shift of her eyes, but Mor had seen it. "But we can only pray that with Allah's guidance and the warmth of the sun they will turn back to light if they find themselves in darkness. But that worry has not been so with yours." Her voice grew light again.

Mor eyed Cheikh beside him on an old, overturned *gaal*. He noticed his friend's head dipped a bit as the women talked. But Mor shared Tanta Coumba's hope and wished for it to be true. He and Cheikh sat quietly, staring out to the surf as Fatima and Oumy giggled. Demba held tight to pieces of cloth wrapped around their middles while they splashed in the water, learning to swim.

"I remember when I tried to teach you." Cheikh raised his elbow toward their sisters. "You bucked and screamed and cried each time I threw you in, and it only rose to your chest. I couldn't make sense of it." He chuckled.

Mor remembered those times. "I was scared if I went under, you would leave me there alone."

"I would never leave. . . ." Cheikh's words could barely be heard over the lapping of the water against the shore. But Mor had heard them.

The smell of Amadou's grilling fish met Mor's nose, and he smiled. Even though his *bàjjan* hadn't made up her mind yet, for Mor it was a beautiful day surrounded by family in a place he loved. He, Amina, and Fatima had done all they could do. At that moment Amina looked up from her reading. Her lips creased in a slight smile as she admired the tiny *sër* Naza sewed for a rock doll, while baby Zal played in the fabric strips on her lap.

Music heavy with sabar drumbeats pinged off the air

around them, coming from a small radio hanging at the front of Amadou's shack. Jeeg lay under one of the tables, nibbling anything she could find.

"Well, well, well." Mor heard Tanta Basmah's full, cheery voice behind him. "Am I finally to meet the wonderful and brilliant *bàjjan* Mor and the girls have told me so much about?"

Mor turned just as Basmah reached out her henna-tipped fingers, clasping both of his aunt's hands, and kissed each of her cheeks. She winked at Mor as she straightened.

"I hear you are doing fabulous things in the city, and these children are doing fabulous things here. Aren't they, Tanta Coumba Gueye?" Tanta Basmah greeted Tanta Coumba with two kisses as well.

"Yes, they are," Tanta Coumba joined in, not missing a step. "Their names are on many tongues, and it is always followed by a smile. They have become an example of what a strong family can do. And you are a part of all that." Tanta Coumba patted the thigh of Mor's aunt. "People applaud your courage to give them the opportunity to grow. Your name is in their hearts as well."

Dieynaba beamed. It was clear she enjoyed the praise.

"Yes," Tanta Coumba said. "By allowing them to sprout, their roots have become strong. They are making a respectable life. One I am sure Allah will reward, Dieynaba."

"If Allah wills." Mor's aunt slowly swayed back and forth. He saw her mind working behind her hooded eyes.

"Amina, *kai fii.* Tell your *bàjjan* of your wonderful painted rocks. And Mor, come tell her of your success in the mechanic shop and out at sea. Come, children, come," Tanta Coumba encouraged.

"I have heard. Mamadou told me all in our brief phone calls," their aunt admitted. "I'm sure he was informed by you. Yes, I am proud. As soon as my sandals touched the dusty earth of Lat Mata, I've heard praise. *Yalla Bakh na.*"

"Yes, Allah is good." Basmah nodded as Mor and Amina made their way over to their *bàjjan.*

"Come and feast," Amadou called out to Demba and the girls kicking in the waves. He lifted the grilling fish from the flames and slid them onto trays, head to tail. Basmah cut one of the lemons she had brought and squeezed it over the fish.

As Demba and the girls reached the table, salt water running down their faces, Tanta Coumba picked up a cloth to pat down both Oumy and Fatima. Tanta Coumba dried Fatima's arms as Fatima asked, "So can we stay?"

Everyone went silent. It seemed as if they all held their breath.

"We shall see, Fatima. There is a lot still to decide," their *bàjjan* said as sweetly as she could, but her smile was tight. She did not appear to like being on a stage, all eyes on her.

"Like what?" Fatima pressed. No one stopped her.

"Many things, child. They will be discussed at home, tonight," their aunt cautioned, staring Fatima down.

"But Mina wants to go to school. She has the money. And she says maybe she'll even be able to pay for me to go one day. Mor brings us fish with Demba. And he learns to fix engines like Baay." She rattled off everything so fast, it was hard to keep up. "And Oumy and Naza and Tanta Coumba and Tanta Basmah are always here if we need help. They give us hugs and kisses, and *sidèmes*, too," she went on.

"Okay, that is enough, Tima," Tanta Coumba whispered, pulling Fatima closer to her side. "Your *bàjjan* is a woman who needs much time to think."

"But she still hasn't said yes and she's been thinking all summer." Fatima pouted.

"Yes, Auntie, Mor has tried so hard," Amina spoke up, a rock doll in her hand. Everyone turned to her. "He has done everything a brother should do and more. Iéna's would still be a dream if he hadn't made it real. Even when I was hard on him, he never stopped trying for me. Can't you see that? Can't you see our home is here? Can't you see how much we want to stay? Please do not be the reason we cannot. We don't want to be separated. We are better together."

No one took a breath as their *bàjjan* shifted uncomfortably on her seat. She stared at Amina as if she were seeing her for the first time.

"W-whe . . . well . . . ," she sputtered, undoubtedly feeling the heat of all their focus.

"And if we get sick," Fatima butted in, "Demba can save us."

Tanta Coumba hugged her close, kissing the top of Fatima's head.

"I still don't know." Their aunt smoothed out the folds in her *boubou*. Then her eyes found Mor. "This is too great a responsibility for you."

"It's a responsibility I want," Mor said, standing taller. "This is where Baay and Yaay are."

"But the *daara* would teach you to be a pious man. Many wise leaders have found their way from there."

"And many children have gotten lost at some too," Cheikh added. He stood above everyone except Demba. "Bàjjan, I know you want what is best for them. It won't be at a *daara* and it won't be cleaning a stranger's floors. It will be here. Amina's mind is like the ocean, you cannot see to its end, and Mor's heart is like the rising sun, bright and shining." He pointed down to the marks on Jeeg's hide. "Just like their *yaay* and *baay*. Do not lock away those things for them. They should be here with us. I will share the responsibility with my brother." He nodded to Mor. "Even though I am older, he has taught me how to never turn away from a true friend. We'll look out for each other, together." He swept his hand over his friends and family. "Please let us."

"Those are kind words," Dieynaba said. "But there is a large world out there that they should see. And it could start in Dakar."

"And we will see it in time, *Incha'Allah*." Mor moved

closer to his aunt. "But for now our life is meant to be here. Our friends and our family are—"

"I am your family," she reminded him.

"And you will always be." He glanced at his sisters.

Amina stepped next to him and placed a rock doll in their *bàjjan*'s palm. It looked so much like their aunt that she let out a small gasp when she saw it. The doll wore a similar *boubou* and *mousore* to the ones she had arrived in.

Mor didn't believe it could ever happen, but as he watched, he saw his aunt softening, as if a shell were cracking.

"It's you, Auntie," Fatima squealed. "It's you!"

"I see, child. I see." She pressed her hands around the doll as if in prayer. "I am not yet sure this is the right thing."

"Please, Bàjjan," Mor urged. "Give us a chance to do more. Do not make us go." He knelt in front of her, clasping his hands. "I need my sisters and they need me."

"You act as if you are being torn apart."

"But that is how it would feel," Mor said. "How it would be."

Their aunt blew out. "I don't think it is as serious as all that." She looked to Tanta Coumba for agreement. Tanta Coumba only shrugged.

"It is," Mor added. "I am better when I am with them. Please let us stay."

Their *bàjjan* searched everyone's faces, and everyone searched hers.

427

"An unclenched fist will let the *pithis* fly." Demba stared up at the sky, his back to the group as though he hadn't been listening.

Their aunt gave the slightest nod of understanding. Then she sighed. "This is still not settled within me, but I would be a villain if I tore you away when you speak so. You have my blessing. You can remain."

Fatima was the first to react, shrieking. She threw her arms around Tanta Coumba and then leaped away, skipping in circles with Oumy. Jeeg, who'd been chewing plastic under a table, bleated, "Meh-mehhh," and went to push against Fatima's back, joining them.

Mor stared at his extended family. He would never have dared believe it would all work out.

When your heart is open, it will continue to fill.

He gasped and stood very still. As everyone else moved about, wrapped in the excitement of the news, he closed his eyes and listened.

When your mind is open, you will experience the wonder of possibility.

His *yaay*'s voice was no heavier than a breath. And smoother than a butterfly's wing. He had to hold his own breath to hear it. Then a faint silhouette of his *baay* as he remembered him, wearing his sky-blue tunic and pants, came into view. Mor rushed forward, reaching out, but only grasped salted air. *When you search for opportunity*, his *baay* offered, *it will find you. Remember this, my son.*

"I will, Baay. I will," Mor said as his family's laughter filled the beach behind him.

We are proud of all you have accomplished. You have kept your promise well and fulfilled so much more.

Mor smiled as his father's spirit flickered like a flame in front of him.

You are equipped for this journey now.

But remember, his *yaay* said faintly. He searched the sky for her image. *You can always find us in here.* Her hand appeared then, shimmering like the sun on speckled sand, and then her arm and the rest of her slowly materialized like sugar when it first falls into a glass of tea. He touched his chest over his heart, where she touched him, filling him with heat.

Yes, that is where we will always be, his father assured him.

Tears welled in Mor's eyes, but he was not sad. Although he knew it was good-bye, he knew it was not forever. For he would always be with them and them with him.

"Mor," Amina called from the table. "We are ready to eat."

After one last look at his parents, memorizing the curve of his *yaay*'s cheek and each sprig of stubble on his *baay*'s chin, he turned to his sister and his family around him. And he knew they were his home.

AUTHOR'S NOTE

When I started writing this book, and created the fictional villages of Lat Mata and Mahktar, I was uncertain of where Mor's journey would lead me. And although this is a story purely of fiction, I wanted to make sure it was based in some reality. I hope all readers, and especially those unfamiliar with Senegal, the land of *teranga* (hospitality), will gain a better understanding of some of its many charms, as well as some of its struggles.

I wanted to showcase not only the importance of things like fish, a staple in most Senegalese homes, and the power of superstitions and *gris-gris*, but also the hardships of some *talibés* (tah-LEE-bays).

Even though my story does not center on the plight of the

talibé, a word that means "disciple" or "follower" in Arabic, I wanted to show how the experiences of some of these children could play a profound role in their lives and the community at large.

Every time I go to Senegal, and the capital city of Dakar, especially, I am struck by the number of young boys who swarm the streets with empty tomato cans or plastic yellow bowls begging for alms. *Talibés* are mainly boys and come from both rich and poor families, but many are from rural villages, sent by parents who are often unaware of the hardships their children might face in the city. They send their sons and (some) daughters to be educated and cared for at a religious school known as a *daara*, under the tutelage of an Islamic teacher, or *serigne*. Although many of the *serignes* who instruct the children in the teachings and memorization of the Koran are fair and pious, and want to instill humility in their pupils, there are some, like the one Papis and Cheikh encountered, who unfortunately exploit the children for their own gains.

In 2010, the international aid group Human Rights Watch estimated that some fifty thousand children begging on the streets of Senegal were students of these *daaras*. Sadly, many of these neglected children live in deplorable conditions, usually cramped in unsanitary shacks with twenty to thirty other boys, sometimes for many years. Some are even beaten if they do not return to the *serigne* after a day of begging with a certain amount of food or money. Memorizing the Koran should normally take two to three years, but because the students are sent to beg for most of the day, they are away from their families sometimes as long as eight years.

Talibés are an accepted norm in Senegalese culture, and many prominent leaders in the country were brought up in this tradition. It is a complicated subject because the beliefs behind these practices are heavily tied to religion, an integral part of the society. In recent years, however, leaders are beginning to take action. During the summer of 2016, President Macky Sall ordered that all street children be returned to their families or placed in transit centers. Although this will not end all the troubles these young people face, it is a definite step in the right direction.

Through writing about Senegal and the *talibé,* my hope is that I will spark an interest in others to learn more about this beautiful country and the grace, richness, and dignity of her people.

—Leah Henderson

ACKNOWLEDGEMENTS

When I first looked out a car window in Saint-Louis, Senegal, and saw a boy sitting on a beach wall and whispered to myself, "What story would you tell me?", I never imagined that the ten-page story I scribbled in my journal would ever go farther than my grad-school professor's inbox. But regardless of my uncertainty about telling this story, my professor Louella Bryant saw something in Mor's journey that I didn't yet see. Ellie, thank you for encouraging me to keep giving you "just a few more pages of Mor." Luke Wallin, Rachel Harper, and Crystal Wilkinson, thank you for teaching me about craft so that I could tell this story. And to the amazing MFA staff at Spalding University (Katy, Kathleen, Karen, and Sena), I will always be appreciative of the warmth and encouragement you have shown me from the first moment I met each of you.

Babs, thank you for sharing your enormous heart and for pushing open a window so I could see and breathe the true beauty of Senegal.

To the Gueye family, from our first meeting in the courtyard of your home, I instantly felt as if I were with family. My love for you cannot be measured.

Grandma, I will always hear you saying: *"Waaw waaw. Namm naa la."* And I miss you too.

Mom and Dad, the words "thank you" will never be enough to express my gratitude for your endless and unconditional love and support. In every way, you told me I could do this. And when I was frustrated, thank you for reminding me that this book is for the kids who don't often see themselves front and center on the page and not to give up. I am honored and blessed each and every day to call myself your daughter.

Moe, since the days of making sure I had the biggest toys in my crib and the best haircut, you have always looked out for me, and I am forever grateful. Derick, just having you push up your glasses and ask, "How's it going, sis?" always leaves me with a smile and lets me know you care. You are the best big brothers a little sister could ever wish for. And it is because of you both that Mor knows how to be an amazing big brother too.

Assa Diaw, thank you so much for agreeing to be an early beta reader. You will never know how much it meant when you wrote that reading my manuscript "feels like a warm chocolate cake dessert for [your] soul; almost like a slice of home." Dr. Babacar Dieng of Gaston Berger University, Saint-Louis, thanks so much for taking the time to review sections of my early drafts and for answering all of the many questions I sent your way time and time again.

I would also like to express a heartfelt thank-you to Rubin Pfeffer for believing in Mor's story and to Melissa Nasson for your thoughts on making it better. John Jay Cabuay, you have given Mor a beautiful coat to greet the world in. Thank you.

And to my wonderful editors: Jessica Sit, thank you for your excitement about this project and for bringing me into the Atheneum/Simon & Schuster family, and Alexa Pastor, thank you for your patience and your guidance. And Erica Stahler, I am in awe of your keen eye. It has been a pleasure working with each of you.

Michelle Edwards, Frank Eposito, docents (Paula Hirschoff, Detra Robinson, Theresa Steverlynck) of the Smithsonian National Museum of Africa Arts, along with Mr. Diaw and Nicole Dewing, I appreciate your quick responses to all of my many queries.

Daning Koite, the day I called the Senegalese Embassy in need of help was a day I made a true friend. Thank you for everything, especially your laugh. Tanaz Bhathena and Papa Sangoné Sene, I am beyond grateful to both of you for taking the time to read through *One Shadow on the Wall* and for all of your comments and thoughts on how to make it a stronger work. Adama Coulibaly, I have always considered you a brother, and I appreciate you never tiring of me asking you an endless stream of questions, no matter how repetitive or random, and no matter the hour. Your kindness will never be forgotten.

And to my kiddies at ACFA orphanage in Bamako, Mali. Although you are across the border from Senegal, the hope and fire I saw in each of you after only a few short months at ACFA greatly informed how I wanted Mor and his sisters to be. My love for you was poured into every inch of Mor, Amina, and Tima. Remember you are always in my heart!

And to Boston, my best buddy. A girl couldn't ask for a better friend to take long walks with, play soccer with, and talk to when humans just couldn't understand.

So many people have had a hand in making this book a reality, but none more than Lesléa Newman, my friend and mentor and Mor's greatest cheerleader. I will never be able to say thank you enough for all the love and support you have shown Mor and me over the years. You are a beautiful, (leopard-print-wrapped) brilliance.

It has truly taken a mighty village to get here.

Jërëjëf, everyone!

wursts and frankfurters, corned beef and corned tongue. In the early days, the cured meats were shipped over from Germany, but as the Jewish community settled in, it became more self-sufficient. During the 1870s, kosher sausage factories sprang up on the Lower East Side to supply the quickly multiplying number of Jewish delicatessens in New York, Philadelphia, Baltimore, and smaller cities as well. In 1872, a German butcher named Isaac Gellis produced some of America's first domestic kosher frankfurters in his sausage factory at 37 Essex Street. As the company was passed down from father to son to grandson, it grew into an empire, with delicatessen restaurants selling nothing but the Gellis brand scattered through Manhattan. One of them, Fine & Schapiro, can still be found on the Upper West Side of Manhattan. Moses Zimmerman, also from Germany, was another early sausage-maker. His factory on East Houston Street opened in 1877, producing bolognas, frankfurters, wienerwursts, corned beef, and corned tongue, along with kosher cooking fat.

In the 1880s, as migration patterns shifted and large numbers of Eastern European Jews sailed for America, they discovered the delicatessen in cities like New York, Philadelphia, and Chicago. The great majority had never seen one before. Older immigrants looked on the delicatessen with suspicion (it was "too spicy" and "too fancy"), while their children were intoxicated by its distinct perfume, a blend of boiled beef, garlic, pepper, and vinegar. Mondays through Fridays, they rushed from school to the local deli for a lunch of pickles and halvah. On Saturdays, the delicatessen was closed for the Sabbath, but it opened again Saturday evenings at sundown. This was a moment that ghetto kids looked forward to with crazed anticipation, famously captured by Alfred Kazin in his food-rich memoir, *A Walker in the City*. Saturdays at twilight, Kazin writes, neighborhood kids haunted the local delicatessen, waiting for it to reopen. As soon as it did, the kids raced in, "panting for the hot dogs sizzling on the gas plate just inside the window. The look of that blackened empty gas plate had driven us wild all through the wearisome Sabbath day. And now, as the electric sign blazed up again, lighting up the words Jewish National Delicatessen, it was as if we had entered our rightful heritage."[19]

The irony here is that the delicatessen was not, in fact, a pillar of

Jewish food culture, at least not for the Russians, or the Poles, or the Litvaks, but the Jews declared it one all the same. If their mothers disapproved—and most mothers did—for Jewish kids, the delicatessen was like a second home, part lunchroom, part urban clubhouse, and at night, an after-hours meeting place for ghetto sweethearts. With their limited pocket money, East Side kids were confined to the cheapest items on the delicatessen menu: a frankfurter with yellow mustard or a salami sandwich. The big-ticket item was a plate of sliced deli meat served with a tub of pickles. The most aristocratic option of all was the "mixed plate": a combination of pastrami, corned beef, and tongue.

Inch by inch, their kids leading the way, the new Jewish immigrants developed a taste for the cured meats of their German brothers and sisters. Those with an entrepreneurial bent looked to the delicatessen as a business opportunity and opened stores of their own. Samuel Chotzinoff, a Russian immigrant and future concert pianist, remembers exactly what that entailed. The Chotzinoff family arrived in New York in the late 1890s when Samuel was around eight years old. A few years later, when his mother decided to open a delicatessen, she paid a visit to one of the local sausage manufacturers. In keeping with East Side custom, the Mandelbaum Sausage factory offered her a kind of delicatessen start-up package. It included fixtures for the store (paid for on an installment plan) and three months of credit toward supplies. The sausage people even taught her how to cut meat into the thinnest possible slices, the delicatessen's key to financial success. A seltzer company lent Mrs. Chotzinoff a soda-water fountain for making syrup drinks. The store kitchen was a backroom with a three-burner stove, where she cooked her own corned beef in a tin clothes boiler. The entire operation cost her only $150 upfront, money that she borrowed from a well-off landsman.

Looking beyond the delicatessen, the Jewish East Side was home to a staggering variety of eating places. Neighborhood restaurants catered to every nameable niche and subniche of the local population—geographic, economic, professional, and even political—attracting a highly specialized clientele of like-minded diners. Every national group had its corresponding restaurant. The more modest establishments were located in tenement apartments temporarily converted into public eating spaces. Blurring the line between home and business, the private restaurant offered diners a truly Old World eating experience: a home-cooked meal prepared in the style of a particular region or city back in Europe. A visitor to the East Side in 1919, who discovered these private restaurants, explains how they worked:

> *A great many of the emigrants from Russia and Rumania, even after years of alienation, have an intense craving for the dishes of their native province. They cannot assimilate the American cuisine, even though they accept its citizenship. It is, therefore, the practice of the inhabitants of particular province to convert her front parlor (usually located on the ground floor of a tenement) into a miniature dining room, where she caters to a limited number of her home-town folk. Her shingle announces the name of her province, such as "Pinsker," "Dwinsker," "Minsker," "Saraslover," "Bialystoker," etc., as the case may be. Here the aliens meet their friends from the Old Country and lose their homesickness in the midst of familiar faces and dialects and in the odors from the kitchen, which evoke for them images for their home and surroundings.*[20]

Parlor restaurants answered the needs of the working person, but the ghetto also provided for the local population of well-off merchants, factory owners, lawyers, doctors, and real estate barons. By the turn of the century, a half dozen glittering eating-places had opened on the Lower East Side, which catered to the downtown aristocracy. Most of them were in the hands of Romanian Jews, the self-proclaimed bon vivants of the ghetto.

The Romanian quarter of the Lower East Side began at Grand Street and continued north until Houston Street. It was bounded on the west by the Bowery, the border between the Jewish ghetto and Little Italy, and by Clinton Street to the east, the thoroughfare that separated the Romanians from the Poles. The streets within this square quarter-mile were unusually dense with pastry shops, cafés, delicatessens, and restaurants,

the most opulent eateries south of 14th Street. Dining rooms were decorated in the sinuous Art Nouveau style, a raised platform at one end for
the house orchestra, the tables arrayed along a well-polished dance floor.
Sunday nights, when ghetto restaurants were at their busiest, the dance
floors were crowded with ample-bodied Jewish women, the grand dames
of the Lower East Side, decked out in their finest gowns and sparkliest
diamonds.

The deluxe surroundings belied the earthy, garlic-laced cuisine typical of the Romanian rathskeller. The following account of Perlman's
Rumanian Rathskellar at 158 East Houston Street comes from a 1930
restaurant guide:

> *The food for the most part is invariably unspellable and wholly deli-
> cious. Sweetbreads such as you never encountered before; smoked goose
> pastrami, aromatic salami, chicken livers, chopped fine and sprinkled
> with chopped onions; Wiener schnitzel; pickled tomatoes and pickled
> peppers; sweet-and-sour tongue; and huge black radishes. Because it's
> so good, you eat and eat until your head swims, drinking seltzer to
> help it along.[21]*

The Romanian restaurants were also known for their "broilings," or
grilled strip steaks, and for their *carnitzi*, sausages that were so pungent
they seemed one part ground meat to one part garlic.

Romanians shared East Houston Street with Hungarians, and
together the two groups transformed a generous chunk of the Lower
East Side into New York's leading café district. Where Russian Jews were
devoted tea drinkers, the Hungarians had acquired a love for coffee, a
habit learned from the Ottoman Turks. (Along with Austria, Hungary
was part of the vast territory claimed by the Ottomans between 1544
and 1699.) Settling in the United States in the late nineteenth century,
the Hungarians brought their coffee habit with them, establishing scores
of coffee houses in immigrant enclaves. Visitors to the East Side counted
at least one café on nearly every block of the Hungarian quarter, while
some streets had four or five. Coffee on the East Side was served in the

European style, with a small pot of cream and a tumbler of water, a symbolic gesture of hospitality. That was for patrons who asked for their coffee *schwartzen*. Coffee with milk was served in a glass. Whichever style, Hungarian coffee was often consumed with pastry, maybe a slice of strudel, apple or poppy seed, or a plate of *kiperln*, the crescent-shaped cookies that we know as rugelach.

After dark, well-heeled New Yorkers descended on the cafés for a night of "slumming," a term coined in the nineteenth century. For the uptown city-dweller, slumming on the Lower East Side was both an opportunity for cultural enrichment, like a visit to the museum, and a form of ribald entertainment. The adventure began as the uptowner crossed 14th Street and entered the foreign quarter, seeking immigrant cafés with olive-skinned waitresses, gypsy violinists, and fiery (to the uptown palate) Hungarian cooking. A favorite destination was Little Hungary, a haunt of Theodore Roosevelt during his term as New York police commissioner. Below, a 1903 guide to the East Side cafés deciphers the menu at Little Hungary for the bewildered uptown diner. First among the entrées is, of course *"Szekelye Gulyas,"* a sharp-seasoned ragout of veal and pork, with sauerkraut. Then there are such things as:

> *Lammporkolt mit Eiergeste*—a goulash of lamb
> *Peishel mit Nockerln*—a goulash of lung
> *Wiener Backhendle*—fried chicken, breaded
> *Kas-Fleckerl*—vermicelli with grated cheese
> *Zigeuner-Auflauf*— vermicelli with prune jelly
> *Palacsinken*—a sort of French pancake
> *Kaiserschmarren*—a German pancake cut into small pieces
> while baking, and mixed with seeded raisins
> *Strumpfbandle*—noodles with cinnamon and sugar
> Among the most noted pastries are *Apfel-Strudel*, *Mohn*, and
> *Nuss-Kipferl*[22]

It didn't seem to matter to the uptown patrons that the café crowd was made up of fellow slummers. High on slivovitz, they tumbled into their waiting carriages and bounced homeward, their taste buds still reeling from the onslaught of garlic and paprika.

The Russian quarter of the Lower East Side hosted its own café network, only here the action unfolded around steaming glasses of amber-colored tea. In his drinking habits, the Russian Jew was the inverse of the Irishman. The Irishman drank his tea at home, but socialized over whiskey in the East Side saloons. The Jew, by contrast, consumed his alcohol around the family table while tea was his drink of public fellowship. Café tea was brewed in samovars and served in glass tumblers with a thick slice of lemon and a lump of sugar that the drinker clamped between his front teeth. The hot liquid was then sucked through the sugar with a loud, slurping sound. In the process of drinking, a few tablespoonfuls always splashed over the edge of the tumbler into the saucer beneath. When the glass was empty, the drinker raised the saucer to his lips and drained that as well.

In Little Hungary, music was part and parcel of the café atmosphere. In the Russian quarter, music was replaced by the sound of talk—feverish, theatrical, and at times contentious. The food and drink were secondary. For this reason, the cafés came to be known as *kibitzarnia*, from the Yiddish verb *kibetzn*. Roughly translated, to kibitz is to banter, in a sometimes mocking or intrusive way. The Yiddish writer Sholem Aleichem, who was born in Russia in 1859 and lived for a short time on the Lower East Side, explains that to kibitz "is to engage in repartee of a special sort, to needle someone, tickle him in the ribs, pull his leg, gnaw at his vitals, sprinkle salt on his wounds, give him the kiss of death, and all with a sweet smile, with a flash of rapier-like wit, with whimsy and humor . . ." In the *kibitzarnia*, he continues, the customer orders a cup of tea and a bite to eat, in prelude to the real action. Now the kibitzing starts:

> *The barbed compliments fly between the tables. Racy stories and witticisms are passed around, each calculated to step on someone's toes where the shoe pinches most . . . The kibitzarnia, dear reader, is a sort of free Gehenna [hell] where people rake each other over the coals, a steam bath where they beat each other with bundles of twigs until the*

blood spurts. Here opinions are formed, reputations are made and destroyed, careers decided.[23]

During the day, the café doubled as a conventional working person's restaurant serving traditional Russian fare: bean soup, borscht, kasha varnishkes, and herring in all its forms. At Leavitt's Café on Division Street, stomping ground of the East Side literary set, patrons could order a plate of chopped chicken liver for a nickel, or meatballs with farfel for 15 cents. After the dinner hour, the café assumed its nighttime role as the local debate club/lecture hall/classroom/salon, where the talking continued unabated until two or three in the morning. In the East Side hierarchy of daily necessities, good conversation trumped a good night's sleep.

A café existed for patrons of every political conviction. All of the "-ists" were represented: Socialists, Marxists, Zionists, Bundists, anarchists, and even the lonely capitalist, odd man out among Russian Jews, could find a sympathetic audience in one café or another. And not just men, but women too, were at home in the politically charged café environment. To the uptown observer, the sight of these "unwomanly women," sitting in mixed company and denouncing this or that government, came as a shock. To the café regulars, hungry for revolution on any front—political, artistic, or social—it exemplified the new world to come. Revolution, however, was for the young. . . . The older generation had their own establishments, where the talk centered on spiritual matters, and men in derbies (the café patron never removed his hat) disputed esoteric points of Talmud over a glass of tea and a slice of strudel. This is where we may have found the pious Mr. Rogarshevsky, president of his synagogue, embroiled in religious debate with his fellow congregants. The café also served the ordinary working people— the factory hands, shopkeepers, and peddlers who were more concerned with earning a living than with Nietzsche or Marx. This last group, repairing to the café at the close of the workday, sucked down glass after glass of hot tea—ten, twelve, fifteen glasses in succession—to soothe their throats, raw from a day of shouting.

Another expression of culinary specialization could be found in the East Side knish parlors, restaurants dispensing that one item and not much else. Starchy and filling, the knish, or *knysz*, was Russian peasant food, a rolled pastry traditionally filled with kasha. Because it was portable, it could be carried into the fields for a calorie-dense midday meal. Adopted by the Jews, the knish was transplanted to America, where it became the quintessential East Side street snack. Hot knishes were initially sold from carts that resembled tin bedroom dressers but were actually coal-burning ovens on wheels. The knishes were stored in the warming drawers. Like other East Side street foods—the bagel included—the knish eventually moved inside to a proper shop, the knishery.

The Jews made two basic types of knishes, *milchich* and *fleishich*, dairy and meat. The dairy knish was filled with pot cheese, the meat knish with liver. Knishes filled with kasha, potato, and sauerkraut could go either way, their status determined by the type of shortening used in the dough, butter or schmaltz. Deep into the 1920s, East Side knish-makers still followed the traditional strudel-like blueprint, stretching their dough, slathering it with one or another filling, then rolling it up like a carpet. After baking, the baton-shaped pastry was cut into sections. But this represented only one possible configuration. When uptowners discovered the knish sometime around World War I, they were baffled by it. A visitor to the East Side in 1919, on a tour of local eating spots, responded to the knish with typical befuddlement:

> Another institution which is part of the multifarious life of the lower East Side is the "knishe" restaurant. The "knishe" is a singular composition. One may look in all the cook books and culinary annals of all times for the recipe of a "knishe," but his efforts will be futile. Its sole habitat is the East Side.[24]

And so began the mythological association between this Slavic pastry and New York City, birthplace of the knish in the American culinary imagination.

Everything about the knish was so well-suited to the mode of life on the Lower East Side that it seemed to have sprung from the asphalt. Its portability was one of its major assets. Another was its price. What other food could deliver so much satisfaction for only three cents? At midday, it was a cheap and filling lunch for the sweatshop worker. At night, theatergoers devoured a quick knish at intermission or stopped by the local knishery for an after-show snack. In fact, an important connection developed between knishes and theater that helped establish a place for the knish in the local ecosystem. The home of the Yiddish theater in the early twentieth century was Second Avenue, the playhouses concentrated between 14th and Houston streets. That same strip came to be known as "knish alley" in recognition of the many knish joints that had sprung up within a few blocks' radius. Knish parlors followed theaters the same way that pilot fish follow sharks. Wherever a theater opened, a knishery followed. In 1910, a Romanian immigrant named Joseph Berger opened a knish restaurant at 137 East Houston Street, directly next door to the Houston Hippodrome, a Yiddish vaudeville house that also showed moving pictures. The restaurant was named for Berger's cousin and former partner, Yonah Schimmel, the knish vendor who had started the business two decades earlier with a pushcart on Coney Island. Berger's son, Arthur, took over from his father in 1924, and continued selling knishes for the next fifty years. Eventually, the business was sold to outside investors. The Hippodrome building is still a movie theater, now a five-screen multiplex. When the shows let out, hungry theatergoers walk the same thirty feet to Yonah Schimmel's, functioning time capsule and last of the East Side knisheries.

One measure of wealth among East Side Jews was how much meat a person could afford. Because they came from a meat-scarce society, its sudden availability in America represented the unlimited bounty of their adopted home, and Jews aspired to eat as much of it as possible. This fixation on meat helps explain the exalted place of the delicatessen in the life of the ghetto. But shortly after the turn of the century, a new type of eating place appeared on the East Side, which served no meat at all: the dairy restaurant. Here, with the exception of fish, the kitchen was strictly vegetarian, concentrating on foods made from grain, vegetables, milk, and eggs. On the face of it, the dairy restaurant was a natural outgrowth of the Jewish dietary law that forbids the mixing of meat and milk. On closer inspection, however, its appearance in New York around 1900 was a product of culinary forces that extended beyond the ghetto.

First, the East Side dairy restaurant was part of a growing interest in vegetarian dining that had recently taken hold of New York. The city's first vegetarian restaurant opened in 1895 and more followed, providing patrons with a meatless menu of salads, nut-butter sandwiches, omelets, vegetable cutlets, and dairy dishes like berries and cream. American vegetarians came to their dietary views by way of religion. One early proponent was the Reverend Sylvester Graham (advocate for whole-grain bread) who helped found the American Vegetarian Society in 1850. Another was John Harvey Kellogg, a Seventh-Day Adventist and culinary inventor responsible for the creation of corn flakes. At his sanatorium in Battle Creek, Michigan, Kellogg also experimented with faux meat compounds made primarily from gluten and nuts, which became a staple of the East Side dairy menu.

The appearance of the first Jewish dairy restaurants coincided with a culinary crisis on the Lower East Side, which centered on the high cost of kosher meat. In the spring of 1902, a sudden jump in the price of kosher beef uncorked the pent-up outrage of East Side housewives. The women organized a neighborhood-wide boycott for the morning of May 15, with picketers stationed in front of every neighborhood butcher shop. Patrons who crossed the picket line had their purchases seized and doused with kerosene. At eleven a.m., a group of women and boys marched down Orchard Street and smashed the windows of every butcher en route, including the basement shop at number 97. Police who tried to stop the women became the target of their anger. The demonstrators pounced on the officers and wrestled them to the ground or pelted them with garbage. That night, five hundred women assembled at an East Side meeting hall. As the surrounding streets filled with angry supporters, tensions escalated between the crowd and the police. The inevitable fight broke out, and within the hour the neighborhood was engulfed in violence. The rioting subsided by the following afternoon, but the meat troubles continued for another decade, sparking boycotts and protests, though nothing on the scale of 1902.

The East Side's first dairy restaurants, born in the midst of the kosher-meat crisis, were shoestring operations, the menu limited to a handful of traditional dishes like blintzes, kasha, and herring. By the 1940s, however, this working person's lunchroom had evolved into a more ambitious enterprise. The most ambitious of all was Ratner's, which had originally opened in 1905 in a cramped storefront on Pitt Street. In 1918, the restaurant moved to its new home on Delancey Street, right next door to the Loew's Delancey, then a neighborhood vaudeville theater. In 1928, the Loew's Delancey became the Loew's Commodore, one of the new and fantastically ornate movie palaces that had begun to appear in the city. That same year, Ratner's received its own renovation at a cost of $150,000, transforming the old-time lunchroom into the "East Side's premier dining place." In its more elegant guise, its menu blossomed, and by 1940 covered a vast gastronomic territory ranging from the traditional herring salad to asparagus on toast to caviar sandwiches, among the most expensive items on the menu. But the most creative dishes to emerge from the dairy restaurant were their counterfeit meats. In place of actual beef or chicken or lamb, the dairy restaurants served meat substitutes that craftily mimicked the original. There was vegetarian stuffed turkey neck, chicken giblet fricassee, or chopped liver, all traditional Jewish foods. Diners with more assimilated taste could have vegetarian lamb chops or meatless veal cutlet. All of these foods were grouped under a section of the menu labeled "Roasts." Under the same heading was a selection of the faux meat products manufactured by Kellogg at his Michigan plant. The most popular was Protose steak, which the dairy restaurants served with fried onions or mushroom gravy. Here's a classic recipe for vegetarian chopped liver, with the "livery" taste surprisingly coming from the canned peas:

LILLIAN CHANALES'S VEGETARIAN CHOPPED LIVER

3 medium-sized onions, chopped
3 tablespoons vegetable oil
I large can sweet peas, drained
I ½ cups chopped walnuts
2 hard-boiled eggs, chopped

Sauté the onions in the oil until they are soft and golden.
Mash peas with the back of a fork. Combine onion and
peas with remaining ingredients and chop by hand until you
have the desired consistency. If you like, you can use a food
processor, but be careful not to over-process. Season with
salt and a generous dose of freshly ground black pepper.[25]

The East Side's vast network of food purveyors satisfied the diverse
culinary needs of the local population with a thoroughness that was
unmatched in most other neighborhoods. People like the Rogarshevskys
had no reason to cross 14th Street to buy their horseradish or kosher meat
or to find a congenial café or a restaurant that met their religious standards.
As East Siders began to disperse, the food merchants followed. Kosher
butcher shops opened in Brooklyn, the Bronx, and along upper Broadway,
in addition to Jewish bakeries and delicatessens. Dairy restaurants began to
appear in midtown to feed the Jewish garment workers, and more opened
on the Upper West Side. But still, former East Siders returned to the old
neighborhood to shop from the downtown merchants and patronize the
restaurants. Immigrants who had moved to Brooklyn or the Bronx or
Upper Manhattan made Sunday trips to the Lower East Side to flex their
bargaining muscles at the pushcart market and buy a smoked whitefish
at Russ & Daughters, the appetizing store on Houston Street. Before the

holidays, they converged on the East Side to buy their matzoh, kosher wine, and dried fruit. When the shopping was done, they went for lunch at Ratner's or Rappaport's, another of the East Side's dairy restaurants.

Accounts of these food-inspired trips to the Lower East Side appear regularly in immigrant memoirs and immigrant fiction as well. A Fannie Hurst story called "In Memoriam" follows the tribulations of Mrs. Meyerberg, a lonely Fifth Avenue matron who returns—by chauffeured limousine—to her former tenement kitchen. Flooded with memories, Mrs. Meyerberg is moved by a sudden impulse to assume her place behind the tenement stove, and she does, but the experience proves too much for her. In typical Fannie Hurst fashion, the matron literally dies of joy. Anzia Yezierska's East Side heroine, Hannah Brieneh, makes a similar voyage. Now an old woman, residing in relative splendor on Riverside Drive, Hannah Brieneh is bereft, a living soul trapped in a mausoleum. The answer to her existential crisis is a trip to the pushcart market. "In a fit of rebellion," she rides downtown, buys a new marketing basket, and heads for the fish stand. The downtown foray is like a splash of cold water for the withering Hannah Brieneh, who returns in triumph, filling the lifeless apartment with the homey smells of garlic and herring.

The subway ride from the tenements to uptown New York proved more disruptive to immigrant food ways than the initial journey to America. Comfortably middle-class, the uptown Jew could eat like royalty, meat three times a day, unlimited quantities of soft white bread, pastry and tea to fill the gap between lunch and dinner. But uptown living came with unexpected constraints. Uptown Jews were plagued by a new and irksome self-consciousness that complicated mealtimes. Americanized children badgered their immigrant parents to give up the foods they had always relished. If the uptown Jew had a craving for brisket and sauerkraut, the aromas of these dishes cooking on the stove wafted through the apartment building and neighbors complained. The once-beloved organ meats became tokens of poverty, and uptown homemakers had to sneak them into the kitchen like contraband on the servant's day off. What a pleasure, then, to escape to an East Side restaurant for a plate of chopped herring and a basket of onion rolls.

CHAPTER FIVE

The Baldizzi Family

"Whoever forsakes the old way for the new knows what he is losing but not what he will find."
—SICILIAN PROVERB

A t the start of the twentieth century, 97 Orchard Street stood on the most densely populated square block of urban America, with 2,223 people, most of them Russian Jews, packed into roughly two acres. One hundred and eleven of them resided in the twenty apartments at 97 Orchard, the oldest building on the block.

By the 1930s, the same East Side neighborhood was a shadow of its former self. Many of the older tenements had been abandoned by their owners, who could no longer afford to pay the property taxes, and were now vacant shells. Others had been demolished or consumed by fire and never rebuilt. As a result, a neighborhood once defined by its extreme architectural density was now littered with empty lots. The tenements that survived the 1920s were languishing too, the victims of changing demographics. Immigration had slowed dramatically by the middle of the decade; old-time East Siders, those who had settled in the neighborhood before the war, had dispersed to the outer boroughs. The number of people living at 97 Orchard, for example, had shrunk from one hundred and eleven to roughly twenty-five, leaving one-third of the building's apartments completely empty. The East Side tenant shortage meant that neighborhood landlords—even the most conscientious—could no longer afford to maintain their properties, and many buildings fell into disrepair.

Built during the Civil War, years before New York had formulated a body of housing laws, 97 Orchard embodied a laissez-faire approach toward lodging for the working class. As the building passed from one owner to the next, it was gradually modernized. In 1905, 97 Orchard was equipped with indoor plumbing. A system of cast-iron pipes now branched into every apartment and connected to the kitchen sink, supplying tenants with cold running water. The same system allowed for indoor water closets. A second major overhaul came in the early 1920s, when the building was wired for electricity. Despite these efforts, 97 Orchard remained an architectural relic. As late as 1935, the four apartments on each floor were served by two communal toilets. None had bathtubs or any form of heat apart from the kitchen stove. Only one room in three had proper windows.

In the years following World War I, 97 Orchard was home to a mix of Irish, Romanians, Russians, Lithuanians, and Italians. Included in this last group were the Baldizzis, a family of Sicilian immigrants that had come to New York to share in the unlimited possibilities of the American economy. Their plans, however, were derailed by the stock market crash of 1929 and the resulting disappearance of millions of jobs.

For most of the nineteenth century, as Germans and then Irish streamed into the United States, the Italian population stayed at microscopic levels. The 1860 census counted only twelve thousand Italian-born immigrants in the entire country, a demographic speck. The great majority of these early settlers were Northern Italians from Genoa, the surrounding province of Liguria, and from Piedmont just to the north. The numbers began to climb in the boom decades after the Civil War as America turned to the work of rebuilding. The rush of postwar construction activity created more jobs than the country could fill with its own citizens. So, America turned to her neighbors overseas. With the encouragement of the United States government, work-hungry Italians—among other immigrant groups—stepped in to alleviate a desperate labor shortage. During the 1880s, fifty-five thousand Italians arrived in the United States, and just over three hundred thousand in the decade following. By the end of the century, more Italians were landing at Ellis Island than any other immigrant group, and the trend continued into the 1900s. The immigrants who belonged to this second wave were overwhelmingly from the southern provinces of Basilicata, Calabria, and Sicily.

Two features of the Italian migration distinguished it from other groups. First was the lopsided ratio of men to women from Italy. During the last two decades of the nineteenth century, that ratio was four to one, with men leading the way. Though the numbers balanced out some over time, they never reached an even fifty-fifty. Lone Italian men came to the United States to work in railroad construction, to build dams, dig canals, lay sewer systems, and pave the nation's roads, "pick and shovel" jobs. The Italian laborer was typically a man in the prime of his working life. Many had wives and children back in Italy, to whom they planned to return once they had saved enough of their American wages to go back home and purchase a farm or maybe start a business. The average length of the Italian's sojourn in America was seven years. Some Italians became long-distance commuters. They worked in America during the busy summer season and returned home for the slow winter months, when construction was put on hold.

The success of this international labor pool hinged on a figure known as the padrone, an immigrant himself who wore many hats. Part employment agent, part interpreter, part boardinghouse keeper, and part personal banker, the padrone supplied the new immigrant with much-needed services while robbing him of half his wages, and sometimes more. The padrone's headquarters were in America but his work began in Italy, scouring the countryside for prospective clients—dissatisfied field workers, in good health, who were willing to travel. This work was often delegated to an Italian-based partner, who worked on commission. The padrone also formed relationships with American employers who kept him apprised of their labor needs, so when an immigrant landed, the padrone knew where to send him. In the cities, he kept boardinghouses where his clients were compelled to lodge, charging extortionist rates for a patch of floor to sleep on. Italians who were sent afield to lay railroad tracks or dig reservoirs in the American hinterland were beholden to the padrone for all their basic needs. Other men who worked on these grand-scale building projects—Slavs, Hungarians, and even the occasional American—lived in camps established by their employer. They slept in the company bunkhouse and ate together in the company mess hall. The one group missing from this international community was the Italians, who followed their padrones to all-Italian camps complete with bunkhouses, a commissary for buying supplies, and a kitchen where the men ate. These boardinghouses in the wilderness, catering to a captive and hungry clientele, were another money-maker for the padrone. At the same time, they answered one very important requirement for the laborer: to eat like an Italian.

Where other groups consumed whatever stews, breads, and puddings they were given, the Italian demanded foods from the homeland. Over the course of one month, the typical laborer consumed:

Bread 34.1 lbs
Macaroni 19.3 lbs
Rice .24 lbs
Meat (sausage, corned beef, & codfish) 2.31 lbs
Sardines 2–5 boxes
Beans, peas and lentils 2.06 lbs
Fatback (lard substitute) 5.13 lbs
Tomatoes 2.13 cans
Sugar 2.8 pounds
Coffee .43 lbs[1]

The men purchased their supplies at the commissary or shanty store, a grocery run by the padrone, where everything on the shelves was triple its normal price. The men took turns behind the camp stove, a group of three or four preparing meals for the entire crew. Some camps ran their own bakeries, using commissary flour. Out west, a similar arrangement could be found among Chinese railroad workers. In their separate camps, faced with the unappetizing prospect of the company mess hall, the Chinese workers assumed the job of feeding themselves, the only possible way to procure food that they considered edible. For both groups of men, Chinese and Italian, cooking became a New World survival skill.

Many of the foods that issued from the communal pot would be familiar today. Various forms of lentil soup, macaroni and tomatoes, beans and macaroni, beans and salt pork, and beans with sausage. Next to the familiar were more uncommon preparations. One ingenious food was a kind of homemade bouillon cube, prepared by Italian workers in Newark, New Jersey, circa 1900. Using a beer vat as their mixing vessel, the men first pounded a large quantity of tomatoes. Next,

> they poured some cornmeal and flour into the vat and stirred until the stuff became a dough. The next step was to throw this on what bakers would call a molding trough and knead it, adding enough flour to make it a stiff pulp. The less said about the state of their hands the better, but that is a trivial matter. The mixture was molded into little pats about the same size of fishcake. These were placed on boards and taken to various roofs to dry.[2]

Come winter, when fresh tomatoes were no longer available, the cakes were dissolved in boiling water, each cake producing enough soup for six men.

A second defining feature of the Italian migration was poverty. After 1865, the great majority of Italian immigrants were poor southern fieldworkers. They arrived at Ellis Island, illiterate and unskilled, with, in 1901, an average life-savings of $8.79. Despite their farming background, most Italians settled in the large industrial cities. Here they found work as street cleaners, pavers, and ditch- and tunnel-diggers—the dirtiest, most dangerous jobs. Immigration officials bluntly referred to the Southern Italian as America's "worst immigrants," a judgment echoed in the daily papers. "Lazy," "ignorant," and "clannish" were just a few of the adjectives most commonly linked with Italians by the popular press. "Violent" was another oft-mentioned Italian characteristic. American newspapers kept a running tally of crimes committed by the Black Hand, an early name for Italian organized crime, paying special attention to any case that involved explosives. (Bombs were a fairly common means of extortion among gangsters of the period.) America's fascination with Italian gangsters helped reinforce the argument that Italians were violent by nature. Following this circular logic, Americans were convinced that "no foreigners with whom we have to deal, stab and murder on so slight provocation," a judgment offered by the *New York Times*.[3]

Among the lowest of this low-grade stock were the men and women who rejected honest work in favor of more shiftless occupations. One character was the Italian organ-grinder, a roving street performer with a hand organ suspended from a strap around his neck. The hand organ worked like an oversized music box, with a rotating cylinder inside it that turned by means of a crank. The more prosperous worked with an assistant, a trained monkey in a red vest and matching fez. The animal perched on his master's shoulder while the music played and collected pennies at the end of the number. The organ grinder's main patrons were the city's children.

Another dubious line of work was rag-picking, an urban occupation dominated by foreigners, beginning with the Germans in the 1850s. The Irish also turned to rag-picking, but in smaller numbers. By the 1880s, the industry had been passed down to the Italians, the country's newest immigrants. America's first career recyclers, rag-pickers made their livelihood by sifting through the city's garbage for reusable resources. The tools of the rag-picker's trade were a long pole with a hook at one end and a large sack slung across her chest. Her workday began before the city was fully awake, when the streets were still quiet. She made her rounds, moving from one trash barrel to the next, examining its contents with the help of her pole, and plucking from it whatever she found of value. Her most fruitful hunting grounds were the cities' wealthier neighborhoods, where the garbage was rife with discarded treasure—old shoes and boots, battered cooking pans, glass bottles, and the rags themselves, cream of the trash barrel. Once home, she emptied her sack onto the floor to survey the day's gleanings. Each type of article was sorted into its own box, one for paper, one for leather goods, one for metal, one for glass, and so on. The bones were put into a large kettle and boiled clean. The rags were rinsed and hung up to dry.

The next stop for the sorted garbage was the junk dealer, a refuse middleman who paid the rag-picker a set sum by weight for each material, then turned around and sold it, at a profit, to assorted manufacturers. Old shoes and boots were retooled to look like new or shredded to a pulp, an ingredient used in the manufacture of waterproof tarps. Paper was sold to local publishers, who turned it into newsprint for the morning papers. Bottles were reused or melted. Bones from the family dinner table were turned into umbrella handles, snuff boxes, buttons, and toothbrushes. Rags, which fetched more per pound than any other item, went to make the era's finest writing paper.

Middle-class America declared the rag-picker too lazy for "real work," or accused her of ulterior motives. All of that innocent rummaging was, they believed, a cover for her real purpose—casing the best homes in the city for future burglaries. The organ grinder was likewise seen as a threat to public welfare, a nuisance at best, but at worst a common street thug, his stiletto tucked in his boot. Bootblacks, chestnut vendors, and fruit peddlers all belonged to the same itinerant class and all were suspect.

Non-Italians found proof of these immigrants' lowly character in the foods they ate: stale bread, macaroni with oil, and, if they were lucky, a handful of common garden weeds. No other immigrant diet was as meager. For his nourishment, the Italian fruit peddler relied on the bruised and moldy fruit that was too far gone to sell, even by East Side standards. Organ grinders, because of their aversion to work, subsisted on a diet "so scanty that had they not been accustomed to the severest deprivation from infancy, their system would refuse to be nourished by food that an Irish navvy would shrink from with abhorrence."[4] Their spare diet acted as an impediment that kept the immigrant from rising in the world. A typical lunch for the Italian laborer, a piece of bread and cup of water, was no meal for a working man. American employers, who could choose from an international pool of workers, came to regard the Italian as second-rate. "They are active, but not hardy or strong as the average man"—a rung below the Hungarian or the Slav. The main reason: "they eat too little."[5]

But no diet was more reviled than the rag-picker's—a hodgepodge of bread crusts, vegetable trimmings, bones, and meat scraps plucked from middle-class trash bins. One particularly desperate class of rag-pickers scavenged only for food, eating some of what they gathered and selling the rest for profit. Italian women from Mulberry, Baxter, and Crosby streets, the food scavengers targeted the city's markets, grocers, fruit stands, butchers, and fishmongers. An 1883 newspaper story from the *New York Times* describes how they operated:

> *Partially decayed potatoes, onions, carrots, apples, oranges, bananas, and pineapples are the principal finds in the mess of garbage that is overhauled. The greatest prize to the garbage-searching old hag is a mess of the outside leaves of cabbage that are torn off before the odorous vegetable is displayed for sale on the stands. The rescued stuff—cabbage leaves, onions, bananas, oranges, &c.—is dumped into a filthy bit of sacking, and the whole carted, as soon as a day's labor is concluded, to the miserable quarters which the old hag is forced to call home. Here a sorting process is gone through with. If the husband or son is sufficiently endowed with this world's goods to be the proprietor of a fruit-stand, everything that may possibly be sold for no matter how small a sum is transferred to him. The remainder is subdivided. The cabbage leaves which are fresh are sold for use in the cheap restaurants to be served with corned beef. Such as will not serve for that purpose is stripped of decayed portions and used as the body of the poor Italian's favorite dish—cabbage soup. In the composition of this dish, often for days at a time the only food save stale bread, which a family has to dine upon, are mixed the portions of the potatoes, carrots, and other vegetables which are not absolutely rotten. The tomatoes*

are used in making a gravy for the macaroni, this delicacy being se-
cured in exchange for decayed fruits and vegetables at the groceries or
restaurants of the Italian quarter. This process of exchange is carried
on quite extensively as the store-keepers prefer it, and find an addi-
tion to their meager profits in the system of barter.[6]

Despite the revulsion of middle-class America, the rag-picker's harvest provided her and her family with a windfall of edible wealth. American queasiness over "rescued food" was a luxury that the struggling immigrant could easily overlook. The heaps of discarded food, some of it perfectly good, which materialized each day in city trash bins, must have left the rag-picker gaping in wonderment. On the one hand, the rag-picker's lack of skills, education, and English left her consigned to the outer fringes of American society. Still, she was able to make a living off America's leftovers. American abundance was so staggering that the garbage that accumulated daily in cities like New York could support a shadow system of food distribution operated largely by immigrants. The rag-picker was a key player in this shadow economy, redistributing her daily harvest to peddlers, restaurants, and neighborhood groceries. In her own kitchen, the rag-picker's culinary gleanings formed the basis of a limited but nourishing diet. (Sanitary inspectors were often surprised by the rag-picker's good health.) Even more surprising, the rag-picker cook was determined to both nourish and delight, bartering for macaroni—a luxury food in the immigrant diet—while turning her rescued fruit into jellies and marmalade.

Expressions of anti-Italian bias continued until the start of World War I, when the nation shifted focus to fighting the Germans. German-Americans, once regarded as model immigrants, were now considered a threat to national security. Suspected of loyalty to the Fatherland, they were declared "enemy aliens" by President Woodrow Wilson and subject to a string of government restrictions. Thousands were arrested or interned. In the anxious years after the war, animosity directed at the Germans spread to other foreigners, placing immigrants and immigration at the center of a national debate. Though many of the old fears persisted, the new nativists turned to the faux science of race studies, a potent blend of anthropology, biology, and eugenics. American prosperity, they argued, rested on the superior mental traits of the Anglo-Saxon, attributes that were passed down from parent to offspring in much the same way as eye color. Alarmed by the recent influx of Southern and Eastern Europeans, the nativists claimed that decades of unchecked immigration had compromised the greatness of America, and the danger would continue as long as the gates stayed open. If they did, the outcome was assured: race suicide. By this reckoning, the settlement workers and schoolteachers who had worked so hard to Americanize the foreign-born were hopelessly misguided. American greatness could not be taught. It was literally in "the blood."

Among the leading voices of the new nativists was a New Yorker named Madison Grant, a lawyer and amateur zoologist who helped found the Bronx Zoo. Alongside his interest in wildlife, Grant developed a taste for politics, chiefly in the field of immigration policy. He encountered like-minded thinkers in such organizations as the Immigration Restriction League and the American Defense Society, a group originally founded to protect America from German aggression. Once the armistice was signed, the group shifted focus to a new enemy, the immigrant. Grant published his manifesto, *The Passing of a Great Race*, in 1916. The book never sold very well, but the ideas laid down by Grant filtered into Washington. Here, they became the quasi-scientific basis for a series of anti-immigration laws culminating in the 1924 Johnson-Reed Act, the most stringent immigrant quota system in United States history. After 1924, the total number of immigrants allowed to enter the United States each year became one hundred and fifty thousand, a minuscule number compared to earlier times. What's more, Johnson-Reed was specific about who those immigrants could be. America was now prepared to admit two percent of each foreign population living in the United States as of 1890, a year strategically chosen to make room for Western Europeans while shutting out less desirable types—Eastern Europeans, Italians, and Jews.

More than other groups, Italians arrived in this country with the firm knowledge that they were unwanted. In the workplace, Italians were paid less than other ethnicities, or denied jobs entirely. Landlords with a no-Italians policy denied them housing. The fact that few spoke English offered little protection against ethnic slurs, sources of the deepest humiliation for the transplanted Italian. The immigrant soon discovered that words like *dago* and *ginny* were accepted features of American speech, and not only in the streets and the schoolyards. "The Rights of the Dago" and "Big Dago Riot at Castle Gate" were the kinds of headlines Americans could expect to find in their morning paper. The quota laws effectively made anti-Italian discrimination the official policy of the United States government.

In the hostile environment first encountered by Italians, food took on new meanings and new powers. The many forms of discrimination leveled at Italians encouraged immigrants to seal themselves off, culturally speaking, from the rest of America. This circling of the wagons, a response typical of many persecuted people, was interpreted by Americans as Italian "clannishness," an unwelcome trait in any immigrant but especially so for an already suspect group—poor, uneducated, and Catholic. The metaphorical walls built up by Italian-Americans served a double purpose. On the one hand, they protected the immigrant from outside menace, both real and invented. On the other, they carved out a space where Italians could carry on with their native traditions in relative peace, away from American disapproval. As it happens, the traditions they seemed most devoted to were those connected with food. Certainly, culinary continuity was important to other foreign groups, but Italian-Americans were bonded to their gastronomic heritage with an intensity unknown to Russians, Germans, or Irish, and went to great lengths to protect it. The Jews had their religion; the Germans had their poets, their composers, and their beer; and the Irish had their politics. The Italians arrived with a strong musical tradition; they also had their faith. But food was their cultural touchstone, their way of defying the critics, of tolerating the slurs and all of the other injustices. It was their way of being Italian.

Harsh critics of Italian eating habits, Americans tried through various means to reform the immigrant cook. The Italians were unmoved. Despite the cooking classes and public school lectures, and despite the persistent advice of visiting nurses and settlement workers, the immigrants' belief in the superiority of their native foods was unwavering. Respect for the skills of the Italian cook, the goodness that she could extract from her raw materials, was one thing, but the immigrants were equally devoted to the materials themselves. For them, good Italian cooking was made from foods that grew from the Italian soil, and they used imported ingredients whenever possible. Olives and olive oil, anchovies, jarred peppers, dried mushrooms, artichokes cured in salt, canned tomatoes and tomato paste, vinegar, oregano, garlic, a variety of cured meats and cheeses, and, above all, pasta, were some of the products found in the Italian groceries that served America's many Little Italys. Here, Italian homemakers, working women of limited means, could stock their pantries with native foods, despite the daunting cost of imported goods. The financial sacrifice was proof of the Italian's dedication. A 1903 newspaper story describing the Italian grocery for readers who had never seen one took note of the Italians' food priorities:

> *No people are more devoted to their native foods than the Italians, and Italian groceries filled with imported edibles flourish in all the different colonies of the city. The price of the imported good is a drain on the purses of the patrons and they wearily try to get the same satisfaction out of American-made substitutes, which have the same names and the same appearance, but never, never, the same taste.*[7]

To the immigrant palate, Italian-style hams made in America were cured too quickly; American-made *caciocavallo*, the cheese beloved by Sicilians, was lacking in butterfat and quickly spoiled; American garlic was tasteless; and American vinegar was the wrong color. But the saddest disappointment was American pasta, much of it produced on Elizabeth Street in Sicilian-owned pasta factories. Made from standard white flour—not semolina—it was pale and, once cooked, it went soft. Domestic pasta was half the price of imported, but Italians were loath to buy it and literally saved their pennies for the genuine article.

Back home in Italy, peasant families had managed to survive another kind of hostile environment. Oppressive landowners, unfairly high taxes, and periodic crop failures meant a precarious life for the *contadini*, the field workers of southern Italy. Even in good times, when the peasant had enough to eat, starvation remained a looming possibility, always one crop failure away. If nothing else was guaranteed to the peasant—and nothing was—the unshakable bond of family was his bedrock. The family patriarch was an unchallenged authority who demanded absolute obedience from his wife and children, his helpers in the fields. The needs of the family came before those of the individual, and loyalty among family was unwavering. In America, as Italians adapted to a new way of life, the old values of family solidarity were put to the test. For the first time, children left their parents' side to attend school. Here they were exposed to a world of people and ideas apart from their family. Italian girls, no longer under the constant surveillance of their elders, were now free—though not entirely—to make their own friends, and eventually to find their own husbands. As Italian women left their homes to work in American factories, they too developed lives separate from the family, discovering a level of independence they had never known in the Old Country.

Despite all these changes, the old values lived on in the nightly ritual of the evening meal, a tangible expression of family solidarity, loyalty, and love. To borrow a phrase from *Blood of My Blood*, Richard Gambino's wonderful book about Brooklyn Sicilians, the evening meal was "a communion of the family." Sicilians, and southern Italians in general, arrived in America with a deep reverence for the preciousness of food. They knew full well the human labor required to coax it from the earth, and how, on occasion, the earth would refuse them. In America, though now removed from the soil, the Italian still labored for his food, working for relatively low wages in the nation's most strenuous jobs. The family meal was an occasion to share the fruits of that labor, and for the Italian, attendance was mandatory. On weekdays, Italian kids often returned home for lunch as well, though they could eat for free in the school cafeteria.

As Italians found their way into the American economy, the family supper took on another layer of meaning. Edible proof of the immigrant's success, the evening meal was a nightly celebration of the triumph over hunger. The price of that victory was not lost on the immigrants, especially the older ones, who still remembered the fourteen-hour work-days. The bounty before him was the Italian's belated reward for build-ing America's subways, her skyscrapers and bridges—in other words, for bringing America into the twentieth century.

Each night, the family dinner table became a stage for all the tempting foods that the immigrant had once dreamed about but couldn't afford. At the center of that dream, there was meat. For early immigrants, meat was used as a seasoning, an ingredient added to soup or sauce to give it body and richness. By the 1920s, a midweek dinner in a working-class Italian kitchen included soup, then pasta, followed by meat and a salad. At the end of the week, Italian families sat down to a banquet of stunning extrav-agance. Sunday supper began in the early afternoon with an antipasto of cheese, salami, ham, and anchovies. Appetites now fully awake, the family moved through multiple courses, leading them to the heart of the feast. If the family were Sicilian, that might include a *ragu* made from marrow bones, chicken, pork sausage, and meatballs, stewed veal and peppers, and braciole, a thin filet of pounded beef or pork wrapped around a stuffing of cheese, bread crumbs, parsley, pine nuts, and raisins.

The Italian writer Jerre Mangione, who grew up in Rochester, New York, in the 1920s, remembers the parade of courses: first, there was soup; then pasta, perhaps ziti in *sugo*; followed by two kinds of chicken, one boiled, and one roasted; roasted veal; roasted lamb; and *brusciuluna*—"a combination of Roman cheese, salami, and moon-shaped slivers of hardboiled egg encased in rolls of beef." When the meat was cleared, there was fennel and celery to cleanse the palate, followed by homemade pastries, nuts, fruit, and vermouth. These Sunday suppers, prepared by the author's father, were more extravagant than the family could realisti-cally afford, and the senior Mangione often had to borrow money to pay for them.[8] Moderation had no place at the Sunday table. The gathered crowd, encouraged by their fellow diners, went back for multiple helpings with not a jot of self-consciousness. Quite the contrary, any guest who refused another helping was given a mild rebuke.

The meatballs, *ragus*, and roasts that were (and remain) a centerpiece of the Italian-American kitchen had never figured in the peasant diet. Rather, they belonged to the kitchens of Italian landowners, merchants, and clergy, who, on important feast days like Easter and Christmas, distributed meat to the poor.[9] In America, immigrant cooks reinterpreted these feast-day foods and, in another expression of American bounty, made them a regular part of the Sunday table. The American larder was so immense that it could literally feed the working class on a diet once reserved for Italian nobility.

One effect of the quota laws of the 1920s was to create a shadow wave of uncounted immigrants, men and women from Russia, Poland, Italy, and other restricted nations, who evaded the authorities and entered the country illegally. The Baldizzis belonged to that wave. Adolfo Baldizzi was born in Palermo in 1896 and was orphaned as a young boy. His professional training as a cabinetmaker began at age five, but the outbreak of World War I put his career temporarily on hold. A wartime portrait of Adolfo shows a young soldier with thick black hair and a neatly trimmed mustache. Rosaria Baldizzi (her family name was Mutolo) was born in

Adolfo Baldizzi in his soldier's uniform, circa 1914.

Wedding portrait of sixteen-year-old Rosaria Mutolo Baldizzi, two years before she emigrated.

1906, also in Palermo, to a family of tradespeople and civil servants. The Baldizzis were married in 1922, the same year Rosaria turned sixteen. A year later, the couple decided to emigrate. To evade the 1921 immigrant quota laws, Adolfo came to America as a stowaway aboard a French vessel. As the ship pulled into New York Harbor, he climbed from his hiding place, jumped over the railing, and swam to shore. Rosaria made the same trip in 1924, with a doctored passport.

For Rosaria Mutolo Baldizzi, the move to America was a step down in life. Born to a middle-class family, Rosaria spent her childhood in a good-size house with a stone courtyard where her mother grew geraniums and raised chickens, selling the eggs to neighbors. Rosaria's father was confined to a wheelchair by the time she was a young girl, but in his youth had owned or worked in a bakery. Her two older brothers were both policemen; her sister was a dressmaker. On Sunday afternoons, still in their church clothes, the family took leisurely strolls, stopping at a local café for coffee and granita. Rosaria's marriage to a cabinetmaker at age sixteen was considered a good match. In her 1921 wedding portrait, she is posed at the foot of an ornate staircase, dressed in a tailored skirt and matching jacket, both trimmed in a wide panel of hand-woven lace. A flapper-style cloche hat, jauntily cocked, with a long, trailing sash, completes the ensemble.

Rosaria's move to New York in 1924 meant the end of a reasonably privileged and protected life. Her first glimpse of Elizabeth Street, center of Sicilian New York, was a sobering experience for the young immigrant. To her consternation, the shoppers who overflowed the sidewalk onto the cobblestoned street were oblivious to the garbage under their feet, a carpet of moldering cabbage leaves and orange rinds. Every window ledge and door lintel was veiled in soot, like a dusting of black snow. But most disturbing of all were the Elizabeth Street stables. The young Mrs. Baldizzi was shocked to find that New Yorkers, presumably civilized people, lived side by side with horses.

The couple's first home was a single room in a two-room apartment. To supplement her husband's earnings, Rosaria took in laundry, a common source of income for immigrant women. Whenever the couple fell

behind in rent, they simply packed up and moved. The two Baldizzi children, Josephine and John, were born on Elizabeth Street, but in 1928,
when John was still in his swaddling clothes, the family left Little Italy
for 97 Orchard Street, a leap across cultures that brought the Baldizzis
into the heart of the Jewish Lower East Side. Living on Orchard Street,
they encountered the challenges typical of an immigrant family. These
were eclipsed, however, by the calamitous events of 1929 and their after-
math. The "land of opportunity" they had expected to find evaporated
before their eyes, leaving Mr. Baldizzi with a wife, two toddlers, and little
hope of finding work.

The Baldizzis remained on Orchard Street through the grimmest
years of the Depression. For most of that time, Adolfo was unemployed,
though he still earned a few dollars a week as a neighborhood handyman. New clothes or toys for the children were out of the question.
When the soles on Josephine's shoes sprouted holes, they were forti-
fied with a cardboard insert. The family food budget was concentrated
on a few indispensible staples: bread, pasta, beans, lentils, and olive oil.
Once a week, the family received free groceries from Home Relief, the
assistance program created by Franklin Roosevelt in 1931 when he was
still governor of New York. For many foreign-born Americans, Home
Relief introduced the immigrant to foods like oatmeal, butter, American
cheese, and, for the children, cod liver oil. It also furnished them with
milk, potatoes, vegetables, flour, eggs, meat, and fish. For the Baldizzi
parents, the weekly trip to the neighborhood food bank (it was actually
the children's school) was a public walk of shame. The food, however, was
necessary, and they accepted it gratefully.

Breakfast for the Baldizzi children was hot cereal, courtesy of Home
Relief, or day-old bread that Mrs. Baldizzi tore into pieces and soaked
in hot milk, with a little butter and sugar. The resulting dish, a kind of
breakfast pudding, was a favorite of the children. Josephine Baldizzi,
who was always thought too skinny by her parents, was given raw eggs to
help fatten her up. The eggs were eaten two ways. Mrs. Baldizzi would
poke a hole in one end of the egg, instructing her daughter to suck out
the nutritious insides. She also prepared a drink for Josephine made of

raw egg and milk whipped together with sugar and a splash of Marsala wine. Breakfast for the parents was hard bread dipped in coffee that Mrs. Baldizzi boiled in a pot. Coffee grinds, like tea bags, were reused two or three times before being consigned to the trash. The Baldizzi children returned home for a lunch of fried eggs and potato, or vegetable frittata. A typical evening meal was pasta and lentils or vegetable soup, which Mr. Baldizzi referred to as "belly wash." On Saturday evenings, he made the family scrambled egg sandwiches with American ketchup.

Though America's bounty eluded the Baldizzis, Rosaria understood the power of food over the human psyche and used it—what little she had—as an antidote to the daily humiliations of poverty. Dinner in the Baldizzi household was a formal event, the table set with the good Italian linen that Rosaria had brought over from Sicily, the napkins ironed and starched so they stood up on their own. If the menu was limited, the food was expertly cooked and regally presented. On occasion, as a treat for the children, Rosaria would arrange their dinners on individual trays and present it to them as edible gifts. One of Josephine's clearest childhood memories is of her mother standing in front of the black stove at 97 Orchard, holding a tray of "pizza"—a large round loaf of Sicilian bread, sliced crosswise like a hamburger bun, rubbed with olive oil, sprinkled with cheese, and baked in the oven. "You see," Rosaria says, "you *are* somebody!" Such was the power of food in the immigrant kitchen: to confer dignity on a skinny tenement kid with cardboard soles in her shoes.

On birthdays and holidays, edible gift–giving rose to the level of ritual. For All Souls Day, when ancestral spirits deigned to visit the living, Mrs. Baldizzi gave the kids a tray piled with the candied almonds known as *confetti, torrone*, Indian nuts, and Josephine's personal favorite, one-cent Hooten Bars. That night, the children would slip the tray under the bed, in case the spirits should arrive hungry. The next day, after the ancestors had presumably helped themselves, it was the children's turn. On Easter, each child received a marzipan representation of the Paschal lamb. Candy was also part of the Nativity scene displayed each December on the Baldizzis' kitchen table, the manger strewn with *confetti* and American-style peppermint drops.

Much of the candy sold in New York in the early twentieth century—Italian and otherwise—was produced locally in factories scattered through the city. In fact, by the turn of the century, New York was the center of the American candy trade, employing more people than any other food-related industry aside from bread. New York candy-makers were tied to another local industry with deep historical roots: the sugar trade. All through the eighteenth and nineteenth centuries, ships carrying raw sugar from the Caribbean delivered their cargo to the refineries or "sugar houses" that were clustered near Wall Street, converting the coarse brown crystals into loaves of white table sugar. Candy factories began to appear in Lower Manhattan in the early 1800s, before migrating uptown to Astor Place, then to midtown and Brooklyn.

By the late nineteenth century, immigrants were important players in the candy business. Some owned factories specializing in their native sweets, but many, many more worked as candy laborers. In New York, Chicago, Boston, and Philadelphia, all major candy-making cities, foreign-born women, chiefly Italians and Poles, worked the assembly lines, dipping, wrapping, and boxing. *Italian Women in Industry*, a study published in 1919 that looked specifically at New York, reported that 94 percent of all Italian working women in 1900 were engaged in some form of manufacturing. While the overwhelming majority worked in the needle trades, about 6 percent were candy workers, a job that required no prior training or skills. The dirtiest, most onerous jobs—peeling coconuts, cracking almonds, and sorting peanuts—went to the older women who spoke no English. For their labor, they were paid roughly $4.50 for a sixty-five-hour workweek. (Women who worked in the needle trades generally earned $8 a week, while sewing machine operators, the most skilled garment workers, brought in $12 weekly or more.) The long hours and filthy conditions in the factories made candy work one of the least desirable jobs for Italian women. Mothers who worked in the candy factories for most of their adult lives prayed that daughters "would never go into it, unless they were forced to."

Another class of candy workers could be found in the tenements. Candy outworkers were immigrant women hired by the factories, who brought their work home to their tenement apartments, completing specific tasks within the larger manufacturing process. This two-tiered arrangement of factory workers and home workers was widespread on the Lower East Side and used by several of the most important local industries. The largest and best-documented was the garment industry, in which factory hands were responsible for the more critical jobs of cutting, sewing, and pressing, while home workers did "finishing work": small, repetitive tasks, like sewing on buttons, stitching buttonholes, and pulling out basting threads, a job that often fell to children. In the candy trade, finishing work meant wrapping candies and boxing them. It also included nut-picking: carefully separating the meat from the nutshell with the help of an improvised tool, like a hairpin or a nail. These were jobs often performed as a family activity, by an Italian mother and her kids, sitting at the kitchen table with a fifty-pound bag of licorice drops lugged home from the factory that morning, a small mountain of boxes at their feet.

Unlike her sisters in the factories, the home worker fell beyond the reach of protective labor laws that regulated the length of her workday along with her minimum wage. Her children were also unprotected. In the Old Country, children worked side by side with their fathers in the fields. In cities like New York, the moment they returned from school they went to work shelling hazelnuts or walnuts until deep into the night. During the rush seasons just before Christmas and Easter, they were kept home from school entirely.

In the eyes of middle-class America, the candy home worker was an ambiguous figure, equal parts victim and villain. Bullied and abused by greedy factory owners, she attracted support from social reformers like the National Consumer League, which advocated on her behalf. At the same time, the outworker was a threat to public safety, the foods that touched her hands contaminated by the same germs that flourished in her tenement home. Pasta, wine, matzoh, and pickles were also produced in the tenements, foods made by immigrants for immigrants. Candy, however, was different. While made by foreigners, it was destined for the wider public, available in the most exclusive uptown stores.

As middle-class Americans became aware of tenement candy workers, panic set in. Tenement-made candy, they surmised, was the perfect vehicle for transporting working-class diseases like cholera and tuberculosis from the downtown slums to the more pristine neighborhoods in Upper Manhattan. "Table Tidbits Prepared Under Revolting Conditions," a story that ran in the *New York Tribune* in 1913, sounded the alarm:

> *Foodstuffs prepared in tenement houses? For whom? For you, fastidious reader and for everybody! A pleasant subject this for meditation. Slum squalor has been reaching uptown in many insidious ways. It was bad enough to think that the clothing one wore had been handled in stuffy rooms, where sanitary conditions and ventilation were deplorable . . . When it is learned, however, that many of the things actually eaten or put to the lips have been prepared by some poor slattern in indifferent or bad health and by more or less dirty tots of the slums amid surroundings that would cause humanity to hold its nose, a brilliant future looms up for some of the scourges scientists are busily endeavoring to stamp out.*[10]

An immigrant family shelling nuts at their kitchen table. This photo was used to demonstrate the unsanitary conditions that prevailed among tenement home workers.

Stories like this one, brimming over in lurid details, enumerated the many sanitary breaches committed by the home worker. She was known, for example, to crack nuts with her teeth and pick them with her fingernails. At mealtime, picked nuts were swept to the side of the table, or removed to the floor or the bed. But most alarming of all, home workers performed their tasks in rooms shared by tuberculosis sufferers or children sick with measles. In some cases, the home worker was sick herself, like the consumptive woman who was too weak to leave her bed but somehow managed to go on with her work as a cigarette maker. The one detail consistently absent from these stories was mention of any documented illness linked to tenement-made goods. They may have occurred, but the looming threat posed by the home worker was more compelling than the actual risk.

While immigrant candy workers fed the national sweet tooth, in their own communities, Italian confectioners made sweets for their fellow countrymen. The more prosperous owned their own shops, or *bottege di confetti*, preparing the candy in large copper pots at the back of the store. Marzipan, *torrone* (a nougat-like candy made with egg whites and honey), and *panforte*, a dense cake made of honey, nuts, and fruit, were specialties of the confectioner's art. The *confetti* shops also sold pastries like cannoli and *cassata*, an ornate Sicilian cake made with ricotta, candied fruit, sponge cake, and marzipan. In the months leading up to Easter, store owners created window displays of their gaudiest, most eye-catching sweets. Herds of marzipan lambs grazed in one corner of the window, beside a field of cannoli. Pyramids of marzipan fruits and vegetables, each crafted in fine detail, loomed in the background. Most eye-catching of all, however, were candy statues representing the main actors in the Passion story: a weeping Virgin Mary in her blue cloak; Christ in his loincloth staggering under the weight of the cross; Mary Magdalene; and even the heartless Roman soldiers brandishing their spears, all cast from molten sugar.

The Easter celebration was a family event centered on the home. More conspicuous occasions for candy consumption were the religious festivals held through the year in the streets of Little Italy. The *feste* were

Nut peddler at an Italian street festival.

open-air celebrations in honor of a particular saint, each one connected with a town or village back home. Sponsored by fellow townspeople, they combined religious observance in the form of a solemn procession with brass bands, fireworks, and public feasting, the exact nature of food determined by the immigrants' birthplace. A Sicilian festival, for example, would include *torrone*, but not the kind made with egg whites. Sicilian *torrone* was a glossy nut brittle made with almonds or hazelnuts, a confection brought to Sicily by the Arabs. There was also *cubbaita*, or sesame brittle, another Arab sweet, and *insolde*, a Sicilian version of *panforte*. Below is a description of the foods, candy included, available at a 1903 festival held in Harlem, the uptown Little Italy, honoring Our Lady of Mount Carmel:

> *The crowd is chiefly buying things to eat from street vendors. Men push through the masses of people on the sidewalks, carrying trays full of brick ice cream of brilliant hues and yelling "Gelati Italiani"— Italian ices. "Lupini," the "ginney beans" of the New York Arab; "cice-retti," the little roasted peas and squash seeds are favorite refreshments.*

*Great ropes of Brazil nuts soaked in water and threaded on a string,
or roasted chestnuts, strung in the same way, lie around the vendor's
neck. Boys carry long sticks strung with rings of bread. All manner of
"biscuitini," small Italian cakes, are for sale, frosted in gorgeous hues,
chiefly a bright magenta cheerful to look upon but rather ghastly to
contemplate as an article of food.*

*Boys at the door of bakeshops vociferate "Pizzarelli caldi"—hot
pizzarelli. The pizzarello is a little flat cake of fried dough, probably
the Neapolitan equivalent of a doughnut. They sell for a penny a
piece. Sometimes the cook makes them as big as the frying pan, putting in tomato and cheese—a mixture beloved of all Italians. These
big ones cost 15 cents, but there is enough for a taste all around the
family. The bakers are frying them hot all through the feast. A certain
cake made with molasses, and full of peanuts or almonds, baked in
a long slab and cut in little squares, four or five for a cent, is much
eaten. So is "coppetta," a thick, hard white candy full of nuts; and the
children all carry bags of "confetti," little bright-colored candies with
nuts inside. Here and there the sun flashes on great bunches of bright,
new tin pails, heaped on the back and shoulders of the vendor: and
the new pail bought and filled with lemonade passes impartially from
lip to lip of the family parties lunching on the benches in Thomas
Jefferson Park.[11]*

Below is a recipe for *croccante*, or almond brittle. It is adapted from *The
Italian Cook Book* by Maria Gentile, published in 1919, among the earliest
Italian cookbooks published in the United States.

CROCCANTE

3 cups blanched sliced almonds
2 cups sugar
1–2 tablespoons mildly flavored vegetable oil
1 lemon cut in half

Preheat to 400°F. Liberally grease a baking tray with the vegetable oil and put aside. Spread almonds on a separate tray and toast in hot oven until golden, about 5 minutes. Heat sugar in a heavy-bottomed saucepan and cook until sugar has completely melted. Add almonds and stir. Pour hot mixture onto greased baking tray, using the cut side of the lemon to spread evenly. Allow to cool and break into pieces.[12]

In the descriptive names that immigrants invented for the United States is a measure of what they expected to find. To Eastern European Jews, America was the *Goldene Medina*, or "Golden Land," a place of extravagant wealth. For the Chinese immigrants who settled on the West Coast, America was "the gold mountain," a reference to the California hills that would make them rich. Sicilians, by contrast, referred to America as "the land of bread and work," an image of grim survival, comparatively speaking. To the Sicilian, however, bread was its own form of wealth. More than other Italians, Sicilians felt a special closeness to this elemental food, a "God-bequeathed friend," in the words of Jerre Mangione, "who would keep bodies and souls together when nothing else would."[13] The Sicilian respect for bread was rooted in a long history. From the sixteenth century forward, bread formed the axis of the peasant diet, sustaining—though just barely—generations of Sicilian field workers. The typical Sicilian loaf was made from a locally cultivated strain of wheat, *triticum durum*, which Arab settlers had brought to Sicily, along with almonds, lemons, oranges, and sugar, back in the ninth century. The wheat grew on giant estates called *latifundi*, and by the Middle Ages it covered most of Sicily's arable land. Durum was a particularly hardy strain with a high protein content, producing a dense, chewy bread with a powerful crust. When mixed with water, it could be stretched into thin sheets that resisted tearing, making it ideal for pasta, too.

Peasants who worked all day in the field packed a hunk of bread and maybe an onion for their lunch. For dinner, there was bean soup, and yet more bread. As minimal as this sounds, the Sicilian pantry became even more spare during periods of famine, which in Sicily amounted to "a time without bread." A Sicilian proverb recounted by Mary Taylor Simeti in *Pomp and Sustenance* sums it up beautifully:

> *If I had a saucepan, water, and salt,*
> *I'd make a bread stew—if I had bread.*

A loaf of bread for Sicilians embodied the basic goodness of life. Where we might say a person is "as good as gold," a Sicilian says "as good as bread." A piece of bread that fell to the ground was kissed, like a child with a scraped knee.

When Sicilians described America as the land of bread and work, they imagined a country without hunger, which, in their experience, was just as miraculous as a city paved in gold. One thing they never imagined, however, was that bread would fall into their hands like manna from heaven. Richard Gambino, describing the powerful work ethic that guided his Brooklyn neighborhood, remembers a phrase often repeated by the local men, *"In questa vita si fa uva,"* literally translated as, "In this life, one produces grapes." In other words, each one of us has been put on this earth to be useful. Gambino also remembers his grandfather's Sicilian friends holding up their calloused workers' hands and saying *"America e icca,"* meaning "America is here—this is America."[14] For the Sicilian, bread and work were locked together in a kind of dance that began early in life, the day the young Sicilian was old enough to contribute.

Sicilians carried their bread tradition to America, where it continued with certain necessary revisions. On Saturdays in Sicily, women did all their baking for the coming week, a way to preserve precious fuel. In cities like New York, the Italian laborer, now on his own, purchased his weekly ration each Saturday in Little Italy. Here, Italian peddlers sold loaves prepared expressly for the "diggers and ditchers," immense crusty loaves nearly the size of a wagon wheel. Anyone who could not afford to buy their bread fresh, bought stale loaves, a special sideline of the retail

Curbside bread peddler on Mulberry Street, selling her wares from a basket.

bread trade controlled by women. Bread that was once thrown away was sold by the larger bakeries and retail houses to middlemen who, in turn, sold it to the peddlers, women who sat on the curbstone, their goods piled in a blanket beside them. As the immigrant's finances swelled, his diet branched out in new directions. Pasta, eggs, and, eventually, meat diverted some of his affection for bread but never replaced it. In the Mangione household, bread was eaten with every course of the Sunday feast, except for the pasta. A bowl of soup without bread was bereft of its faithful companion. Meat without bread was considered sinful.

Elizabeth Street in the 1930s hosted two groceries, two butcher shops, one fish store, and one candy store, but six bakeries. In New York, the typical Sicilian loaf was a simple round bread sprinkled with sesame seeds, weighing roughly two pounds. On holidays and feast days, however, the baker's imagination took flight, and the Elizabeth shops offered fantastic bread sculptures, each shape tied to a particular saint. One resembled a curving bowl of flowers, another was shaped like a swirling backward *S* with frilled edges. Though each of these fanciful shapes was created for the saints, the baker hedged his bets by including breads that were braided or knotted, traditional forms of protection from the evil eye.

When they lived on Orchard Street, the Baldizzis relied on bread as a food of survival in much the same way it had been for generations of Sicilian peasants. It was eaten at every meal, and for breakfast it *was* the meal. Stale or hard bread was never thrown away. Instead, Rosaria would rub it with a little water and oil and put it in a warm oven to soften it up. Bread that was too far gone to revive was turned into bread crumbs, the indispensable ally of all Sicilian cooks. Bread crumbs were used to stretch more costly ingredients like meat, and sometimes to replace it entirely. Combined with oil, parsley, and garlic, bread crumbs were used as a stuffing for peppers, zucchini, artichokes, and other vegetables. Bread crumbs, parsley, and eggs were used to make frittata, a standard mid-day meal for the Italian laborers who dug the New York subway system. Bread crumbs were also toasted in hot oil and sprinkled over pasta or pizza as a replacement for the more expensive grated cheese. Even as their incomes rose, Sicilian-Americans continued to cook with bread crumbs, a former food of necessity. Nothing made a crunchier coating for fried calamari or *arancini*, the creamy, fist-size rice balls filled with ground meat or cheese, sold as street food and prepared in the home for holidays and parties. Today, they appear on the menus of old-time Sicilian restaurants and delicatessens. Below are two bread crumb recipes. The first is for a bread-crumb frittata.

Zucchini Frittata

4 large or 6 small zucchini
1 small onion sliced
3 tablespoons olive oil
5 eggs
½ cup grated Romano cheese
⅓ cup bread crumbs
Salt and pepper

Rinse and grate zucchini using the large holes on a hand-
held grater. You could also use the shredding disc on a food
processor. Place grated zucchini in a colander over the sink.
Sprinkle with a teaspoon of salt, toss, and let sit 15 minutes
or longer, until the zucchini begins to "weep." Squeeze out
the extra moisture with your hands. Put aside.

Sauté the onion in 2 tablespoons of the olive oil until lightly golden. Add the zucchini. Cook until zucchini
is slightly browned in spots and most of the remaining
moisture has cooked away. Season with salt and pepper,
and remove from the stove. Meanwhile, beat the eggs in
a large mixing bowl. Add the warm zucchini, along with
the grated cheese and bread crumbs. Let the mixture sit a
minute or two, so the bread crumbs can drink up some of
the egg. Add remaining oil to the frying pan, and let it get
hot. Add egg mixture, then turn down the heat. Cook over a
low flame until frittata starts to set around the edges. Place
under a hot broiler to finish cooking the top. Slide onto a
plate. Eat at room temperature.[15]

The pasta recipe below comes to us from Concetta Rizzolo, an immigrant from Avellino, a town east of Naples, who settled in New Jersey
in the 1910s. The toasted bread crumbs can be stored in the refrigerator
for several weeks.

SPAGHETTI CON AGLIO E OLIO

½ cup olive oil
6 cloves garlic, minced
½ to 1 tsp red pepper flakes
10 black peppercorns
1 pound spaghetti

½ cup chopped parsley
½ cup toasted bread crumbs

To toast bread crumbs, coat a frying pan with olive oil and
heat over a medium flame. When the oil is warm, add 1
cup homemade bread crumbs. Stir bread crumbs to prevent
them from burning or sticking. They are ready as soon as
they turn a uniform golden-brown.

Boil water for spaghetti. Meanwhile, heat oil over low
flame. Add garlic and peppercorns. Cook garlic over a very
low flame until it is soft and translucent, but do not allow
it to brown. Add pepper flakes and continue to cook for
about five minutes.

Drain pasta but reserve about a cup of cooking water.
Add to oil and garlic mixture and heat over low flame. Toss
with spaghetti and serve immediately with parsley and
toasted bread crumbs.[16]

Living on Orchard Street, in the heart of the Jewish East Side, the
Baldizzis formed close relationships with their Jewish neighbors, Fannie Rogarshevsky in particular. After her husband died, when Fannie
assumed the role of building janitor, Mr. Baldizzi, a trained carpenter,
often helped her with repairs. The two became good friends. Sometime
in the early 1930s, to alleviate crowding in the Rogarshevsky household,
one of Fannie's grandsons was sent to live with the Baldizzis. Conversely,
Fannie regularly fixed school-day lunches for the Baldizzi kids when their
mother was at work. (Rosaria Baldizzi worked for a short time during the
Depression but had to give up her job or forfeit her check from Home
Relief.) The young Josephine, Fannie Rogarshevsky's designated *shabbos
goy*, was fascinated by the way the Jewish homemaker koshered her chickens, scrubbing them at the kitchen sink the way an Italian mother might
scrub an especially dirty child. Every evening, Mr. Baldizzi stopped by

Schreiber's Delicatessen on Broome Street for a glass of schnapps, his
ritual nightcap. On weekends he took the kids on long walks that carried them over the Manhattan Bridge and back again, stopping along the
way for hot potato pancakes, that quintessentially Jewish snack sold by
the East Side vendors. Even so, when it was time to shop for groceries,
Mrs. Baldizzi found limited use for the pushcart market directly below
her window. Instead, the food she depended on could be found a few
blocks away, in the Italian pushcart market on Mulberry Street. By the
time of the mayor's pushcart commission in 1906, Mulberry Street was
already a full-service open-air market catering to the Italian homemaker.
Satellite markets sprang up on Elizabeth and Bleecker streets and along
First Avenue below 14th Street. The largest of all, however, extended
for nearly a mile from 100th to 119th streets on First Avenue in East
Harlem. The pushcart markets were the single most important source

Clams on the half-shell, a common street food in Little Italy.

of food for immigrant New Yorkers from the 1880s through the late
1930s, when Mayor La Guardia, the son of immigrants himself, finally
prevailed in the decades-long battle between the pushcart peddlers and
the city government. In anticipation of the upcoming World's Fair and
the multitudes that would soon descend on New York, La Guardia shut
down one market after another, consolidating some and moving others into newly built market buildings more befitting a modern city. The
Mulberry Street market fell to the mayor's ax in 1939, the year the fair
opened. In the meantime, however, the Mulberry Street pushcarts supplied Italian cooks like Mrs. Baldizzi with foods unknown in the Jewish
quarter. The Italian peddlers, for example, did a brisk business in mus-
sels, periwinkles, conch, oysters, and clams. The last two items were sold
as street food, the Italian equivalent to the Jewish knish.

In the Old Country, Italian women foraged for snails, a free source
of precious protein. In America, the snail peddler became a fixture of the
Italian pushcart market. His mode of advertising, unique among street
vendors, was an upright board with the snails clinging to it. The bulk of
his delicate stock could be found in a crate under the pushcart to keep
the snails shaded and cool. Italian cooks soaked their snails in cold water,
prompting the animal to inch out of its shell, then fried it with garlic,
creating a savory and inexpensive topping for pasta. Other sea creatures
sold at the market were squid, octopus, and eels, which the Italian cook
stewed with tomatoes.

But the most remarkable feature of the Italian markets was the selec-
tion of greens and other vegetables that figured so prominently in the
immigrants' diet. Early accounts of the pushcart markets offer a par-
tial list of the many forms of plant life sold by Italian peddlers. There
was cabbage and cauliflower—though no mention of broccoli—cow
peas, cucumbers, celery (distinct from American celery), fennel, peppers, tomatoes, eggplant, onion, garlic, chickweed, beet tops, lettuce, and
many other forms of leafy greens which the Americans had no names for.
As a convenience to the homemaker, beans could be purchased dried or
already soaked to hasten the cooking time. The Italian vegetable peddlers,
many of them women, were fastidious in the presentation of their goods.

As one observer noted, "They clean, cut, and freshen the vegetables, constantly rearranging them so that they appear to the best advantage on the stands."[17] The women scrubbed their celery and their fennel until the stalks gleamed; they buffed the peppers and sprinkled the lettuce with water to keep it from wilting. Americans, who still thought of salads as an assemblage of vegetables and meats, often bound with mayonnaise, were struck by the Italians' more restrained approach to the same dish. "No other people in the world," one observer remarked,

> use so many salads. They never mix tomatoes, lettuce, and cucumbers as Americans do in their salads. Each is kept separate. For their tomato salad, they clean the tomatoes, but do not peel them, split or slice them, and dress them with oil, but no vinegar. Then they strew over them stems of "regona," a herb of aromatic taste and smell which comes dried from Italy . . . Cucumbers they peel and eat with both oil and vinegar, regona, and garlic. The heart of the lettuce, which they call "lattuga," is a prime favorite, dressed with olive oil and Italian vinegar.[18]

The Italian's devotion to these simple preparations was also noteworthy. "The Italian invariably has a salad for dinner if he can afford it," our observer adds, "and it seems often to supply the place of meat to him." To the American, the Italian salad habit was a source of puzzlement. How could a plate of lettuce, they wondered, take the place of a good roast? More curious still, how could a diet so lacking in substance provide the nourishment required to sustain human life?

Come spring, immigrants scoured the vacant lots of Brooklyn and the Bronx for wild dandelions, a food they had once gathered in the fields around their native villages. In New York, dandelions were a source of income for Italian women who collected the greens, cleaned them, and sold them at the pushcart markets, a washtub's worth for a nickel. Italian cooks used the wild green for dandelion soup, or fried them in olive oil with tomatoes and pepper. When boiled for several hours, the filtered cooking liquid, *"acqua di cicorie"* was used as a tonic for "dyspepsia and general weakness."[19] An Italian summer delicacy was *cucuzza*, an extremely long squash with smooth, pale green skin and a hook at one end like an umbrella handle. Peddlers displayed the *cucuzze* by looping the hooked ends over a horizontal pole so they hung like stockings on a wash line. The leaves of the plant, sold as a separate vegetable, were heaped in crates on the pushcart below. *Cucuzza* was especially popular with Sicilian cooks, who added it to soups or fried it with garlic and tomatoes. Sicilian confectioners, meanwhile, chopped the squash into small pieces or shaved it into ribbons, then boiled it in sugar syrup until the opaque white interior had turned deep gold and was almost transparent.

Much of the produce sold on Mulberry Street was grown on immigrant "truck farms" in Brooklyn, Queens, Long Island, and New Jersey, a few hours commute from the wholesale markets in Lower Manhattan. A bit farther out from the city, Italians established a vibrant farming community in Vineland, New Jersey, which by 1900 comprised two hundred and sixty immigrant families. The Vineland farmers cultivated fruits and vegetables for the immigrant market using seeds imported from Italy. Their crops included garlic, peppers, cauliflower, cabbage, beets, fennel, cardoons (a relative of artichokes), chestnuts, figs, plums, and ten varieties of grapes.

In the nineteenth century, immigrant Jews carried their goose-farming tradition to America, establishing urban poultry farms in the East Side tenements. Several decades later, Italian immigrants brought their treasured home gardens to urban America, now reconfigured as a tenement window box. In wooden planters made from discarded soapboxes, Italian homemakers grew oregano, basil, mint, peppers, tomatoes, and lettuce. (The more ambitious urban farmers planted their gardens on tenement rooftops.) The tradition of the home garden continues today in Italian neighborhoods like Hoboken, New Jersey, and Bensonhurst, Brooklyn, where second- and third-generation immigrants grow basil and plum tomatoes in emptied institutional-size cans of *pomodori pelati*.

Though removed from the soil, transplanted Italian women moved to the rhythm of the agricultural year. Each fall, in New York's Little Italy, they bought up great loads of peppers and preserved them for the coming winter. The peppers were split and brined in tubs of saltwater or packed in jars filled with vinegar. The women also dried their peppers in the sun, just as they used to in the Old Country. In New York, however, they threaded the peppers onto long strings and suspended them from the fire escapes in great dangling loops. Tomatoes were also dried in the sun, along with eggplant, which the women first cut into strips. Each of these dried vegetables was soaked in water for several hours prior to cooking, then fried in olive oil or added to soup. The eggplant recipe below is from Maria Gentile.

Eggplants in the Oven

Skin five or six eggplants, cut them in round slices, and salt them so that they throw out the water that they contain. After a few hours, dip in flour and frying oil.

Take a fireproof vase or baking tin and place the slices in layers, with grated cheese between each layer, abundantly seasoned with tomato sauce.

Beat one egg with a pinch of salt, a tablespoonful of tomato sauce, a teaspoonful of grated cheese and two of crumbs of bread, and cover the upper layer with this sauce. Put the vase in the oven and when the egg is coagulated, serve hot.[20]

The contempt for Italian cooking that prevailed in this country a hundred-plus years ago is a buried fact in our culinary history and a surprising one, too, considering how much attitudes have changed. In the United States today, no immigrant cuisine is more embraced by the American cook, her kitchen stocked with tomato paste, canned tomatoes, jarred marinara sauce, olive oil, parmesan cheese, garlic, and above all pasta, mainstay of the American dinner table. And what food, if not pizza, is more beloved by American schoolchildren?

This national love affair unfolded in two overlapping yet disconnected chapters. Chapter one began in the mid-nineteenth century, as immigrants from northern Italy settled in New York, Philadelphia, Baltimore, New Orleans, Boston, and San Francisco. Italians who belonged to this first wave were largely people of culture—artists, musicians, teachers, doctors, and other professionals. Among the early immigrants were restaurant-keepers. In the 1850s and 1860s, as the Italian settlements gathered critical mass, they opened eating places to feed their transplanted countrymen. New York's first Italian restaurants were clustered near Union Square, close to 14th Street, then the city's main entertainment thoroughfare and home to the Academy of Music, the nation's first official opera house. In 1857, an Italian named Stefano Moretti opened a pleasingly shabby second-floor restaurant directly across the street from the Academy, which became New York's first important Bohemian dining spot. The favorite haunt of Italian opera stars, Moretti's began to attract native-born musicians, artists, and writers. The avant-garde of their day, they were drawn to Moretti's by the delightfully foreign atmosphere as well as the food, a five-course dinner for a dollar, a fair price for the time though well beyond the means of the working class. The dishes they encountered were typical of the northern kitchen. Risotto with kidney was a house specialty, along with wild duck and quail, both served with salad. But Signor Moretti was also known for his spaghetti, "tender as first love" and "sweet beyond comparison." Though nineteenth-century Americans were generally familiar with macaroni, the pipe-stem-shaped pasta used today for mac 'n' cheese, spaghetti was still utterly alien. American diners were simultaneously baffled, alarmed, and enchanted by these attenuated strands of dough that they discovered in Italian restaurants but still had no name for. If the food itself was bizarre, the complicated procedure of eating it left Americans awestruck. The following description of a New York Italian restaurant circa 1889 captures the air of adventure surrounding this novel food. The second course consisted

> of a substance resembling macaroni that has been pulled out until each
> piece is at least two feet long, while the thickness has proportionally di-

minished. You are told that it is wholly bad form to cut this reptile-like food; you must eat as the Italians do. Thereupon you suddenly cease to feel hungry, and spend the time in observation. They, to the manner born, lift a mass of this slippery thing upon the fork, give the wrist several expert twists, and then, with lightning rapidity, place it in the mouth. If by misfortune a string escapes, it is gradually recovered in the most nonchalant manner imaginable. It is a fascinating operation, though by no means one to inspire a desire to emulate the operator.[21]

The only thing more diverting than this queer new food was the foreign crowd, a collection of singers, ballerinas, professors, journalists, and businessmen.

As the city's theaters migrated from 14th Street to Broadway, the restaurants followed. For New Yorkers out on the town, tired of their native chop houses and oyster saloons, Italian food was a refreshing change of pace, and much cheaper than French, the foreign cuisine favored by elite society. Italian food, by contrast, along with German, was the foreign cuisine of the American middle class. The kind of food New Yorkers could expect to find at the new Broadway restaurants was more attuned to American tastes. For the less adventuresome eater, they offered both chops and oysters. The rest of the menu was still rooted in the more mildly flavored and buttery cuisine of northern Italy. An inventory of recommended dishes that ran in the *New York Sun* advised diners to stick with the cheaper items on the menu, like spaghetti in meat sauce, "a chopped-up soupy compound," and to skip the more expensive meats in favor of veal, lamb, and giblets:

The leg of veal, usually used for a soup bone, is delicious when it comes on the table as osso buco. The leg is roasted, there is a suggestion of herbs and garlic and a sauce of brown butter over the risotto that accompanies it. Then there is the delicious marrow in the bone that has been opened in order that it may easily be eaten.

The veal cutlets, whether they are served à la Milanaise, with cêpes cut up over them and put into a sauce of butter and cheese, or with herbs, are superior to any that can be eaten at the best of Fifth avenue restaurants.

Arostino, which means a little roast, is a slice of the veal served with the kidney embedded into it and cooked with thyme and a thick brown sauce covering it and a bed of risotto. Such a cut of veal is unknown to American butchers.

The kidneys au sauce Medere are made in accordance with an Italian formula and are remarkable from the fact that only very small kidneys are used and they are served with champignons of about the same size.

It is in such dishes as these that the Italian restaurants excel, and to them they owe their present popularity, for they alone are able to serve them in such excellence in cooking and at such prices.[22]

The Broadway restaurants offered just enough novelty (and garlic) to stimulate the imagination while providing diners with the niceties of New York's finest eating establishments, including an Italian menu printed in French.

After 1880, an entirely different kind of Italian eating place could be found in New York. These were the basement restaurants on Mulberry and Mott streets that catered to the new wave of Italian immigrants, peasant farmers from the southern half of the country who began to settle in New York's notorious Five Points neighborhood, moving into the ramshackle tenements once occupied by American blacks and poor Irish. The Italians also took over the low-paying jobs once held by the Irish to become the city's new street cleaners and ditch diggers. Native-born New Yorkers drew a firm distinction between these new immigrants and the Italians they already knew, "honest," "industrious," and "orderly" people. An 1875 editorial that ran in the *New York Times* presented this thumbnail portrait of the new arrivals:

They are extremely ignorant, and have been reared in the belief that brigandage is a manly occupation, and that assassination is the natural sequence of the most trivial quarrel. They are miserably poor, and it is not strange that they resort to theft and robbery. It is, perhaps, hopeless to think of civilizing them.[23]

While the north vs. south distinction was rooted in historical fact (southerners *were* poor and uneducated), it became the foundation for pernicious stereotypes imposed on southern Italians, which Americans returned to again and again, using the immigrants' birthplace to explain everything about them, from their violent nature to their deplorable eating habits. As a result, several years passed before Americans were able to gather up their courage and sample the fruits of the southerners' kitchen.

The first restaurants in Little Italy reflected the immigrants' meager earnings. A visitor to the Italian colony in 1884 counted four neighborhood restaurants where laborers could buy a two-cent plate of macaroni, three cents worth of coffee and bread, or splurge on coffee and mutton chops, the most expensive item on the menu, for a total of six cents. Basement restaurants also provided laborers with a place to gather, to smoke their pipes, play cards, and enjoy the talents of their musical peers. (The neighborhood's busiest social spots, however, were the stale-beer dives, as they were known, where the house drink was made from the beer dregs collected from a better class of saloons.) The dining rooms attached to boardinghouses and cheap hotels were another eating option for the transplanted Italian. A typical menu consisted of coffee with anisette and hard bread for breakfast, and for supper, minestrone, spaghetti or macaroni, followed by a stew made with garlic and oil.

The early restaurants reflected the strong connections that immigrants felt for their native villages. As they settled in New York, Italians recreated the geography of home, with Neapolitans on Mulberry Street, Calabrians on Mott, Sicilians on Elizabeth, and so on. Within these regional encampments, Italians from a particular town or village tended to cluster on the same city block and sometimes in the same building. At their *festa*, villagers came together to honor their local saint, but also to celebrate their ties with each other. Italians have a word for the special connectedness felt among townspeople. *Campanilismo*, from the Italian word for "bell," describes the bonds of solidarity felt among people who live within hearing distance of the same church bell.

Restaurants preserved these regional loyalties. Some of the first restaurants were hidden within the Italian groceries that began to appear in New York in the 1880s, the provisions lined up on one half of the room, the other half set aside for tables. Like many immigrant restaurants, these were family-run businesses. The store/café occupied the front room of a ground-floor apartment, while the family slept in the back. This was also where the proprietor's wife cooked for her customers. An 1889 article from *Harper's* magazine describes the convivial scene inside one of these store/cafés, this one owned by a family of Sicilians:

> *Notwithstanding the poverty of the place, it is as busy as a beehive. At the long table, a number of men, who probably work at night on the scows of the Street-cleaning Department, are drinking the black coffee, which, despite its cheapness, is palatable enough to the drinkers. A handful of Italian women, whose dresses and shawls are bright with the gaudy colors so dear to them, are chaffering with the proprietor's wife over a string of garlic or a pound of sausage. The chairs about the room are occupied by friends and customers of the house, who are smoking villainous short pipes and talking so loudly that one ignorant of the language would suspect them to be on the point of a riot.*
>
> *The air is blue with tobacco smoke, and the place reeks with the conglomeration of stenches that no language can describe, yet all the people appear to enjoy the best of health, and even the children display a robustness and physical vigor that would do credit to those born with silver spoons. The food served in this, as in all places of a similar sort, does not lack nutrition, though the materials gathered would not recommend themselves to the fastidious. The stew, made up of scraps gathered here and there, is spiced until savory to a hungry man, and the macaroni, though manufactured from the cheapest and coarsest flour in some eastside shop, is usually wholesome.*[24]

If Americans were charmed by the Italians' earthiness, an establishment like the Sicilian café was best experienced in the pages of magazines.

Once confined to the Five Points, New York's most notorious slum, by 1910 Little Italy stretched north toward Houston Street and west toward Greenwich Village. As the colony expanded, its physical character also changed. In 1895, the tenements surrounding Mulberry Bend, the heart of the Five Points, were torn down to make way for Columbus Park, Little Italy's new "town square." Two blocks west of the Bend, more tenements were razed to widen Elm Street, creating a broad thoroughfare known today as Lafayette Street. Now open to light and air, Little Italy was no longer the "foul core of New York slums" that Jacob Riis described in the 1890s. What's more, Little Italy was no longer the bachelor community it once had been. By 1900, Italian immigrants were largely men and women who came to the United States to start a family and lay down roots.

Chapter two of the American romance with Italian food began at the turn of the century, as native New Yorkers wandered into the now-expanded Italian colony. One stop on their itinerary was the Italian grocery, which exposed the visitor to enticements they had never known existed. The heart of their education, however, took place in the Italian restaurants that served as culinary classrooms. For Americans who believed that Italians subsisted on bread and macaroni, the edible delights available in the downtown restaurants came as a revelation. Published accounts of these gastronomic forays were quick to warn readers of certain possible pitfalls. To quote one newspaper reporter: "The Italian taste in cookery is not always such as pleases the native American palate."[25] Properly advised, however, American diners could find an array of delectable dishes: minestrone that was "thick and tasteful"; kidneys, liver, and veal, prepared southern-style with peppers and onions; simmered *polpette*, or meatballs; fried calamari; and a host of tantalizing vegetable dishes based on eggplant, tomatoes, and peppers. But the dish that most enchanted American diners was spaghetti.

Discovered by an earlier generation of adventuresome eaters, in the early 1900s spaghetti reentered the American culinary consciousness and quickly moved from restaurant kitchens to the family dinner table. Recipes for spaghetti began to appear in American cookbooks, including *The Boston Cooking School Cook Book* by Fannie Farmer published in 1896. In her 1902 cookbook, Sarah Tyson Rorer, a leading voice of the domestic science movement, explains precisely how this still-novel food should be cooked:

> *Spaghetti is always served in the long form in which it is purchased. Grasp the given quantity in your hand; put the ends down into boiling water; as they soften, press gently until the whole length is in the water; boil rapidly for twenty minutes. Drain, and blanch in cold water.*[26]

Around the same time, recipes for spaghetti began to appear on the women's pages of American newspapers. Many sent in by readers, newspaper recipes leave a vivid record of the creative, often zany applications that American home cooks found for spaghetti. There was "Mexican Spaghetti" with tomatoes, paprika, peppers, and bacon served in a chafing dish; "Chicken and Spaghetti Croquettes" made with cooked spaghetti, finely chopped; and the popular "Tomatoes Stuffed with Spaghetti." In 1908, the women's page of the *Chicago Tribune* featured a reader's recipe for "Spaghetti and Meat Balls," one of the earliest references to this future staple of the Italian-American kitchen:

SPAGHETTI AND MEAT BALLS

> Take one pound of round steak, run through meat grinder
> two or three times; one egg, three rolled crackers or grated
> stale bread, one small onion grated, four sprigs parsley
> chopped fine, and pepper and salt to suit taste. Mix and
> form into small balls, a teaspoonful and a half each.

Prepare sauce as follows: One can tomatoes, one green or red pepper, one onion, two bay leaves, and a quart water. Boil one hour, then strain through colander. Add small piece of butter, and pepper and salt to suit taste. Return to fire and place meatballs in it and boil slowly for forty minutes.

Spaghetti: take one pound of spaghetti, boil it in two quarts of saltwater for twenty minutes, drain, pour over sauce and all, and serve hot.[27]

The Baldizzis' financial prospects improved considerably when America entered the war in 1941. By this time, the family was living in Brooklyn. Adolfo found work in the wartime naval yards, while Rosaria returned to her job in the garment district. With both parents employed full-time, the pall cast over the Baldizzi household began to lift. On Orchard Street, the family had owned a radio, which Rosaria kept tuned to the opera stations.

Josephine and John Baldizzi on the roof of 97 Orchard Street, 1935.

In Brooklyn, she bought a record player and kept it running whenever she was home, filling the house with music. On holidays, the Baldizzis hosted family parties complete with music and dancing. The new prosperity brought very welcome changes to the family dinner table. At last, Rosaria could afford to buy the meat that was so conspicuously absent from the Orchard Street kitchen. The most festive meal of the year, however, was entirely meatless. Christmas dinner traditionally began at ten o'clock, to coordinate with the midnight mass. The first course was octopus salad, followed by a pan of lasagna, rich with ricotta, eggs, and mozzarella, but the climax of the meal was a stew made with *baccala*—salt cod. Here is the Baldizzi family recipe for the holiday staple:

CHRISTMAS *BACCALA*

> 1 stalk celery, diced
> ½ cup chopped onion
> 2 cloves garlic, chopped
> 1 tablespoon salted capers (or more to taste)
> 2 small cans tomato sauce
> 2 ½ to 3 pounds *baccala*
>
> Two days before Christmas, soak the *baccala* in cold water, changing the water at least two times a day. Cut *baccala* into pieces.
> Sauté celery for five minutes. Add onion, garlic, and capers and cook a few minutes, until soft. Add tomato sauce. Cook over a low flame fifteen minutes. Add *baccala* and cook until fish comes apart with a fork.[28]

On New Year's Eve, the Baldizzis celebrated with *sfinge*, a kind of hole-less doughnut. Rosaria started the batter in the afternoon, mixing the flour, yeast, and water in a large pot, then covering it with a blanket and leaving it to rise. Just before midnight, she put a pot of oil on the stove, testing the temperature with a drop of water. When it splattered, the oil was sufficiently hot. The second the clock struck twelve, she dropped the first spoonful of batter, which caused the oil to bubble wildly, producing a loud *zhoosh*-ing sound. It took roughly a minute for the *sfinge* to cook up, puffy and golden. After scooping them from the pot, she dipped them in sugar. Then she fed them to the kids, still hot, so their first taste of the New Year would be sweet.

Notes

CHAPTER ONE: THE GLOCKNER FAMILY

1. Henriette Davidis, *Practical Cook Book: German National Cookery for American Kitchens* (Milwaukee, 1904), 131.
2. Davidis, *Practical*, 11.
3. Gesine Lemcke, "Cooking Correspondence," *Brooklyn Eagle*, January 1, 1899, 23.
4. Author's recipe, adapted from Davidis.
5. Davidis, *Practical*, 318.
6. Gesine Lemcke, "Cooking Correspondence," *Brooklyn Eagle*, March 26, 1899, 20.
7. "Uncleanly Markets," *New York Times*, May 22, 1854, 4.
8. "Market Reform," *New York Times*, March 29, 1872, 4.
9. "Local Intelligence," *New York Times*, December 19, 1865, 2.
10. Junius Henri Browne, *The Great Metropolis* (Hartford, 1869), 408.
11. Thomas F. De Voe, *The Market Assistant* (New York, 1862), title page.
12. "How New York Is Fed," *Scribner's Monthly*, October 1877, 730.
13. Mrs. Emma Ewing, *Salad and Salad Making* (Chicago, 1883), 37.
14. "Our City's Condition," *New York Times*, June 12, 1865, 1.
15. "Sauerkraut Statistics," *Chicago Tribune* (reprinted from the *Philadelphia News*), December 29, 1885, 5.
16. "The Sauerkraut Peddler," *Washington Post* (reprinted from the *New York Evening Post*), August 24, 1902, 10.
17. Charles Dawson Shanley, "Signs and Show-Cases of New York," *Atlantic Monthly*, May 1870, 528.
18. "Vienna Bread," *New York Times*, January 28, 1877, 6. ("Mackerelville" is a nineteenth-century term for the neighborhood that became the East Village.)

19. "The Household," *New York Times*, January 30, 1876, 9.

20. "Toothsome German Dishes," *New York Times*, July 11, 1897, 10.

21. "The Million's Beverage," *New York Times*, May 20, 1877, 10.

22. Browne, *Great Metropolis*, 161.

23. "History of Beer," *United States Magazine*, August 15, 1854, 180.

24. Jacob A. Riis, *How the Other Half Lives* (New York, 1890), 215.

25. "German Restaurants," *New York Times*, January 19, 1873, 5.

26. "Where Men May Dine Well," *New York Sun*, April 5, 1891, 23.

27. Emory Holloway, ed., *The Uncollected Poetry and Prose of Walt Whitman*, 2 vols. (Garden City, New York, 1921), II: 92.

28. Gesine Lemcke, *European and American Cuisine* (New York, 1933), 543.

29. "Luchow's," Benjamin DeCasseres, *American Mercury*, December 1931, 447.

30. "Germany in New York," *Atlantic Monthly*, May 1867, 557.

31. "The Yearly Turn-Fest," *New York Times*, August 26, 1862, 8.

32. "Jovial Souls," *Brooklyn Eagle*, July 14, 1891, 2.

33. "Sixth Plattdeustche Festival," *New York Times*, September 7, 1880, 8.

34. "New-York City. Germans in America," *New York Times*, June 27, 1855, 1.

Chapter two: The Moore Family

1. Andrew Carpenter, ed., *Verse from Eighteenth-Century Ireland* (Cork, Ireland, 1998), 248.

2. Nancy F. Cott, *Root of Bitterness: Documents of the Social History of American Women* (Lebanon, New Hampshire, 1996), 154.

3. Letter from P. Burdan, 1894. Personal Collection of Kirby Miller.

4. Letter from Cathy Greene, 1884. Personal Collection of Kirby Miller.

5. "Those Servant Girls," *Brooklyn Daily Eagle*, March 12, 1897, 3.

6. Johann Georg Kohl, *Ireland* (New York, 1844), 13.

7. Kohl, *Ireland*, 45.

8. Charles Loring Brace, *The Dangerous Classes of New York* (New York, 1872), 168.

9. Seamus MacManus, *Yourself and the Neighbours* (New York, 1914), 70.

10. Letter from Alice McDonald, 1868. Personal Collection of Kirby Miller.

11. Charles Fanning, *The Irish Voice in America* (Lexington, 2000), 127.

12. Louise Bolard More, *Wage-Earners' Budgets* (New York, 1907), 173.

13. "Cheap Pudding," *Irish Times*, February 1, 1879.

14. "A Day in Castle Garden," *Harper's New Monthly Magazine*, March 1871, 554.

15. John F. Maguire, *The Irish in America* (London, 1868), 190.

16. Jeremiah O'Donovan, *A Brief Account of the Author's Interview with His Countrymen* (Pittsburgh, 1864), 367.

17. "Saturday Night at Washington Market," *New York Times*, March 17, 1872, 5.

18. Maria Parloa, *First Principles of Household Management and Cookery* (Boston, 1879), 87.

19. "Restaurant Calls," *Brooklyn Daily Eagle*, July 3, 1887, 13.

20. J. C. Croly, *Jennie June's American Cookery Book* (New York, 1870), 76.

21. George Foster, *New York in Slices* (New York, 1850), 70.

22. William Ellis, *The Country Housewife's Family Companion* (Totnes, Devon, 2000), 97.

23. Kathleen Mathew, "New York Newsboys," *Frank Leslie's Popular Monthly*, April 1895, 458.

24. "Tempting Hotel Menus," *New York Times*, December 26, 1890, 8.

Chapter three: The Gumpertz Family

1. "Hester Street Market," *New York Times*, July 27, 1895, 12.

2. Ladies of Congregation Emanuel, *The Fair Cook Book* (Denver, 1888), 7. (Reproduced courtesy of the Beck Archives, Penrose Library, Special Collections, University of Denver.)

3. Leah W. Leonard, *Jewish Cookery, in Accordance with Jewish Dietary Laws* (New York, 1949), 166.

4. John Cooper, *Eat and Be Satisfied: a Social History of Jewish Food* (Northvale, New Jersey, 1993), 80.

5. Marx Rumpolt, *Ein new Kochbuch* (Frankfurt am Main, 1581), 120. Translated by the author.

6. Florence K. Greenbaum, *International Jewish Cookbook* (New York, 1919), 84.

7. "Where Strict Jews Eat," *Current Literature*, March 1881, 408.

8. Bertha Kramer, *"Aunt Babette's" Cook Book* (New York, 1914), 513.

9. Matthew Hale Smith, *Sunshine and Shadow in New York* (Hartford, 1869), 456.

10. National Council of Jewish Women, *Council Cook Book* (San Francisco, 1909), 48.

11. Fannie Hurst, *The Vertical City* (New York, 1922), 262.

12. Albert Waldinger, ed., *Shining and Shadow: An Anthology of Early Yiddish Stories from the Lower East Side* (Cranbury, New Jersey, 2006), 142.

13. Michael Ginor et al., *Foie Gras, a Passion* (New York: 1999), 41.

14. Albert H. Buck, ed., *A Treatise of Hygiene and Health* (New York, 1977), 400.

15. During the early decades of the twentieth century, ethnically based food rackets were common in New York City. Taking advantage of their fellow

immigrants' fear and insularity, Jewish gangsters at various times took control of the kosher poultry industry, soda-fountain syrup manufacturing, and wholesale bakeries. Italian racketeers controlled artichokes, grapes, and pasta manufacture. All these rackets raised food prices mostly for that part of the population that could least afford it. Most food rackets were eliminated during the late 1930s, thanks to a concerted effort by the La Guardia administration.

16. "Some Queer East Side Vocations," *Current Opinion* (reprinted from the *New York Post*), August 1903, 202.
17. Greenbaum, *International Jewish Cookbook*, 12.
18. Author's family recipe.
19. Anya Yezierska, *Hungry Hearts* (New York, 1997), 116.
20. Henry Harlan, *The Yoke of the Thorah* (New York, 1896), 205.
21. Kramer, *"Aunt Babette's,"* 24.
22. Kela Nussbaum family recipe, contributed by Betsy Chanales.

Chapter four: The Rogarshevsky Family

1. "Humanity and Efficiency," *The Outlook*, March 28, 1908, 627.
2. Menu, Ellis Island archive.
3. "Their First Thanksgiving," *The Sun (New York)*, December 1, 1905, 2.
4. Frederick A. Wallis, "Treating Incoming Aliens as Human Beings," *Current History*, April–September 1921, 443.
5. "Feast of the Passover Celebrated," *New York Times*, March 26, 1899. 6.
6. Kosher menu, Ellis Island archive.
7. Frieda Schwartz family recipe, contributed by her daughter Francine E. Herbitter.
8. Regina Frishwasser, *Jewish American Cook Book* (New York, 1946), 47.
9. Bertha M. Wood, *Foods of the Foreign-Born in Relation to Health* (Boston, 1922), 90.
10. Jennie Grossinger, *The Art of Jewish Cooking* (New York, 1960), 147.
11. Elsa Herzfeld, *Family Monographs* (New York, 1905), 33.
12. Fannie Cohen family recipe, contributed by her granddaughter, Francine E. Herbitter.
13. Hinde Amchanitzki, *Text Book for Cooking and Baking* (New York, 1901), 30.
14. "East Siders Don't Approve Cookbook," *Hartford Courant*, January 17, 1916, 3.
15. John C. Gebhart, "Malnutrition and School Feeding," *Bulletin, United States Bureau of Education*, 1922, 14.
16. Emma Smedley, *The School Lunch* (Media, Pennsylvania, 1920), 147.

17. "Poor Meals Break Homes," *New York Times*, September 16, 1920, 8.

18. "Queer Dishes in Shops," *New York Tribune*, December 12, 1897, 40.

19. Alfred Kazin, *A Walker in the City* (New York, 1951), 34.

20. "Along Second Avenue," *New York Tribune*, August 31, 1919, F12.

21. Rian James, *Dining in New York* (New York, 1930), 32.

22. William Reiner, *Bohemia, the East Side Cafes of New York* (New York, 1903), 20.

23. Sholem Aleichem, *Wandering Star* (New York, 1952), 233.

24. "Along Second Avenue," *New York Tribune*, August 31, 1919, 68.

25. Family recipe of Lillian Chanales.

CHAPTER FIVE: THE BALDIZZI FAMILY

1. "Unskilled Laborer," *Washington Herald*, February 2, 1908, 12.

2. "New Recipe for Soup," *New York Times*, August 19, 1900, 15.

3. "Undesirable Immigrants," *New York Times*, December 18, 1880, 4.

4. "Phases of City Life," *New York Times*, November 4, 1871, 2.

5. "Italy's Invading Army," *New York Sun*, June 28, 1891, 23.

6. "Found in Garbage Boxes," *New York Times*, July 15, 1883, 10.

7. "Things Little Italy Eats," *The Sun (New York)*, August 23, 1903, 5.

8. Jerre Mangione, *Mount Allegro* (New York, 1981), 131.

9. See Hasia Diner's *Hungering for America*.

10. "Table Tidbits Prepared Under Revolting Conditions," *New York Tribune*, May 11, 1913, D4.

11. "Quaint Italian Customs of Summer Festal Days," *New York Times*, July 12, 1903, 30.

12. Maria Gentile, *The Italian Cook Book* (New York, 1919), 133.

13. Mangione, *Mount Allegro*, 131.

14. Richard Gambino, *Blood of My Blood: the Dilemma of the Italian American* (Toronto, 1996), 92.

15. Author's recipe.

16. Concetta Rizzolo's family recipe, contributed by her grandson Stephen Treffinger.

17. Jeannette Young Norton, "Going Marketing in 'Little Italy,'" *New York Tribune*, July 23, 1916, C5.

18. "Italian Housewives' Dishes," *New York Times*, June 7, 1903, 28.

19. "Do Fiery Foods Cause Fiery Natures?" *New York Tribune Illustrated Supplement*, December 6, 1903, 5.

20. Gentile, *The Italian Cook Book*, 76.

21. "A Bit of Bohemia," *The Vassar Miscellany*, February 1889, 154.

22. "March of the Italian Chef," *The Sun (New York)*, December 20, 1908, 8.

23. "Our Italians," *New York Times*, November 12, 1875, 4.

24. "A Sicilian Café in New York," *Harper's Weekly*, November 2, 1889, 875.

25. "The Italian Cook's Best," *The Sun (New York)*, June 20, 1909, 2.

26. Sarah Tyson Rorer, *Mrs. Rorer's New Cook Book* (Philadelphia, 1902), 301.

27. "Spaghetti with Meat Balls," *Chicago Tribune*, February 21, 1908, 9.

28. Baldizzi family recipe.

Bibliography

Barnavi, Eli, *A Historical Atlas of the Jewish People*. New York: Schocken, 1992.

Barr, Nancy Verde, *We Called It Macaroni: An American Heritage of Southern Italian Cooking*. New York: Alfred A. Knopf, 1990.

Bayor, Ronald H. and Timothy J. Meagher, eds., *The New York Irish*. Baltimore: Johns Hopkins University Press, 1996.

Beecher, Mrs. Henry Ward, *Motherly Talks with Young Housekeepers*. New York: J. B. Ford and Company, 1873.

Bolino, August Constantino, *The Ellis Island Source Book*. Washington, D.C.: Kensington Historical Press, 1985.

Browne, Junius Henri, *The Great Metropolis: A Mirror of New York*. Hartford: American Pub. Co., 1869.

Brownstone, David M. and Irene M. Franck, *Facts About American Immigration*. New York: H. W. Wilson Company, 2001.

Burrows, Edwin G. and Mike Wallace, *Gotham: A History of New York City to 1898*. New York: Oxford University Press, 1999.

Cahan, Abraham, *The Rise of David Levinsky*. New York: Harper & Brothers, 1917.

Clarkson, L. A., and E. Margaret Crawford, *Feast and Famine: Food and Nutrition in Ireland 1500–1920*. New York: Oxford University Press, 2001.

Coan, Peter Morton, *Ellis Island Interviews: In Their Own Words*. New York: Checkmark Books, 1997.

Cohen, Rose, *Out of the Shadow: A Russian Jewish Girlhood on the Lower East Side*. Ithaca, New York: Cornell University Press, 1995.

Cordasco, Francesco, ed., *Studies in Italian American Social History: Essays in Honor of Leonard Covello*. Totowa, New Jersey: Rowman & Littlefield, 1975.

Cowan, Cathal and Regina Sexton, *Ireland's Traditional Foods*. Dublin: Teagasc, 1997.

Dembinska, Maria, *Food and Drink in Medieval Poland: Discovering a Cuisine of the Past.* Philadelphia: University of Pennsylvania Press, 2002.

Diner, Hasia, *Hungering for America.* Cambridge, Massachusetts: Harvard University Press, 2001.

Dolkart, Andrew S., *Biography of a Tenement House in New York City: An Architectural History of 97 Orchard Street.* Santa Fe: The Center for American Places, 2006.

Ernst, Robert, *Immigrant Life in New York City, 1825–1863.* New York: King's Crown Press, 1949.

Ewen, Elizabeth, *Immigrant Women in the Land of Dollars: Life and Culture on the Lower East Side, 1890–1925.* New York: Monthly Review Press, 1985.

Fanning, Charles, *The Irish Voice in America: 250 Years of Irish-American Fiction.* Lexington, Kentucky: University Press of Kentucky, 2000.

Foner, Nancy, *From Ellis Island to JFK: New York's Two Great Waves of Immigration.* New Haven, Connecticut: Yale University Press, 2000.

Gabaccia, Donna R., *From Sicily to Elizabeth Street: Housing and Social Change Among Italian Immigrants, 1880–1930.* Albany, New York: State University of New York Press, 1984.

Gabaccia, Donna R., *We Are What We Eat: Ethnic Food and the Making of Americans.* Cambridge, Massachusetts: Harvard University Press, 1998.

Greenspoon, Leonard J., Ronald A. Simkins, Gerald Shapiro, eds., *Food and Judaism: A Special Issue of Studies in Jewish Civilization, Volume 15.* Omaha, Nebraska: Creighton University Press, 2005.

Hecker, Joel, *Mystical Bodies, Mystical Meals: Eating and Embodiment in Medieval Kabbalah.* Detroit, Michigan: Wayne State University Press, 2005.

Homberger, Eric, *The Historical Atlas of New York City.* New York: Henry Holt, 1994.

Hundert, Gershorn David, *The YIVO Encyclopedia of Jews in Eastern Europe.* New Haven, Connecticut: Yale University Press, 2008.

Isola, Antonia, *Simple Italian Cookery.* New York: Harper & Brothers, 1912.

Jackson, Kenneth, ed., *The Encyclopedia of New York City.* New Haven, Connecticut: Yale University Press, 1995.

Joselit, Jenna Weissman, *The Wonders of America: Reinventing Jewish Culture 1880–1950.* New York: Hill and Wang, 1994.

Joselit, Jenna Weissman, Barbara Kirshenblatt-Gimblett, Irving Howe, Susan L. Braunstein, *Getting Comfortable in New York: The American Jewish Home 1880–1950.* New York: The Jewish Museum, 1990.

Kagan, Berl, ed., *Luboml: The Memorial Book of a Vanished Shtetl.* Jerusalem: Ktav Publishing House, 1987.

Kessner, Thomas, *The Golden Door: Italian and Jewish Immigrant Mobility in New York City 1880–1915.* New York: Oxford University Press, 1977.

Maffi, Mario, *Gateway to the Promised Land: Ethnic Cultures in New York's Lower East Side.* New York: New York University Press, 1995.

Maguire, John Francis, *The Irish in America.* New York: D. & J. Sadlier & Co., 1868.

Mangione, Jerre and Ben Morreale, *La Storia: Five Centuries of the Italian-American Experience.* New York: HarperCollins, 1992.

McCabe, James D., *Lights and Shadows of New York Life.* Philadelphia: National Publishing Company, 1872.

Moreno, Barry, *Encyclopedia of Ellis Island.* Westport, Connecticut: Greenwood Press, 2004.

Nadel, Stanley, *Little Germany: Ethnicity, Religion, and Class in New York City, 1845–80.* Urbana, Illinois: University of Illinois Press, 1990.

Nathan, Joan, *Jewish Cooking in America.* New York: Alfred A. Knopf, 1998.

Parker, Cornelia, *Working with the Working Woman.* New York: Harper & Brothers, 1922.

Parloa, Maria, *First Principles of Household Management and Cookery.* Boston: Houghton, Osgood and Company, 1879.

Pitkin, Thomas, *Keepers of the Gate: A History of Ellis Island.* New York: New York University Press, 1975.

Plunz, Richard, *A History of Housing in New York City.* New York: Columbia University Press, 1990.

Rischin, Moses, *The Promised City: New York's Jews, 1870–1914.* New York: Corinth Books, 1964.

Roden, Claudia, *The Book of Jewish Food.* New York: Alfred A. Knopf, 1996.

Roskolenko, Harry, *The Time That Was Then.* New York: Dial Press, 1971.

Sarna, Jonathan D., and Nancy H. Klein, *The Jews of Cincinnati.* Cincinnati: Center for the Study of the American Jewish Experience, 1989.

Schneider, Dorothee, *Trade Unions and Community: The German Working Class in New York City, 1870–1900.* Urbana, Illinois: University of Illinois Press, 1994.

Simeti, Mary Taylor, *Pomp and Sustenance: Twenty-Five Centuries of Sicilian Food.* New York: Alfred A. Knopf, 1989.

Strasser, Susan, *Never Done: A History of American Housework.* New York: Pantheon Books, 1982.

Ware, Caroline Farrar, *Greenwich Village, 1920–1930: A Comment of American Civilization in the Post-War Years.* Berkeley: University of California Press, 1994.

Photo Credits

Library of Congress: 150

Library of Congress: 203

Library of Congress: 205

Library of Congress: 209

"Ludlow St. Hebrew making ready for the Sabbath Eve in his coal cellar—2 loaves on his table, c. 1890," Museum of the City of New York, The Jacob A. Riis Collection: 90

National Archives: 127

Photography Collection, Miriam and Ira D. Wallach Division of Art, Prints and Photographs, The New York Public Library, Astor, Lenox and Tilden Foundations: 117

Picture Collection, The New York Public Library, Astor, Lenox and Tilden Foundations: 18

Picture Collection, The New York Public Library, Astor, Lenox and Tilden Foundations: 213

Provided courtesy of HarpWeek., LLC: 78

Provided courtesy of HarpWeek., LLC: 84

Provided courtesy of HarpWeek., LLC: 85

Rare Books Division, The New York Public Library, Astor, Lenox and Tilden Foundations: 73

Science, Industry & Business Library, The New York Public Library, Astor, Lenox and Tilden Foundations: 16

"Street Vendors, 1898," Museum of the City of New York, The Byron Collection: 106

"The Oyster Stand, 1840," Museum of the City of New York, Gift of Francis P. Garvan: 75

Index